CEROLIAN
SAGAS
THE NEVARRIAN WAR

MAP OF CEROLIA

By Mathew "Vieryon" Ruley

Copyright © 2018 by Mathew E. Ruley
"Cerolian Sagas" is a registered trademark. All Rights Reserved.
No part of this book may be reproduced or used in any manner without written permission of the Copyright owner except for use of quotations in a book review.
For more information, address: vieryon@ceroliansagas.com

First paperback edition May 2020

Book design by Mathew E. Ruley
Map, Logo, and Cover Design by Eleanor J Mathews
Cover Art by Ramon Macairap "Hachiimon"
Concept Art by Mylene Olavere "Mikurei"
Beta Reading by Jia Yue He
Editing by Heather Romanowski

Military Advisers:
Emora Dantelino - US Army, PMC
Adam Scott Lewis - US Army
Daniel Kinsmen - USMC

WEBSITE

FACEBOOK

YOUTUBE

ISBN 978-1-7348122-0-6 (Paperback)
ISBN 978-1-7348122-1-3 (Hardback)
ISBN 978-1-7348122-3-7 (Audiobook)
ISBN 978-1-7348122-2-0 (E-Book)

Library of Congress Control Number: 2020905832

First Edition

In Loving Memory of James Dorsey

CONTENTS
Cerolian Sagas
The Nevarrian War

Warnings:

Casual violence and gore
The use of cigarettes and alcohol
Mild swearing
Mild nudity
Death and tragedy
War related themes
Sexual themes

The Nevarrian War

Written by Vieryon
Cerolian Arts

***

Daybreak | Viano 24, 1238 - Temple of Aludra
Operation Chromia: Zero Hour

The slow and melodic sound of Sofie's violin filled the misty air as the young girl practiced her favorite instrument. Her ruby-red hair danced in the wind alongside her long, soft tail that matched it in color, forsake its white tip. Adorning her hair were a pair of white feathers that held steadfast in front of her right ear. She was an Aluni, one of the thirteen races that called the planet Cerolia their home. Her ears were long and pointed with a coat of thin fur, the back of which was black with a single streak of green from the tip to the base, and the inside was light gray. These feathers were a source of pride for her, as they signified her position as an Acolyte of the Temple of Aludra.

While other temples existed, this was the only one that taught its practitioners the skills they needed to wield their Symbiont's energy in combat. Only those who were trusted among their small isolationist society were allowed to progress through the ranks, as the power that one could attain by mastery in their art could potentially sway the tide of war. Advanced practitioners, called Paladins, were only permitted to utilize their abilities in the immediate defense of those around them as a last resort.

She stood alone upon a circular stone platform that was surrounded with patches of flowers and flowing water. Being at the furthest edge of the temple's garden, her platform was on the precipice of a manufactured waterfall. Before her was the great fountain that pumped water back up to the gardens as it was captured in a large pool below.

The temple, which was devoted to the Protector of the West, was built out of the side of a mountain that overlooked the exquisite coastal city of Nevarria and its harbor. It was protected by pristine white walls while the fruit-bearing gardens themselves were situated in steppes beyond the Temple's main gates. Tending to the gardens outside of the walls always kept Sofie in a pleasant mood, and she preferred to practice her music away from others so that her mistakes wouldn't be a bother. Her motions were slow and deliberate, her stance was strong, and she was focused on bettering herself.

"So close...." Sofie muttered in frustration as the last few chords of her tune missed their mark.

She was good at getting back on track after a screeching mistake would attempt to pull her away from her goal. Every time it happened; she would make a mental note of the chord she missed for later. It was upsetting that she couldn't get through a single song without issue, but she was determined to master the violin. Mulling things over was her way of pushing beyond her mistakes and turning her negative feelings into something productive. Next time she would get it, next time she would finish the song in its entirety. Slower compositions like the one she had chosen were easier for her to pick apart.

Moving the instrument from beneath her chin was almost a relief, as her sore neck was not yet accustomed to the position it needed to be in to hold the violin in place. She quickly slipped her bow into a holster she fashioned to her black corset so that she could use her now free hand to rub the nape of her neck. Her fingertips slid across the thin fur of armored bone-like plates that protected her spine. They were layered like a single row of defensive scales that started at the base of her skull and ended just beyond the small of her back.

Sofie quickly realized how stiff she was as she used the violin's sling to secure it on her back as though it were a rifle. The leather strap came to rest on layered bones plates that adorned her shoulders like natural pauldrons. They were red and formed much like the scales of her spinal armor. She rotated her wrists before tightening a special set of muscles on the top of her hands. This pulled her forearm blades forward slightly, locking them in so that they would now follow her hand movements. Like the plates on her spine, these large bones were covered in a layer of thin red fur. The blades were more like that of a dull spear, though, and were only dangerous at the sharpened tip situated near her elbows. It was a shield as well as a weapon, something she was being taught to use as effectively as possible within the walls of the temple.

After she was a bit more comfortable, Sofie gently patted some dust off of the vibrant green skirt that she wore. She imagined that it came from her time tending the garden today, even if she was careful to keep her Acolyte's uniform as clean as she could. It was tapered from the front to the back, nearly trailing on the floor behind her. As her stance shifted idly, she felt a small pop beneath the dusty skin of her right foot. It was a very familiar sensation to her: one of the smaller denizens of the planet belonging to a race called the "Mek'Vatir" had wandered far too close to her and disappeared beneath a casual footfall. Green spirals that resembled tattooed vines across her arms and legs shimmered to life with an eerie glow as the being beneath her perished. She had absorbed its soul, adding its life to the reserves of energy that she used to practice her magic.

Sofie loved her life at the temple studying under the High Paladin, Lady Zara. She had only recently been allowed to live within the Sanctum Astrona, which was an honor bestowed upon her when she became an Acolyte. Zara was the one who founded the temple and was the only one on Cerolia who knew the arts trained in the temple before its construction.

 CEROLIAN SAGAS

"You were great, comrade," a familiar and upbeat voice broke the silence, as one of the temple's newcomers crossed the bridge to Sofie's platform.

"Thanks, Kiera," Sofie replied meekly. "You didn't hear all of that, did you?"

"Most of it," Kiera said proudly, feeling the embarrassment that surrounded her friend. "Don't worry, you've really come a long way since you started practicing."

Kiera's long, purple hair was pulled back in a tight ponytail to keep the wind from taking it. She offered her hand to Sofie with a polite smile as her tail swayed. The Acolyte happily accepted her gesture, taking her hand without a moment's hesitation. Together, they began their short walk through the garden toward a dirt path that ran alongside the temple's walls.

"I just don't think I'm ready to have an audience. I feel like I bother people when I mess up, and it makes me nervous."

"It's so awesome that you're already working from memory though," Kiera replied quickly as they passed the trees that formed a natural fence between the dirt path and the cliff's edge. "You'll get it sooner or later, and when you do, you'll be the best violinist out there."

"You're doing well with your studies too, right? I wonder how many empaths there actually are."

"Yeah, Lady Zara's really helped me learn to focus so I don't feel so many unwanted emotions from the people around me.

It's only the super-strong ones I have problems with... I think she said that I'm the only one she knows of though, but that can't be right, right?"

"You arrived four cycles ago, right? I'm sorry I haven't really been paying attention to your Aikua classes recently, I'll try to be more attentive."

"Well, you have a lot on your plate. It'll be four cycles tomorrow; Alexis and I are kicking butt together in class. I won our last match with this really awesome leg sweep that caught her off guard, but she's been beating me a lot. Zara says we fight well together when we're paired up though so there's that. We even beat one of the masters!"

"You did?" Sofie asked excitedly as she hopped a bit to catch up.

"Yep! It was Master Vari," Kiera proudly stated as they reached the enormous black gates of the temple's outer walls.

"Now I know you're lying."

"No! For real, we did! You can ask him."

"I'm just joking," Sofie replied joyfully, "I bet you couldn't beat me though."

"I wouldn't even wanna' try."

Kiera loved looking up toward the machicolations when she approached the wall since they were so hard to actually see against the white stone normally. Every so often, she could catch a glimpse of one of the Paladins that were stationed on the wall in their meditative pose. It was inspiring to know that Sofie would someday be counted among their ranks. 'Master Caren' had a nice ring to it in her mind. After passing the black gate, the two began their trek up toward the main temple where Alexis was waiting for them.

"Race you to the top!" Kiera shouted, nudging Sofie gently before breaking into a dead sprint up the stairwell.

"Hey wait!" Sofie squeaked, quickly giving pursuit.

"Nope!" Kiera laughed as she ran. "It's more training!"

Sofie's footsteps patted up the stairwell as she ran, trying to skip steps to give her a boost. There wasn't much she could do to catch up to Kiera though, who had a decent lead starting out. Kiera's ascension faltered as she misplaced her footing with a surprised yelp. As the young purple-haired Aluni fell forward, she resisted the urge to grab for the stairwell. Instead, she moved her wrists so that the strong bone of her forearm blade made contact with the ground, keeping her head from bouncing off of the steps. Sofie quickly caught up and crouched at her side as their jovial race to the top of the stairwell abruptly ended.

"Are you alright?" She asked in a worried tone.

"Yeah… I scraped my knee a bit."

"Can I help?"

"Sure," Kiera replied as she pulled her pant leg up to reveal her bloodied knee. "I just…."

Sofie brought her hands down to her friend's knee as tendrils of green energy bridged the gap between her palm and the cut.

Healing was an ability Sofie was able to tap into without much special training. Within seconds, the spirit she had taken in down in the garden was used to mend her friend's wound. All the major races of Cerolia had attunements, or special abilities granted to individuals by birth based on the color of the patterns throughout their bodies. Her shade of green was considered 'Terra Attuned'. Some with the color were able to heal, and others were able to help plants quickly grow to maturity. These denominations were referred to as 'Terra Medical' and 'Terra Botanical' respectively.

"There," Sofie said proudly, "better?"

"Sofie, something's wrong," Kiera said breathlessly as her eyes widened. She was visibly tense as they looked back toward the enormous black doorway they had just passed through while quivering like a leaf.

The Paladins on the wall stood at the ready with their staffs in hand as the echoing sound of the portcullis descending reverberated through the temple grounds. The heavy black doorway then began to close for the first time in Sofie's life.

All eyes were on the city as steel vessels lay in the harbor surrounding the island of Vastari off of Nevarria's coastline. It was normal to see a military ship or two in the harbor, as the city was a renowned tourist destination that served as a choice location for shore leave. This was different. An entire fleet of battleships had positioned itself at sea while airships emerged from the clouds above as though the mist was positioned delib-erately to mask the fleet's approach. The two watched together as flashes of light erupted from canons and trails of vapor arched toward the city's shores. Silent fire engulfed the coastline, turn-ing the beaches into a burial ground as civilians could be seen running for their lives.

Kiera screamed, curling up into Sofie as the overwhelming emotion of an entire city in peril washed over her. The thun-derous sound of explosions and cannon fire finally reached the temple while the healer held her writhing friend as tightly as she could. Paladins on the walls stood together, huddled around large crystals on the ramparts as a hostile airship appeared from around the corner nearest the cliff on their right. Its turreted cannons began to rotate toward the temple, just as a wave of sil-very spiritual energy fell like a curtain from the cliff face above. The barrier covered the entire temple just as the deck guns of the vessel acquired their target and began their assault.

The two cowered on the steps together as Paladins on the wall fought to defend the temple itself.

"Get Kiera inside!" a commanding, feminine voice shouted as the woman who spoke reached down and gripped Sofie by the arm. Then, she was lifted to her feet.

Sofie stumbled slightly, nearly dragging her purple-haired friend to a standing position as she looked up to the High Paladin. Her snow-white skin made her appear as though she were glowing, only contrasted by her jet-black hair and piercing blue eyes. As the two girls frantically made their way up the stairwell, the High Paladin lifted her right hand toward the air-ship that was battering the newly erected barrier.

Black tendrils of smoky energy wrapped around her out-stretched arm as Lady Zara held her staff tightly in the other hand. The same black smoke began to dance around the airship's main deck cannons. With a subtle motion of her fingertips, the High Paladin began to slowly warp the barrel of the canons to the point where they were inoperable. The workers aboard the ship didn't realize the damage as they loaded another round for a subsequent salvo. Once the cannons fired, the shells exploded in the tubes causing twisted metal to fly out around the turret like shrapnel. All of the High Paladin's movements were focused and concise, slowly blanketing the airship in an eldritch snare that left the entire vessel under her control like a monster of the sea enveloping its prey. Smoke spiraled around her arm from a crescent-like black pattern near her shoulder as she drew more spiritual energy into her task. The airship began to descend toward the beaches, though she would not allow it to come down in a blaze of fire.

The High Paladin, though her people were under attack, instead chose to guide the ship to a safe landing where assaulting the Temple would be nearly impossible up a sheer cliff.

The crew were all spared by her mercy.

 CEROLIAN SAGAS

Kiera looked back to the High Paladin and the defenders through teary eyes as she did all she could to block the overwhelming emotions battering her from all sides. She could hardly walk up the stairwell, only making progress toward the safety of the Temple's armored residential chambers by Sofie's tenacity. It was horrendous, a collective outcry of suffering that shook her to her very core.

It was tearing her apart....

May the Goddess Bless the Republic.

Serendipity

S E R E N D I P I T Y

C H A P T E R   I

Morning | Alerio 10, 1240
Nevarria City – Recreational District

The walls of the lobby shook as a mortar landed nearby, freeing more dust from the hotel's once-pristine ceiling and adding to the debris that littered the building's red carpet. The lobby was a grand room with a single wide stairwell in the center leading to the upper levels. Cycles ago, this hotel had beautiful ornate brass decorations throughout the walls of the room. Now, those decorations were riddled with bullet holes. This dilapidated hotel played host to dignitaries from all across Cerolia, and now hosts the front-lines of a major war between the nations of Novalus and Aestellus.

Barely a centimeter tall, two little beings moved across the grand red carpet of the lobby. They were the Mek'Vatir, and they were the only current residents of this establishment under siege. Blissfully unaware of the ongoing conflict around them, the pair continued their endeavor to survive in a world where everything conspired to tear them down. These two were special among their comrades, having learned to work together despite their lack of language. They each held tightly to their edge of a piece of food as they made their way toward the lobby's main counter, a shelter out of sight that they called home.

Though, they were far from safe in their travels.

The sound of gunfire and roaring explosions had desensitized the little ones to their surroundings. The fact that they were not alone in the lobby didn't dawn on the creatures until it was far too late, and the sky above them darkened. A moment of fear washed over them both as they looked up to see the sole of a boot block out the sky after having been lifted a mere five centimeters off of the ground in its owners' gait. One of the Mek lost its footing and fell to its back just as the light gray tread of Kiera's boot pressed its body into the carpet below. The other dropped its end and ran as quickly as it could to the side in hopes of taking the shortest path to safety.

As Kiera moved forward, her heel lifted from the carpeted floor to reveal the damage done. The one who ran had its arm caught beneath her rubberized tread and crushed flat; its black blood filled the small and dusty gray alcove that it now was forced to inhabit. The space was barely too thin for the rest of its body, making breathing a terrible chore for the pained being as it was taken along with its tormentor.

It was the unlucky one, as the one who had fallen had already been killed. It had been caught directly beneath a flat part of the Aluni's tread and was now reduced to a small black splatter on her sole. The tiny creature's white intestines dangled from what now only resembled a pelt of gray skin. A small string of black blood and white gore connected the Mek to its lower half on the ground for only a few seconds before the distance became too great. Like a small rope being pulled past its limits, the connection was quickly severed.

Kiera moved forward in a crouch, listening for anything that she thought might be dangerous to her. Being careful paid off in a warzone, especially for a relatively unarmed youngling that had just passed into adulthood. She was twelve cycles of age, which was the equivalent of eighteen earth years. Her yellow eyes scanned the upper level of the lobby for any sign of enemy soldiers as she proceeded with her search. Inky tendril-like arms constantly swayed and moved as though they were reaching across her iris from her darkened pupil. This was a trait all Aluni shared, pupils that constantly changed like a tiny eldritch creature swirling beneath the surface of her eye. It was as though they had a consciousness of their own. Light-blue crystalline formations just below her palm's skin began to glow as she took in the soul of the Mek'Vatir that was crushed to death, trapping its spirit within her own body while she didn't acknowledge the little one's presence. The survivor was forced to endure as though it were a sentient pebble trapped deep within the tread of her shoe with no hope of escape.

Kiera quickly made her way up the staircase in a crouch. Her heels didn't touch the ground as she ascended, giving her passenger a view of the red-carpeted staircase. When she arrived on the second floor she began to step fully again, pressing the Mek deeper into her boot's tread and further devastating the corpse of the one that had already been crushed. Another shell landed near the hotel, shaking the walls and forcing Kiera to shuffle toward the nearest wall in her crouched state. She kept low, looking up and around to make sure that nothing was about to fall on her before she resumed her search. She knew this building well, having vacationed in it several times with her family before the war began. Her goal: the lunchroom on the second level of the hotel. She wasn't a soldier, she was a survivor.

She was in search of anything she could find to help her family keep on living.

After the quaking stopped, Kiera shifted the bag on her shoulder back over her layered purple bone plates. It had slipped down her arm when she braced herself for the impact, and while it was light and empty now, she was hopeful that she would be able to scavenge enough food and supplies to fill it to the brim. She then gently rolled the sleeves of the light gray shirt she wore up to her elbows, freeing the two purple fur-coated forearm blades. When her weapons were at the ready, she tucked the bits of her purple hair back down into her shirt's collar and cinched up her scarf a little more to keep the strands from falling out once again.

"Right...." Kiera said under her breath as she resumed her journey, staying close to the wall.

She still had a decent mental map of the entire building; having an explorative soul during her stay here, she wandered the premises rather thoroughly. The level she was on had a gym, a lunchroom, and several long hallways filled with guest rooms connecting them all. Kiera stopped in front of the large metallic door that headed deeper into the facility, and slowly pushed the handle downward.

Nothing.

The handle wouldn't budge, as it was locked from the other side. It was designed to always allow anyone within to leave, but she needed a physical key to gain entry from her side.

"Damn," she said under her breath, "maybe it's downstairs."

She leaned over the ledge slightly, using the railing for support as she scanned the ground floor from her perched position. The check-in desk was a mess, though it was the best bet of finding a way to access the upper level's rooms. Her silver tail swayed back and forth in hope, its purple tip almost wrapping around to her chest. She had spotted a small wooden box on the table that was labeled 'Keys'. Not saying another word, the happy Aluni quickly descended the stairwell to take a seat at the desk.

She dusted the seat off before sitting down, as it had accumulated some debris from the bombardments. Her tail fit perfectly into a space in the back of the chair as she sat down and rolled her seat forward. Kiera knew that it may take a bit of work to get into the key box, so she was set on getting comfortable. When she moved her chair, she felt her right boot come to rest on a piece of stone or something beneath the desk. The sensation hardly registered in her mind as noteworthy as she lifted the box and began her attempt to examine its mechanism.

There was an ornate latch on the front of the container made of bronze that locked the lid down to the box's structure. It was just barely loose enough to allow her to pry the top of the box open so that the keys could slide out under the right conditions. When she lifted the box and moved it around to examine it further, the sound of keys rattling inside the container could be heard. Using her thumb's purple claw, she carefully pried it open and shook it. Kiera hoped that the keys were just on little hooks or something. Making noise was about all she succeeded in doing, as they were secured by something she couldn't quite see.

While she worked, she subconsciously began to tap her foot on the debris underneath her. It was good for some entertainment while she focused, since the object she had was soft enough to compress yet strong enough to toy with. Then, as she idly rolled it around in circles, it collapsed like a crunchy-yet-soft bit of stale food and the light sound of a squeak filled the air.

A chill of energy ran up her spine that was soothing enough to stop her from her current task. She took a deep breath in, then moved the box around in search of a way to get inside of it.

"This is hopeless...." she groaned as she found the keyhole to the device on the back of the box.

She wanted to break the thing open, but it was such an ornate box that she felt like destroying it would be a crime. Someone put a lot of hard work and effort into making this thing, only to have someone come along and break it open for the chance of finding more food upstairs. It looked like, with a bit of repair, the latch could be made to fit solidly and keep everything secure inside. She knew the pub still had some food left over, and there were a few other stops she was planning to make on the way home. All she had to do was take the box back to the pub and see if her friend Alexis would help her get it open, then return at a later date to get in the lunchroom. Alexis had a hobby of woodworking and tinkering, though it died down a bit since the war began and craft supplies were no longer readily available.

Then, she noticed it. A purple glow was coming from beneath her, and it was bright enough to cause immediate concern.

Kiera dropped the box on the table and jumped to her feet in a fit of terror, realizing that whatever she crushed was now stuck to the bottom of her boot. She stomped her foot on the carpet, dragging and twisting it around in a frantic attempt to get the glowing liquid off of her.

"No, no, no," she said to herself as she continued to grind her boot into the carpet. "Not like this, please Goddess…."

The soothing sensation, the glow. One of the few things she knew about radiation was that she wasn't immune to it as a Nuclear Attuned individual would be. If she was this close to the source, she felt like it was only a matter of time before she would die. Kiera ran toward the nearby stairwell and gripped the railing tight, leaning on it as she looked back to the glowing desk and her purple footprints leading up to where she was now. It wasn't as intense as she initially imagined, though: each splatter of glowing purple was only around five centimeters in diameter aside from the smears she left on the carpet during her panicked attempt to get the radiation off.

It was still with her.

Trying to calm herself down, the hyperventilating Aluni slowly lifted her right foot. She cocked it to the side so she could see the bottom of her shoe, revealing the vague shape of a person's body. It was around three centimeters in height, three times the size of an average Mek'Vatir. She had utterly demolished the creature in her haste, but there were a few things she could tell from the being's remains. The creature had pale skin, with long white hair and a bushy black tail. It looked like an Aluni, but the ears were more animal-like than one of her kind. Whatever it was must have been using the desk as a shelter when she sat down and unwittingly crushed it.

"What in Cargasso...." she said in a hushed tone as she lowered herself to have a seat on the stairwell without stepping back down on the creature's remains.

The crushed being's tail twitched, though it was probably more akin to a death rattle. Its organs were jammed into the canals of her shoe's tread, and the little one's kidneys resembled miniature purple beans. Intestines that looked like impossibly thin noodles were spread across the mess, and its skull was crunched up underneath the tread. All of its facial features were buried in a mess of sprawling white hair and glowing purple brain-matter that trickled down its little neck. The most peculiar thing though, was that the creature was wearing clothing. A gray toga-like dress adorned its flattened body with a red sash around its abdomen, but her stomping had undone the outfit enough to allow its insides to filter out.

Shifting so that her ankle was resting on her other leg's knee, she held her hand out beneath the shoe to catch any bits that might fall. Then, she carefully slid the claw of her other hand's index finger into the space that was beneath its clothed chest. Kiera winced as it was pried free, watching intently while the three-centimeter-tall creature's demolished form plopped like a slab of meat into her waiting palm.

She could make out more details about the little one from here, even though its body was nearly a perfect clay print of her shoe's tread. Kiera ran her claw tip along the intricate tattoos on the creature's chest, which disappeared beneath the toga around his midriff. She regretted not being able to interact with the little one while it was alive. It was a curious-looking little creature, and immediately her mind began to wander to ideas of what sort of race it belonged to. Were there others like it? Did they have a society of any kind elsewhere, or was this the last of its kind; unlucky enough to be snuffed out under a careless wanderer.

Then, the intricate patterns across the carcass' chest began glowing bright blue. The light radiated out from the center of its body to encompass its entire broken form. Upon seeing this, Kiera immediately yelped and shook her hand wildly as though she were afraid it would sting her. The glowing bright-blue blob fell to the carpet with a light and unassuming plop while Kiera resumed backing her way up the stairwell in case the thing was harmful. When the light disappeared, the little one was left lying next to a pile of his internal organs. They were separated from his body as though he had recreated everything about himself from scratch. Barely three centimeters tall, the little one simply lay there gazing upward at the ceiling as though he was a tiny breathing doll.

A few moments of tense silence passed as Kiera tried her best to rationalize the situation in her head. There was a tiny creature that looked like it was a hybrid of her race and another, though it was ridiculously small and seemingly immortal. It wasn't quite a Mek'Vatir, but it also wasn't anything she had come across in her life up until this point. Just because she hadn't heard of it though, doesn't mean it wasn't discovered before her.

Either way, she was here with it, and she had hurt it badly.

Taking a deep breath, she slowly approached the tiny being. Step by step she came back down the stairwell before she was standing directly over it, where she then crouched to get a better look. He was breathing and shaking; his little eyes were open and his ears were perked up attentively. While he looked like he had seen better days, he didn't seem to be afraid. In fact, his little red-tipped black tail was flopping about lightly like a pet lazing about the home. Another realization dawned on her as she looked into his heterochromatic eyes.

She couldn't feel his emotions.

The Mek'Vatir were the only creatures she really couldn't feel, other than wild animals. Cautiously, she reached down to the little one beneath her and pinched his chest between her fingertips. Lifting him from the ground, she then made her way back to the desk she was sitting at before and set him down.

"What are you...?" she asked rhetorically as she pulled herself closer and wiped the glowing blood off her hands and onto her pant legs.

"I'm not sure, entirely," the tiny being responded as he struggled to sit upright. "I can't remember much, just vague flashes of experiments and conditioning. I've been wandering around the city for days trying to get someone's attention."

She wasn't expecting a response from him at all. When he spoke, she shot up to attention in her seat and her tail began to sway quickly behind her. Her eyes were wide as she looked him over with her mouth opened slightly to reveal her two sharp canine teeth. She wasn't trying to intimidate him, she was simply startled and confused.

"You speak?" Kiera asked breathlessly. "I must be hallucinating or dreaming, or something."

"Yes, I do," the little one said. "Are – are you here to take me back to the laboratory?"

"I don't know what you're talking about."

"I...." the tiny creature began, stopping to hold his head before continuing. "I want to go back to her, the scientist with red hair and curled gray horns. She's your height with green crystals on her back and gray eyes. I think I saw her have wings once, but I'm not sure."

"That sounds like a Sarin."

"Her name was Sarin?"

"No little comrade," Kiera chuckled lightly. "That's her race, a Sarin. They're the only ones I know of who only have wings when they want to have them. They just sprout from crystals on their backs at will. I've only seen it happen a few times because it's pretty rude to ask them to do it a bunch. Most of them live on the island nation of Sari."

"Can you help me find her?"

"I'm sorry," Kiera said nervously. "Things really aren't great right now. We're in the middle of a warzone and my family needs me, I can't just abandon them at the drop of a hat."

"I understand," the little one replied solemnly, "I shouldn't have asked, sorry."

"It's okay little comrade. Can I ask you a question though?"

"Of course."

"You aren't radioactive, are you? You're glowing an awful lot and it's got me a bit worried."

"I don't think I am. Is radiation an issue around here?"

"Not exactly a comforting answer, but I'll take it as a no. There are a lot of radiation zones around the world, specifically one south of the mountains from where we are. Unless you're Nuclear Attuned, it's a big problem."

"Attuned?"

"I, uh," Kiera replied in a defeated tone, looking around the lobby a bit nervously. "Well, attunements are like special abilities everyone gets when they're born. You can tell someone's attunement by the color of the markings on their skin. I'm Frigid Attuned, which means I can't get uncomfortably cold and I'm immune to cold-related problems like frostbite and stuff."

Kiera then lifted her hand so that he could see the light-blue pattern on her palm.

"That's incredible!" he replied enthusiastically. "So, what are the others like?"

"Well, red is Blaze. It's basically like my opposite, where the person can't get burned at all and doesn't get uncomfortably hot. My friends Alexis and Lain have that ability, which I am super jealous of when it's muggy and gross outside. Nuclear is the immunity to radiation thing, and that's bright green. Darker green can either be Terra Botanical or Terra Medical, Botanical makes plants grow faster and medical heals people. Aquatic is dark blue and lets you breathe underwater. That's Maya, she runs the bar I stay at. The only other one I know of after that is a Prime, but it's really rare. It's all of the attunements combined into one super-attunement."

"That sounds fantastic! I'd love to have any of those abilities."

"So, what should I call you?" Kiera asked as she leaned forward to rest her chin on her hands.

As she waited for him to reply to her, she brought her index fingertip's claw around to the back of the little one's ear and gently scratched at the black fur. The action caused his tiny ear to flick slightly, but he eventually began gently pushing his head up toward her finger as he closed his eyes. From this distance, she could easily make out details that she hadn't noticed before. He had markings on his forehead that matched the style of the markings on his chest, as well as fluffy red fur inside his little black ears. He seemed a bit saddened by the question she asked, even though his tail was still swaying back and forth at her attentions.

"Adriel," Kiera said, breaking the long silence. "That's your name now, okay?"

"Adriel?" the little one replied, looking up to her in wonder.

"You don't know your name, do you? Or the name of the person who had you before?"

"No, I don't," he replied, still nudging into her fingertip a bit with his head as she gently massaged behind his ear. "If I'm Adriel, what should I call you?"

"My name is Kiera Azah Rovanoe. So then, what do you think of your new name? Do you like it?"

"Oh yes, I love it!" Adriel replied enthusiastically, looking up to his new companion. His eyes were each a different color, the left one was red and the right was light gray.

"I'm glad then," Kiera said. "Sorry about hurting you earlier."

"You don't need to worry about hurting me, I heal. Besides, I've been conditioned to like it anyway. Pain doesn't feel the same for me as it does for others. It's like a drug."

"Like a drug? So when I crushed you earlier, you enjoyed it?"

"I did," Adriel replied nervously. "I don't know how to explain it any better than it being an addiction. I just feel like I want to help others, like it's what I'm meant to do."

"Can I try something really quick?" Kiera asked. "I think I might know why someone would want to make you."

"I am at your service, Kiera. You may do with me as you will."

CEROLIAN SAGAS

S E R E N D I P I T Y

C H A P T E R   I I

Without saying another word, Kiera slid her hand up so that the palm was hovering just over the little one's face. With her fingers outstretched, Adriel gently pressed his forehead against her skin with his eyes closed. He smiled, feeling a warmth within himself as the Aluni began drawing energy from the little being. All of the patterns across Kiera's body began to glow as misty arcs of light passed through the air from his body and into her palm, soothing her as well. It wasn't anything like the shimmer of a soul passing into her. The light was constant while she drew in his energy, staying lit throughout the entire process as calming spiritual rays entered her through the palm of her hand. After Kiera had a decent amount of the energy stored up in her body, she drew her hand back and let out a contented huff. She then leaned back in her chair, taking in all that had just happened. Kiera felt as though she spent the day at a spa, every muscle in her body had relaxed to the point where she almost felt too calm and peaceful about her surroundings.

"Woah," Kiera said softly, "you're amazing."

"Can I ask something else of you?" Adriel said, using his arm to prop his little body up shakily. His tail was still swaying back and forth, though it too was a bit slower now.

"Sure, ask away, little guy," Kiera replied, her tail swaying across the floor behind her. "I'm sorry if I took too much."

"If you can't take the time to help me find her, can I call you my new owner?"

"Your what?" Kiera replied quizzically. "You don't want me as your owner. I mean, I don't want to hurt you or anything like that. There are a lot of better people you can choose."

"I don't have anyone, and I don't want to be out here alone," Adriel replied in a solemn tone. "I promise I won't be in your way. My old owner used to store me in her shoes when I wasn't being used. She had me massage her feet too as a way of getting me used to being near them."

"As mean as that sounds, it actually makes sense."

"It does?"

"Yeah. The bottom of our feet, the palms of our hands, and the inside of our digestive tract are all of the 'pure gathering points' we have. We don't get all the benefits of taking in a spirit anywhere else, and we need to take at least two lives a day to survive. It's the same for all of the races here."

"What happens if you don't?" Adriel asked curiously.

"I've never seen it happen really, but I've read about it. We call it Æther Sickness, and it's fatal if you let it go on for too long. The first day or so isn't anything terrible, just some really bad headaches and nausea. After that though, people spiral out of control pretty quickly. They start to get aggressive and after a few more days they can't even speak. You're a lost cause at that point. Beyond that, people go brain-dead."

"So, the little ones running around—"

"The Mek'Vatir. We really need them to survive, yeah," Kiera replied. "Pretty much everyone is taught to drop a Mek in each shoe in the morning, or your slippers if you're being lazy around the house. The heat and pressure make them basically disappear after they get crushed, and once you get used to feeling them down there you hardly notice. It's a bit less personal for most people who don't want to see them break."

"Where did they come from? Please, can you tell me as much as you can?"

"Alright then, how about I start at the beginning? A long time ago, the Anunnari created two races to inhabit Cerolia. They were called the Mek'Va and Ali. Then, they constructed a series of cities and structures that drew on the life essence of the planet to power everything. It was a seemingly inexhaustible supply since the planet was able to regenerate everything just as quickly as it was used."

"That sounds like a utopia."

"Yeah, until the Mek'Va decided they were above everyone else. The majority of their race formed an aristocracy called the 'Elite.' They fought to either eradicate or enslave all the Ali and any sympathizers they could find. The Mek'Va Elite were disgustingly successful in quelling any rebellions they came across. They eventually became curious about the city's technology and tried to figure out how it worked. Their studies brought them to find a series of substations throughout the planet that managed the flow of power to all of their civilization. Inside of these substations were portals to another realm called Cargasso."

"They opened them?"

"Of course they did," Kiera continued. "On the other side they found a crystalline substance that they could turn into a drug. It didn't have any immediate effects when injected, but whatever the stuff was made them completely reliant on it. Naturally, they tried to use it to further guarantee their rule over the Ali."

"That sounds terrible...."

"It was. They didn't know how to work the portals though, and since they weren't designed to stay open indefinitely, they began to drain Cerolia of its life. When the planet wasn't strong enough to maintain the portal network anymore, all of the portals collapsed at once. It released radiation all across the planet, with the most dangerous places of all being the exclusion zones we have today."

"What happened after?"

"Well," Kiera said softly, "the radiation caused the entire planet to become sterile. Nobody was able to have children, and that meant the entire population of Cerolia was about to disappear. The Ali were successful in fighting back at this point, but when they won, they were the victors of a desolate wasteland."

"How did they fix things?"

"The Four Protectors. They were all drawn to a single spot, the records aren't really clear on how or why they all came—nor their races. I think they were a group of mixed slaves, some Ali and some enslaved Mek'Va. They discovered a command center for all of the other substations that still functioned and disappeared into its portal. Shortly after they made it to the realm of the dead, each found a weapon that protected them from the spirits on the other side."

"Do you know what their names were?" Adriel asked.

"Yep! I know their names, and what their weapons were made of, too! All of this was required learning before I moved in at the Temple of Aludra. She's the Protector of the West, and her weapon was made out of physical shadow. Then there's Astrona. She was the Protector of the North who had one that was made of pure light. Kine of the South found one made from stardust while Hitara of the East had a weapon made from hope."

"Stardust and Hope?" Adriel said dismissively. "It sounds a bit far-fetched."

"Honestly, I'm talking to a miniature immortal right now so I'm a bit open to far-fetched ideas."

"You have a point there."

"They're tales that weren't written by the Protectors themselves, so they're bound to be a bit fantastical."

"So how did the Protectors manage to save the world?"

"They never returned, so we don't really know for sure. About a cycle after they disappeared, crystals that were made of something completely foreign to the planet began to appear all over. A pair of scientists, who were married, were among the people researching them. They handled a crystal at the same time and their willing spiritual connection activated it, making new life. The Symbiont Crystal eventually came to term and the first Aluni was born. We're all descendants of the Ali and the Mek'Va who were injected with the poison. I don't really know how they made children before Symbiont Crystals started forming, I just know it needed a male and a female to work. We don't have that problem anymore since all of the thirteen races that are around now are single-sex."

"What happened to the slaveholders?" Adriel asked quickly, and Kiera dismissively motioned toward a small Mek'Vatir that was scurrying along the ground nearby.

"When any of the slaveholders tried their luck, they made them. The Mek'Vatir are their prodigy. Without them, we would fall prey to Æther Sickness. The crystals inside of our body are what we call a Symbiont, they're in everyone. It's what remains of the crystal we're born from, and if it doesn't get enough spiritual energy, it takes from the host and tries to force you to kill anyone you come across in desperation."

"So, you think I was supposed to replace them? The Mek?"

"Maybe. I do think it's why she was so interested in keeping you underfoot, since that puts you right up against a pure gathering point all the time. Are you really sure you'd want to go in there with me? I've already had my sacrifices for the day so I wouldn't mind just carrying you around."

"Honestly, it makes me feel useful," Adriel said softly. "So does that mean you'll be my new owner?"

"Just until we find your old one, then you can figure out who you want to go with," Kiera replied with another toothy smile.

"Thank you!" Adriel squeaked, bowing slightly as his tail flailed back and forth with vigor. "You can do whatever you'd like with me, I just want to be able to help."

"Oh!" Kiera said sharply as she remembered the box of keys. "I'm trying to get a key from this box and I can't quite manage it. I can open the lid enough for a key to slip through, but I think they're fastened down inside."

"I can help if you'd like," Adriel replied triumphantly as he stood up and stumbled over to the little box. "Can you open it enough for me to get in? I might be able to hand them back through to you, or at least unfasten them."

"Let's see...." Kiera said as she reached over to the box and slid her thumbnail into the crack.

It opened slightly, just barely enough for a standard-sized key to fit through but not much else. She moved her other hand over for Adriel to step onto and lifted him up so that he could attempt entry. He reached his arms inside, though there wasn't enough space for his head to fit through the gap. The sight of their near-miss was disheartening, but even if she had to go back home with Adriel as her prize, she would be able to call it a very successful scavenging trip.

"Not quite," Adriel said under his breath, before hopping off her hand. He looked to the various items on the desk, and then back up to Kiera. "I have an idea."

"What is it?"

Adriel then wandered over to a small sheet of paper, laying down atop the notice as though he were about to get some rest. He then looked up to the confused Aluni with a proud smile.

"Alright. Set a piece of paper down on top of me, then crush me between them. After I'm flat, you should be able to slip me inside so I can heal. Then, I'll be able to free the keys."

"You'll be trapped inside," Kiera pointed out.

"Look there," Adriel said, pointing to a small strip of leather nearby. "If you fold that over and push the looped side through the crack, I'll be able to climb in. Then, when you pull it back out, it'll crush me through and I'll heal again."

"That sounds horrifically painful," Kiera said, wincing slightly as she took a longer slip of paper in hand. "I guess it'll work, and if we do get the keys I won't have to come back out here later."

"I'm ready when you are."

Kiera was a bit skeptical about the whole plan, but decided to go along with it. She watched him disappear beneath the paper as she set it on him like a tiny blanket, then she slid both toward the edge of the table. Part of her hoped that he would reconsider everything if she waited long enough. When it was clear that he wasn't going to go back on this, she gripped the desk's edge and set both of her thumbs on his little body. She could feel him breathing beyond the paper, chest heaving in and out as he lay there waiting to be crushed down.

Slowly, she began to do just that. Her thumbs kneaded down on his body, gently at first. The sound of his little bones breaking sent chills up her spine as a glowing spot of purple began to form around where his mouth would be beneath the paper. She was being far too gentle, and inadvertently making this last longer than it really needed to. Realizing this, she covered his torso with her right thumb and pressed down until she felt it flatten in a tiny burst of purple blood. Her patterns came to life again as the liquid made contact with her skin, but she needed to do more to make him thin enough to fit.

"Sorry," Kiera apologized, still working up the courage to completely flatten her new tiny pet.

She then set her thumb on his skull, took a deep breath, and began to squeeze as tightly as she could. It was incredibly frail, succumbing to the pressure in a mere instant with a chilling crunch. Her pointed ears lowered and her tail curled up underneath the chair as she kneaded down his legs, and soon the little creature was as thin as a tiny purple coin.

"Alright then, in you go little comrade," Kiera said, mostly to herself as she lifted the thin bit of paper.

She slotted it into the space between the lid and the base of the box, using her thumbnail to pry it open in an attempt to give Adriel as much space as possible to fit through. She didn't have to wait long for the glowing light to shine from the inside. Then, once it dissipated, there was nothing but silence.

"Adriel?" Kiera asked, "Are you alright?"

"Yeah," he replied, his voice sounding a bit winded, "I'm just a bit tired is all."

"Are you sure this is going to work? If you get stuck in there, I'll have to break the box to get you out."

"Don't worry, I can be helpful," he replied promptly.

The sound of paper shifting emanated from the interior of the box as Adriel moved around. She couldn't see anything other than the faint glow from his blood, which was slowly fading. Several small clicks echoed from inside as he worked, before the nervousness finally got to Kiera again.

"Is everything going okay?" she asked.

"Last one! You can send in the leather now," he replied.

Kiera quickly took the small bit of leather that was on the table nearby and folded it in half. It was thin, like something one would use to make clothing from. Then, she slid the looped end into the box and waited until she felt it move. Adriel quickly pulled himself up into the looped section so that he could lay down on his back. He flattened himself out as much as he could, taking in a deep breath as his tail tucked up between his legs.

"Ready!" Adriel shouted.

Kiera then slowly started pulling the leather back out, just until she felt his body begin to resist. Instead of holding the top of the box open, the Aluni focused on using her other hand to steady the box itself while she tried to get her new pet out of it. Adriel grunted slightly, followed by a small wheeze as she began to force him through the crack. He could feel the box's sharp edge pressing into his shoulders as she pulled. However, Kiera was still trying her best to be gentle, which was once again doing more harm than good. The leather began to glow purple with his blood as she felt him breaking through small vibrations in the strap. Then, his entire body gave way in a single 'crunch' that seemed to echo in her head. With that, the leather slid through easily and Kiera cautiously set it to the side and opened it up so that her new companion could heal in peace.

Now that Adriel was safe and ready to repair himself, her attention shifted to the box of keys.

She picked it up like she did before and pried it open with her thumbs. This time, the keys inside felt like they were rattling around loosely. Her ears perked up, and her tail began to sway back and forth feverishly as she shook the box.

Several metallic keys came falling onto the table in front of her. Kiera laughed happily as she celebrated her miniature victory, shaking the container until there were none left inside. When she finally set the box down, however, she noticed that her little comrade hadn't healed yet.

"Adriel?" she said in a worried tone. "Adriel, are you alright?"

The blue light then began to wrap around him just as it did before. It enveloped his broken form on the leather's surface, then faded away to leave him whole again.

"Sorry," he whimpered out, "I don't know why it took so long for me to come back."

"It's alright," Kiera said, her tone still a bit concerned.

"Kiera?"

"Hmm?"

"I'd like to ask you something. It may sound strange, though."

"I like strange."

"Alright," Adriel said, clearing his throat after. "I would like it if you treated me as my old owner did. I want to be helpful, and the best way I can think of doing that is to keep you safe from Æther Sickness until we find her. Maybe even after that! Please, don't take it easy on me at all. All I need is to serve someone to feel like I'm doing my part. I don't even need food, or air, or anything else. I just want to be useful to someone, and if you want to show me to others, please be sure they do the same."

"Hold on, so let me get this straight. You're asking me to torture you, make you pamper me, and ensure that everyone else I tell about you does the same? You realize that the majority of Cerolians would rip you apart without a second thought, right?"

"Yes...."

"You are the strangest little thing, aren't you? I think it's kind of cute. Are you absolutely sure you want me to do that?"

"Undoubtedly. Do you promise you will?"

"I promise. If you want me to be ruthless, I'll treat you like you're a Mek. I was planning on showing you to my friend Alexis as well, so I'll be sure she knows. Oh, and if we decide to let anyone else know about you and your powers, I'll do my best to get them to torture the crap out of you. Any preferences?"

"Cerolians most commonly step on Mek, right?"

"That's right, little comrade," Kiera said, "Our entire culture is basically centered around keeping them underfoot or cooking them into meals. That's your preference?"

"Yes."

"Alright buggo, 'smashed like a Mek' is priority number one then. I really hope you know what you're getting yourself into."

"Thank you," Adriel said. "You and whoever else you let use me can take all the energy you want, whenever."

"Understood. Maybe we should name your race as well since we're setting things in stone for you."

"A different name?"

"Well, you're still Adriel, but something more like a species. Maybe you're an Ætherbug?"

"That sounds cute. I like it!"

"Ætherbug it is, then," Kiera happily replied as she began to unlace the straps of her left combat boot underneath the table. "We should get going, I can't wait to show you off to Alexis."

Kiera took off her boot while still sitting down and set it to the side, before bringing her foot up to rest her ankle on her other leg. She then gently wiped the debris from the bottom of her sock, including a few discarded Mek carcasses. There was one still alive near her toes that she callously pinched between her fingertips and tossed aside, causing her blue patterns to glow through the sock's fabric.

"Thanks again for your help," Kiera said with a smile.

She picked her boot up off the ground and set it on her lap before reaching over to the little one, who was now sitting on the leather strap in a puddle of faintly glowing blood. Instead of picking him up immediately, she gently ran the tip of her index finger along the side of his face. His tail flipped back and forth happily as she did so, and she gently pressed his cheek into her soft fingertip for a few moments. He was amazing, a living being that was truly immortal.

She was trying her best to change her mindset. Adriel wanted her to be ruthless to him, so she couldn't be worried about every little thing that happened. Kiera closed her eyes, took in a deep breath, then exhaled.

She could do this.

Without warning, she pinched the hair behind the back of the little one's head and lifted him by his white locks. He let out a sharp yelp of surprise as she pulled him up to eye level, watching him writhe like a worm on a hook. At this range, the little one got a great glimpse of her ever-changing pupils. They shifted like inky black tentacles beneath the surface of her eye as she looked him over.

"If I ever go overboard, tell me."

"Don't worry," Adriel said, trying to smile as he gripped at his hair.

She couldn't feel his emotions at all, but she could see his tail still swaying back and forth behind him and his ears hadn't flattened atop his head. Instead of carefully lowering him into her boot, she tossed him inside. He hit the inside wall of her footwear and tumbled to his back onto the well-worn heel of her insole. The air was swampy and the saltiness made his eyes immediately water. All he could smell was the musky smell of sweat, as one might expect from a place like this. He could hear Kiera gathering the keys they had managed to pry from the box outside as he pushed himself up to his feet and looked around.

A perfect print of Kiera's foot was permanently pressed into the insole, complete with darkened grooves for each of her toes. He could see dozens of spots where the Mek had lost their lives spread across the ground. Some of them were flawless imprints of the victim's form, and were far more visible in the lighter areas. They looked like simple shadows, and it was eerie to the little Adriel how much he could recognize about them. There were other bodies spread across the insole as well, though most looked like they were disappearing into the darkened footprint.

They weren't all dead.

Near the side of her boot, a single Mek had managed to get its upper body lodged between the insole and the leather wall. The Mek's lower half was gone, smashed into the damp fabric where the ball of her foot would naturally rest. It was still breathing though, even with its white innards laying behind it. He didn't get much more time to assess his surroundings before Kiera was ready to move. The moment she picked up her boot, Adriel fell face-first into the floor.

The plight of the Mek in her shoe was the furthest thing from Kiera's mind as she set her boot on the ground.

"Good luck, pipsqueak," Kiera cooed down into her footwear as she gripped the leather opening by each side and slid her sock-clad foot into the darkness.

She felt Adriel's body beneath her arch as she strapped her boot on tight. It was such a strange, surreal sensation to have a living being his size trapped where he was. Kiera had killed hundreds of thousands of Mek'Vatir this way over the course of her lifetime, as she had to in order to survive. However, she could never feel their breath passing through the damp fabric of her sock, or the minute movements of their hands as they gripped at her sole.

The sensation of his tail attempting to wiggle made her laugh. It wasn't that it tickled, she was just overwhelmed with all of the new and strange sensations this sort of thing entailed. Ideas began circulating through her mind of ways she could accommodate his request, focusing more on how she was going to trick herself into treating him like a Mek.

Gently, she set her foot down on the ground next to her chair and flexed her toes. Then, she stood up.

It took a lot of courage for her to willingly stand on someone like Adriel, but she managed. The sensation of his lungs emptying under her weight made her feel uneasy. His bones flexed, allowing him to spread out instead of breaking immediately. Kiera's ears were low and her tail was still as she shifted her weight back and forth, which forced him to breathe.

"This is so weird," she said to herself. Then, she slipped her backpack off of her back and snatched the box up from the table. It was meaningful to her now, a reminder of the first time that she met the strangest creature on Cerolia. Besides, she knew she could ditch the box if she needed the pack space later.

CHAPTER III

The lovely sound of metal tumblers falling into proper place was like music to Kiera's ears as her eyes lit up and she hopped in place out of joy. She cringed when the act caused Adriel to puff out a bit of air under her foot, but buried it in her mind. He must be holding up pretty well so far since she didn't feel any dampness from blood quite yet. Gently, Kiera pressed down on the handle and slowly opened the door.

The hallway she entered looked very familiar, and she felt that it was unlikely anyone else would be in here since the doorway was locked. That, and with her heightened state of awareness, she would be able to feel anyone if they were hiding in a room nearby. Her fluffy tail swayed idly as she walked down the main corridor toward the lunchroom. It too had a locked door, but this one was made of wood instead of metal. She grumbled and lowered her ears when she discovered its locked state, then pulled a small key from her pocket. To her delight, the first one she tried worked and the door swung open with ease and her long, pointed ears perked back up once more.

Kiera ran through the dining area toward the kitchen, pushing the batwing doors open with vigor as she went directly to where the food may have been stored. The freezer was her first option, as the hopeful Aluni thought it may have been attached to a generator of some sort. She gripped the handle, pulled open the door, and was met with a wave of rancid stench so horrendous that she could feel it on her skin. She gagged, immediately shutting the door to the freezer just as quickly as she opened it.

"Gross," she groaned to herself, her ears lowered as she held her nose in disgust.

The next stop was canned goods. She hopped over toward the pantries near the back, still filled with hope as she neared the doorway only to be met with disappointment once more.

"Ugh," she lamented, "they took all the good food with them?"

Her tail was motionless behind her as she slowly wandered out of the kitchen, leaning against the wall with her arms folded across her chest. She sighed slightly, looking up to the doorway she had entered the lunchroom from. Tapping the foot Adriel was trapped in, she spent this time trying to train her frustrations on him. Her tail began to sway back and forth after a few moments of tossing the little one around and toying with his breathing. She must not have been heavy enough to flatten him outright while he was there under her arch, or her fabric insole was soft enough to absorb most of the blows.

"Alright, let's try the bakery," Kiera said, loud enough that Adriel could hear her.

It was oddly comforting to know that she wasn't alone, and he did help relieve her stress. As she wandered back to the door, Kiera felt bright and optimistic about this arrangement.

Then, a wave of anxiety hit her. Her tail stopped as she scurried to the side of the door, placing herself as flat against it as possible. She could hear footsteps. They were moving quickly toward her position, which got her immediately thinking of some place to hide. The black pupil of her eye began to disappear behind a sheen of yellow as adrenaline filled her system, and her thoughts of Adriel completely fell by the wayside.

"Clear," a muffled voice said on the other side of the door.

The footsteps sounded like they were heading toward one of the nearby rooms. She held her breath for what seemed like an eternity, then slowly crept toward the handle in the center of the door. Gently, she put her fingertips on the metal and slowly pressed down until she heard the latch mechanism give way. Then, Kiera carefully opened the door just enough so that she could see into the hallway.

Nobody.

She could feel their emotions, so she knew they were still inside the hotel. By the sound of their footsteps she counted two, but there was no real way for her to be sure. Breathing as softly and quietly as she possibly could, Kiera opened the door.

Creak-

Her heart felt like it stopped as the sound echoed through the hallway and her expression shifted into pure fear.

"No," Kiera mouthed breathlessly.

Maybe she should stay until they left?

Hide somewhere nearby?

This wasn't her fight to begin with, she was just a civilian trying to survive. Coming out here was a dangerous task and she was doing it against Maya and Lain's best wishes. They knew she did this, they protested, but she did it anyway. She should have listened to her adoptive parents when they told her to stay put and not sneak away to fill the supply shed for them. She just wanted to help!

Tears began to well up in her eyes, though she noticed that the two soldiers hadn't approached. Their energy could still be felt, however, as they were in the other room.

Taking another deep breath, she continued to carefully open the doorway before her.

The hinges didn't creak again as the door moved, allowing the girl to have a clear look down the pathway toward her escape. There was another stairwell halfway down the hall that lead to the ground, but it was likely locked. With no time to fumble around trying to find the right key among the dozens she had,

Kiera thought it best to leave the same way she came in. Most of the doors were ajar down the hallway though, which meant the soldiers could be occupying any of the rooms from her position all the way to the exit. Relying on her unique senses would be the only real way that she could get out of the hotel without a potentially life-threatening confrontation.

Perhaps if she just ran now? They were busy with whatever they were doing, and if they saw that she was young, they may not bother with chasing after her.

No, that was too much of a risk to take. In a slow and deliberate crouch, she began to make her way down the long hallway. Every step she took was accompanied by the sound of her heart beating violently in her chest as adrenaline spiked. The overwhelming dread only got worse when she came to the first open doorway. She flattened herself against the wall like a plank, took in a deep breath, and crossed the gap quickly. Kiera was light enough on her feet that the movement was silent, and she angled herself so she could see inside the room for the split second she passed the doorway.

It was empty.

Taking another meek breath, Kiera continued to press on. She came up to the next doorway and the feeling of anxiety was almost crippling.

She was confident that the soldiers were inside.

"There she is," she heard one whisper, and she froze.

"Wind north, less than two knots. Distance one hundred and twelve meters."

She was relieved that they weren't talking about her, but something else dawned on her....

She'd let them in.

By the Goddess, if she hadn't been so greedy in her search for spoiled food these two soldiers wouldn't be where they were now. She was in territory controlled by Novalus, which was her own home country. If these two were about to take someone down, they were Aestellan.

Kiera ran.

She turned the corner into the room and saw them. They were wearing Aestellan uniforms; one was standing near the corner of the room with a pair of binoculars while the other was on the bed with the rifle in hand, set back enough that the barrel was nowhere near the glass.

"Fire!" the spotter yelped as she dropped her binoculars and reached for her automatic rifle.

Kiera ran onto the side of the bed and set her foot square on the sniper's back between their wings. They were a Kavar, an androgynous race of bat-like sentient beings and one of the thirteen races of Cerolia. The boot to the back was enough to throw off the sniper's aim as Kiera used them as a springboard. The muscles in her wrists tightened, shifting her blades so that they would follow her hand's movements as she angled them for the fall. The Aluni spotter turned with an automatic rifle at the ready as Kiera came down, and each of her blades landed right above the collarbone. The only part that was sharp was the tip, and with the entire weight of the girl behind them, she was easily able to puncture the skin. She felt her blades dig deep into the Aestellan spotter's neck as both of them fell to the ground. Kiera looked right into her opponent's eyes as the pupil disappeared just like hers did, leaving only a blue disc as adrenaline filled the soldier's body. She could hear the spotter's hoarse breath as she collapsed to the corner of the room while her arms knocked over an old unlit lamp. As soon as the two hit the ground, Kiera quickly pulled her blades out of the spotter and turned toward the sniper.

"Ash!" the spotter sorrowfully shouted.

Kiera could feel their anguish at the sight of their comrade falling in a pool of her own blood. They lifted their rifle, already closing the distance as they positioned the firearm so that they could use it to club Kiera over the head. Kiera launched herself toward them in a roar with her claws at the ready. She lifted her right arm just over her head as the rifle came down on her, and in response, she tightened the muscles in her wrist and rotated her hand down. The stock skimmed her forearm's blade, and the extra pop from the defensive bone caused their attack to slide right over her head as she ducked.

This left their entire torso open to attack.

Kiera brought her left hand up into the sniper's kidney, her claws digging into their flesh as she slashed across the uniform leaving only torn fabric and blood in their wake. The sniper recoiled and growled as they swung their wings forward in an attempt to disorient the girl.

She grabbed the arm that still held the rifle tightly as she attempted to maneuver herself so she could use her left hand to get at their throat. The Kavar shifted their stance just as Kiera saw a flash of steel out of the corner of her eye. She dropped her elbow instead of going for the throat just in time to bury her forearm blade in the sniper's arm. The blade of a dagger fell to the ground as they wailed in pain, stumbling back again as Kiera continued her offensive.

Two strikes to the chest in rapid succession. She could feel the leading edge of her knuckles as they sent shock waves through her opponent's torso. The solider then attempted to get an upper hand by pushing forward, though Kiera anticipated their show of force. She stepped to the side, and using the Kavar's own momentum, she managed to trip the soldier.

The glass window shattered as the Kavar fell into it, ripping the vibrant blue membrane of the bat's wings in passing while Kiera fell to her knee. Their wings fluttered and flapped in an attempt to stop their spinning descent, but it only aided in keeping their head aimed directly at the cobblestone below. They landed with a crunch, shattering their neck on impact.

Kiera then stood, panting with her tail tucked between her legs as blood dribbled off of her clawtips. As the adrenaline subsided, her pupils returned to their normal state. The empathic abilities she had began to effect her more as well. Waves of fear and hopelessness washed over the young Aluni from the corner of the room as she heard the pained sounds of someone trying to breathe with a mortal neck wound. She looked over to the other soldier, who was still clutching her automated rifle which lay at her side. Her other hand held the wound on her neck in a feeble attempt to buy herself precious seconds of life.

Kiera got caught up in the moment, and now she had done something she could never undo. She stepped back slowly toward the bed and looked to her blood-coated fingertips. Her forearm blades were stained all the way down to her wrists. Tears blurred her vision as they welled up in her eyes, and she finally took a seat on the bed in the same place that the sniper had been just a moment before. It was one thing to take the life of a Mek, but it was another thing entirely to kill a fellow Cerolian. Her face was flushed, and the tears began to stream down to her chin as her heavy breathing turned to a shaky whimper.

"Bring...." the soldier began, her voice strained. "Bring me the knife, please."

Kiera hesitated; her eyes wide as she looked down to the object that the sniper had dropped in the melee. The blade was engraved with swirls that ran from the sharpened tip down to the handle, and it had a name etched into the steel. Kiera gasped when she heard the sound of the soldier dropping her rifle, immediately looking up to Ash as the soldier used her free hand to remove her gun belt.

"I...." Kiera whimpered.

"There's ammunition. In the pack next to you."

Kiera then looked down to a small backpack that was quite like her own. It had some spare magazines strapped around the interior wall of the pack, as well as a few other items inside. Ash then tossed her gun belt over toward Kiera's feet.

"I can't," Kiera replied quietly, quaking as she tried her best to maintain her composure.

"You did what you had to do."

Kiera could feel Ash's fears washing away to an eerie sense of acceptance and steady calm. The young Aluni stood from the bed, shaking as she crouched down in front of the knife. Then, she picked it up and slowly walked it over to the soldier. It was as though she were watching herself from outside of her own body, and when she neared Ash, she collapsed to her knees and offered her the blade.

"I'm sorry," Kiera squeaked out as the soldier took the knife.

"I knew what I was getting into when I signed up," Ash set the blade on her stomach. She then pulled a small mirror from her pocket and offered it to Kiera, who took the object and held it tight against her chest.

"The other soldiers are coming; they can help you." Kiera reasoned, her voice cracking as she spoke.

"I refuse to be a prisoner of war," the soldier huffed as she grabbed her rifle, shakily offering it to Kiera while the young Aluni slid the small mirror into her pocket. "Hurry, leave me. You don't want to see what comes next."

"I'm sorry."

"Take what you can, we won't need it anymore."

Kiera took the short-barreled automatic rifle from the soldier and slid it onto her back via its sling. It came to rest between her tail and the bottom of her backpack easily without sticking too far out either way. Then, she turned back to grab the gun belt that had been tossed a moment ago. She donned that as well, which fit comfortably on her hips. Instead of taking the time to transfer ammunition from one pack to the other, Kiera simply grabbed the entire backpack and threw it over the one she had on already. Her pack was relatively empty, so it fit with little trouble. She then picked up the long-range rifle from the floor, threw it over her shoulder, and ran toward the hallway.

She killed them.

She killed them with her own hands, with skills she was trained to use only in defense.

She felt like an absolute monster.

The soldiers were most likely coming in through the front door, so she decided to take an alternate route before they could surround the building's entrances. She reached into her pocket for the keys, dropping a few of them in the process as she began shoving them randomly into the keyhole one after the other.

None of them seemed to fit.

She frantically dropped to her knees and began fumbling with the ones that had fallen before a thought crossed her mind. Kiera had assumed that the door was locked; she didn't know that for sure! She stood back up and tried the doorknob, and sure enough, the door swung open. Without bothering to retrieve all of the fallen keys, she ran down the stairwell to the ground floor. The doors were probably only locked from the outside so that people could escape in the event of a fire. Once she reached the final doorway to freedom, she pulled the small mirror out that Ash had given to her and slowly opened the door. Angling the mirror to the right, she was able to see the hotel's main entrance.

Novalin Defense Force (NDF) soldiers had already stacked up on the doorway and were getting ready to breach inside. They all had black uniforms on, with their signature green arm-band that sported a white circle with a triskelion in the center of it. It was a black symbol made of three spiral arms that twisted out from a singular center point. The group of soldiers kicked the door in, allowing Kiera to run for it.

She pushed the door open and looked to the left.

Another group of NDF soldiers were around the far end of the building with their rifles drawn. One of them, in particular, stood out among the rest. She wore a long, black coat like the other officers. However, her jacket had no rank pins or badges. The uniform looked quite like a militaristic dress, it was an outfit that Kiera recognized immediately.

It belonged to the Consular of War, and those soldiers that Kiera had killed were likely targeting her.

Her name was Aurora Rose Vinneral, the only Consular in their nation's history to personally lead her troops into battle. She was also one of the few Cerolians who had a Prime Attunement, making all of the patterns across her body a snowy white. At her side was her bodyguard, who wore a standard black officer's trench coat. They were both Aluni, and both had long blue hair. Aurora had hers pulled in front of her pointed ears, and her bodyguard generally wore her hair in a ponytail with the same style of bangs.

While Aurora gave orders to her soldiers with rifle in hand, her bodyguard had a rifle trained on Kiera from the moment she exited the building. Kiera couldn't breathe, as the soldier had her dead to rights. She was well within the mid-range rifle's effective distance. However, she didn't fire. She lowered the firearm and allowed Kiera to run toward the safety of a nearby alleyway.

All she wanted to do was get to the bakery.

**Midday | Alerio 10, 1240
Nevarria City – Business District**

Kiera wandered down the streets of Nevarria like a ghost with her automatic rifle in hand. She trekked around the husks of burned-out automobiles that were already being slowly overtaken by weeds and other bits of plant life. The young Aluni had a hard time keeping her head held high. Her tail felt like it was dragging on the ground behind her as she walked and each step felt as though it were a chore. Her mind trailed back to the hotel she had just escaped as sweat rolled down her dirt-coated forehead. The blood on her claws and forearm blades had now dried, and all she could do was hope that she could catch a break at her next destination. The bakery was the last stop, then back to the meeting place in the woods.

She had forgotten about her little comrade entirely through all the chaos. Her lack of attention had cut off his healing abilities, unwittingly leaving the poor Ætherbug in a state of being half crushed yet completely conscious. He tried his best to claw at her sock between steps, but it seemed the young Aluni simply wasn't paying enough attention to notice through the stress of her day. His glowing blood had at least illuminated all of the space he had between the arch of her foot and insole. Every step she took forced him to breathe; inhaling when she would lift, and exhaling when she would step down. It was horrendously hot, humid, and all the air he was forced to take in was foul.

It's what he asked for, though; it's where he wanted to be.

Kiera knew this part of town all too well. Her eyes trailed off to the left as she passed an abandoned shop. A sign above the entryway read *Romanov's Sweets*. It was as though she could see her younger self running inside, dragging her friend Alexis along as their parents followed suit. Running off ahead was something she would always get scolded for, which never really seemed to help her habit of doing so. In truth, her younger self might have thought the quiet of her current life to be a blessing since going out during the day wasn't something she enjoyed.

She looked further down to the courtyard at the end of the next block. She didn't have any intention of visiting it, but it was her favorite place to be at night with her parents before she went off to the Temple. There were times she regretted leaving them, losing four cycles of their love to return to charred structures where her home once stood. She let go of her rifle with one hand and pulled her scarf a bit closer to her face, the last memento she had of her biological family before the shells fell.

Kiera strayed over toward the right, walking up the back of an automobiles husk and over the roof to get to the corner of the intersection labeled Halifax Street. She slipped her fingers into her pocket and pulled out the sniper's mirror, then leaned up against the wall so she could angle it around the corner. There was a walkway that normally connected the upper levels of the bakery to a shopping center on the other side of the street. It had collapsed, blocking the road beyond the bakery's front door. Other than that, the roadway seemed to be completely devoid of soldiers.

She cleared her throat nervously as she dropped the mirror back into her pocket and held her rifle tight in hand. The patterns on her palm began to glow as she slid her foot to the right slightly in preparation for her trip into the bakery. The Mek that had been jammed up in the tread of her boot since she first entered the hotel perished. After having held on for so long, its tiny body finally dislodged from its torturous prison, only to meet with the same fate as its comrade beneath Kiera's heel.

Kiera noticed the glow from her palm, but she didn't care. The young Aluni brought her rifle to bear as she quickly dashed across the street, scanning the rooftops and nearby areas for any potential attacker. The bakery had a small 'diner' style entrance where most of the bread and energy tonic had been sold. The windows were opaque due to the dust and debris that had coated them during the conflict, so instead of trying to clear them off, the girl moved toward the front entrance. It simply pushed in, allowing her to easily move through the aperture with her rifle up and at the ready.

Her eyes darted back and forth through the darkened diner as she slowly moved forward, letting her empathic ability feel the room for any sentient presence. She came up empty, which made her feel a bit more at ease. The diner itself was set up in the shape of a horseshoe with the center being the main counter. There was a dividing wall between it and the entrance, so Kiera had to walk around to the right to see if there was anything of use here. Behind the counter were air-tight glass containers filled with assorted loaves of bread and bagels. She'd hit the jackpot, as the products behind the glass hadn't been exposed to too much of the moisture in the air. The display case was much like the one used for cigars, nearly vacuum-sealed from the outside world.

Once she realized the bread was well-kept, she let out a long sigh of relief and took off the sling that held her automatic rifle to her body. She walked over to the counter and set it down, along with the sniper's rifle and the heavy backpack of ammunition. The added weight wasn't too bad to begin with, but having walked so long with it made her absolutely exhausted and sore. Her shoulders ached horribly as she took her regular backpack off and set it on the countertop as well. She kept the gun belt on though, since it had a revolver in the pouch and she didn't want to be caught without a firearm. It was still dangerous in Aestellan-held territory, though this area was mostly deserted.

Her tail finally began to sway back and forth again as she looked to the right to see a door labeled 'Lavatory.'

Quickly, she walked over and pushed the door open to see a fairly well-maintained room, complete with a Sani-Pot and Sanitation Bowl. She reached over to the wall nearby and pulled a small lever, which activated the lights and illuminated the room she was in. The building must have had a generator that was running, and if that was the case, the water pump should be working as well. She walked over to the Sanitation Bowl and gripped two leavers for the water, one for the hot and the other for the cold. She brought both to the center of their settings to mix into a warm flow of water, and her suspicions were confirmed.

Clean water, beautiful clean water.

She smiled as her tail swayed behind her, and her ears perked up when she reached over for the soap. Immediately she put her arms beneath the flowing water and began to scrub away all of the blood she could. The water beneath her arms turned red as it filled the very bottom of the container before being hurried down a series of pipes and out of mind. She saw a Mek slip into the tides out of the corner of her eye, its little arms flailing in the warm liquid as it rushed toward the drain, but she was too worried about getting the blood of the soldiers off to care. It disappeared into the depths while she blissfully splashed warm water on her face in an attempt to wash away the grime and sweat that had accumulated through her trip in the city.

When she finished, she turned the water off and pulled a bit of disposable towel from a dispenser nearby. As she dried off, she looked at herself in the mirror and let out a light sigh. Her tail stopped swaying once more, and she turned back toward the doorway she came through while tossing the crumpled bit of paper into the nearby bin.

The bread behind the glass was indeed well preserved as she began packing it away into preservation bags she found beneath the counter. After each bag was filled, she would seal it up and place it into one of her two backpacks. She had moved the box she got from the hotel to the ammunition pack and filled the remaining space with bread so that she could devote her older bag to the food entirely. It was the one she planned on putting on her back, so the one with her bread would have to be light enough that it wouldn't be cumbersome to carry. After this task was done; she hung both bags over her shoulders, took her rifles from the countertop, and walked all of her items over toward one of the booths.

She returned to the preservation chamber after that to grab a single sugar-glazed bagel from the rack before pressing a button on the side of the device. A large pane of glass moved as gears churned behind the walls. Normally, it wasn't something one would notice, but since it was so quiet in the building, she could hear it clearly. When the pane of glass was in position, a hiss of air could be heard as the preservation chamber resumed its task of keeping the food good for as long as possible.

Kiera sank in the seat cushion of the booth as she sat down, wrapping her tail onto her lap for comfort. The large and fluffy appendage was a bit matted from her adventure, but it was still quite soothing to embrace. She then leaned back, kicking her feet up on the seat across from her as she bit down into the bagel and immediately began to salivate.

She hadn't thought of how hungry she was until this point with all that had happened, and the desire for some sort of liquid to make her meal a bit more complete caused her to look around. The dispensers that normally served such things were locked behind a small gate though, so she didn't bother.

The tip of her tail flicked every so often as she let one arm rest on it, gently running her now-clean fingertips through the fur, like petting a beloved house pet.

Bzzzzzz....

The sound of a flying insect near her ear caught her attention, and she waved her hand a bit to the left to deter its approach. There were plenty of bugs that stung nearby, and most of them were simple annoyances.

Bzzzzzz.

The sound came again, followed by the sensation of something landing on her neck. Kiera swatted at it there, trying to catch it before it could fly away. She felt the insect pop under the palm of her hand, and out of curiosity, she brought her hand up so that she could see what kind of bug it was.

Laying on her palm was a little gray body, mostly smashed but still alive. It looked identical to a Mek, with long white hair and white intestines spread across her skin to match. It even had the same horizontal scales that coated its chest and ran down between its legs. However, this one had wings. It writhed in pain as Kiera took a bite of her bagel, before bringing her hand down to her pant leg. With a single wipe, the Mek's entire form was turned into a smear of black on the fabric of her pants and Kiera's blue patterns began to glow.

"Hmph," Kiera said under her breath as her tail flicked again.

She had certainly never heard of Mek that could fly, but just because she didn't know they existed didn't mean it was a new discovery. As she sat there and thought of her aches and pains, she felt something else. Adriel's little hands were kneading at the arch of her foot within her shoe, desperately trying to do something to help her relax.

She then smiled and slid a bit further down in her seat, warmed by the idea that he was still doing his best. With him, she was never truly alone. Someone else nearby, even if she wasn't talking to them at the moment, was exactly what she needed right now to get over recent events. Shortly after remembering he was there; she felt his body begin to repair itself. She slid her heel a bit on the seat so that her foot wasn't pressed up against the arch of her shoe, giving him room to breathe. Kiera realized it was probably a quagmire of humidity inside of there, but since he requested that she treat him like a Mek, she resisted the urge to take him out.

Adriel seemed fine after healing, but there was something else she loved about having him around all the time. He was the one person on Cerolia that she could be around without guarding herself against their emotions.

She could relax, she could breathe and just exist with him around, and that fact was simply relieving beyond words. The patterns on her hands began to glow as she felt energy flowing from his body into her, sending chills up her spine as it moved through to her muscles. Aches from her shoulders began to fade away almost immediately, and everything simply seemed right.

It wasn't long before she felt him moving again, and after taking her last bite of the bagel she had in her hands, she shifted position. Kiera rolled to the side, wrapping her arms around her fluffy tail as she curled herself up on the bench seat. The cushion was more comfortable than she had initially thought.

She sighed in exhaustion as she got comfortable, then slowly fell to sleep.

The Mek had survived for nearly a full cycle on Nevarria's war-torn streets. Even with a lack of food, it still had enough to keep it going for quite some time. The little one's tiny black eyes peered from the shadow, before it ran headlong into the open. Most of the cobblestone street had been torn up by explosions and bullet holes, which worked quite well in its favor. It had made a small home from the rubble of a fallen building's sky-bridge, and it was time to start looking for some food to snack on. However, just as it stepped out into the street, the sound of something sliding against steel caught its attention. It looked up just in time to see the velvety underside of a neon green cloven hoof slide off the slanted rooftop of the fallen structure that it called home. For a mere second, it was cast in shadow.

Life seemed to go in slow motion as adrenaline filled its tiny body. The Mek could make out every detail of the bottom of her hoof as it filled the sky. Two hoof 'toes' were separated by a tuft of black fur, each having a hard outer wall with a softer velvety sole for traction. Hers were adorned with dirt and dust from their trek through the streets.

Clop.

"This street's such a mess," Rina said as she stood atop the broken skybridge that her companion had just crossed.

She looked down at Sandra who was already crouched with her rifle to her shoulder, sweeping the barrel across the street. She immediately noticed a pulse of neon green from Sandra's hooves and smiled softly. The sight of her shimmering like that always felt magical to her ever since they first met as children. She let out a subdued yelp as she slid after her companion while holding her own automated rifle close so she wouldn't lose it.

They were both Edoraii, a feminine race that resembled the Ibex. Their uniforms were the same as the snipers—Aestellan soldiers on patrol through the occupied streets of Nevarria.

"You need to get out of the base more often, Rina. I know you're not so big on actually fighting, but part of both intelligence and being a soldier is actually being able to pull the trigger on someone. What if our forward base gets overrun?" Sandra said as Rina came to a sliding halt behind her.

"How did you even get approval to have me out on a patrol? I'm not a grunt, Sandra, I'm a codebreaker," Rina complained as she dusted some of the dirt out of her hair with her left hand, keeping her rifle tightly held in the right.

The tips of her fingers were of the same material her hooves were instead of actual skin. She had horns that curled back around her ears and came up with the pointed tip ending near her jawline. Her horns, hooves, and fingertips were all the same deep red color. Rina's long black hair was pulled back into a ponytail, its color matching most of the fur on her body aside from the lighter gray fur on her chest. Her neck was marked as well, with a diamond-shaped patch of white fur.

"I thought it'd be good for you. It's an honor to be out in the field," Sandra said, getting a glare from her companion. Rina's red eyes could be fairly intimidating, even if she was mostly harmless even when angered. "What?"

"If I have to kill someone just because you thought it'd be 'good for me' I'm going to beat you," Rina threatened, getting a chuckle from Sandra as they continued down the street.

Sandra was a lot like Rina in appearance, though her attunement was Nuclear. Her horns were pointed upward and neon green, matching her fingertips and hooves. Her hair was black as well and cut significantly shorter than Rina's. Sandra held her rifle a bit more professionally than her squad mate did, walking down the streets with more caution.

"Your threats are so hollow," Sandra teased. "Don't worry, this area's been abandoned for a while. The only things we're likely to find out here are looters and Mek."

Rina walked up close enough to Sandra that they were nearly shoulder to shoulder and looked down to the ground. As if on cue, there was a pair of Mek trying to scurry their way through the cobblestone path. She couldn't remember if she got her two kills in for the day, so this was a perfect opportunity.

 CEROLIAN SAGAS

Sandra Auri

While Sandra looked off into the distance, Rina gently patted her hoof on the ground. She felt one of the little ones writhe its way up between her hoof-toes but paid it no mind as she shifted herself forward. Sandra looked back to her companion just in time to see her red horns glow with the soul of at least one of the Mek.

"Scratch two targets, can we go back yet?" Rina jested, looking back to Sandra who simply chuckled.

"How about this. We'll clear the bakery just for practice and then we can head back to base."

"If there's still food in here, I say we snack."

"Alright. We clear the bakery, have a snack, and then we can go back."

"Right! I'll go first. But you have to stay close to me."

"Acceptable, I'll tell you what you did wrong after we're done. If we ever go on patrols closer to the combat zone, we shouldn't talk so much. Alright?"

"You'll never get me anywhere near that area. Besides, if I happened to get hurt, you'd never forgive yourself," Rina quipped in a pseudo-pompous tone.

"Stay low and slow, check all your corners, and keep your guard up," Sandra said in a matter-of-fact tone. "There's still a chance someone might be in there, so I'll keep close."

"Right, right," Rina said as she crouched with her rifle up and began her approach on the bakery.

Kiera felt her arms still tight around her tail as she was slowly roused from sleep by the sensation of nervous energy coming closer. Her eyes flickered as she gained consciousness, which was punctuated by a yawn that showed off her sharpened canine fangs to an unseen audience. It took her a moment to remember where she was and what she was doing. As she stretched her legs out lethargically, she could feel her sock had been wadded up at the arch. She smiled a contented smile as she lay back, feeling Adriel move and cuddle closer into the fabric.

Oh no!

The sense of calm she had shattered when her real situation dawned on her. The black pupils of her eyes disappeared behind yellow immediately as the shock settled in. Quickly, she sat up and grabbed whatever was closest to her on the desk. The sniper rifle's strap was the first thing her left hand fell onto, and her right managed to find the bag of ammunition. She then stood up in a frenzy as shadowed figures appeared on the other side of the opaque windows. Immediately, she ran toward the sales counter and slid behind it. She kicked at the ground in an attempt to push herself against the cabinet, held the sniper rifle in hand, and tried her best to calm herself down.

Damn. She left her bread pack and the automated rifle.

The doorway to the bakery opened with a creak as Kiera frantically looked around the bakery for a place to escape. Directly to her right was a door, so that was naturally her first option.

She could hear the two soldiers beginning their search, though there was still a divider between her and the intruders. With her tail tucked down, the young Aluni reached out for the handle and tried it.

Locked!

Rina moved into the room quickly, keeping a low stance as she made her way directly to the divider in the center of the diner. She stayed left with her rifle drawn while Sandra came over and took the right side. Rina went first, slipping around the corner and bringing her rifle to the ready as Sandra kept watch on the side that had the actual counter. When the codebreaker got to the dead end, she turned back around and made her way back over to her companion.

"Clear," Rina whispered.

Sandra didn't say anything as Rina came up close to her side. The experienced soldier brought her green fingertip up to her lip, then pointed toward the booth that Kiera was occupying. Rina gripped her rifle tightly as her eyes widened and her chest felt as though it were tightening. Sandra looked back, sensing Rina's hesitation she closed her hand into a fist. Rina recognized the gesture as 'Hold Position' and nodded.

Kiera was in full-on panic mode as her eyes darted around for any hope of finding a key. At this point though, she wouldn't even have time to put the key in the keyhole before being apprehended. She could feel them on the other side of the counter as their emotions radiated through like a beacon. One felt terrified, while the other was calm and focused. The calm one began to move, keeping against the counter as the other stayed put.

There had to be a way out of this.

Kiera shifted herself so that she was in a crouch and her backpack was on her right shoulder. She lifted the long rifle and held it steady. Just as she did, she could sense the person who was approaching had made it to the edge of the counter. Letting out a small huff of air, she clicked off the safety and pulled the trigger twice in rapid succession.

Two rounds entered the wooden door near the handle as Kiera pushed herself off the floor in a dead sprint. The hinges on the door looked like they would swing away from her, and she hoped that was the case. Sandra stood up with her rifle drawn just as Kiera jumped out and slammed her shoulder into the door, which shattered open on impact. The two rounds had weakened the door just enough that when she hit it, the entire handle simply snapped off.

Bang!

"Contact!" Sandra growled. "Move, move!"

Rina quickly jumped up from where she was with her rifle trained on the damaged aperture. The shattered door had swung closed again as the two moved toward it. Sandra took the far side before pushing it open, then she stepped through with her rifle to the left while Rina followed looking right.

The bakery's production center was huge, set up with large ovens on either side of the hallway that lead into a larger two-story kitchen area with metal catwalks above. The soldiers came through just in time to see Kiera's tail disappear heading left around the last brass steam-powered oven, followed closely by the sound of boots on a steel catwalk.

"How many?" Rina asked as the two ran after their target.

"One, I didn't get a good look at them."

As they made it to the corner, Rina brought her automatic rifle up to the catwalks above while Sandra ran over to the stairwell. The inexperienced soldier had Kiera in her sights as the Aluni ran across the upper catwalk. The moment she got a good look at her target, she felt a knot well up in her throat.

"Sandra, wait!" Rina yelped, running after her companion who had just reached the top of the stairwell. The moment that Sandra was in good place to stand, she aimed her rifle.

Bang!

The round from Sandra's rifle slid right above Kiera's head, close enough that she could feel the bullet's shock wave displace her hair. Kiera lost her footing and fell to her knees in front of the main door to the upper administration office. The stray bullet landed in one of the windows that surrounded the room, splintering the glass without shattering the pane. Rina had dropped her rifle while running up the stairs and was now forcing the barrel of Sandra's toward the ceiling with both of her hands.

"What are you doing!" Sandra growled as she shoved Rina back down the stairs with her elbow and ran after the Aluni. Rina didn't fall, she caught the railing and pulled herself back up to her hooves.

Panting, Kiera didn't have many options. She momentarily considered standing her ground, but didn't want any more blood on her hands today. There were several crystal processing consoles nearby that looked like older models, designed only for simple computing tasks and running the equipment nearby. Toward the back of the room, though, there was a large window that looked relatively thin.

She could hear the approaching soldier's hooves as she made up her mind. Kiera ran forward and lifted her rifle to her shoulder to launch two more bullets through the window in front of her. They weren't enough to break the glass, but she didn't need them to. Kiera moved the rifle to her back mid-run and pulled her scarf up over her head to protect her face and neck. Before she reached the window though, she heard the sound of another rifle firing behind her.

Thwap!

A sharp, jarring pain shot through her back as her footfalls faltered slightly. She managed to force herself to jump though, tucking her head and hands down as the weakened glass shattered all around her. She couldn't breathe as she soared through the air toward the bombed-out ground below. The last thing she thought about before impact was her makeshift family at The Isarean Pub, and that her scavenging trip out into the warzone wasn't worth leaving them behind.

She landed on her side, with her back and left shoulder blade taking most of the force as her body rolled down a soft decline. The road she fell to had been hit with a mortar, leaving the ground open for her landing. It was a stroke of fate she jumped where she did, as the dirt acted like a ramp allowing her to roll to a safe stop at the bottom in a small puddle of muddy water.

Adrenaline kept her from stopping. Quickly, she rolled to her front and began to claw her way out of the mortar's pit. She could feel her back where the bullet made an impact. It was wet from the water and ached, but there was no exit wound on her chest. The concept of being shot didn't stop her though as she pulled herself onto the cobblestone street with all the strength she had. There were no alleyways to duck into, so she had to run as fast as she could in the direction of home.

Sandra made it to the window first, taking aim at Kiera's retreat and squeezing her trigger. Bullets landed close to the young Aluni, but she was too quick. Sandra's rifle wasn't rated for the distance she had traveled. The rounds fell short, and when she adjusted for the distance they seemed to drift left or right of their intended target. When Kiera disappeared around the corner, Sandra slammed the stock of her rifle into the window's frame, shattering the rotten wood.

"What in Cargasso was that?" Sandra growled as Rina approached from the doorway. "If you hadn't interfered, I would have had her! Screw the 'list of things you did wrong,' that was downright treason!"

"I stopped you from committing a war crime!" Rina said in absolute disgust. "I can see capturing a kid for questioning, but shooting her in the back as she fled is a capital offense. You can't tell me you couldn't tell her age just by looking at her, she couldn't be more than fourteen cycles! That's barely an adult, and she certainly wasn't wearing a uniform!"

"Dammit!" Sandra shouted, looking back out to the dirt Kiera kicked up from the crater. "We're going back to the wire."

The Isarean Pub

THE ISAREAN PUB
CHAPTER I

Nightfall | Alerio 10, 1240
Nevarria City – Residential District Outskirts

Kiera's hands were shaking as she held her rifle in a death grip. The safety was off and her index finger was resting along the rifle's frame, ready to drop down and squeeze at a moment's notice. With the adrenaline rush subsiding, she was left alone in the woods with her aches and pains. All her mental barriers were down, allowing her empathic abilities to feel everything around her in the forest. While she couldn't feel the animals or insects, she could feel if someone was stalking her.

That's what she was afraid of the most now. Soldiers.

"I hope you're doing alright," Kiera said under her breath as she trudged along.

She couldn't feel Adriel anymore, which in her mind meant that he had wound up in an unfortunate position beneath her. Her suspicions were confirmed when she felt his body begin to reform beneath her heel. She paused in her stride, setting her foot back a bit so that her heel was off the ground. His breath was all that she could feel before his tiny hands began to pull at her sock to drag himself back down to the safer area off to the side beneath her arch.

"I'm sorry," she said softly, "I wish I could have warned you."

She felt him cuddle up to her arch again, pulling the fabric of her sock down as a response to what she had said. Kiera's solemn face turned into a soft smile as her tail began to sway slightly behind her, knocking off some of the dried-up mud that had accumulated from her fall. She was a mess, but at least he was with her still. A large tree was right next to her, so instead of proceeding to the meeting spot, she decided to give Adriel a moment to recover. She simply let herself tilt to the side and put her shoulder against the behemoth for support.

The leaves of this tree and those surrounding it weren't all that thick right now, which gave her a good view of the night's sky. Dark storm clouds were slowly rolling in from the east over the ocean, but that didn't obscure her view at the moment. Looking south, she could see Cerolia's rings in all their splendor. The planet was in the center of an active part of the galaxy, which made the night's sky immensely vibrant. It looked as though someone dotted twinkling white paint all over a canvas of purples and blues. One of her favorite books growing up took great care in telling the names of each nebula and constellation, as well as those of the stars. She was never able to remember them all, but that didn't stop her from trying.

As she took in the magnificence of the universe, Kiera deeply inhaled. The patterns on her hands began to steadily glow with an icy blue light as she let Adriel's energy flow into her. It wasn't enough to cure every ache that she had, especially the one on her back, but it helped calm her down.

"We should go," Kiera said calmly. "Are you ready?"

Adriel pulled the sock tight to his little body, and she could feel his tail sliding back and forth. Even through all this, he still seemed quite content. With that, she resumed her journey. Kiera felt his lungs empty with each step she took, and she didn't quite know what to think of that yet.

The sound of running water was a relief as Kiera saw the glow of the river through the trees. She recognized the patterns they made and the radiant fungi that dotted the bark like spirits through the woods. It was only a few more steps until she made it into the clearing and saw the two cut logs that they used as a place to sit. There was a small fire pit near the logs as well, though they weren't planning on making a fire tonight. With a long, satisfying sigh, Kiera took a seat on the log facing the river.

They both loved this spot, especially at night. Spectral flowers always formed on the rivers in the area; their petals were luminescent much like most of the fungi on the trees.

"Ugh...." Kiera groaned, nearly falling off the log as she set her backpack and rifle to the side. Her body still ached despite Adriel's abilities. Kiera arched her back, reaching her right arm behind her to see what the damage was. It felt as though her skin was on fire.

No blood.

Kiera sighed in relief, looking to the backpack on the ground next to her. There was a bullet hole in it for sure, but she could see where the round hit one of the magazines and ricocheted out the side. The pain in her back was likely a major bruise or a broken rib from the impact.

Far better than the alternative.

"Thank the Goddess," she mumbled as she looked over the flowing river to the mountains and beyond.

She slid her feet forward and crossed one leg over the other, stretching them out and flexing her toes within her combat boots. It felt like Adriel had weathered this part of the journey better than the last. Kiera then reached over to her backpack, tugging it closer so that she could see what's been damaged and if the bread she packed in the sniper's bag was still good. She opened it up and pulled out her damaged magazine to examine it closer. The indent that was made by the bullet wasn't deep enough to affect the magazine's operation, so instead of tossing it, she opted to keep it.

"Saved me once, maybe it'll do it a second time."

The next item on her list was the bread. She moved the box over to the side and frowned when she saw the state of the food. The preservation bags had all opened during her escape, and the mud that soaked through had made its way inside. All the bread that hadn't been crushed was in a terrible state.

"I guess we did alright, even without the food."

Kiera fished out the soggy bread from the preservation bags and set it all out on the ground nearby. If she wasn't going to eat it, there was likely an animal that would be more than happy to take care of the mess. Then, she felt her friend's bright energy approaching her from behind.

"Find anything good?" Alexis asked as she came out of the woods with a bag over her shoulder.

Although she was the same age as Kiera, she was shorter by five centimeters. She had light brown hair that came down to the middle of her back, and an olive drab t-shirt that had holes cut in the shoulders so that her natural red-layered pauldron bones could be seen.

"I thought I was going to be late. When I saw you weren't here, I got a bit worried," Kiera said as she swayed her tail.

She looked over her shoulder to her friend who made her way into the little campsite they had. Alexis had a limp, though it was only obvious if you were looking for it. She walked to the log across from Kiera, set her bag down, and took a seat while she swayed her tail as well.

"I'm better than that," Alexis replied with a smile, though it faded when she saw the firearm nearby. "You found a rifle?"

Kiera froze for a moment as she slid her feet back and rested her elbows on her legs. Her hair drooped down, having fallen out of her shirt and the scarf around her neck. Noticing her silence, Alexis grabbed her bag and walked over. Crouching down near Kiera, she set her hand on her friend's back.

"Hey," she said softly. "It's ok, you're safe now. What's wrong?"

"I killed them," Kiera whimpered. "I... I killed them both."

"By the Goddess...."

"I'm never going out like that again."

Alexis had no idea what to say to Kiera, who sat in silence. Instead of speaking, she did her best to comfort Kiera by gently rubbing her back and staying nearby. Her hand slid across the bruise, which caused Kiera to wince.

"Maybe you're right," Alexis said softly. "I think we *have* been a bit too reckless."

Kiera began unfastening the gun belt from her waist, and once it was off, she offered it to Alexis. Still taken aback by all she just heard, Alexis took the belt and looked back to her friend who was forcing a smile.

"We can't be unarmed anymore if we do anything away from home," Kiera said sternly. "I want you to have this, alright?"

Alexis tugged at the flap of the gun belt's holster until the button snapped open to reveal the handle of a revolver. It was

 CEROLIAN SAGAS

engraved with ornate swirling patterns that looked like they were designed to help enhance the user's grip on the gun. Slowly, she pulled it out of the leather to reveal the bright silver firearm in all of its splendor.

"Are you sure? This thing is beautiful."

"Of course. I had a rifle for you, but I lost it at the diner."

Alexis looked to Kiera's backpack, immediately noticing the bullet hole and how different it was from the pack that she always carried. Figuring it was better not to ask about it after Kiera's somber reaction to her previous inquiry, she left it alone. Her light brown tail swayed in the grass as she focused on how beautiful the gift was, keeping her thoughts on the positive. Managing her own emotions always helped Kiera whenever she was down, as though she could feed off others joy.

"I'll keep this with me whenever I can. How are you doing on energy? Need any Mek?"

Kiera took a deep breath as Alexis took a small pouch off a loop that was sewn into her pants. She opened it up with her pinky finger and reached inside, pulling a struggling Mek out by its hair before closing the pouch up once more.

"I'm more than good for that."

"Good," she replied before turning her attention to the Mek. "Sorry, tiny comrade."

Alexis slid her right foot toward herself through the dirt. She had a pair of brown leather boots that came up to her ankles.

Above that was a lighter brown section of fabric that flared out, which made life a bit more convenient on a day to day basis. After she used her index finger to pet the top of the Mek's head, it was set on the lip of her shoe and nudged until it slid toward the back of her ankle. Instead of struggling against her, the Mek kept still while she loosened the top leather strap of her boot. She then lifted her heel enough to create a gap so that the Mek would fall in. Once the deed was done, Alexis tugged her shoe back on and tightened the strap.

"I think the soldiers I attacked were trying to assassinate the Consular of War," Kiera said softly as she looked down toward the boot Adriel was trapped inside. "I let them in the hotel on accident. They came up to one of the guest room's windows to take the shot. I could have run away if I really wanted to, but instead, I ran inside and—"

"You're a hero," Alexis replied in shock.

"I don't feel like it. Anyway, there wasn't much left in the hotel to scavenge. I did come across something weird, though."

Adriel couldn't breathe. The weight of Kiera's foot kept his chest from expanding, and his lungs were on fire as he tried to tug at the fabric of her sock. Blood from his previous injuries illuminated his tiny crawl space though as he desperately tried to pull in air. Kiera's striped sock then slid off of him, and he instinctively took in a deep breath of the foul air. Before he could get up though, he could feel something pinching his tail.

Alexis' eyes widened when her friend pulled a small *person* out of her combat boot by the tail. As she tried to process everything, Kiera set the little being in her open palm.

"Adriel, meet Alexis. Alexis, Adriel," Kiera said as she brought him over so that her friend could get a closer look.

The little one in her palm pushed himself up to a seated position as he adjusted himself to the new, cooler environment. When he was comfortable, he looked up to see Alexis' eyes less than thirty centimeters away. They were like his, heterochromatic. Her left eye was yellow and her right was a very bright and vibrant shade of blue.

"Pleasure to meet you," Adriel said with a shy smile as his matted tail began to wag.

"He can talk?" Alexis squeaked out. "This is amazing. I mean, I've never heard of anything like him before."

"It gets better," Kiera replied as the patterns on her palm began to glow.

Paths of glowing blue vapor slid from Adriel's body and into the palm of Kiera's hand as she closed her eyes. She let out a sigh, draining more spiritual power from the little Ætherbug while Alexis watched on in amazement.

"Beautiful," Alexis began. "Wait a minute."

"Something wrong?" Kiera asked.

"Yeah. So you found a tiny person capable of speaking and making clothes, and the first thing you do is trap him in your shoe for a walk around the city? That must have smelled awful for the little guy, I'm surprised he's still alive."

"Oh! He's immortal, I crushed him a bunch during our trip."

"That doesn't help your case."

"I've given myself to Kiera and whomever she chooses to share me with until we can find my previous owner," Adriel said, instantly gathering Alexis' attention. "I actually asked her to keep me there, since I can't feel pain like others do. It's where I'm most useful, and I feel most at home there since that's where my old owner used to keep me."

"Your old owner?" Alexis asked.

"She's apparently a Sarin scientist with red hair, and either a Medi or Botanically attuned," Kiera chimed in again. "He also asked me to treat him like I do the Mek."

"You're awful to the Mek."

"Your point?"

"Adriel, are you sure that you want this?" Alexis asked. "I can make you a comfortable place to stay, you don't have to subject yourself to this sort of stuff."

"I wouldn't be useful there," Adriel said sternly. "Being helpful makes me feel like I have a purpose."

"Besides, nobody's going to accidentally find him if he's always with one of us," Kiera added.

"I'm still not sure about this," Alexis nervously replied, "are you sure he comes back?"

"Here," Kiera said as she offered him to her friend, "You can try for yourself."

Alexis gently took Adriel and looked to him as if asking for approval. The Ætherbug smiled back up to her and nodded, his tail swaying slowly behind him. Swallowing deeply, Alexis used Kiera's log to pull herself back up to her feet. She highly favored her left leg as she did so, using her left arm to hoist herself up while carefully cupping Adriel in her right hand.

"How does it work? His healing, I mean," Alexis asked.

"Drop him and twist him out like a cigarette, you'll see."

"Alright."

Alexis hesitated, looking to the little one in her hand before finally giving in. She tilted her hand until Adriel lost his footing and fell to the ground. The little one gasped as he landed on his back, and looked up to the two towering above him. Wheezing, he tried to catch his breath again in the mossy grass as Alexis lifted her boot over him. The tread underneath was a bit different than he had expected. It looked like an adorable paw; with four distinct 'toe' prints, a 'ball pad' print that was stylized to point near her arch, as well as a teardrop-shaped print on the heel of her shoe. Several flattened corpses, which he only spotted due to the shimmer of their broken bodies, were stuck in bits of mud between her toe prints as well.

Kiera stood up to help steady her friend's stance, able to feel her anxiety welling up inside.

"I promise you, he'll be alright," Kiera said calmly.

Alexis nodded and set her foot down on the little one, pinning him directly beneath the ball pad of her boot's tread. She then slowly began to press down into the dirt, shifting her weight forward as she held her breath.

Pop.

The moment she heard his body give way underfoot, a wave of soothing energy rushed up to her spine and washed through her body. Alexis let out a long breath as her tail began to sway once more. She cleared her throat when she lifted her foot from the ground and looked to the impression it made in the dirt. Curiously, she cocked her foot to the side so they both could see his body stuck to the bottom of her shoe.

"That felt amazing," Alexis said under her breath.

"See why I'm okay with keeping him in my shoe?"

"Yeah. This is going to sound morbid though."

"What?"

"I actually think his tiny insides look cute," Alexis said sheepishly, wiggling her shoe around a bit to get them to move.

"Ahaha! You of all people."

"It's like a tiny wad of glowing yarn, I'm sorry."

"I can see it; I just didn't expect that from someone who apologizes to every Mek she encounters."

Alexis watched him intently as the glow encompassed his crushed body. It only took a few seconds for Adriel to return to his former self, though the glowing intestines were still flattened next to him on the sole of her shoe. His tail, soaked with glowing blood as well, began to flop back and forth while his healed body remained attached to her.

"Oh my Goddess," Alexis chuckled as she saw the motion.

Kiera reached down, swiftly catching his tiny tail mid-swing before slowly peeling him off the bottom of her friend's paw-printed shoe. Once he was clear of her foot, Alexis stepped back down and went to sit once more. She looked to the dangling little guy in amazement as Kiera offered him back to her.

"So did you find anything good out there?"

"Nothing like him," Alexis replied as she took the little one in her cupped hands, happily bringing him in close.

She then crossed her legs and gently set Adriel down on her knee. After, she reached over to her filled shoulder bag and slid it closer. Kiera watched as her friend opened the top flap to reveal a large slab of meat wrapped in cooking foil. She had small sealed bags of ice to keep it preserved, and there were pouches that seemed to have spices and additives all around it as well.

"I found a butcher's shop that still had an active freezer in it," Alexis said as she looked up from the bag to Kiera. "Lain will love cooking it up for breakfast or something!"

"Ooh! Laya meat?" Kiera said excitedly. "I haven't had that stuff in cycles."

"I haven't either, but other than that I don't have much else."

"Well, I had some bagels and bread...." Kiera replied, trailing off a bit as she motioned to the gross pile of soggy mush.

"I still think you did well though!"

Alexis smiled brightly and changed her focus to the little creature on her knee. She gently began running her red claw tip along his back, letting him lie face-down on her pant leg as his tail slowly swayed back and forth.

"Yeah. I still can't believe he actually asked me to treat him like a Mek," Kiera said as she leaned closer to Alexis to look at the little one. "Are you going to?"

"Nope," Alexis happily replied, "I'll probably step on him from time to time and wear him around a little bit, but I think he deserves some peace and quiet sometimes too. I'll leave the unnecessarily cruel stuff to you as long as he's ok with it."

"He mentioned something about giving massages too."

"That sounds sweet."

"I'm not sure I'd be too keen on that, but it seems like a massage would be right up your alley."

"As long as he's happy doing it," Alexis smiled, still gently scratching at Adriel's back. "I'm sure you can handle picking him apart or whatever it is he wants you to do."

"Little stress reliever."

"What an interesting job title."

A flash of light filled the sky, and shortly after the sound of thunder off in the distance growled through the forest. They both could feel the air pressure begin to drop and came to the same conclusion: it was time to head home. Alexis gently began to fasten the flap of her pack as Kiera leaned over to get her supply bag back on.

"How about you try him out on the walk back to the pub? I'm sure he wouldn't mind," Kiera suggested as she lifted her rifle and slid the sling over her shoulder.

"Would you like that?" Alexis asked down to Adriel, who simply gave a gentle nod from her knee.

"It feels a bit weird at first but you get used to it."

Alexis leaned forward and unfastened one of the belts that strapped across her left shoe. It was just enough that she could get her heel out of the confines. Her tail was still and her motions were a bit slow as she gently picked up her new little friend in her right palm. Adriel sat down until he was brought over to the funnel-like mouth of her shoe and presented with the option.

"Be careful, alright?" Alexis sheepishly said as Adriel got to his feet and walked toward the edge, then he sat down with his legs dangling over the side.

Adriel looked back up, his tail swaying back and forth as the sound of thunder filled the air once more. He then pushed off, sliding right toward the entrance her heel had made for him. The little one leaned back when he reached her heel and slipped right inside, landing in the humid enclosure directly on his back. It was much softer than Kiera's insole, which made his landing a lot easier than it would have been otherwise. Instead of sealing him in immediately, Alexis waited so that the little one could get comfortable.

Kiera stood up, looking to the sky as the clouds began to obscure their sight of the moon and the planet's rings.

"Come on, if we don't get moving, we're going to get soaked."

"Ok," Alexis softly said as she slid her heel into place.

The sensation of a person-shaped object against the arch of her foot was quite strange for her. As she cinched the small belt around her shoe up, she could feel his little legs and arms shifting to get comfortable. Being acutely aware of his struggle to breathe in there was unsettling as well. She looked to her shoe for a moment, gathering the courage to stand up. Knowing that Adriel would heal from whatever she did to him, and that this was where he wanted to be, wasn't comforting to her. Like Kiera, she had to resist the urge to remove him.

"Let me help," Kiera said as she offered a hand to Alexis.

The purple-haired Aluni had stepped in front of her friend while she was still in deep thought. Alexis accepted, taking Kiera's hand to be hoisted up to her feet. The sensation of Adriel's body compressing caused Alexis to let out a tiny squeak and a whimper. Instinctively, she lifted her foot so that she could keep pressure off of him. Kiera chuckled, kneeling to pick her friend's shoulder bag up from the floor while staying at the ready to catch her if she fell.

"Are you sure you're alright with this?" Kiera asked as she helped Alexis get the pack on her shoulder.

"Y-yes," Alexis whimpered as she gingerly stepped back down. "It was just shocking, that's all. I wasn't expecting it to feel like that. I'll be fine."

"I warned you."

"I know," Alexis replied as she held her chilled bag close.

"Why did you put him under your sensitive side? Might be easier if you switched."

"I wanted to be sure he was alright," Alexis replied sweetly. "If he were in the other shoe, I wouldn't be able to feel him."

"Here," Kiera crouched, fetching her friend's gun belt. Once she had it, she offered it to Alexis to take.

"Thanks."

Alexis then took her belt off and donned the new one, making sure the revolver was near where her right hand would naturally rest in case she ever needed to draw it quickly. The distraction was enough for her to shift all of her weight onto Adriel's body, forcing the air from his lungs once more in a tiny puff. Her tail came to a stop, and her ears lowered as she winced at the potential of feeling him break down there. In response, Kiera chuckled and set her hand on her friend's arm to steady her.

"What?" Alexis asked sheepishly.

"You're a bad liar."

"Turn around," Alexis huffed. "I need your pack."

Kiera complied, turning so that Alexis could unfasten the strap that sealed her backpack. She opened it up and set her old belt inside, pausing for a moment to look at the box that was tucked away before closing the pack up as it was. Kiera turned back around when she was sure that her friend was done, chuckling again when she saw Alexis favoring her right leg still.

"If you keep putting weight on that leg, you'll collapse."

"I'm fine," Alexis said in a matter-of-fact tone.

"That was the first thing you said after you got shot."

"And I was fine then too."

"You were decidedly *not* fine."

"*Fine*," Alexis said as she shifted her weight back onto Adriel and sympathetically winced.

She made sure that most of her weight was on the blade edge of her foot so that Adriel could have enough space to breathe. Kiera stood back a bit with her arms folded, an eyebrow raised, and a smirk still gracing her lips.

"You know you *can* take him out if you want, I wouldn't mind using him for the walk home."

"But I don't really want to. He likes it and I want him to be as comfortable as possible."

The glowing fungi and plant life made the mist shimmer as it began to fill the air around the two. Kiera stepped forward and took her friend's right hand in hers. Her tail swayed behind her happily, causing Alexis' tail to sway in turn.

"Alright then, I'll make sure you don't fall," Kiera said as she pulled her scarf off of her neck with her other hand and draped it over Alexis' head and shoulders.

Alexis tugged the scarf down with her free hand, holding it as rain started to patter through the trees and the smell of the dampening forest floor surrounded them. Then, she looked down and took her first step in the soil with Adriel in tow.

Holding hands, the two departed for home.

THE ISAREAN PUB
CHAPTER II

The doorway to the pub's storage building creaked open as Kiera entered. She quickly took off her soaked backpack and set her rifle to the side so she could remove her shirt. Kiera wore a gray tank top underneath, which was still fairly dry aside from sweat. Alexis followed, immediately sealing the door behind the two with a deadbolt. She still had Kiera's scarf, so she took it off and set it aside. The rain echoed through the little building as Alexis pulled two towels off of the nearby shelves and tossed one to Kiera across the way.

"That was refreshing," Kiera said as she caught the towel and began drying herself off.

"At least the rain was warm."

"Wouldn't have bothered me."

"Of course not," Alexis chuckled, "you prance around bare-foot in the snow wearing a summer dress. Must be nice."

"Speaking of which...."

As Kiera finished drying her hair, she approached her friend and took the bag from her shoulder. She set her damp towel aside then made her way over to a large steel door on the left side of the room. There was a circular valve-style lock next to the door with a thermometer above it that read well below freezing. As she turned the lever, the lock was slowly disengaged inside of the walls. Alexis bundled herself up in her now-damp towel as Kiera opened the doorway, which spewed fog from the refrigeration chamber.

Frozen, yet still alive.

The eyes of the Mek were forced to stare forward as it saw the door open to reveal Kiera's silhouette. Blinding lights flickered overhead as its tiny, frozen eyes attempted to adjust to the brightness. It was used to winters where it would spend months frozen in place beneath the snow to await the thawing. However, this winter never ended.

The darkened outline became clear as Kiera stepped inside. Across the ground were other Mek that had been frosted in place like small statues. They were all in various positions, some reaching out in pain while others were laying down curled up for warmth. The jovial tune of Kiera's humming voice filled the frigid air, echoing through the empty chamber as her boot came down upon two of these frozen figures. The patterns on her hands shimmered to life as their souls entered her body. Kiera purposefully altered her path just so she could step on more, like hopping on leaves in the fall. Her frost-covered sole lifted over the frozen Mek's body as it desperately tried to break free of its prison, but there was no hope.

Crunch.

Kiera hummed happily to herself as she placed the slab of Laya meat in the back near some sausage rope and a few other skinned carcasses. There wasn't much in the chamber other than that, most of the meat hooks were empty forsake one to the side that they had been sparingly using for their meals. Her tail swayed back and forth happily as she made her way out, hopping on the little frozen bodies along the way. She had no idea they were still conscious; in her mind, they were simply dormant and not worth cleaning out.

"There we go," Kiera said cheerfully as she closed the door.

Alexis sighed in relief as her friend worked on tightening the valve-like lock. Just having the door shut made it easier for Alexis to remove the towel-blanket she wore and resume drying off her tail. Kiera patted her hands together to dust them off when she was done and went over to gather her things so that they could return to their room.

"I wonder if Aestellus is going to let Maya get a shipment of food in," Alexis said.

"I hope so," Kiera replied, "we still have that whitegrain in the storage if things get too bad."

"Yeah. They seem to really like Lain's cooking, so I don't know why they're taking so long."

"Major Christoph said that they were considering helping us out. She still makes me nervous, but I think we can trust her for that at least. With how much she's been helping us, we might as well give her the benefit of the doubt."

"I'd hate to think what she would do if she found Adriel."

"Just another reason to keep him where he wants to be. Let's get you downstairs and dried off."

Kiera donned Alexis' shoulder bag and her own backpack before taking her wet shirt and draping it over her arm in front of her like a clothesline. With her free hand, she picked up her rifle while Alexis retrieved the scarf she had set down earlier.

"Right," Alexis said as they both made their way toward another metal door.

It was set up just like the refrigeration chamber, though it didn't have a temperature gauge near the lock. As Alexis spun the valve to release the lock, Kiera used her shoulder to open the doorway. It was the emergency supply room, which mostly had a few bags of whitegrain as well as canned goods spread sparsely around the shelves.

The floor of the storeroom was made of brick as opposed to the wooden floor of the rest of the shack. It was placed so perfectly that you couldn't see the mortar between each piece. Alexis made her way to the back of the room as Kiera pulled the doorway they entered through shut. It was well-oiled and maintained, so it didn't make nearly as much noise as the freezer's door when she shut it and secured the valve. Alexis immediately went to the back wall to press a single brick switch until she heard an audible 'click'.

Steam could be heard hissing through the walls almost as though it were singing a light tune. After a few moments, bricks on the floor began to slowly lower one by one in an empty corner near a large wine rack. The mechanism they used was old, though it was well cared for and reliably effective.

"So," Alexis said softly, "I saw a box in your pack too? What's that all about?"

"I was going to see if you have the tools to open it up," Kiera said as she made her way down the brick staircase toward the hidden basement chambers.

"I might be able to!" Alexis said excitedly. "I'll have to look at it a bit before I have a go at it though."

Her footfalls were somewhat uneven as the bricks continued moving beneath her to form a proper stairwell. Alexis followed, and as soon as she hit the bottom of the stairwell she pulled a lever to reverse the mechanism. Brass rods pushed the bricks upward, each having a leather pouch filled with dirt attached to them that would fool anyone testing the ground for a trapdoor.

Alexis pressed a small button on the wall once. The mechanism made a deep 'click' again, and as soon as it did, the path to their room was illuminated with buzzing electric lanterns. The door to their miniature home was made of ornate brass bolted into the brick structure around it. Kiera stood in front of it and pulled another small lever. As soon as she did, the door moved forward slightly as the lock released.

Kiera pushed it open revealing a small brick corridor. Off to the left was a personal little boiler room that produced the steam and electricity for their abode. To the right was a small storage room that contained a few more emergency supplies, and directly ahead of the two was a white door that led into their retrofitted bedroom.

Kiera stepped through the door and into their living quarters first. It wasn't large, just big enough to fit two small beds and an end table between the two. There was a closet on either side of the room, as well as a lavatory off to the right. A clothes-washing station filled with fresh water was set up to the left near Kiera's closet. It had a rigid metal board inside, and next to it was an empty bucket. As Kiera approached the rig, she tossed the wet shirt she had into the bucket and set her rifle in the corner. She then set her backpack on the foot of the bed and tossed Alexis' shoulder bag over to hers.

Alexis wandered over to her closet and unbelted her shoes so that she could step out of them and removed the wet clothing she

   CEROLIAN SAGAS

had on. After pulling a tattered black nightdress from her closet, she threw it on over her shoulders and slid her tail through a slit in the back. It swayed as she knelt down and picked up her boots along with the dirty clothes she had just discarded. Quickly she ran over to the clothes-washing station, hardly noticing her red patterns shimmer as she inadvertently trampled several Mek in the process. She added her wet clothes to the bucket before going back to her bed to have a seat.

"Hey," Alexis said softly as she set the boot that Adriel was in on her lap.

"Yeah?"

"I've been thinking about joining the military...."

"Oh?"

"Yeah. I think I'd join the Aeronaut Corps. I hear airships are getting more and more advanced, and they were planning to go into space soon with rockets before the war started."

"Where did you hear that?"

"I found a few publications while I was out."

"I'd rather be here with Maya and Lain taking care of the pub."

"I wanna be a captain," Alexis said with marvel in her voice. "Leading an airship would be an awesome job. I could help make Nevarria safe in a bigger way and do so much good."

"Those things keep getting shot down over the city. They're not strong enough yet," Kiera replied skeptically. "You should at least wait until they make airships that can take a beating."

"They will someday, I'm sure of it."

Alexis then peered inside her boot. She was expecting to see Adriel moving around, but all she saw was darkness. A bit worried, she reached in and felt around.

"Gross," Alexis groaned.

Adriel winced as her claw tips slid up around his chest to begin the process of peeling him free. He had survived the entire trip without breaking a single bone thanks to Alexis' softer insole and smaller frame. She had beaten him down enough to leave an impression of his body on her insole, and he was exhausted.

"How is he?" Kiera asked as she sat next to her backpack.

"I think he's alright."

Alexis pulled her pillow to her side and gently set Adriel down next to her. He slowly roused himself, sitting up with his tail flipping behind him from side to side. The little one let out a few meek coughs before looking up to the worried Aluni.

"I'm fine," he said, his voice a bit shaky.

"He didn't cough when he came out of mine," Kiera jested, "maybe you should take the first shower."

"Sorry," Alexis said shyly as she tucked her tail up to her lap. "I hope it wasn't too bad."

"Not at all!" Adriel replied. "Your shoes are soft inside."

"He's probably more comfortable in that environment than he is out here," Kiera said as she pulled her shoes off, tossing them aside haphazardly on the ground.

"Blegh," Alexis groaned again, but her tail resumed swaying behind her on the bed.

She reached down to Adriel, running a claw down his back gently a few times as though she were cautiously petting a tiny rodent. His ears flicked, which immediately made her switch to gently using the tip of her claw to massage behind them and straighten his matted hair.

Kiera pulled her socks off and straightened them out so they weren't bunched up. There were still a few Mek bodies that had been crushed so deep into the fabric that they were already beginning to disappear. They would be easy enough to get out, so she simply tossed both of her socks over to the dirty clothes bucket and turned her attention to her backpack. She fetched her box, stood up, brought it over to Alexis, and took a seat on the bed next to her.

"Do you think you can get it open?" Kiera asked curiously.

Alexis took the box and spun it around, looking at the thing from all angles before she could give a clear answer. She set it down in her lap, looked to Kiera, and smiled.

"Only if we can make it into a house for Adriel."

"Deal," Kiera snorted in laughter.

Alexis then opened a small drawer on the side of her night-stand and pulled out a leather roll of tools as well as a small pair of magnifying glasses. She then took a second pillow and slid herself up against the wall. Crossing her legs to be comfortable, she donned her glasses and flipped a few of the little magnifying lenses so she could see better.

"I think it's about time to get clean," Kiera said as she stood up from the bed.

Adriel hopped off his pillow and made his way over to Alexis' pillow. He tried to climb it, struggling a bit before she reached down and lifted him to her shoulder. Once he was there, the little one cuddled up against the soft fur of her shoulder's red bone pauldrons and watched her unroll the leather toolkit.

"I should have this open by the time you get out," Alexis replied confidently as she began bobbing her left foot.

"Oh, and Alexis?" Kiera said as she pulled her tank top off over her head.

"Yeah?"

Kiera tossed her shirt to the dirty laundry bin and looked back to her friend, who still had her glasses' magnification down. The sight of her eye magnified several times made Kiera chuckle a bit and sway her tail faster.

"For what it's worth, I think you'd make a great captain."

"Really?"

"Yeah, just don't get in one of those things until they find a replacement for that weak air bladder they use."

"Would you be disappointed if I left to conscript?"

"I want the best for you, and a life in the military isn't a bad one. It has to be better than just barely scraping by like we're doing now. Lain will be serving 'Gourmet Rations' as our house special soon if we don't get another shipment in."

"Thanks," Alexis said happily as she resumed her work.

Kiera ran her fingers through her grimy purple hair as she looked down to the ground, stretching her neck from side to side and rubbing near her armored spine. There were quite a few Mek scurrying around, searching for food and going about their tiny little lives.

"I think we can start culling the Mek soon. How's your pouch doing? Need to top it off?"

"It's a little low. Think there are enough for a refill?"

"Yeah. I'll start collecting tonight before I get to the dirty clothes. In the meantime...."

Kiera consciously picked three Mek that were between her and the door to the washroom. She then started walking, aiming for them as they ran away from her footfalls. Her tail swayed back and forth behind her as she chased them down in a one-sided game of cat and mouse.

Pat.

The first one burst against her heel, stuck to the ground as she left it in her wake. The other two looked back, freezing in perfect order as the patterns on Kiera's sole shimmered with the soul of the deceased. A small splatter of black could be seen with the vague shape of a Mek on the skin of her heel.

Pat.

The second one disappeared beneath her arch. The patterns across her body shimmered to life again as she finally made it to the doorway and stood in the aperture over the last little Mek. Kiera pinned it down beneath her great toe, then slowly began rolling it around against the ground like a pebble. She could feel it struggling, but that didn't faze her at all. Eventually, the Mek stopped fighting against her. She opened the door and leaned against its frame for support.

Tap, Tap, Tap.

The tiny one stuck to her toe due to the moisture with every other tap, before she finally pressed it flat into the ground. She felt it spread out beneath her and stick to her skin. Another shimmer crossed her body as its soul was brought to her voracious Symbiont. She then removed the rest of her clothes, tossed them into the bucket, and closed the door behind her.

Alexis' left foot continued to bob idly as she carefully pulled the locking mechanism from the wooden frame. She had a series of small tools nearby, as well as a pile of parts that were removed from the box itself. Her ears were low and her tail was still as she concentrated entirely on her task, successfully removing the barrel with a satisfying click. She had some specialty tools to get into little boxes like this as a hobby. It wasn't lock picking per se, more like lock repair and replacement. As soon as that part was done, she pulled her bands out of her hair and let it fall behind her shoulders from the pigtails she had it up in.

"Hey Alexis," Adriel said.

"Hmm?"

"Can I ask you a personal question?"

"Of course, squirt."

"What's wrong with your right leg? I felt you walking with a limp, and overheard something about you getting shot earlier. I'm sorry if asking is out of line."

"Oh, not at all," Alexis replied, still focusing on getting the rest of the locking mechanism out without breaking the wood around it. "I startled an Aestellan officer while out on a scavenging run. He drew his pistol and shot before he saw what he was shooting at, and hit me in the leg. When I told him where I came from and why I was out on my own, the soldier felt so bad that he patched me up and brought me back to the pub."

"Ouch, I'm sorry that happened to you."

"We didn't have access to a Medi so we had to make do with what we had. The soldier went out and got one of his friends to help us, but when they returned the damage had already progressed to the point where all they could do was heal the initial wound. I haven't been able to feel anything below my right hip on that side ever since."

"That's terrible...."

Adriel's tail remained still as he looked to Alexis, intently focused on what she had to say.

"I'm able to walk just fine now aside from a bit of a limp. Running is dangerous if I'm not paying attention, since I might kick something and fall over. I can usually hide it pretty well if I'm focused enough on what's going on around me."

"Is that why you wiggle your other foot around a lot?"

"You noticed that, huh?" Alexis chuckled. "Yeah, it's just something I do without thinking about it. If you spent more time in my shoe, you'd probably have noticed it a bit more firsthand."

The lid to the box popped open, revealing a small piece of folded paper. The center had gotten wet and dried up, leaving it wrinkled. Curious, Alexis picked it up and opened it to see if there was anything written in there. Once she did, she looked over to Adriel on her shoulder with a smirk.

"Missing some parts, squirt?" She chuckled as a few crushed and tiny purple organs fell out onto the bed. They were dried-up too and dissolving away.

"I didn't need them."

"Hahah, I bet not. Hang on tight for a second, alright?"

Adriel nodded and held onto her shoulder pauldron as she moved to set the open box and paper on the nightstand. Leaning toward the ground, she grabbed her left boot and pulled it onto the bed. Alexis reached inside, removed the insole, and set it on her lap before placing her boot back on the floor nearby. The insole had a perfect imprint of Alexis' foot with little toe-claw marks toward the tip, and was littered with Mek carcasses. She dusted the ones that would come off onto the floor, before picking Adriel up from her shoulder and setting him down on the arch of her insole.

"What's going on?" he asked as he sat down.

"You're adamant on having us walk on you, right?"

"Yeah."

"Well, I don't like the idea of hurting you all the time," Alexis explained as she pulled out a small razor pen from her toolkit. "So I'm going to fix the problem. Lie down in your favorite spot."

Adriel looked around curiously, before making his decision. He crawled up to the deep indent where the ball of her foot would naturally rest and lay on his back with his head in the space between where her great toe and first toe met. She then carefully brought the razor down to the top of Adriel's head and pressed it into the fabric.

"Stay really still," Alexis said as she flipped her glasses magnification so she could see better.

She then took her time tracing an outline of his entire body, exactly the way he was laying. Adriel kept still as he was asked, holding his breath as she cut up around his legs and abdomen before making it back to the starting point. When she finished, she plucked the little one back up and set him on her shoulder. Alexis then began to cut deeper around the shape she made, carefully digging it up so that a perfect outline of his body was pulled out without cutting all the way through. She set the little cutout aside and picked him back up, laying him down so that he was flush with the rest of her insole.

"This is surprisingly comfortable."

"Perfect," Alexis replied brightly. "This way I don't have to worry about hurting you. Now, you can ride with me anytime!"

"Thanks," Adriel said as he sat up in his new indentation. "You know you don't have to do all this stuff for me."

"Yep. Kiera can be rough with you all she wants, but I don't want to be. I'm ok with stepping on you when I'm wearing my shoes, but actually feeling you squish against the skin is just a little bit too much."

"Speaking of which. What did Kiera mean about culling the Mek?" Adriel asked curiously.

"The Mek have these tiny spores in their body that only work when they die. If they get crushed by us and we leave their bodies alone, they make more Mek. It may seem a little bit mean, but sometimes when the population down here is low we have to crunch a few extra to get more of them. When there are too many around, we gather them up and give them to Lain in the pub for meals or put them in small pouches. The pouches are nice because then we always have them around when we need them and don't have to worry about running out during the day."

"Kiera likes toying with them, though?"

"She does, but she's not a mean person. A lot of Cerolians find funny ways of justifying our need to kill the Mek. Really, we spend all our lives distancing ourselves from their suffering. I don't blame anyone for turning it into a game as she does. She got the idea from reading old action books about giant monsters rampaging through cities stomping around. Fantasizing about being in control helps her cope with the war, I think."

"So, does that mean you like doing that too?"

"Absolutely not," Alexis said sternly. "I can't even walk around here barefoot because I'm afraid I'll feel them squish. I've got some slippers I wear, which they still manage to get trapped in all the time. Fortunately, I never really notice them when they do until they're already smushed, so I don't mind so much. Socks, slippers, or stay in bed for me."

"How many do you really need in a day?"

"Just two, but even I have a bad habit of killing more than I need. We're all kind of gluttonous with them since everyone is afraid of Æther Sickness."

"Kiera told me about that earlier."

Just then, the doorway to the washroom opened up revealing a cloud of mist. Kiera stepped through, drying off her hair and body as she made her way over to her closet and opened it up. She tossed her wet towel on the clothesline before grabbing her favorite purple dress. It slipped over her shoulders and laced up the sides underneath her arms with a little bow.

She didn't mind being naked in front of her friends since it wasn't a taboo in Cerolian culture. All of the races of Cerolia were devoid of genitalia, so they had nothing to be ashamed of. Children were born from special crystals, which give them life and follow them into the world in the form of a Symbiont. When gender is referenced in conversation, it spoke of the individual's race as a whole and not the individual themselves.

"I'm going to head up to the pub and get a drink before I start on laundry," Kiera said as she donned a pair of torn-up white socks and her regular black boots.

"I'll probably be asleep when you get back."

"I won't be too long. Did you manage to open up the box?"

"Yep!" Alexis said proudly as she lifted the box from their nightstand. "I'm going to try and make a little bed and everything for Adriel tonight before I sleep."

"You're the best," Kiera said as her tail swayed. "See ya soon."

Alexis set the box on her lap and gently pulled Adriel from his new personal insole alcove. She then set the little one on her shoulder and picked up the cutout. It was quite intact, so the next task was to find a way to secure it back on the insole for when Adriel wasn't with her. As she did this, Kiera grabbed a black umbrella from the closet before entering the hallway leading back to the upper level.

THE ISAREAN PUB
CHAPTER IV

Kiera held the open umbrella under her arm as she slid a skeleton key into the supply building's main door. The sound of the lock clicking could be heard over the rain pattering above her. Then, she fastened her key to the bow on the hip of her dress before walking through the woods toward a cobblestone pathway nearby. The smell of the rain in the wet forest was one that she absolutely adored, and one of the little joys she had living away from the city. Her tail wrapped around her hips so that it wouldn't be out in the rain. As she progressed through the woods, she came upon the embankment leading up to the main road. The rain had soaked it enough for the incline to be slick, but her combat boots were pretty good for traversing inclement environments like this.

She only made it halfway to the top before stopping dead in her tracks.

The feeling of foreign emotion urged her to take cover in case there was a reason to fear the source. She heeded its warning as she always did and stepped to the side behind a large oak tree. Being half way up was enough to give her a good vantage point while allowing her to keep her umbrella open. Under its protection, she could see the cobblestone street lit by automated lamp posts. The intense sound of thunder ripped through the sky, causing her to jump in anticipation of what may come.

It was probably nothing to be concerned about.

"We got a message earlier that they're calling for a cease-fire," she heard over the rain as the emotions source approached.

The voice was oddly familiar, accompanied by the sound of clopping hooves on the cobblestone path. A moment after she heard it, she saw them. Two officers clad in green, one with silver markings on her uniform's jacket and the other with gold.

"Who's calling for it?" Sandra asked, her green patterns giving off a haze through the rain as she held Rina up so that she wouldn't topple over.

"Our side," Rina sheepishly replied.

"Why! We're still in the fight here. I know the assault on Sanova ended miserably, but we can still win this."

"The... The northern front is held up at Indara," Rina replied while slurring her speech, "an' we haven't been able to break their lines here and close the gap. They said we shoulda' cut them off by now. Their supplies and stuff. N' not to mention, Admiral Creed Deimos isn't letting us get to Sanova on the west coast."

"If they hold off a bit longer, we can still push through the gap and cut off the northern peninsula. We already hold three of their major cities, the fact that the first attempt at Sanova failed shouldn't stop us."

"We hold them for now," Rina said. "That special operations base to the south is sending troops up through the radiation zone. Osa, I think it's called? The attack there failed too and Admiral Victoria Lozen is coming for blood. If they get here before we push out, they're going to start taking back the city starting at this little pub here. There's some news from brass that they're keep... Keeping under wraps too. That's probably the real reason but they won't tell me."

"How long do we ha—"

"Does it matter? Why are we here anyway? You shot at a little girl earlier. A little girl!" she barked at Sandra as her friend simply let go of her.

Rina stumbled a few steps before falling into the light pole. The hollow sound of metal being struck made Kiera cringe even from the distance she was eavesdropping. Her horn hit the metal, and she simply slid down to a seated position.

"You need to watch your tone or I'll have you court-martialed for insubordination," Sandra growled at Rina.

"Insubordination?" Rina replied, looking up to Sandra as rain fell on her face. "What you were about to do was an offense that could have gotten you executed by our military's standards. Shooting a civilian in the back as she ran from you? A kid? Why did you want to pull the trigger on her? She looked like she was just there to get something to eat."

Sandra knelt in front of Rina and put her hand on her shoulder, gripping it tightly.

"It's not your place to question my actions. You're an inexperienced desk jockey with a rifle and I outrank you. She had a rifle, she was a combatant, we're leaving it at that," Sandra barked.

"It's called 'Escalation of Force!' You can't just—"

"I said drop it."

"Why are we here anyway? Dying and killing for one goddess forsaken patch of land. Yay, we're the victors of the day, we almost have the city and there's a whole load of hurt coming down around our heads from the south. We've won a city we can't sustain, filled with enemy forces crawling out to slit our throats. Why don't we just go back to our peaceful Vineyard? Back to where it's safe, and we can just live our lives again. Together."

"We have an airbase and reinforcements of our own from the south. If you want to go back to squashing Mek-filled grapes all day, run back home and desert. I should have never taken you out of that bunker and onto the streets."

"You're right, you shouldn't have."

Sandra then drew a knife, causing Kiera's heart to stop as she saw the reflection of a blade come to Rina's neck.

"One more word about this and I'll kill you myself," Sandra said coldly as she held her comrade at knife-point.

"What has this war done to you? I grew up with you, we went to school together and played together. Now you're calling me a traitor and threatening my life? Shooting at children over a war we know nothing about? What is this place to Aestellus?! I just want to go back home.... I want *us* to go back together! Sandra, I lov—"

"I've heard enough," Sandra sharply replied. "Go back to the pub if you want to drink your worries away but don't bother me with them. I'm going back to base to confirm this.... Don't show up to your post tomorrow, take the day to sober up."

Sandra then stood up and put her knife back into its sheath and her hands in her pockets, before walking away with her head low. Kiera couldn't see Rina's face, but she could feel the sorrow welling in her heart. It was enough to even make her begin to tear up.

"Fine," Rina said lightly enough that Kiera could barely hear it. "Leave... war is more important than people. Shoot kids and kill civilians because why not, right?"

As Sandra made her way down the road, Rina looked down the path she was walking. The sound of her hooves began to fade off in the distance as Rina let the rain drench her uniform.

When it was clear Sandra wasn't going to turn back, she reached out toward her comrade. Her red hooved fingertips shimmered in the rain as like from the lamp reflected off of them.

"Come back… I didn't mean it, Sandra! Please… please don't go…." Rina said with a light whimper.

Sandra disappeared from view and the fact that she was now alone was fully realized. She began to weep. The rain felt soothing to her at least as it pattered down. Kiera could feel the sorrow and loneliness envelop her like a black fog.

Kiera waited until she could no longer feel Sandra's presence at all before climbing the rest of the way up the embankment to the cobblestone pathway. She glanced in the direction Sandra went to make sure she wasn't returning, then emerged from the woods completely. The closer she got to Rina, the deeper her cloud of hopelessness felt. Sorrow from another person as different from her own sorrows, but one thing was abundantly clear to the young Aluni.

It wasn't a soldier she was approaching; it was a person.

When Kiera arrived, she crouched down next to Rina and used her umbrella to shield her from the rain. The Edoraii flinched away when she felt Kiera's touch, too intoxicated and lost in her worries to have any real sense of what's around her. She looked up, seeing the purple-haired girl standing over her as her quivering began to slowly subside.

"You…" she said under her breath, her face riddled with fatigue. "How much did you hear?"

"Let's get you out of the rain. You'll catch a cold," Kiera said as soothingly as possible as she gently brought an arm underneath Rina's to help her stand.

The Mek that had unwillingly hitched a ride between Rina's cloven toes still clung to its last threads of life. It was injured severely, each step the Edoraii had taken since the bakery had worked to grind it down more and more into her musky fur. The little creature now lay on its back upon the cobblestone pathway looking up to the bottom of Rina's red hoof; its eyes were locked on another Mek's crushed body that had been flattened far beyond recognition. Her hoof was doing a good job at keeping it safe from the rain that threatened to wash it away… but when she stood, its shelter had vanished.

The Mek heard the sound of hooves and a pair of boots on the pathway slowly begin to fade in the distance as the water worked to wash its broken body down into the woods. It was done…. Too injured to live without medical attention, it was now food for whatever animal would happen across it next.

 CEROLIAN SAGAS

Maya whistled to herself as she stood at the bar cleaning a small shot glass with a sanitary rag. The tables had already been cleaned, and when she was finished with the last glass she would be set to open the next day. Not that there was a huge morning rush at the bar, they were normally lucky to get a single customer before evening on average. She sighed as she set the shot glass down on the countertop with the rest of them and swayed her enormous bushy tail.

She was a Jalar, and her tail wasn't the same as Kiera and Alexis'. It was thicker and fluffier, with alternating shades of dark and light blue that went all the way to a black rounded bushy tip. She pulled one of her dreadlocks back so it was tucked behind her ear and leaned forward onto the countertop with her elbows against the wood. Her dreads alternated in color between black and cobalt blue, and were mostly pulled back into a ponytail.

"I hope those two got home safe," she said softly to herself as she looked to the front doorway.

Just then, a Mek on the countertop caught her eye. It was running across near the edge toward something that Maya couldn't quite see. She plucked it up from the counter between her fingertips and groaned, throwing it to the floor next to her paws.

"Not on the counter."

The little one landed on its back, and before it could get up to run away, the sky was blocked out with the underside of Maya's paw. A few corpses of other unfortunate Mek that had wandered too close were mangled inside her fur, their presence only made known by a hanging limb or a strand of gore. The underside of her paw was completely covered in fur from her four toes all the way to her heel. It was black, except for a patch of white fur that covered the underside of her toes and the ball of her paw.

Pat.

Her paw swatted the ground directly on top of its body with her heel raised in the air. The Mek survived the initial step, only having the wind knocked out of its lungs which couldn't expand to help it recover. As it tried desperately to breathe, she shifted her weight onto its body and began to twist. This was the little creatures ultimate downfall. The white fur on her paws and hands began to glow dark blue as she absorbed its soul. Each of the cobalt blue dreadlocks she had illuminated as well as the inside of her maw when she groaned in disdain.

The glow signified her attunement: Aquatic.

Pouring rain had nearly drowned out the sound of the pub's front door unlocking. She heard it, though, and immediately felt relief wash over her as her own over-fluffed tail began to sway. The doorway opened immediately after, and Maya looked up expecting to see her two adoptive children waltz through with their packs of supplies.

"You know how we feel about you two wandering into a war-zone," she said, preemptively scolding Kiera and Alexis. "Next time at least leave a...."

Her eyes widened as she saw Kiera struggling to carry an umbrella... and one of the Aestellan soldiers that had held her up from closing the bar down. She immediately ran from behind the counter toward the two, sliding herself underneath Rina's other arm as the drunken soldier nearly fell.

"Oh girl, please let this be worth it," Maya said under her breath as she guided Rina toward the closest available chair.

"I found her collapsed against a light post. The other soldier she was with got into an argument with her and left her out in the rain," Kiera explained. "She definitely had too much to drink."

"Telling a soldier they can't drink anymore isn't easy," Maya said as she pulled a chair of her own over. "Go fetch a towel from the back please."

Kiera nodded and disappeared into a corridor on the right side of the bar that led to a storeroom and the public lavatory, leaving Maya and Rina alone to talk.

"I'm sorry, I don't want to be a bother," Rina said under her breath, still slurring her words.

"You're alright, dear, just relax. What's the matter?"

"There's no justice in this war," Rina said sharply, though her anger seemed more directed toward herself. "I'm a codebreaker, I listen. I've picked up on thousands of radio broadcasts, both military and civilian. Soldiers trying to find their families among the rubble and chaos of war. Whenever I ask what we're fighting for, I'm told to be a good soldier and mind my own business."

"War is ugly...." Maya replied as she leaned forward to push some of Rina's wet hair out of her eyes.

"Sandra was the only one keeping me together, and she just held a knife to my neck. All because of this place. We're monsters, not soldiers. All of us...."

"You don't feel like a monster to me," Kiera said as she ran back over with towel in hand.

She set it down on Rina's shoulders and the soldier began to carefully dry herself off. She leaned forward with the towel and wrapped it around her legs, attempting to dry the large tufts of white fur on her calves. In doing so, she nearly fell off the chair and had to be helped back to a proper seated position by Kiera.

"I am though. I'm wearing this uniform, I'm one of them. Even behind a desk I've been the catalyst of countless slaughters. Their blood is on *my* hands. I should have stayed home at the vineyard, with Kali."

"Kali?" Maya asked.

"My baby sister. Protecting her and the nation is why I signed up for the military, not to invade. I feel like I'm the last one here that's clinging onto sanity."

"But you feel," Kiera said with a smile. "If you didn't feel, you'd lose what makes you a Cerolian. It's a sick state of affairs really. The less you cling onto what you were, the more of a mindless automaton you become. I think that makes you tough."

"Tough? I'm a blubbering soldier, I'm anything but."

 CEROLIAN SAGAS

"I know you saved my life," Kiera replied, looking Rina in the eye as the Edoraii returned her gaze.

"What?" Maya gasped.

"If you hadn't interrupted Sandra's shot, she'd have hit me. I saw you when I was running," Kiera proudly said. "You stood up to your friend and a superior officer, and because of your selflessness, I'm still alive."

"You've barely started your life, I can't let a bullet take that away from you. It's the least I could do to ensure you aren't added to the long list of atrocities I've been involved with."

"I'll be right back," Maya said as she stood up.

She patted Rina on the shoulder as she made her way toward the two swinging doors to the left of the bar itself. The soldier said nothing while she was gone, keeping her head down and eyes closed as Kiera stood behind her. After a few minutes, Maya emerged from the double doors holding a steaming cup of tea. She grabbed another chair for Kiera, positioned it next to the group, and took a seat.

She set the cup of tea down in front of Rina before reaching into a small pouch on her hip. Maya then dropped two live Mek in the steaming liquid.

"Drink this," Maya said cheerfully, "it'll make you feel better. You saved my girl, so free room and board is the least I can do. The tea should help you avoid a nasty hangover in the morning. Better than nothing."

"Are you her mother?" Rina asked as she took her tea from the table and brought it to her lips.

She gently blew the steam away before taking a sip of the warm liquid. Afterward, she held the cup in her hands and enjoyed its warmth as the Mek inside writhed. They attempted to swim toward the side for safety, but the edges were so smooth that reaching the edge was simply wasted effort.

"My friend Alexis and I were at the Temple of Aludra when the invasion began. Maya knew both of our families, and with no home for us to go back to, she adopted us," Kiera solemnly said.

"Why are you helping me?" Rina asked. "You have every right to want to see me dead."

"And risk losing the last sane Aestellan soldier here? I'll pass, thanks," Kiera replied as her tail swayed.

"Will you be missed in the morning?" Maya asked.

"I was graciously given the day off by my lovely superior officer," Rina replied as she took another sip of the tea.

One of the Mek surfaced after having been submerged, its skin scalded by the hot liquid. It saw Rina's lips on the edge of her cup and began to panic, trying to swim away from the inevitable. The current fought against it, however, and the little one came tumbled face-first into her skin. Rina was now confident in her drink's temperature, so she parted her lips to take in more.

The little creature struggled against the tide as the hot liquid cascaded over her tongue and beyond. It was smaller than a pill and easier to swallow as well. Rina could feel the warmth slide down her throat and into her stomach as she enjoyed her beverage. The sensation completely masked the Mek's descent as her esophagus broke its bones and the liquid continued to burn it alive. It took in a deep breath once it was able, but was met with a toxic environment of acidic air and oppressive darkness. It didn't survive long. After a few more sips her horns and fingertips let out a single pulse as the little one's body dissolved in all the alcohol she had consumed earlier.

"Let's get you upstairs to sleep," Maya said, getting a nod from Rina as the Jalar stood. "You should get some sleep too, Kiera. I'll look after Miss Rina."

The teacup wasn't all that big and with one more taste, the drink was finished. The surviving Mek managed to get caught between her cheek and her molars, a very bad place for it to be. Rina set the cup down on the table as Maya helped her to stand on her own two hooves.

The Mek struggled, clawing at the inside of her mouth as it did everything in its power to try and escape its fate. Her breath reeked of alcohol, and it failed miserably to get any type of footing in its new environment. Her tongue slid up underneath it, helping it out of the gap and onto the flat surface of her tooth. It was trapped, fighting against an immeasurably stronger adversary as it struggled to get onto her tongue before it was too late.

Crunch.

It's lower half disappeared between her vicious teeth, sending a shock wave of pain through what remained of its body. Aided by a torrent of saliva, her tongue forced the little one back with ease. Unable to do anything more, the Mek was forced to look upward to the shadowy white bone that would be its demise.

Squelch.

As her teeth parted, strands of white gore and black blood began to mix with her alcohol-infused saliva. Using her tongue, Rina dislodged the flattened carcass stuck to her tooth and swallowed it, savoring the salty taste the Mek gave off.

Their flavor made them a wonderful additive for food, as they were a healthy alternative to salt.

Crossroads

CROSSROADS
CHAPTER I

Time Unknown | Date Unknown
Location Unknown

Howling wind outside of the barred windows woke her from her slumber. Kiera pulled the blankets up close to her as she sat up, though when she scanned her new surroundings, she was incredibly confused. The walls of her room were dark and made of a strange smooth stone that wasn't found in modern Novalin construction. It was without lines from mortar of any sort, as though the room itself was cut from a single stone. Her gaze lifted toward the barred window on the wall high above, which allowed the wind to pass through even though it was shut.

"Hello?" Kiera said, her voice cracking slightly as her long ears lowered. "Is anyone there?"

The only response to her question was the empty howl of wind as it passed the secured window of this strange room. She felt stiff and sore as she rose from her small bed, which was far too solid to get any sort of restful sleep on anyway. When her skin was exposed to the air, she gasped and instantly bundled herself up in the blankets she had available to her.

She could feel the chilling cold.

"What's happening to me?" Kiera said under her breath as she held her fabric close.

She had never felt cold in her life other than the slight chill of a cool breeze. Her blankets kept her warm enough to be somewhat comfortable, but the chilly air on her feet was more than enough for her to quake uncontrollably.

The creaking sound of rusty steel hinges echoed through the small chamber she occupied as the door to her cell cracked open. Her bright yellow eyes fixated on it, expecting something to come through as she tried her best to keep warm. To her relief, nobody came, but now it was time to figure out exactly what she had to do here.

Before she left the room, she glanced around for any hints of what was going on. The Mek'Vatir scurried around, some already having been crushed. The gray floor camouflaged them well, but their presence didn't raise any red flags.

Her mind then trailed to the clothes she was wearing, which weren't part of her normal wardrobe. She reluctantly opened up her shield of a blanket to glance over herself for clues, trying her best to keep warm while doing so.

"131351," she said as she looked to her chest.

     CEROLIAN SAGAS

It was embroidered in white on a gray dress over her collar-bone. The dress wasn't formal in the least, however; it was tattered and torn like it had been used for cycles. On the right side of her chest was a strange insignia she didn't recognize; it was triangular with a circular glyph on the inside.

"Prisoner?" Kiera said softly, her voice was still hoarse.

She pulled her blanket back up, breathing out as she did so. Her palms were visible from her cocooned state, and the light-blue markings were still present throughout her body.

Why didn't her abilities work? Why was she so cold?

Kiera's filthy bare soles slid across the floor as she cautiously made her way over to the doorway. When she started to reach out for the door's edge she paused, looking down to her feet while still wearing the tattered blanket like a jacket. One of the Mek was trying to scale her form and was already dangling from the clawed toenail of her pinky. It slipped, then got its footing and pulled itself up to the top. Kiera only noticed it when it kicked her skin, and her current state of hyper-vigilance caused her to react.

She was curious though.

Kiera watched it as it slowly crawled across the swirling blue markings on the top of her foot. She could feel its little footsteps against her skin as it approached the purple crescents of exposed bone that ran from the top of her foot up to the outside of her calves. Before it reached its destination, she set her other foot atop the tiny creature and pinned it down. Her piercing yellow eyes were locked onto her prey as she felt it squirm for its life between two layers of skin, one of which was thickly covered in dust and debris. Slowly, she slid her foot toward her toes and back to the ground. A streak of black blood was left in its wake trailing unrecognizable white organs. The rest of its body was stuck steadfast to the bottom of her foot along with all the dust.

The patterns beneath the blood pulsed to life as they always did before dimming back to their flat colors. If she still needed to feed on them, how could she feel the cold chill of the air?

The young Aluni reached out to grab the edge of the door and pull it toward her, like a prison cell it had no handle on her side. A chill ran from her hand to her spine as she felt the cold steel of the door in her grip, but she ignored the strange sensations and pushed the metallic obstruction from her path.

Kiera hesitated for a moment and listened to the hum of the air, closing her eyes to try and see if she could sense anyone around her as she had always been able to do. She began to put herself into the state of meditation she had become accustomed to using in order to amplify her abilities.

Incoherent whispers filled her mind, and the more she tried to focus, the louder they became. It wasn't long before the nonsense was so loud it felt as though she were surrounded by rambling lunatics. She could feel them around her, their breath on her neck raising the hairs of her skin.

 CEROLIAN SAGAS

"Damn," Kiera grumbled.

She let her blanket fall to the ground and moved forward. Carefully, she peeked around the corner to her right to see a long hallway of prison cells lit by electric light bulbs. Each cell had a metal plate above it, but instead of any numbers signifying the occupant's identification, they all had sayings etched into them in common script.

'Save Us.'

'End Our Suffering.'

The scripts were sloppily written. Some were scratched in as though they were done by a rock while others were written in blood that trailed back beneath the metal plaques. After reading a few of them at a glance, she closed her eyes and took in another deep breath to calm herself.

Her room had to have a placard too, right?

She opened her eyes again, assuming that the voices would return if she tried to focus too much. She stepped out and looked up to the plaque above her door and read it aloud.

"Lluvia of Ætheria," she said under her breath.

The script of this one was written in a different way. It looked as though it were carved through, and beyond was a sparkling galaxy. The chamber she stepped out of was at the very end of the hallway with only a single window that gave extra light to where she stood. Beyond the glass though, Kiera could see that snow was falling feverishly.

"How?" she whimpered out under her breath. "There's no snow in Alerio. It's Alerio still, it has to be. The month started a few days ago...."

She turned to face the long hallway of prison cells and kept her vision low so she didn't have to accidentally read the terrifying scripts etched above each room. It was sickening to think of what might be going on here, but what was more sickening was the fact that she was here at all. What happened to Alexis and Maya? What became of Lain and Rina? Did the soldier betray them and get them all locked up in this horrendous place?

Questions. All she had were questions, with little answers.

The hallway was dark, hardly lit by the strange electric chandeliers that were placed after every sixth cell down the hall's length. It ended in a large set of brass and wooden double doors with a pair of tiny windows toward the top. She could see shadows moving behind the windows and hear muffled noises behind the door, things she didn't want to get closer to if she could help it. If this was a military base, there had to be some sort of airstrip somewhere that she could commandeer a vehicle from.

That would be her escape.

She didn't know how to fly an airship or drive a Steamtrack, but she was confident she'd figure it out under pressure.

Carefully she made her way down the hall, keeping to the left side as she closed the distance to the first intersection. She held her tail close as her body shook, but she forced herself through the fear and moved around a hostile area without her empathic abilities. Kiera slid herself up to face the wall, still quaking from the cold as she set her palm on the right side of the stone at the corner. Slowly, she peered around to see what was in store.

The chandelier at the end of the hallway flickered, intermittently casting light on the smooth stone of the walls and floor. She let out a soft sigh of relief before committing herself to take the path before her. At the end of the hallway was another intersection that split left and right, and what looked like an obscure stairwell guide that pointed to the latter. She couldn't be sure though, as the common script was mostly scratched away. Just as she emerged from the corner, the sound of metal creaking warned her to move back to her safe place for observation. She crouched to make herself less visible as she watched one of the metal prisoner's doors open inward.

Something emerged, something strange.

She couldn't make out what it was exactly, but it was tall and feminine in form. The flickering light shone on its skin only long enough for her to tell that it was wet and synthetic. Its pace staggered as it turned to look back to the cell from which it came, revealing her back to the girl. There was a large circular section between its shoulders missing, replaced with what looked like the enormous glass face of a pocket watch. Gears and springs of various sizes roughly ground together behind the glass window. There was a heart beating in time with the springs that twisted inward and outward, as well as a pair of heaving organic lungs. The clockwork abomination crouched down, slowly backing away from the door as the hallway was filled with the sound of flesh sliding across stone.

Whatever the creature was turned back to the hallway facing away from Kiera, having a better grip on its prize. It began to walk, revealing what it was dragging.

It was a Jalar.

Kiera instantly choked up a bit, stifling herself as the individual was pulled from the cell. She was missing her lower half, dragging green entrails while barely clinging to consciousness. Kiera covered her mouth as a sickening feeling entered the pit of her stomach. She was relieved it wasn't Maya, but the fact that the Jalar was still moving made Kiera nauseous.

She wanted to cry, she wanted to scream and run back for the safety of her prison cell to hide beneath the bed. At this point, she could tell that hiding there would simply mean waiting her turn for a similar fate. She had to be proactive if she wanted to survive. All she could do was watch as the Jalar was pulled out of sight by the unidentified creature.

The movement of all the Mek'Vatir on the ground caught her attention again, if only because they were so oddly spread around. Most buildings had Mek wandering about for people to trample through their day simply as a courtesy, but this was different. There were so many of them it would be hard not to step on the wrong spot. Some were huddled together while others moved about separately.

"No...." she whimpered as their true purpose dawned on her.

The lights were dim by design, and she could hear the footsteps of more of those things patrolling the area. She stood back up and checked the bottom of her own feet for additional bodies. Sure enough, five flattened corpses were tattooed in the dirt on her sole that she hadn't remembered killing.

"They're signals."

One step in the wrong place and she was caught. She likely only got away with the ones she already killed on accident because of the window behind her. If she were to kill any more inadvertently on her journey in the darkness, she would glow bright enough to illuminate the hallway and give away her position. All the races glowed when they absorbed a soul bright enough to trip this insidious alarm.

"What's going on here?" Kiera whimpered to herself as she stepped back down.

"You don't belong," a voice came from behind her as though someone whispered over her shoulder.

It was spoken in countless of languages from countless voices all at once, though the loudest one spoke so she could understand. Kiera cringed and stumbled forward when she felt breath slide across the back of her neck as those words were uttered. She quickly turned to face whoever said it, bringing her arms up in defense. She was greeted by an empty corridor leading to the same snow-covered window as before.

It was time to move.

She glanced back down the hallway that the creature had emerged from with the poor Jalar and swallowed deeply before proceeding. Instead of crouching down, she stood up straight and slowly walked along the pathway. Kiera started each step with the heel and slowly shifted her weight forward to the ball of her foot. Hopefully, by moving like this, she could feel them beneath her before she killed them. Three steps down the darkened hall she felt something pop beneath her arch though, immediately freezing her in her tracks. Kiera nervously exhaled as she moved her foot to the side. The Mek was laying there looking back to the young Aluni, its insides had spewed out to the floor as it writhed there in pain.

The sound of stone grinding against stone then filled the hallway. She stayed where she was until the noise dissipated, then stepped over the green trail of blood. It was hard to even breathe as she approached the corner that the clockwork abomination had just taken.

Cautiously, she peeked around that corner.

It was gone.

The trail of blood ended against a wall in the middle of the hallway directly opposing a door that had a plaque with the word 'Warden' etched onto it. The first thing that came to mind was

     CEROLIAN SAGAS

a secret chamber of sorts, but what lay behind wasn't something she was keen on seeing. An object on the floor nearby caught her attention though, it was a small skeleton key made of copper with a string attached to it like a necklace. She quickly picked it up and slipped it over her neck in the event it could be useful.

"Futile."

Kiera whimpered while reaching to the back of her neck to shield it from the legion's breath. She stumbled forward as she turned to face the source of the noise, still very uncomfortable with all of the new sensations she had to deal with. The corridor she was in now resembled the first; a long pathway with prison cell doors and plaques that ended in a set of reinforced double doors. These were ajar though, and the sign that was above them read 'Stairwell.'

Kiera took another long, deep breath as she gathered the courage to proceed. The methodical and heavy footsteps of more of these beasts felt like the beat of a drum. She was listening closely, as their noisy nature was her best bet at knowing where they were. Carefully, she pushed on. Her tail was draped behind her motionlessly as the young Aluni focused her attention on the noises around. It was incredibly hard to see the Mek'Vatir in the darkness though, and she often had to change the way she was moving to avoid outright crushing them. The lucky ones were simply knocked to the ground and pinned before she felt them, while others were broken and left to die on the cold floor.

Just a few more hallways. The monsters sounded as though they were walking the opposing path, so she should be clear.

Squelch

She felt the little one a second too late as her heel pressed its body into the ground. She quickly tried to ball her fists in an attempt to block the glowing light they produced as its soul was brought into her. Kiera stayed where she was, waiting with bated breath as she desperately tried to listen to any changes in the clockwork abomination's rhythm.

Pap, pap, pap, pap.

She felt a wave of immediate anxiety befall her as her body released copious amounts of adrenaline. Her eyes glazed over with their yellow sheen and her pupils disappeared. The sound of heavy footfalls approaching from behind her felt impossibly close. Her fight or flight response kicked in immediately, and she turned to face the beast with her clawed hands at the ready and her fanged teeth bared.

Nothing.

She panted more and more as she slowly backed toward the double doors with her ears down and her tail tucked between her legs. All she wanted to do was know where these things were so she could dodge them or stand and fight. The patterns on her hands and legs came to life time and time again, her main focus now on her opponent. There was one more hallway left to cross before getting there, she was so close.

She turned and pressed herself against the wall, then peeked around to see if it was indeed empty. To her relief, she was alone. Adrenaline in her system began to subside, and the black pupil in her eye resumed its normal movements.

Pap, pap, pap.

Kiera turned back the way she came and was now face to face with the slick sheen of an abomination's skin. Her knees gave out beneath her as she stumbled backward just in time to dodge an enormous blade. It collided with the wall where her head was just as she hit the ground, and that adrenaline sheen of her eyes immediately returned. This creature was enormous, much larger than the feminine one she had seen earlier. The blades were attached to its arms, which made it a temporary prisoner stuck in the wall as its expressionless face remained trained on Kiera. Black beady eyes flickered back and forth at an unnatural speed, sunken deep in darkened eye sockets as it stood.

Instead of trying to free its arm, it lifted the blade attached to its other hand high enough to scrape the ceiling. Kiera scurried back with her tail between her legs as it came down. She watched the blade slice through its own arm at the wrist in a single slash, freeing it from the burden entirely.

There was no way she could fight this thing.

Kiera scrambled to her feet and ran toward the opened double doors. She could hear its heavy footsteps behind her just as she reached the doorway and threw it open. Knowing that putting anything between herself and this beast would be helpful, she held onto the door and slammed it shut the moment she was on the other side. She ran down the stairwell, nearly tumbling when she heard the doorway she had just closed be ripped from its hinges. Even in her panicked state, she was increasingly careful about how she stepped down the stairwell. A single foot out of place could send her tumbling to her death, or worse.

It could leave her crippled, at the beast's mercy.

The stairwell was just as filled with the Mek as the prison cells. She could feel their bodies sticking to her like dirt on her skin, though she didn't care how many she killed. All she knew was that her Symbiont was flashing frequently, absorbing soul after soul and calling out for the beasts to come to take her back for execution.

There were no doorways on the way down. The stairwell went on forever it seemed as the sound of the clockwork terror behind her grew closer and closer.

"Solumna will rise...." the voices whispered.

The end of the spiraling staircase came to another set of doors much like the first. She ran into them at full speed, pushing the right one open with all the weight she could muster. They were heavy and poorly maintained, making moving them a chore. Calling forth all the strength she had left, Kiera let out a cry of desperation. As soon as she could fit inside, she slid through and pushed it shut.

There was a hole in the doorway for a key to fit into, and without hesitation, she leaned in so that she could use her skeleton key necklace.

It fit.

She turned it with the hope that it would cooperate.

Click.

She leaned against the door with all her weight. Just as she did, the sound of the abomination's body slamming against it echoed through the room. The heavy doors lurched forward, throwing her to her back as the hinges barely held it in its frame. She stared up at the only thing separating her from the massive clockwork horror as dust fell from the ceiling.

Bang.

Bang.

Kiera panted quickly as each loud slam shook the walls around her. A single roar filled the room muffled only by the doorway between the two, and after that display of primal anger, the room grew silent. The only noises that reached the young one's ears now were that of steam hissing through pipes and larger cogs clacking nearby.

She curled up, bringing her knees to her chest and wrapping her arms around them while she wrapped her tail around her legs. Her light whimpering was masked by the cogs churning. Within seconds her cheeks were wet with tears, which dripped from her chin to the shirt below.

"I wanna go home...." she meekly said to herself as she pulled her tail in tight.

After taking a few minutes to recuperate, she slowly pushed herself to her feet and used the back of her hand to wipe her burning eyes clear so she could see.

Kiera scanned the room she was in for the first time since she arrived in it. It was about twice the height of the hallway she was in a moment ago and had large machines along all of the walls. Enormous vats of an unknown liquid were across from her that smelled of sulfur. Steam rose from the bubbling liquid to the ceiling above, which was scorched from extended use. There only seemed to be one exit to the room, so with no other choice, she made her way there.

She opened it slowly, revealing a long hallway made of stone that ended in a t-shaped intersection. From around the corner, she saw someone run and turn her direction, though this person seemed different. She looked like an Aluni and wore a long black trench coat with the sleeves rolled up so that her white forearm blades could be seen. She had long white hair that slowly faded to various sparkling shades of blue, purple, and black. The cosmic pattern matched her tail, and she wore a white mask that was tapered perfectly to fit her jawline. A pair of ethereal white handguns with cleaver-like blades on the end appeared in her hands as she started running toward Kiera, lifting them as the doorway shut on its own.

Kiera turned to look back into the steam room. Mere centimeters away from her face was a pelt of slick, gray skin and gears churning behind a pane of glass. It lifted it's right arm high into the air and Kiera immediately stepped to the side, running underneath it so that her back wasn't up against the wall. The creature phased in front of her, its form blurred and distorted as though it was having a hard time staying within the realm of Cerolia. She reared back, unable to think clearly.

The blade swiftly came down across her neck, and she fell.

**Daybreak | Alerio 11, 1240
Nevarria City – Isarean Pub**

Kiera's eyes shot open as she sat up in her bed, gripping her sweat-soaked sheets while her disheveled purple hair covered her face. Her eyes were wide as her chest heaved in and out. She was in darkness, but the gentle hum of the boiler room's generator nearby allowed her to figure out where she was...

Home.

"By the Goddess," Kiera groaned to herself as she reached over to a nearby electric lamp.

The light buzzed on, illuminating the immediate area around her. She had no idea exactly what time it was since there were no windows down in the shelter. Kiera gently felt at her neck so she could see if there were any markings or issues before sliding to a seated position on the edge of the bed. Alexis had gone, the light beneath the washroom door indicated that's where she was.

Her slippers were gone and all of the clothes had been washed. They were hanging on the clothesline in the corner of the room to drip dry, and there were several small leather pouches on the nightstand next to Adriel's box. She assumed he was inside, but wasn't entirely sure. Alexis' shoes were sitting next to her bed, and an Adriel-shaped cutout was hanging by a string tied to a belt-like strap near her heel so that it wouldn't come off. Several tiny silver bars came out the side of the cutout, as though it fit in somewhere like a key.

Just then, Alexis stepped out of the washroom with two Mek in her hands. She leaned against a nearby wall, bringing her leg up behind her so the back of her heel was near her tail's base. There was a small slit on the heel of her slippers that lead to an internal pocket underneath the worn-out sole. She slotted the first little one into the small alcove between the layers of leather like a coin. As she stepped back down to do the same with her other slipper, the red patterns on her body shimmered with their ethereal glow. The second one slipped into place with little resistance and was met with the same fate as Alexis' attention turned back to her friend.

"Good Morning comrade, glad to see you're up!"

"Ugh," Kiera groaned, "sorry about not washing last night."

"It's alright. I culled a bit this morning so you wouldn't have to worry about that either."

"Have you been upstairs yet?"

"I went up to get something to drink from the storeroom but I haven't been in the pub this morning. Why?"

"Well," Kiera started, her speech groggy and slow, "remember when I said that I had a rifle for you but I lost it at the bakery?"

"Yeah?"

"Long story short, two Aestellan soldiers came in. One was trigger-happy and tried to kill me, and the other one stopped her from doing that. She got drunk last night and she stayed in a room upstairs."

"So, which one is here? The one who shot at you or the one who saved you?"

"The one who saved me."

"Oh good," Alexis sighed, "I'm already nervous enough with Heather working here as a waitress. I know she knows all about our escapades but she still freaks me out. Do you think the soldier upstairs is trustworthy?"

"Yeah."

"We should still leave our guns down here. I doubt Heather would be happy if she walked in and saw us sporting some Aestellan military hardware."

"I wasn't planning on bringing the rifle.... Were you?"

"Just wanted to be sure we're on the same page. I think Lain might be up cooking breakfast already, and Heather should be coming at around noon to help out with the evening rush and relax a bit. You alright?"

"Yeah, just a bad dream is all," Kiera groaned.

Before her memory of her dream faded, she looked to her nightstand and opened up the drawer and rummaged through its contents. She retrieved a small pad of paper and an ink jotter. Then, she began to write.

131351
Solumna - Lluvia of Ætheria
Might be useful, don't forget.

Humming to herself, Alexis walked over and opened up the top of Adriel's box to see him curled up in the corner clutching the rag she had given him as a blanket. He looked up to her with an empty stare, and she immediately scooped him up into her hands. His ears were flattened atop his head, he was shivering, and his tail was coldly static.

"What's wrong?" Alexis asked as she held him close.

In response, the little one lay down in her palm and wrapped his arms around her index finger tightly. Alexis gently used a claw on her other hand to rub his back, hoping to calm him down.

"Please don't put me back in there," the little one pleaded.

"I won't, I promise."

"I can't sleep," he said as he quaked. "It was agonizingly dark and lonely. I don't want to be useless, please."

"You're anything but useless squirt," Alexis replied, "I didn't think you'd be so lonely in there. From now on you'll stay with one of us, alright? At least until we can find a better option."

"Thank you."

Neither noticed one of the captured Mek escaping the confines of its leather pouch. It ran across the countertop toward Kiera's bed and jumped. When it landed, it bounced a few centimeters before rolling to its feet. Panting, the tiny one tried its best to navigate Kiera's bed on its path toward the wall where it would climb down to safety. Then, the bed around it shifted enough to cause it to tumble to its back. Kiera's hair came back down, burying it in purple as the tired girl tugged her blankets back over her. She didn't feel it at all as it struggled, desperately trying to get out from underneath her back while she cuddled with her pillow.

"You get to ride with Kiera for a bit this morning alright? Then maybe we can test out our little insole invention together," Alexis said as she held Adriel up at eye level in her palm.

Adriel nodded as his ears perked back up and his tail's tip began to gently sway again.

"Dammit," Kiera complained as her stomach growled, "I don't want to get up."

"If you want something to eat you will," Alexis replied.

"Ugh. Can you bring food back to me please?"

"Don't be so lazy. Lain might need some help too and I already did all the chores down here."

"Do I have to?"

"Yes."

Alexis sauntered over to Kiera's boots and gently lowered the little one inside. She thought that Adriel might be reluctant to let go of her, but he readily transferred into the darkness of Kiera's footwear. She then proceeded over to the side of Kiera's bed and sat down on the side near where her arm was. The little one under her back wheezed out as Kiera shifted in protest. Alexis smirked, before repeatedly prodding at Kiera's shoulder with her index finger.

"Mrghn," Kiera groaned again.

"Up."

"Ugh."

"Adriel's waiting for you. Up."

"Nope."

"Fine then, starve," Alexis slyly cooed.

Kiera rolled over to face Alexis, and in the process, the Mek beneath her back was torn in half and spread across her purple dress' fabric. It was still alive, though the fight was taken out of it instantly by her lackadaisical motion. Alexis pulled a hairbrush from the nearby nightstand and began combing Kiera's purple locks. As she did so, she ran the brush over the Mek and ended its suffering. Neither Kiera nor Alexis' patterns reacted, as it died too far away from either of their pure gathering points.

"I can comb my own hair, thanks."

"You're too busy pretending to be tired."

"Goodnight," Kiera grumbled as she rolled back over.

"Nope," Alexis said as she wrapped an arm around Kiera and pulled her back up to a seated position, "I just combed your hair, dork. Come on."

"Ok, I'm up. Head on upstairs without me, I just need to brush my teeth."

"I'll have Lain start on a plate for you," Alexis said as she stood up and put the brush away. "You'd better get up."

"I will, I will."

Kiera hoisted herself to her feet as she heard the sound of hissing steam lowering the stairwell off in the distance. Alexis didn't bother shutting the door, as she assumed Kiera would be right in after her. The purple-haired Aluni shambled over to her boots and stepped into them. She was still wearing her torn up white socks from the night prior, which were much thinner than the striped ones. Her tail swayed for the first time this morning as she felt Adriel in his place underneath her arch.

"You're cute. Strange, but cute..." Kiera said as she tightened the leather straps around her ankle. "I think I'm getting used to you already, not sure if that's good or bad."

She yawned a long, loud yawn as she reached up toward the ceiling and rolled up onto her tip-toes to stretch. As she did this, she drew energy from Adriel causing all of her patterns to steadily glow and shimmer.

When she stepped back down, she rocked herself forward and back while swaying her arms a bit. She could feel his body crackling under her as she did so. Kiera tapped her foot on the ground to toy with him more and smiled. She felt awake now, energized by siphoning Adriel's spirit just a little longer than she ever had in a single pull.

The young Aluni turned on her heels and energetically jogged over toward the washroom to brush her teeth and prepare for the day ahead.

 CEROLIAN SAGAS

Lain hummed gently to herself as she watched the Laya meat sizzle on the multiple skillets in front of her. She spent most of the morning preparing a good breakfast for five, and the kitchen's air was filled with the savory scent of her art. The meat's juices were enough to oil her skillet so that she didn't have to. It crackled and sizzled, splashing bits up onto her tan freckled face as well as her hands. She didn't flinch though, as her blaze attunement helped her immensely in the kitchen. Her fluffy green tail's white tip swayed back and forth behind her as the Aluni master chef reached over to a small glass container.

It was filled with Mek that were mostly submerged in alcohol. They had been soaking for a while, but she needed to be sure their taste was right for the meal. The little ones had long since stopped struggling as they lost the coordination needed to escape their fate. She plucked a single one out without even looking and slipped it between her lips, continuing to hum her merry tune. Though it was drunk, it still ferociously struggled against her as she easily overpowered it. In seconds it was caught between her molars, its now sweet taste spread along her tongue.

"Mmm," She smiled in approval, "you're all ready I think."

She had a small pan that was already heated to the side but was waiting until the Laya steak had finished before cooking anything else. Lain casually picked the first skillet up with her bare hand. She held it by its edge as though she were holding a dish and used a spatula to move the cooked Laya onto each of the five plates she had ready and waiting. When she was finished with that, she poured the juices from one of her pans into the smaller preheated one before turning off the burners and setting them aside to cool.

Everything was almost ready!

Lain's blissful humming filled the air as she held the skillet's handle and lifted the jar of spiked Mek over it. She poured them all in, sending a few dozen of the little ones directly into a terrible bath of hot juices to be sautéed alive.

The alcohol numbed their pain to a degree, but it wasn't nearly enough as they struggled to reach the edge. The chef then took a small spoon and continuously shifted the pan underneath the little tortured creatures. She never let them stay in one spot, and on occasion would flip them with a quick forward shift of the pan itself. The spoon was used to keep them moving as well, gently being run along the top of them until they stopped their futile struggles. The whole process lasted less than a minute before she lifted the pan up over the Laya meat and began to pour them out.

She was sure to spread them evenly like the little bits of well-cooked sentient seasoning they were. The master chef kept one of the meals bare for Alexis though since she knew of her preference toward Mek-free dining experiences. The Mek had lost their will to fight, unable to even move as they simply garnished the family's breakfast.

A pair of them working together managed to avoid succumbing to the same fate as their companions. They had escaped before being exposed to too much alcohol early on, and were now running away across the open floor.

Lain drizzled a light brown colored sweet homemade sauce over the top of the steak to create a swaying pattern over the seasoning. She then returned to the fridge, walking past the fleeing Mek'Vatir as they cowered beneath her. She returned to the meals after retrieving a bucket of boiled eggs, a clear pitcher of blue liquid, and a container of cooled breakfast salad. The eggs were each ten centimeters in diameter, and the breakfast salad was made of sweet pink leaves that were chopped up and mixed with an oil dressing designed to maximize the vegetation's flavor.

First, she peeled three of the enormous eggs and sliced them in half. She put the extra half of an egg back in a sealed container she had nearby. When she placed each of the five remaining pieces on the plates, she made sure the yolk was facing upward so that they could scoop it out with a spoon. The remaining space on each plate was accented with the pink breakfast salad, and the pitcher was just enough to fill five glasses before it ran out. After that, she placed each plate and glass on a nearby multi-level pushcart and started toward the batwing doors that separated the kitchen from the main dining area.

The escapees had resumed their trek toward a small crack in the wall nearby. The one in the lead knew where it was, while the one following was simply trying its best to stay among the living. Neither noticed Lain as she approached this time until it was too late. The straggler looked up at the last second to see a wheel bearing down on it. Unable to signal for help, it disappeared silently underneath the cart's rough wheel and came out the other side with the majority of its tiny bones broken. It feebly reached up as the second wheel came, only to have it continue without remorse.

This was only enough to mortally wound the little one, leaving its insides lying next to it as the underside of Lain's dusty moccasin blocked out the light from above. It was unwittingly crushed in her stride, its soul causing the red-winged diamond pattern that was on her chest to glow. The little one's body was callously taken along with her, leaving only a black stain of blood to mark its grave. The sole survivor turned around and was momentarily confused by its comrade's absence.

Believing the other one had simply abandoned it, the Mek hastily resumed its quest for a safer life in the walls.

CHAPTER III

The morning air was crisp and cool, which would be a refreshing feeling were it not for the sound of gunfire in the distance. Gunfire and explosions were just a few small staples of Nevarria's current status quo. Kiera's tail swayed back and forth behind her as she walked along the cobblestone path leading to the pub's front door. There was an Amethya Crystal sign above the entrance that was shaped to read 'The Isarean Pub', which glowed no matter the time of day. The crystals came in various colors and were given their illumination by the souls of Mek'Vatir trapped inside. Everything was still damp from the rain that had fallen through the night, which made it dreadfully muggy in the sun's heat.

The familiar smell of breakfast Laya steak hit her like a wall the moment she stepped inside. Lain was setting one of the tables off to the right side of the main bar with plates. Just beyond her was a small performance stage in front of a dance area that was surrounded by railing. This was to prevent drunken customers from tripping over the trap edge since the dance floor was recessed so that the Mek'Vatir that entered couldn't leave on their own accord. There was a music box nearby as well for when live performances weren't available. It was currently on, playing instrumental music as everyone already seated at the table spoke amongst each other.

"Hey, she's up!" Rina said as she waved over to Kiera.

Alexis and Maya turned to see Kiera in the doorway while Lain took a seat. Since they wouldn't open for another hour or so, Kiera locked the front door and made her way over to an open chair to join them.

"I thought you fell back asleep," Alexis chuckled as she took a sip of her bright blue drink.

"Nope," Kiera replied, "I just had to get ready."

Kiera sat at the empty seat between Alexis and Lain, then looked down to her plate. The Mek that were sautéed on the top weren't moving much, though they were all still very alive. As Rina took her first bite and began to chew, her horns and fingertips started glowing bright red.

"This is amazing!" Rina said as she looked to Lain, who smiled brightly in response.

"Thanks! I love cooking this dish in particular."

"How do you get the Mek to taste different?"

"Oh!" Lain squeaked. "You can make them taste sweet, savory, or sour if you let them soak in different types of alcohol. It helps keep them docile too when they're cooked."

"Really?" Rina replied as she cut into the steak again, slicing one of the little ones in half in the process. "We use them at the vineyard to help make our wines."

"Oh?" Lain inquisitively replied. "I've heard that they're used in some wines but never understood why that was. You run a vineyard at your home?"

Maya looked quite interested as well since she didn't know much about winemaking herself. She had already almost finished half of her meal, and was in the process of slipping a Mek-covered piece of steak into her maw. It rolled onto her blue tongue, and as she began to chew, both the inside of her mouth and her dreadlocks shimmered to life.

"Yep! My family lives on an island off of Aestellus' southeastern coast called Sorovia, and we're the only manufacturers of Sorovian Wine. It's all made by trampling Mek in with the Valeberries that grow there, the old-fashioned way. When their blood mixes with the juice and ferments, it takes the bitter edge off of the wine and makes it taste much sweeter. I was never told why the Mek were added other than that."

"Would you be open to letting us import some when the war is over?" Maya asked. "I never really liked wines personally because of how bitter they usually are."

"Of course! There are some sweeter wines out there, but they normally use sugar or other unhealthy additives. I'd love to set something up later." Rina replied, then looked to the blue drink she had in hand. "What kind of drink is this, by the way?"

"Aquamelon," Lain said cheerfully. "We have a small patch out back and they're in season. You don't have them in Aestellus?"

"We don't, it's delicious though," Rina replied as she took another sip of her blue drink.

"Can you pass the Mek?" Lain asked, looking up to Maya.

The Jalar happily obliged, sliding the small dish of stunned Mek'Vatir over to the green-haired Aluni. When she had them, she poured a small handful into her palm to measure them out before dropping them onto the large egg in the center of the yolk. The majority of them were lethargic from ingesting a salty toxin that was completely harmless to everyone else. Lain then used a spoon to stir them under the yellow surface, before scooping them up to bring them to her mouth. Three of the little ones had overcome their toxins though, and one of those three was now struggling for its life in the scoop of yellow. It managed to surface in time to see Lain's fangs passing by.

The chef enjoyed the salty taste of the Mek bursting between her teeth as it mixed with the egg yolk. Her tail swayed, gently dusting the ground as she looked over to Alexis.

"We wouldn't have this meal if it wasn't for our two scavengers," Lain said brightly.

"Now that I think about it," Rina chimed in, "I do remember hearing about a couple of kids wandering around in an official report. It was about reducing the number of civilian casualties and working with the populace to better their conditions."

"Maybe they should send out more," Kiera said as she finished up her pink salad, "your comrade didn't seem to remember."

"I apologize for her. She's been acting strange lately, getting more and more agitated at just the smallest of things. I don't know what's going on in her head."

"How long have you known her?" Maya asked.

"Oh, all my life. We aren't related or anything, but I really do care about her a lot. I'm just praying to the Goddess that we both get back to the vineyard so we can move on. My family runs the vineyard itself, and we're planning on adding to the roster when we get back."

"Your uniform says Sato," Lain said as she cut up some more of her Laya meat, "I've heard of that name in the culinary world. You're royalty, aren't you? Second only to the Xanham lineage?"

"Technically yes, but I really doubt my family will ever get to see the throne."

Kiera's attention was caught by an escaping Mek'Vatir on the table as the little one ran toward where she was seated. Its tiny locks of white hair made it easy to spot during its attempted jailbreak. Kiera simply watched while sipping from her glass, waiting for it to get close. When it did, she set her glass down.

The little one fell onto its back beneath the cold, wet prison she had just constructed for it. The idle weight of the glass itself pinned the creature to the table with relative ease and threatened to break its tiny form.

"You'd probably do a better job than the tyrant you have on the throne now," Kiera said as she watched the little Mek beneath a sheet of blue.

"I've met both King Ivan Xanham and his son Prince Iosif," Rina said solemnly. "I feel like our nation would be better off lead by the prince than his father, personally."

"So you're in the military because of Sandra, not some jingo-istic devotion to your ruler?" Kiera replied.

"She wanted to enlist, and I hated the idea of letting her ship out alone. Bosservon Castle was just across the strait on the mainland, so we went there together and signed up. She did everything she could to try and talk me out of it."

"That doesn't sound like the person I saw."

"That's why it's so strange," Rina replied, "she's been overly protective of me all her life. Normally she would have killed someone for pulling a knife on me."

"Maybe it's the war itself? Killing someone isn't easy to cope with," Kiera coldly replied.

Slowly, she pressed the glass into the table and began to compress the Mek'Vatir underneath. Kiera watched with the same attentive curiosity one might expect from a student taking in all of the information available to them. The small creature started struggling for its life as she brought it beyond its breaking point. It popped like a small fruit, the sight tinged blue by the Aquamelon juice that remained in her drink. Too far away from Kiera's hand, its spirit was not taken into her directly. However, her glass was specially designed to trap wayward souls so that none were wasted. The clear Amethya crystal glass had a faint, cloudy glow as Kiera lifted it along with the Mek's body stuck to the bottom. Her bright-blue patterns illuminated as she drank what remained of her beverage accompanied by the spirit.

"I don't think I have what it takes to pull the trigger on a living person," Rina replied. "Maybe in self-defense, but I really don't know. They train you to distance yourself from combatants in basic but I went through it knowing that I would be applying for a desk job."

"I believe you," Kiera said as she looked back up from her glass to the soldier.

"I think you've done well if you get back without shooting anyone," Maya said as she stood up and began collecting some of the empty plates.

"Are you married?" Lain asked curiously as she took the last sip of her drink.

"Not yet, but that'll be changing soon. My little sister's running the vineyard while we're away and I have some really big things planned for when I go back," Rina said as she lifted a crystal necklace from the white diamond fur pattern on her chest, "Sandra gave me this before we left. It's blessed green Amethya, I never take it off. I don't know why, but it never seems to catch any spirits like it should. She was so proud she found it in green though, because she's nuclear attuned and said it was so I could always have her with me. It's actually a—"

Rina was cut off by the sound of someone knocking at the door. It startled Kiera, who looked to the entryway. Maya had already finished gathering plates, and instead of wheeling them back into the kitchen, she went to answer the door.

"Is something wrong?" Alexis whispered to Kiera.

"I don't know yet," Kiera replied in a hushed tone.

"I'm sorry, we aren't open yet," Maya said, cracking the door open to see who was there.

"I don't mean to intrude; I'm just looking for my comrade," a feminine voice echoed.

"Sandra?" Rina said as she stood up.

After realizing who it was, Maya stepped to the side and welcomed the soldier in. The tall Edoraii entered with her arms outstretched as Rina quickly made her way over. She wrapped her arms around the newcomer's waist and held her tight.

"Sober up yet, luv?" Sandra asked.

"Yeah. Listen, Sandra, I'm sorry about last night. I should have handled myself better," Rina said as she stepped back and looked up to Sandra while both of their stubby tails wagged.

"You have nothing to be sorry for. I left you in the rain and I felt absolutely horrible about it all night. When I came back you were gone, so I assumed you went in and dried-up."

"You came back?"

"Yeah, and I managed to pull some strings with the brass this morning for you."

"What?"

"How does a nice little promotion and a safe desk job back at Bosservon Castle sound?"

"That sounds fantastic!" Rina squeaked. "But what about you? Are you coming back too?"

"I'll be fine," Sandra replied as she looked to the table.

The soldier lost her train of thought when she saw Kiera staring back at her. She froze, only being brought back to reality when Maya started to speak again.

"Can I offer you a drink, Officer?" Maya asked.

"Oh no, I'm on duty."

Lain saw how uncomfortable Kiera looked and stood up, setting her hand on her shoulder after doing so. Kiera looked up while the chef smiled down to her.

"Why don't you and Alexis come help me clean up in the kitchen? I could use a few hands."

"Right," Kiera replied without hesitation.

Alexis and Kiera both stood, making their way toward the kitchen while Lain pulled a damp rag from a bucket filled with soapy water on her cart. She quickly wiped down the table, gathering any of the stunned Mek that had fallen before reaching a plate during their meal into the cloth. Once the chef had finished, she tossed the rag back into the bucket along with any of the Mek'Vatir that were still trapped inside.

"Did you sleep well? The rooms here must be better than the barracks, right?" Sandra asked.

"Oh, absolutely!" Rina replied. "If I could stay another night out here, I would."

"Let's head over to the bar and have a seat," Maya suggested. "I have some work to do before we open."

"Right," Sandra replied.

Lain scraped some of the excess food off their plates and into a nearby compost bin, along with several of the surviving Mek. She then set the plates into the sink, pinning any of them that remained down between the ceramic dishware. The chef rolled up her sleeves, pulled the hot water lever, and added some soap while steam filled the air.

Alexis leaned back against the countertop nearby. She crossed her legs, letting a slipper dangle idly as Kiera stepped up next to her with her ears low and her tail tucked down nervously between her legs.

They were joined by one more. From a crack in the wall came a tiny gray-skinned Mek pulling itself through. It whimpered, scraping its skin as its tiny scaled chest rubbed against the outside of the crack leaving some blood behind. Just as it freed itself, it stumbled through and caught its heel on the back of Alexis' dangling slipper. Unaware of the severity of its situation, the tiny one rolled onto the well-worn fabric.

The slipper moved before it could recover, taking it along for a dangerous ride. Alexis went back to standing upright, though her heel hadn't fully pressed down on the insect. Its struggles normally would have at least caught the attention of someone who was paying attention. However, all of its efforts were lost on Alexis' nerve-dead foot.

"You look like you've seen a wraith," Alexis said.

"I really don't like her."

"That's the soldier who shot at you, right? Maybe she's just here to apologize? Not that apologizing for an attempted murder is enough to get her off the hook—"

"That's not it," Kiera replied, "last night I could feel every emotion she had, just like everyone aside from Adriel."

"Adriel?" Lain asked curiously.

"I'll tell you later," Kiera said, "my point is—"

"You can't feel her?" Alexis interjected.

"How did you know?"

"Do you really have to ask?"

Alexis tapped the front edge of her slipper on the ground to ensure it wouldn't accidentally fall off. This threw her unwitting passenger forward, wedging it near the ball of her foot against a red swirl that ran the length of her arch. Desperately, it reached toward anything nearby in an attempt to escape its fate while Kiera and Alexis conversed above.

"I guess not," Kiera replied in a low voice, "it just bothers me that one day she feels like a normal irrational person, and now it feels like she doesn't even exist."

"Do you think she knows about your abilities?"

"There are only a handful of people who even know something like what I have is a possibility. Most of those people are Paladins, and all of them have an extremely strict honor code."

"Maybe she's like Lady Zara then?"

"Lady Zara is a High Paladin who knew about my empathic abilities before I even arrived at her temple, she probably has some kind of technique she knows to make me feel more at ease."

"I'm just saying that maybe she might not be the only person who knows how to block you," Alexis rationalized. "There's just so much we don't know about your powers that Zara could have taught us if we had more time."

"Even if Sandra knows how to trick my empathic abilities, how would she know to use it now? Why wouldn't she have been using it before when she was trying to kill me?"

"I don't know, I'm just trying to help."

"I know, I'm sorry," Kiera huffed. "I'm just worried. It's new, and strange, and I don't understand it."

"I'm here for you comrade, always," Alexis said as she shifted to stand closer to Kiera.

The Mek that was trapped in her slipper was unsuccessful as her movements pinned it down completely. It was slowly being compressed into the fabric, able to hear its own skeleton resist in a feeble attempt to keep its structure. The pressure forced its tiny mouth open as it whimpered out its last breath.

"Do you think we should go out and talk with her?" Kiera asked, still nervous about everything.

"If you do, I'll be right by your side alright?"

"Thanks," Kiera replied as she wrapped her arms around Alexis in an embrace.

"Hey," Lain said, "you two can use work as an excuse to come back in here if you need to. Just holler and I'll come running."

"Hopefully it won't come to that," Kiera replied.

Lain pulled her arms out of the hot water and reached for a rinsing faucet when she noticed a speck on her forearm blade. The third Mek that was coherent from before was now trapped in her fur, struggling to keep a hold of the chef while the scalding water burned its skin. Without a second thought, Lain dusted the little one off. Her fingers slid over its form roughly, ripping it in two as it fell to the ground near her feet. Still alive, the little one reached weakly up toward the green-haired chef whose mind had already shifted elsewhere.

C R O S S R O A D S

C H A P T E R   I V

———————————

"Yeah, I'll help you out with the finances when you get the place," Sandra's upbeat voice carried through the batwing doorway as the girls went through. Alexis went first, holding it open for her friend to follow.

"I think we should expand. We don't have enough tanks for storage and pressing, so we can hire some more people and add two new wings," Rina said as she took a sip from a non-alcoholic tonic Maya put together for her.

"Sounds like a plan, we'll split everything when it comes to duties and income," Sandra replied.

Then, everything felt as though it were in slow motion.

Kiera looked to Maya as the doors behind them came to a close. She felt someone grab her wrist and pull her with a surprising amount of force, knocking her from her feet.

As she fell, the sound of a gunshot rang through the pub.

Alexis had pulled Kiera with her toward a nearby hallway, which lead to Maya and Lain's bedrooms. During the fall, Kiera saw everything. Rina's blood-coated tonic shattered on the floor, spewing liquid at their hooves as she held her chest and fell from her barstool. As soon as Kiera hit the floor she tore herself away from Alexis' grip and stumbled to regain her footing. She was just in time to see Sandra's revolver aimed across the bar at Maya, who had gone for the repeating rifle hidden beneath.

A second round left the chamber of Sandra's revolver and cut through the side of Maya's hip, spraying dark blue blood across the wall just below where the alcohol was stored. The Jalar fell to her knees as Kiera's pupils disappeared behind a sheen of yellow.

Her reaction wasn't fear, it was *anger*.

Rage.

Adrenaline.

"Monster!" Kiera growled as she broke into a dead sprint toward the soldier.

"Kiera, get back!" Lain shrieked as she emerged from the kitchen using her shoulder to push through the swinging doorway. Although Maya was shot, she was able to get her rifle and disengage the safety. It was loaded and ready, so the wounded Jalar pushed herself up from the ground to return fire.

Sandra looked down her revolver's sights with a murderous glare. Kiera's purple hair was clear as daylight, and now Rina was no longer there to interfere with her shot. Lain was too far away

 CEROLIAN SAGAS

to help, and Alexis was paralyzed with fear in the nearby hallway. Nothing was stopping her now as she gently pulled the trigger.

Bang.

Maya had her rifle at the ready, but she didn't fire. The chilling sound of a body hitting the floor echoed through everyone as crimson and gray gore flew through the air. Kiera shuffled forward, her boots scuffing at the ground as she fell to her knees.

"Why...." Kiera said, her voice crackling.

The sheen of yellow over her eyes dissipated as Rina's revolver gently fell to the ground, still smoking at her side. Maya set her rifle on the counter as she looked to Lain, who simply stood in the middle of the room with her hands covering her mouth.

"Quick, the med kit!" Maya shouted as she ran to Rina's side, breaking Lain out of her daze.

"You're hit," Lain replied as she ran over to the hallway leading to the pub's back exit. The medical pack was close, so she didn't have to travel far to retrieve it.

"Don't worry about me, I'm fine," Maya replied.

Kiera felt Alexis' arms wrap around her from behind as she attempted to comfort her. Lain ran past them with the medical bag in tow, opening it up immediately when she arrived at the wounded soldier's side.

"Why did she do it?" Kiera asked, her voice distant as Alexis squeezed her tighter from behind.

"What do I do?" Lain stammered out.

"Give me some gauze, quick!" Maya shouted as she leaned over the soldier with both hands pressing down on the wound, "Damn she's lost a lot of blood."

Sandra's lifeless eyes were locked on Kiera and Alexis from the floor, staring at them with the same ferocity they had just a moment ago. Kiera wept, holding her tail as tightly as memories of the two soldiers she had killed flooded back into her mind.

Minutes seemed to last hours as Maya and Lain moved Rina upstairs and set up an emergency medical room. The door creaked ever so slowly behind the green-haired chef as she exited with an exhausted sigh, looking to the two girls down the hall- way to the right as they sat in somber silence.

"We've got her hooked up to a drip and she's stabilized for the time being," Lain said softly.

"I'm glad I didn't use all the medical equipment up when I got shot," Alexis calmly replied. "Has Maya ever had a patient like this? Is she going to be alright?"

"She's not exactly working at a hospital," Kiera interjected.

The doorway opened once again as Maya stepped through, latching it closed behind her with the light click of a handle.

Her own bandages were hidden behind a black dress she had changed into, and her hands were covered with bloodstained white disposable gloves.

"The bad news is, she's lost a lot of blood. She might recover without a transfusion but I can't say for sure," Maya said somberly. "According to her military ID, her blood type is pretty universal but we'll need to get another Edoraii if we want to go that route. Otherwise, we'll need the help of a Green Medi within the week."

"What can we do?" Alexis chipped in. Her ears were low, and worry riddled her face.

"We need to clean up downstairs first and foremost," Maya said. "Then, we can figure out what our next step is."

"Sofie can help," Alexis suggested. "We can go get her!"

"I don't want you two traveling outside the walls at night," Maya sternly replied. "You'll have to stay the night at the Temple if you do go, though."

"We have guns," Kiera replied.

"You know you're not supposed to be looting Aestellan military camps!" Maya said in a hushed growl. "The only reason they're letting you gallivant around the warzone is because we aren't bothering them. If you get caught in one of those places, we can kiss any hope of supplies goodbye and you jeopardize our intelligence agreement with the Novalin Defense Force."

"I didn't take them from a camp!"

"It doesn't matter how you got them; I don't want you carrying around Aestellan equipment."

"Believe me, Maya." Kiera replied, "I am incredibly grateful for what you've done for us since we lost everything, but we're adults now. You can't keep treating us like children."

"I know. I know you're both adults, but I also know you're both inexperienced and in the heart of a warzone. The older you two are the more of a target you become for people like Sandra with an itchy trigger finger and I wouldn't be able to live with myself if you got hurt again!"

"Enough," Lain said sternly, "Kiera, Alexis. I need help cleaning up downstairs, we can talk about this when we don't have a dying friend in the other room and a dead body in the pub."

"Right," Maya said in a huff, "I'm just worried."

"It's alright Maya," Lain replied as she made her way toward the stairwell. "We all are, it's impossible not to be. Let's just get everything taken care of before we get any visitors alright?"

Alexis swept broken bits of glass from the fallen tonic into a small dustpan while Kiera scrubbed at blood that remained on the floor where Sandra's body once lay. It was hard to keep herself from puking as she cleaned up bits of brain matter and skull fragments that were left on the ground. Neither of them spoke as they worked, with the sound of a scrubbing brush and a sweeping broom all that accompanied them.

Lain was out back, leaving the two cleaning inside as she searched for a place to store Sandra's body until they could organize a proper burial. Kiera had a soapy bucket next to her, the contents of which were already quite red. Stained towels were draped over the side of the bucket that would have to be thrown away after they finished cleaning. As the pair worked, Kiera could feel Alexis' anxiety radiate from her like a dark cloud.

"Are you alright?" Kiera asked as she continued to scrub.

"Not really," Alexis replied. "I was hoping I could get through this whole thing without seeing anything like that."

"Why can't we all just move up to the temple and claim sanctuary? Leave all this crap behind?"

"Because then we couldn't help the NDF."

"I don't care about them, or this stupid war," Kiera growled. "I just care about us."

"You don't mean that."

"Alexis, we've already lost our parents and our home. We've been surviving here for so long and I'm tired of worrying every day whether or not we're going to get caught and put in a detention center like all the others who step out of line."

"There isn't a day that goes by where I don't think about what we had," Alexis whimpered as she stood over her friend with broom in hand. "It's gone, though, it's never coming back. People are still counting on us to give them the tools they need to fight, if we just cut and run, we're taking that hope with us."

"I'm sorry," Kiera said softly as she stood up, tossing her sponge in with the rest of the water.

"You said it yourself. We're adults now, we need to start acting like it. Glory, we live as one." Alexis sternly said, reciting part of Novalus' mantra of unified strength.

Kiera walked over to Alexis and wrapped her arms around her friend, who set her broom aside and returned the gesture. Wrapping her arms around Kiera's waist, she buried her eyes into her comrade's shoulder.

"Glory, we thrive as one," Kiera replied. "You, Maya, and Lain are the only things I care about. I'll do anything to protect you."

Then, Kiera turned to look at the doorway as she felt a presence just beyond. The sound of knocking echoed through the room as her eyes widened and ears lowered. Alexis looked to Kiera with concern riddling her face as her tail tucked firmly between her legs again.

"It's Heather," Alexis whispered, "we need to hurry."

Heather Christoph

CROSSROADS

CHAPTER V

The Mek was still alive, struggling to breathe in its swelter-ing confines as the red paw pad it had been trapped against for nearly a kilometer of walking began to glow. Its comrade wasn't as resilient, succumbing to the torture that this little one was forced to endure. Moisture had glued it to her skin, which refused to end its life. Instead, it beat down on its little body with every step she took and left it broken, bleeding, and wishing for an end to its suffering.

Heather tapped her foot gently on the ground as she stood in front of the main entryway to the pub. Her long, slender tail swayed behind her like a snake as she uncaringly tortured the little thing with each tap of her small paw.

"Ugh, really?" Heather grumbled when she realized one of her Mek had burst. "I haven't even started out and you've already gone flat? Just my luck, shoulda' looked for a tougher one."

She was an Incana, a feminine feline race that was prevalent throughout the planet. They were all lightweight and fairly petite by nature, with fur patterns and colors that varied wildly from individual to individual.

"Hello?" Heather curiously shouted as she knocked on the doorway again. "Maya? Lain? Is everything alright?"

There was no answer. She could hear something going on beyond the doorway and some whispering, which piqued her suspicions. Although she was in civilian attire, she was required by Aestellan military doctrine to always carry a revolver on her person while in a combat zone. She unbuttoned her black holster, keeping her hand near the grip of her firearm as she decided to investigate further.

Every morning she came to help, they were almost ready to open up by now.

Heather walked to the building's west side, keeping close to the edge as she peered around its corner. There was a path which led to the back of the building near the aquamelon patch and a large grassy field. Cautiously, she made her way around the pub to the back. The inspector crept to the final corner, then peeked around to the rear of the building.

The doorway to the shed was cracked open, and Lain was crouched near a fountain in the back of the patch washing her hands off. Heather sighed, then buttoned up her service revolver's holster and stepped away from her cover.

"Hey," she said as she approached.

Lain squeaked in shock, nearly falling over as she turned off the water and wiped her hands on her pant legs. Heather stopped in her tracks, holding up her hands with a light chuckle.

"Woah, are you alright?" Heather asked.

"Oh, yeah. Sorry, comrade Christoph, I just wasn't expecting you so early."

"I come here around the same time every day."

"Oh gosh, it's already noon? I haven't had my energy tonic yet, sorry. The time must have gotten away from me."

"Fair enough. Is Maya inside? I have something I want to talk to her about."

"She's getting stuff ready in the ops room."

"Good, I'll be right back to give you a hand alright?" Heather said as she stepped over to the open doorway.

"I could really use your help now," Lain suggested, standing up and dusting off her legs a bit.

"I guess it can wait," Heather replied as she walked back over to Lain, "how can I assist, luv?"

"We're low on Aquamelon juice and these are ready to be harvested I think. Sorta' wanted to get them all taken care of before we open up for the day. Think you can help me trim them back and collect the melons? I already have the cart out here so all you'll have to do is carry them over and put them in."

"Sure, I'll go get some tools from the shed?"

"Ah, don't worry about that," Lain said as she started toward the cracked doorway. "Just wait here and I'll get what we need. Hate to see you work too hard as a volunteer."

"I'm here to work anyway, it's really no trouble."

Heather made her way over to the shed as well, following Lain to the doorway. The chef tried her best to keep her anxiety in check. Too much worry could make her pupils disappear and give away her troubles to the Aestellan officer.

"I think I might have put some of the tools in the Pub's storeroom just inside the doorway, would you check and see there while I look in here? Save some time?"

"Alright. Want me to get a few glasses of water too? I know we're both Blaze but we should still keep hydrated. It's supposed to be hot today and I already feel like a walking bog."

"No, thanks. Just the tools."

"That's fine," Heather said dismissively as she made her way back toward the pub.

In passing, Heather looked to the fountain where Lain was when she arrived. There was nothing but mud, mixed to the point where she would need a good chemical analysis in order to find anything of use. A gut feeling told her something was amiss, so she decided to be vigilant through the day.

"Goddess help us," Lain said under her breath as she entered the shed and closed the door to resume her work. They had a small storage freezer, which was normally used to keep meat chilled so that they could access it quickly during a rush. It now housed Sandra's corpse, and Lain hadn't been able to clean up the blood that was all across the floor leading to it.

Heather rummaged around in the pub's internal storeroom. There were some assorted medical supplies, a single broken drip-tree for medical use, and several med packs. However, she couldn't find anything that would help with the melon patch. Cool air was being circulated through the pub's ducts, which she found to be relieving even though she couldn't overheat. With her tail swaying slowly, Heather decided to investigate further. The Incana made her way down the hall toward the Ops room and an open door which led directly to the pub's barroom.

The medical kit was missing on the doorway near the hall.

Her gray eyes turned red and illuminated as her boot found a stray Mek scurrying along the ground. The feline slits focused while the crystalline gray coloration came back to her.

Maya then rounded the corner, stopping in her tracks when she saw the feline Aestellan inspector lurking down the hall in shadows. She jumped, nearly stumbling back as she held her hand over her heart.

"Heather! Oh Goddess, you startled me."

"Seems to be a running theme," Heather said as she folded her arms, "is everything alright Maya? The med kit's down."

"Oh, I fell earlier and scraped my hip pretty badly on some cooking equipment in the kitchen."

"Can I see?"

"It's really not too terrible, we wrapped it up and I'm sure it'll heal well enough."

"We could take you to a medical facility on base if you need, or I could call in a Medi."

"No, that's quite alright sweetheart. Thanks."

"While you're here, I wanted to talk to you about something."

"Oh?" Maya replied nervously. "What is it?"

"You don't need to be worried, just take a breath. Everyone's on edge around here today and it's pretty bothersome."

"Right, we're just running a bit late today getting the place ready for customers. Besides, you *were* lurking in the dark."

"I understand."

"So what is it?"

"I've pulled enough strings and got Aestellan brass to agree that this pub is a great boost to the soldier's morale," Heather said as she pulled a letter out from her pocket and handed it to Maya. "You're officially in the supply loop."

"That's wonderful!" Maya said, still holding her chest while reading the letter.

"Hey!" Lain said from behind as she approached with the gardening tools in hand. "I found 'em. They were in the shed just like you thought."

"When will the first shipment be?" Maya asked. "Half of our menu isn't available because our supplies are so low."

"We're thinking tonight," Heather responded with a bright, cheerful smile. "The second division is coming down from the frontlines and we have an airship coming in to make the delivery. If we need any help offloading when it arrives, I'll have some soldiers lend a hand."

"We're getting supplies?" Lain said as her ears perked up.

"Yep!" Heather chirped. "It might get a bit busy around here at night since you're the only working modern bar in the city."

"We might need more volunteers," Maya said as she folded up the letter and slipped it into her dress' pocket.

"I'm sure the soldiers would be more than happy to oblige," Heather replied. "We'll even bring some extra Mek so you can keep us glowing all night."

"That sounds fantastic," Lain said as she beckoned Heather to follow her. "We still need to tend to the aquamelon though. Wanna' come help?"

"Gladly," Heather replied as she followed the chef around the corner toward the exit.

Maya accompanied them to the exit and closed the door after they passed through into the oppressive heat outside. She then turned to the shelves nearby, procuring a new saline drip bag as well as a syringe of painkiller for Rina. With medical supplies in tow, the bar owner returned to the pub's main hall and peeked beneath the counter to the two Aluni who hid with their cleaning equipment held close.

"Finish up, quickly," Maya whispered before heading back to the stairwell to tend to Rina on the second floor.

Kiera and Alexis crawled out and began scrubbing Maya's blood from the floor with their bucket of water. Both of them lost their pupils from the adrenaline they had wreaking havoc on their systems. They had no idea what would happen if Heather found out about all of this.

"Goddess, that was entirely too close," Kiera groaned as she flopped down on her bed.

Alexis pulled their now-dry clothes off the line, folding Kiera's neatly on her bed before doing the same with her own. She took a seat and kicked her slippers off, much to her passenger's relief. The Mek had survived the entire day so far, but it was so broken and stuck in the fabric of Alexis' slipper that it didn't have the energy to even move.

"If the guns are coming along, we're going to have to take another route to the temple."

"I still can't believe Heather didn't catch us."

Kiera lazily rolled to a seated position and pulled her folded clothes over while Alexis changed back into her green t-shirt and black pants. The purple-haired Aluni unstrapped her boots before stepping out of them, taking Adriel along for the ride as she did so. He stuck to her sock, half crushed while his tail tried its best to continue swaying.

She brought her foot up so that her ankle would rest on her knee and caught his tail mid-swing to peel him off. The little one was enveloped in healing light the moment he was set aside.

"Can I wear him on the trip?" Alexis asked.

"Sure," Kiera said as she pulled her tank top on.

Shortly after, she lifted Adriel's doll-like body and tossed him over to her friend. Alexis squeaked, catching him out of the air a bit rougher than she had expected to. She felt his spine snap when she got him, and immediately she opened her hand to see if he was alright.

"I'm so sorry, little comrade!" she said to Adriel before looking up at Kiera. "You didn't have to throw him."

"He literally asked for it."

"Well, yeah. I guess you're right, but—"

"He's probably already healed now anyway," Kiera said as she tugged her boots back on over her newly-cleaned striped socks. "Are you bringing your revolver?"

"Of course."

Alexis pulled her insole out of her boot and set it on her lap. Adriel had healed in the time they were talking, though he still looked quite exhausted. She gently placed him in the spot that they made earlier, making sure he was flush with the rest of her insole as she smiled down to him.

"You want to ride here, or in a pocket?" Alexis asked.

"Here would be best," Adriel replied, his voice a bit shaky.

"Are you sure you're alright?"

"Yeah, it just takes a while for me to heal after I've been hurt. I'll be fine recovering in here, don't worry."

"Have a safe trip then, squirt," Alexis said as her tail swayed.

She put her left boot back together and slipped it on, before tightening the strap around her ankle. Alexis flexed her toes to assess how comfortable her new specialized insole was. When she donned her other boot, she stood up and could feel as his breath wheezed out under pressure. She then lifted her heel up and twisted her foot down to test him, shifting all her weight on that one spot he was under. He was struggling to breathe in his confined space, but overall, he was safe!

Most importantly, it was still comfortable.

"I'll get some water from the tap for us," Kiera said as she fished some canteens out from beneath the bed.

"I should be alright," Alexis replied.

"You're getting one anyway."

Kiera took two canteens into the washroom as Alexis donned her gun belt. Shortly after she entered, the purple-haired Aluni returned with two steel bottles filled with water and tossed one to her comrade. They had clips on the back, so it was easy for Alexis to hook it on her belt opposite her revolver. When it was securely fastened, she closed her eyes and took a deep breath. The red patterns on her face began to glow as she fed her Symbiont using Adriel.

"Make sure you're drinking enough water, alright?" Kiera said as she put on her belt.

"I'm usually pretty good about that."

"And that's a lie," Kiera chuckled. "How many times have I had to carry you back because you were too dehydrated to walk? You still sweat."

Kiera didn't have her long-sleeved shirt on, instead opting for a gray tank top that had a black leather band around the abdomen for extra pouches. She wrapped her scarf like a sash around her hip before taking one of the Mek pouches from the nightstand. After she had the pouch, she looped it around a special string underneath the scarf to tie it in place. Finally, she retrieved her rifle which was still leaning against the wall near her closet.

"Well then, are you ready?" Alexis asked as Kiera tossed her rifle over her shoulder and grabbed some rolled up climbing rope that was attached to a small grapple.

"If we don't leave now we'll have to wait for the morning," Kiera replied. "We're probably going to arrive near dusk as is."

"Then lead the way."

The stairwell hissed closed as Kiera and Alexis made their way to the storage shack's exit. Alexis went first, peeking through the cracked door slowly to make sure nobody was wandering around nearby. She then stepped out with her tail swaying back and forth quickly behind her.

"You're excited about this?" Kiera asked.

"I just can't wait to see the temple again," Alexis replied, "Sofie's probably grown up so much."

"Let's swing wide around the pub and follow the river until we get closer to the wall."

"Right."

Alexis ran off to the right, heading away from the pub and deeper into the woods as Kiera followed her closely in a sprint. It was a hot day and they were about to embark on a very long walk. Their biggest concern at the time was nightfall beyond safety of the walls.

The wildlife was far more docile during the day, but the moonlit forest was *their* domain.

Sanctuary

SANCTUARY
CHAPTER I

Evening | Alerio 11, 1240
Southern Gothan Forest

The little creature struggled in vain as it tried to fight against the webbing that had entrapped it. The flying Mek's wings fluttered as it attempted an escape, but everything it did only seemed to hasten its demise. Its tiny gray chest heaved in and out as its beady black eyes remained open wide. It had no idea what was about to come its way.

"Think Lady Zara will be happy to see us back?" Alexis asked.

She watched a large, black arachnid begin to crawl toward the Mek stuck in its web. The moment the little one saw the beast approaching, its struggles intensified. Alexis kept a healthy distance away, knowing the arachnid's bite was likely dangerous. It would be foolish for her to try and intervene when they're so far away from help were she to be injured.

"She didn't really like the idea of us leaving the temple in the first place. I think she'll be happy seeing that we're alive," Kiera responded as she sat upon a fallen log.

She brought a metal canteen to her lips and took another drink of the crisp, clean water within. They could easily refill it when they got to the temple, so she wasn't too concerned with conservation. She sat her rifle down next to her, loaded and ready to fire in the event they needed it.

Alexis watched as the arachnid wrapped the Mek in a layer of its webbing. The victim's struggling slowly stopped as the process went on, burying the Mek in a thick layer of white. When it was completely engulfed, the arachnid sunk its large fangs into the wiggling cocoon. It stood no chance against the beast, its life was forfeit when it fell into the predator's trap.

"How old is she anyway?" Alexis asked as she turned to her comrade when the spectacle ended. "She looks to be about Lain's age but that can't be right."

"I never really put too much thought into it. She's a High Paladin and an Apostle of Aludra; those titles aren't just given to you, ya know."

Kiera capped her canteen as the purple tip of her large tail flicked from side to side. She then hooked it back on her hip underneath her scarf and watched as Alexis came over to have a seat as well.

"Think she's older than the Consulars?"

"Probably. Aurora's the youngest at around ninety-two cycles, I think. The oldest one is.... Two-hundred and three? Maybe?"

"Which book did you get that from?"

"I have a few political books, but I think the one I got that from was called 'Novalin Politics, Volume Something-rather'."

"Volume something-rather?" Alexis chuckled as she took a drink of her canteen. "So what you're saying is, your information is extremely out of date."

"I mean it might be around fourteen cycles old?"

"So, it's older than both of us?" Alexis quipped.

"I'm just glad we have books to read."

"Where did 'volume something-rather' go anyway? I don't think I've ever seen it."

"Probably under my bed or something."

"Alright. Are you ready to head out comrade? I think we're almost to the wall."

Kiera nodded as she took her rifle back into her hands and stood up. Together, they made their way through the small clearing that was chosen so that Kiera could catch her breath in the heat. Alexis was significantly more resilient to the temperature all thanks to her ability, though she was still coated in dirt and sweat. Kiera took the lead with her rifle, slowly pushing through the foliage so her rifle wouldn't snag anything.

"Still... Ninety-two is way older than us," Alexis said while stepping over a fallen log. "Didn't you just turn twelve?"

"Yeah," Kiera replied, "if this war wasn't going on we probably would be flat-mates in the city somewhere struggling to make ends meet. Ya know?"

"I'm still older than you," Alexis said with a smirk.

"But I'm taller."

"You're also an alcoholic."

"Ouch," Kiera groaned, "I didn't realize we were picking each other apart like that. I'd try and get you back but you don't really burn too easily."

"That's cold."

"Goddess help me," Kiera laughed as she came through some dense foliage to the defensive wall.

The grass around the wall's walkway had grown more than she had expected since the Citizen Defenders weren't here to walk them anymore. It was rare for anything to get over them and into the city though, especially with the war waging in the distance. Kiera walked over to the battlement, peeking her head through to look at the forest's canopy below.

"Are you sure we can't just go around to the main gate and take the usual path?" Alexis asked nervously.

"It's probably guarded."

"How do you know?"

"I'd rather take my chances here."

Alexis' red patterns began to glow as she took in energy from her roasting comrade so that she could help calm herself.

She took a deep breath and nodded as her comrade affixed the top of the rope to the inside of the battlement. Kiera then hoisted herself over the side, grabbing onto the pointed edge with one hand and the rope with the other.

"Be careful!" Alexis said with her ears lowered.

"I'll go down first. When I'm on the ground, you follow."

"Just don't fall."

"I wasn't planning on it, but now that you mention… It would get me to the bottom faster."

"Stop joking, please."

"Don't worry, it wouldn't be a very comfortable trip down anyway," Kiera chuckled as she leaned back with the rope held tightly in hand.

Alexis watched with bated breath as her comrade backed down the wall. It had a slight slant, which made it easier for her to traverse. Kiera's tail confidently swayed as she disappeared beyond the forest canopy, then there was nothing but silence. Alexis quaked, leaning over the edge to scan the foliage while the rope in front of her shook.

"Kiera?" Alexis shouted. "Are you alright?"

"Yeah!" Kiera hollered back. "It's all clear down here. You can come down now."

Alexis inhaled deeply, holding it for a moment before letting herself exhale in a prolonged and shaky sigh. After trying her best to delay the inevitable, she carefully climbed over the edge and held onto the rope with all the strength she could muster. Subconsciously, she tried to wrap her tail around the rope as she built up the courage to begin her descent.

"It's ok, it's ok," Alexis whimpered out. "It's not too far."

She opened her eyes and shifted her grip so that she was only holding onto the rope. One hand after the other, Alexis began her trek to the forest floor. She could hear the leaves behind her rustle and sway as fresh air from the sea graced the treetops. That breeze turned into a strong gust, pushing her to the side when she was only a meter from where she started. The sudden burst of air made her look down, and she instantly felt weak.

Alexis squeaked, becoming dizzy as she pulled the rope tight and wrapped her legs around it as though she were clinging to a pole. She bounced off the wall, hugging the rope for dear life while panting. The black pupil of her eyes disappeared, leaving blue and yellow adrenaline disks in their place.

"You're going to be alright, just breathe!" Kiera shouted up. "Take a deep breath in."

Alexis inhaled deeply, listening to her friend's voice.

"Now, breathe out," Kiera shouted up again.

Alexis did so, letting the air pass by her lips as she heard wind rustle through the treetops again far below. On the ground, Kiera paced back and forth. She hadn't seen the rope moving as it should be if Alexis was making progress, and she could feel a waterfall of anxiety showering over her. Her mind was racing, since she didn't realize her friend was this petrified of heights. They had always taken the path through the main gate before. Perhaps it really was unguarded, and this whole ordeal was just an unnecessary risk in itself?

Kiera didn't know what to do.

"It's going to be alright, just keep your feet on the wall and slowly walk backward. You can do this, I know it!" Kiera shouted up to her comrade.

"I can't," Alexis whimpered back in response.

She could feel her rapid pulse in her neck as her head began to ache from stress and her arms started to cramp. Without realizing it, Alexis breathing started to become quick and shallow. Before she could hyperventilate though, her mind trailed to a little tinge of motion beneath her left foot. Her red markings began to glow as she felt Adriel's energy flowing through her. The strength she had lost was returning to her arms as her passenger persisted, calming her down and bringing her back to a place where she could think clearly. Alexis' tail unwrapped from the rope slowly and her breaths resumed a normal pace.

Cautiously, she placed each foot against the wall and pushed herself back up to a standing position. She was still shaking as she walked backward, looking directly at the wall in front of her. As she progressed, she felt the canopy brush by. Alexis looked up and watched as a sea of green leaves larger than she was replaced the sky and obscured Cerolia's rings.

She was going to make it!

Alexis smiled, whimpering out a happy little chuckle as she descended. Kiera held her hands over her mouth as she looked up, and when she saw Alexis finally come through the foliage she jumped in place and let out a triumphant laugh. Pride in her companion's accomplishment welled up inside of her as Alexis rappelled meter after meter.

Snap.

Her elbow hit a hardened branch which sent a jarring shock of pain through her arm and up her armored spine. The impact caused her to let go of the rope. Alexis screamed, her voice echoing through the woods as she plummeted to the ground below.

Thump.

"Oh Goddess Alexis, are you ok?" Kiera asked breathlessly as she ran over to her comrade's side. She wasn't able to react fast enough to intervene.

Alexis coughed and rolled to her side with her arms wrapped around her chest. She wheezed and gasped, trying to gather the air that was knocked from her lungs in the impact. Not sure what she could do to help, Kiera took her friend in an embrace and gently pushed her hair from her face. The red patterns on her skin were constantly glowing as she subconsciously drained Adriel in her attempt to recuperate. When Alexis felt her friend's touch, she sat up and wrapped her arms around Kiera with a grip tighter than the one she had on the rope moments ago.

"Graceful landing," Alexis sputtered as she flopped her tail around in the dirt.

"Yeah," Kiera replied, keeping her arms wrapped around her fallen friend, "if you tell anyone this story later, I caught you."

"My hero," Alexis chuckled, then gasped for air again as she tried to get back to her feet.

Kiera helped her, standing up with her friend as Alexis weakly attempted to get up. She now was covered in dust and dirt, and her motions were slow and pained. As she got to a standing position, Alexis winced and held her lower back.

"Let's take another break, alright?" Kiera suggested, helping Alexis over to a patch of moss nearby.

"Probably a good idea."

"Do you feel like anything's broken?"

"My self-confidence. I'm ok though, just sore."

"Well, I think I can help with that."

Kiera gently helped Alexis to sit down in the moss, before sitting next to her. She pulled the pouch of Mek'Vatir from her hip and dangled it in front of her friend, who chuckled.

"You are the best friend I've ever had, you know that?" Alexis said with a sweet smile.

"Someone has to take care of you."

Alexis then pulled her tank top off, revealing a black wrapping she had over her chest. She set her top off to the side and leaned forward as Kiera slid in behind her. The purple-haired

Aluni opened the pouch and set it on the ground next to her for quick access, making sure it wasn't tilted so the little occupants couldn't escape. Kiera then licked her thumbs and gently slid them both into the pouch. When she lifted them out, she had a single Mek'Vatir stuck to each of her thumb tips.

"Ready, comrade?" Kiera asked.

"Yeah."

Kiera then wrapped her hands around the back of her friend's neck and placed a thumb on either side of her red armored spine. She focused, feeling Alexis' spiritual energy beneath her skin while drawing upon a special soothing pleasure that only Cerolians could access in others. The skin on Alexis' back began to glow bright blue wherever Kiera touched, and as the Mek struggled to escape, Alexis let out a contented sigh. Being directly between the two, the Mek were both completely engulfed in this blue aura. The overwhelming blast of euphoric energy was nearly enough to give them a heart attack, though Kiera was careful not to overwhelm their senses.

Rubbing her thumbs into her friend's back in small circles, Kiera began the massage. Alexis could feel soothing energy radiate from Kiera's fingertips as they traced around her skin leaving waves of relief. Every muscle in her shoulders felt as though they were melting, and the slow drag of the little ones writhing bodies made it all the more potent for her. As Kiera increased her thumbs pressure, the pops of breaking bones sent echoes of tranquil energy through her. The glowing blue markings of Kiera's palms reflected off of the skin as both of the Mek were crushed to death, allowing Kiera to press deeper into the muscles of her friends back. She drug their bodies around on her comrade's skin, using them as moisturizer as their black blood spread like paint from a brush.

Kiera could feel her friend's emotions fading into a drowsy state of tranquility as she plucked two more of the Mek from her pouch. Keeping them stuck on the tip of her thumbs, she moved her attention to her comrade's lower back and pressed them in near her spine. She let her other fingertips fan across Alexis' skin as she drew upon the pleasureful side of her friend's spirit.

Alexis arched her back with her eyes closed and let out a soft sigh when she felt the burst of soothing, euphoric energy radiate through her body. The Mek's continuous writhing caused a cascade of relaxing sensations that made her feel as though every ache and pain she had experienced was draining away from her. It was smoother than her upper back, as the blood from the previous two sacrifices acted as a lotion allowing her friend's fingers to glide across her with ease.

The Mek stopped fighting as Kiera's thumbs left them stuck to Alexis' soft skin. She spread the blood that was on her thumbs across her palms and sprinkled more Mek into each hand, then her attention returned to the two that were already well used. Pressing her palms into Alexis' lower back, Kiera sent a powerful burst of euphoric energy into her friend. It radiated throughout Alexis' entire form, leaving Kiera with a slight headache.

Manipulating spiritual energy came at a steep cost, and that was Æther Sickness. She could only store so much energy at a time before the excess radiated away, and all the souls she had at the ready were now expended. Kiera knew this was bound to happen, which is why she gathered so many sacrifices to recover. She pressed her palms into Alexis' back and slowly worked them in circles near her spine, sliding up to where her black chest wrappings were. One by one the bodies of the Mek'Vatir gave way to the pressure, immediately allowing Kiera's headache to subside as the little ones were reduced to massage lotion.

"Feel any better?" Kiera asked as she moved her inky, bloodied hands up near Alexis' neck again and started massaging closer to the shoulder blades. They both felt several more pops as the survivors were smeared into paste.

"Immensely," Alexis said lowly, "thanks for the Aura massage."

Mek's blood adorned Alexis' back like mud mixed with white specks of gore. The constant motion of her massage spread them quite thin across her skin as Kiera began to hum gently and sway her tail through the grass of the forest floor. They both enjoyed every second they had together as the symphony of insects and animals off in the distance played. When she was finished, Kiera pulled her scarf from her hip and used it as a towel to wipe away the mess she had made on her friend's back.

     CEROLIAN SAGAS

Kiera stood up and wrapped her scarf back around her waist, giving her friend some time to decompress. Alexis eventually got to her feet, donning her shirt before stretching like she had just awakened from a restful slumber. After she was clothed again, she stepped in front of Kiera and grabbed both of her hands. Their patterns began to glow and pulse with life as Adriel's spirit was once again siphoned.

The little one felt like he was being roasted alive as Alexis' sweat made it impossible for his body to cool off. He weakly gripped at the fabric of her sock from his recessed alcove as her patterns illuminated the space around him. Adriel could only take in small breaths of air as the pressure from her standing in one place kept his lungs from completely expanding. As she took a step to the side, he took in a deep breath before having the air ejected from his body when she stepped down. Alexis had drained him to the point where he could hardly fathom moving, though the little one never seemed to reach the end of what he was able to give.

"You should open up an Aura Spa after the war ends," Alexis chuckled as her tail swayed.

"Nah," Kiera replied, "people I don't know annoy me way too much for something like that. Cerocide isn't something I want on my record."

"Yeah, I'd rather not visit you in prison."

"That's if they catch me."

"Well," Alexis said, "if we want to get to the Temple before nightfall we should get moving."

Kiera then looked down at the canteen on her hip and pulled if off. After uncapping it, she offered the water to Alexis who took it graciously.

"Drink before we go."

Alexis nodded and brought the canteen to her lips.

The refreshing, crisp taste of water helped immensely as the heat continued to bear down on the two. It was harder for Alexis to judge her condition on hot days like this since she didn't experience heat the same way others did.

"I don't know what I'd do without you," Alexis said.

"Shrivel up like a dried sentoberry?"

"Yeah, probably."

Alexis turned away and began to walk in the direction of the temple. She felt a soft, round object under her shoe compress as she took a step and froze in place. The patterns on her body illuminated again. Gritting her teeth, Alexis nervously lifted her shoe to see Kiera's Mek pouch flattened in the dirt.

"Dammit! I forgot," Kiera squeaked as she scooped the Mek pouch up from the ground.

She peered inside, and with a defeated sigh, she turned the bag over to let the bodies tumble out to the ground. Kiera then ran her boot across the grass to see if she could stir any awake, but none of them seemed to respond at all.

 CEROLIAN SAGAS

"Sorry," Alexis whimpered.

"It's not your fault, I left it down there," Kiera replied as she strapped the empty pouch on her hip again.

"I guess we can always just share Adriel if you need to."

"We'll be at the temple long before it's a problem," Kiera said as she brought her rifle to the ready again. "I'll go first, alright? Just in case."

Alexis nodded, drawing her revolver so that it was in hand just in case she needed it. They both carefully proceeded deeper through the forest, leaving the pile of Mek bodies alone so the dead could spawn new life.

The canopy high above wasn't helping shield them from the summer heat as much as they had hoped. Alexis followed Kiera closely as they passed through the foliage, hyper-vigilant of the sound of insects and shuffling wildlife in the distance. Alexis still had some water remaining in her canteen, so she pulled it off her hip and took a drink of the warm liquid.

"Are you sure we're going in the right direction?" She asked.

Kiera stopped suddenly and turned to face Alexis with a fingertip to her lips. On her tip-toes, Alexis peeked around her friend in an attempt to see what lay ahead. A pack of animals slept together in a clearing, six in total. Each of the beasts were easily twice their size, with spines lining the back of their fur-coated bodies. One of them was awake, looking to the two as they happened upon their pack. Kiera could feel her friend's fear growing, even though they both knew the animals were more docile during the day. However, even with that fact in mind, startling them would likely lead to a bloodbath.

The two stepped back into the foliage, changing their route to head due east so they could circumnavigate the group. They both remained quiet, placing their footfalls methodically so that they could avoid breaking twigs and making any unnecessary noises. They pushed through another bit of brush, coming directly to a wide river.

"Damn," Kiera groaned as she looked back at Alexis.

"We're at the fork, aren't we."

"Yep."

"Oh Goddess," Alexis said as she held her forehead, looking off to the river. "Why haven't they made more bridges? Maybe ones that aren't guarded by a pack of Ishar."

"We can make it through, we just need to be careful alright?" Kiera said as she set a hand on Alexis' shoulder. "Just stay close to me, I won't let them hurt you no matter what happens."

Alexis held her revolver tightly. She pulled back the hammer with her thumb, forcing the cylinder to rotate a live round into position as Kiera disengaged the safety on her rifle. With that, the pair turned back.

With the revolver in her right hand, Alexis held Kiera's tail near the center like a fluffy rope as the two pushed their way toward the pack. The Ishar that was awake on lookout immediately stood up, stretching the spiked quills on its back as a warning to the two during their approach. Kiera remained crouched, keeping her rifle trained on the watchdog while Alexis followed nervously. The red patterns on her face and arms continued to glow as she siphoned energy from Adriel at a constant rate, just to keep her nerves in check.

The watcher remained vigilant, keeping low in its perch as its gaze was met with their own. If Kiera had to shoot, the unsuppressed firearm would startle the entire pack. Although it was awake and on watch, the beast seemed tired in its movements.

Slow, steady steps were the key. They had already made it halfway through the pack when Kiera saw some movement out of the corner of her eye. They stopped when one of the sleeping animals stood from its rest, stretching as it awoke. Its cold gaze turned to the two as Alexis had her revolver in its direction. They were trapped in the middle of the pack, with an Ishar on either side of them. Slowly the beast lumbered in their direction, the quills on its back up and at the ready as it walked along.

However, it didn't strike.

Kiera and Alexis both kept their firearms trained on the beast as it moved past them toward the watch point above. The weary watcher then hopped off to a nearby shaded area and curled into a ball. It didn't sleep, instead choosing to keep an eye on the two Aluni that were traveling through their area. The rejuvenated Ishar stood proudly upon its perch, gazing down to the trespassers who were not yet deemed a threat to their safety.

Finally able to relax, Kiera and Alexis resumed their trek to the clearing to the other side. Their ears perked back up when they took in the sweet sound of flowing water and pushed through the brush to the actual beaten path leading to the Temple of Aludra. They now stood together on a thin dirt road facing a fork in the river. Enormous mountains off in the distance were accented by the daylight rings of Cerolia arching beyond the clouds. There was a waterfall visible that kicked up a constant glowing mist around its base, even during the day. They knew it as Soria Falls, but the two had never actually been there to see the mist up close.

Before them was a set of bridges, one leading to the left and the other to the right. They connected all three sections of land at the fork along an overgrown pathway.

"Goddess..." Alexis whimpered out as she let go of Kiera's tail.

"That turned out better than expected," Kiera replied as she turned toward the bridge to their left.

Alexis nodded than ran off ahead of her friend, hopping onto the wooden bridge first. She held onto the thick intertwined ropes as it began to sway over the rushing water beneath them. Her tail had resumed its normal back and forth sway as she walked across the bridge, which was still in fairly good shape. Kiera followed cautiously with her rifle in hand, using her left to stabilize herself as she crossed. The flowing river below kicked up mist from the rocks, filling the air with the soothing smell of the sharp, clean freshwater directly from the glacier beyond the waterfall in the distance.

The sound of rustling leaves gave away the presence of a nearby animal in the trees. Kiera looked up to see a creature with white fur and dark blue glowing wings descend from the canopy toward her. Its arms were outstretched and the animal's wings were glowing as though they were made of energy. Kiera let go of her rifle, which was still slung over her shoulders, and brought her forearms up to defend herself as the small creature made contact. Its wings disappeared as it completely bypassed Kiera's arms and crawled around the rifle to her back. Kiera twisted, trying to grab the little thing as it scurried around her.

Alexis came over quickly to help, though the animal was a bit too fast for her to capture. It came to a stop near Kiera's hips though, burying its nose in the layers of her scarf's fabric. She lifted her arms, and Alexis reached for the curious little being.

"Wait," Kiera said, waving her away.

Alexis stepped back and looked to the little creature as it held onto Kiera like she were a tree. The animal was roughly the size of a house pet with a soft coat of white fur. After waiting a few seconds, it pulled its head out from Kiera's scarf and looked up to Alexis. A single blue gem in the shape of an oval adorned its forehead and shimmered with a cloudlike essence, and its big blue eyes darted to the ground near Alexis' feet to scan the grass. The white entrails of a crushed Mek'Vatir dangled from between its lips. Blue feline ears flicked atop its head as it listened to the surrounding area, before the animal buried its face back into her scarf and rummaged around for more. Its fluffy tail flicked from side to side, tipped with a tuft of fur that always seemed to point upward no matter its orientation.

"I think it likes you," Alexis said as her tail danced behind her.

"It's probably after the Mek I wiped up earlier," Kiera replied. "Are there any live ones nearby?"

"There usually are somewhere."

Kiera brought her hand down to the little being and gently ran her claw tips through the fur on its back. It began to purr as it continued its search, which only encouraged Kiera's attentions. While she entertained the newcomer, Alexis crouched and started a search through the grass for any little test subjects. She ran her hand along the top of the grass nearby before noticing a speck of gray hanging onto one of the green blades. It was a single Mek'Vatir that had climbed up, presumably to get a better look at its surroundings. The tiny one was on its way back to the ground when Alexis' fingertips gently pinched its arm.

"Aha!" Alexis said triumphantly as she stood back up.

"Found one?"

"Yep!"

Alexis offered the little prisoner to her friend, who carefully caught its hair between her index claw's tip and thumb. It struggled, holding its white locks in a feeble attempt to escape.

"Hey there," Kiera said sweetly as she brought the Mek over toward the newcomer, "you hungry?"

The critter peeked out from the fabric to its offering. It repositioned itself, grabbing onto Kiera's shirt with a tiny fluffy paw as it reached out with the other for its prize. The Mek struggled frantically as it was engulfed in fur and tiny purple pads, which wrapped around its body as though the animal was picking fruit from a tree. Once it had the Mek, Kiera let go of the little thing and the two girls watched to see what it would do.

The Mek struggled helplessly as it felt invisible hairs sticking to its chest. They were like glue that could be activated at will by the animal, ensnaring it until its struggles ceased. The creature purred happily when its fingers let go of the Mek, which was now stuck to the forepaw's pad like gum with its legs and arms uncomfortably spread out. Its tiny face was forced to the side as the invisible hairs adhered to its entire form, only allowing it the ability to breathe and see.

The flying feline then gently licked at the Mek's back before hopping down to the ground from Kiera's shoulders. It landed gracefully and started prancing around in the grass, each step battering its prey more and more. Whenever the animal passed near Kiera, it would rub its side against the Aluni's ankle and purr loudly. Once it had weakened its target, it hopped back up to Kiera's shoulder and resumed licking at the paw that the Mek was firmly attached to.

One impact from the animal wasn't enough to break its tiny body, but the constant trotting managed to fracture and shatter every bone that the little one had. It was awash in agony as it felt the animals teeth begin to nip at its side, tearing into the flesh until white organs squeezed out onto the animal's paw pad. They were quickly lapped away as though she were happily eating a berry while her tail flicked slowly behind her. When there were no more easily accessible goodies from her teeny snack, the feline nipped off the Mek's legs and used its petite fingers to squeeze until everything had been pushed out.

Just as the Mek's consciousness began to fade away, it felt its body fall from where it had been stuck. The crystal on the animal's forehead illuminated like the girl's patterns while it violently chomped what remained of its snack into little bits and licked its forepaw clean. When there was nothing left to snack on, the newcomer cuddled up to Kiera and purred as it rubbed its forehead gem on the Aluni's cheek.

"Do you know what the animal is?" Alexis asked.

"Adorable and oddly violent." Kiera replied, laughing as it gave her several licks of appreciation.

"I asked about her, not you."

"Thanks?"

Alexis stuck her tongue out and reached over to gently scratch behind the animals ears, which caused the flying feline to push its head up into the attention. Eventually, the ear that wasn't being petted gently flicked a few times and the purring grew louder. The gem on its forehead still had a constant glow as the souls of the Mek it had hunted through the day lingered on to power its wings.

"Can we keep it?"

"I was just about to ask *you* if we could."

Alexis hopped in place and squealed with excitement before leaning in a little closer to the newcomer. She nuzzled up to the animal, and in return, the furry creature set its forehead on hers and pressed forward slightly in a gentle headbutt. The animal hadn't stopped purring and still held onto Kiera tightly with its little forepaw hands.

"It's going to need a name."

"Any suggestions?" Kiera asked as she looked to the little fluffball on her shoulder.

"Not really. It seems to like you, though, so maybe you should think of one?"

The animal looked back to Kiera before rubbing its head on her cheek in a gentle little push as well. It cuddled up close to her neck, using her rifle's foregrip to steady itself as Kiera thought about what to call it.

"What do you think of Pearl?" Kiera asked.

"I think that sounds perfect," Alexis replied as she turned her full attention to Pearl on Kiera's shoulder. "I wonder what Maya and Lain will think of it."

"I would say the bar needs a mascot, but I think it'll eat up all the Mek in the main building. We might just have to keep it around our room and let it play with them in there."

"Think either of them would know what it is?"

"Maybe. We might be able to find out more about it at the temple though," Kiera suggested as she reached for the rifle on her back. "Let's get going."

Pearl moved to her other shoulder to get out of the rifle's way, holding onto her shirt and shoulder pauldron bones for support. The animal licked its lips as the three wandered down the pathway leading deeper into the woods.

CEROLIAN SAGAS

SANCTUARY

CHAPTER III

———————————

"Why did it have to be so hot today?" Kiera complained as they walked beneath the forest canopy.

"I think the breeze makes it feel a bit chilly," Alexis replied with a smug tone.

"Chilly? You think a Blaze Sauna is chilly and that stuff burns the dirt off your skin. Remember when you splashed me cycles ago? I still have a scar," Kiera groaned, pointing to a scar on the back of her arm that could hardly be noticed.

"Hey, you got me back when you shoved snow down my shirt the next Ultir."

"Snow doesn't scar," Kiera groaned again half-heartedly.

"You could complain about anything," Alexis jested, giving Kiera a playful push from behind.

"Didn't work the same when you retaliated, did it? The world before the shells fell was a different place for sure."

"I miss our family," Alexis replied solemnly, "remember how hectic it was? Your parents and mine all living together trying to keep the two of us in line."

"Then I got us sent away to the temple."

"It was my idea though. Well, Sofie suggested it after we got to know her a bit while she was visiting and I brought it up."

"Did you? I thought I saw something about it."

"Nope. Sofie was doing some sort of group thing in the city with some Paladins remember?"

"Vaguely."

"I think I spent more time with her at first so that doesn't surprise me," Alexis replied as her patterns started solidly glowing. She wasn't shy about using Adriel's abilities to keep herself from tiring on the grueling journey.

Pearl held onto Kiera's shoulder tightly as the purple-haired Aluni deviated from the main path and up a hill. She was well acquainted with the area, having played in this portion of the woods a lot during their stay at the nearby temple. The alternate path wound upward to a large, twisted tree that was taller than any other they had seen before. It was an old iron oak, the same type that the Acolytes grew at the temple to make their nearly indestructible staves from. Alexis looked up toward her friend as she traversed the high road like a professional with rifle in hand and a fluffy companion in tow.

"Careful!" Alexis hollered up as the paths diverged even more.

"I am being careful," Kiera replied.

Alexis continued down the path to the bottom of the cliff while keeping an eye on her friend high above who disappeared through the forest's canopy. Kiera could hear the waves of the Glaciatic Sea as they crashed into rocks off in the distance from her vantage point. She shouldered her rifle, peering through the scope while Pearl crawled up her hair to lay atop her head like a fluffy white hat. Through her optic, she could see all the way to the Temple of Aludra which was built out of the side of a mountain. Although it seemed tiny from where she was, she could still make out the Paladins who walked along the temples walls.

"See anything up there?" Alexis shouted up.

"The doors are still closed. I can see some wreckage and scars from a fight in the kinlily fields too, probably had a few more airship visits since we've been gone. There *are* some Acolytes and Paladins moving around inside though, so they're probably alright! Think they'll recognize us when we get back there?"

"After the impression you left on the place? I'm pretty sure you're the only one who jumped off the waterfalls there for fun. I'd be surprised if there was a single person there who didn't remember you after all that."

Kiera slid the rifle's strap up over her shoulder and carefully made her way to the cliff's edge to see if the path they had always taken when they were younger was still available. She peered over the edge, and Pearl leaped from her head over to the canopy below. The white-furred animal's glowing blue wings flashed on its back as it glided down safely to the canopy's enormous green leaves. They were so thick and wide that they could support the animal's weight with ease, allowing it to bounce off of them like a springboard and dive into the space between.

The path that Kiera had remembered was still there. It was a section of cliff she was on that had eroded to make a steep sandy slide. It ran along the entirety of the cliff face and came to an end near the path Alexis was taking below. With a grin from ear to ear and an uncontrollably waving tail, Kiera sat on the edge of this path and pushed herself over. She slid down the long dirt wall causing a cascade of sand in the process, passed the canopy, and came to a stop on the ground where Alexis and Pearl were waiting for her.

"Having fun?" Alexis asked as she helped Kiera to her feet.

"Just a little."

Pearl hopped up from the ground and flapped her ethereal blue wings so she could return to Kiera's shoulder. Once she was secure in her perch, she let her wings dissolve and yawned. Kiera gave her a gentle pat on the head before the group continued along on their journey.

Life in the war zone had robbed Kiera and Alexis of their childhood in a way neither of them could truly comprehend. They couldn't forsake a chance at true relaxation, even with the gravity of their mission weighing on them both.

"At least we're almost there," Alexis said.

When they neared the edge of the forest, the path curved sharply to the left so that it could meet up with the main brick path that connected the city to the temple. Instead of following the curve, Kiera continued through the thin foliage that led to an enormous field of purple flowers which were all over two meters in height. From here, the temple wasn't visible through the field.

"Where are you going?" Alexis asked while she followed Kiera off of the dirt walkway. "The pathway is over here."

"You're telling me you *don't* want to walk through the kin-lilys?" Kiera responded as Pearl playfully pawed at the passing stalks covered in purple flowers.

"Of course I do! You just blend in, violet-head," Alexis replied in a snarky tone and grabbed Kiera's tail again. "Let's go."

The wind blew through the field of purple flowers as the two traversed the spaces between each stalk. As soon as they entered the field, the smell of the air changed to a crisp and subtly sweet odor that lofted all around them along with a rain of vibrant purple petals. The ground was covered in these petals as well, which danced around their ankles carrying Mek along with them like flying carpets. Occasionally, Kiera and Alexis' patterns shimmered to life as they walked through the floral forest when unfortunate petal riders would land in their path.

"I forgot how beautiful this place was," Kiera said in awe as she looked up and around to the clouds high above.

Alexis let go of her friend's tail and broke a small kinlily branch off, which was covered in little purple flowers. Afterward, she jogged out in front of her friend with the branch behind her back and held a hand out to stop her.

"Hold on, hold on. You're missing something very important."

"What?" Kiera replied as she tilted her head, letting one of her pointed ears droop down while the other perked up.

Alexis reached out and gently tucked the floral branch into her friend's hair above her left ear. The pace of Kiera's swaying tail picked up as she did so and her lips spread into a bright smile. Stepping forward, Kiera wrapped her arms around her friend in an embrace, which allowed Pearl to nuzzle and purr at Alexis' cheek with joy.

"Do I wear it well?" Kiera asked as she stepped back.

"Nope," Alexis stuck her tongue out and turned on her heels to resume their walk through the field.

Kiera followed, and with her rifle secured on her back, she reached out and took Alexis by the tail. This caused the young Aluni to freeze in place and turn to see what she was caught on. She saw Kiera innocently smiling behind her, and they both let out a hearty laugh. Together they walked through the shower of purple petals until they finally met with the red-bricked road that led to the temple.

The bricks were worn down from the automobiles that towed trailers of supplies to and from the temple back before the war.

The pathway still looked maintained though, likely by the denizens of the nearby establishment. The snow-capped peaks of Mt. Luara were slightly obscured by mist in the distance, leading down to an overhanging cliff face that the temple was built into. As the pair stepped out onto the wide pathway, Pearl hopped off of Kiera's shoulders and began to hop around on the little Mek'Vatir that were mixed in with the fallen petals. The animal swatted at them playfully like they were toys and rolled around, kicking up clouds of purple petals.

"It really likes those little things," Kiera chuckled as she watched Pearl bat one around until it stopped fighting.

"I guess she'll fit right in at home then," Alexis replied mischievously as she eyed her friend with her hands hidden behind her back. Then, she broke into a sprint past the two. "Last one to the temple's a rotten Varog!"

"Hey!" Kiera shouted as she ran after.

Pearl hopped into the air and spread its ethereal wings to swoop past both of them to the ground. The fluffy white animal then kept pace with its newfound pack, prancing along the pathway as it did so.

Its white hair danced in the breeze as it gazed up to the massively tall flower's corolla while laying on a fallen petal. The Mek didn't know anything about the war or care about the plights of giants, all they cared about was the moment.

Laughter from the two approaching Aluni caught its attention as it grew louder and louder. It was far from the only Mek in the area, of course. There were many of its kind that wandered through the fields outside of the temple. Like all of the other major cities, the Acolytes bred them so that the general population would always have a form of Æther sustenance. They were also fed to the livestock within the temple's walls.

"Cheater!" Kiera shouted as she ran, watching the black tip of Alexis' tail swish about as she maintained a steady lead.

The Mek'Vatir laying on the ground sat up just in time to see Pearl's joyful blue eyes locked onto it as the creature descended. The soft purple pad of its forepaw came crashing down, slamming the little one into the red brick beyond the petal. It felt the Mek's body stick to its pad and lift with its paw, then descend violently into the stone below time and time again. Pearl ran with the victim until the Mek's body broke open and it began to trail a thin string of white gore speckled with black blood through the air. The feline wasn't interested in a snack though, so it allowed the Mek's broken body to fall to the ground. Still barely alive, it rolled to a stop on its back while Pearl blissfully hopped onto another sacrifice. The blue sky above was obscured for the last second of its life by another paw, this one speckled with bodies belonging to its former comrades.

Alexis looked back to Kiera for a quick second. The red patterns on her face illuminated as the Mek'Vatir succumbed to its fate beneath her footfall, joining the others as debris following the sprightly Aluni in her dash.

She maintained her lead up until they reached the temple's enormous shadowy gates. Her gait slowed to a walk as Kiera caught up, and both of them took a moment to catch their breath from the long run. Alexis doubled over to her knees, resting her hands on them as she laughed through each gasping breath while Pearl pranced around them in an excited circle.

"I won," Alexis said as she stood back up and looked to Kiera with a smug and exhausted smile.

"Nah, I let you stay ahead."

Alexis shoved Kiera, who stumbled to the side in a fit of laughter. They then turned their attention back to the black gate in front of them. In an attempt to recuperate quickly, Alexis drew more energy from Adriel and took in a deep breath of air. She could feel her passenger do the same, and was happy that he hadn't fallen from his protective alcove during their competition.

"This place doesn't really change, it's almost like it's stuck in time...." Alexis' voice trailed off as she gazed upward.

While still out of breath, Kiera approached the doorway. From a distance it was so black that it looked to be unnatural, but up close she could see waves of shadowy substance and texture. She pounded the side of her fist into the doorway in hopes of gathering someone's attention on the other side.

"Hello?! Your prodigal daughters have returned!" She yelled.

There was no answer.

Kiera could feel people nearby. They were up on the walls and moving beyond the gate as normal, but nobody came to let them in. They did, however, feel as though they were being watched.

"Maybe we should check the garden?" Alexis suggested, and Kiera swiftly nodded in agreement.

There was a dirt path that led down to the gardens starting immediately to their left. It was both well-traveled and well-maintained. Instead of a full fence, there was a short hedge row with trees that hung over the pathway to keep travelers from falling. Both Kiera and Alexis had fond memories of this path from their childhood, and the faint sound of a violin off in the distance flooded the two with feelings of nostalgia.

As Kiera started down the path, Pearl hopped up to her shoulder and trilled while swaying its tail back and forth slowly. Kiera looked out over the city far below near the ocean, the first time she saw the totality of the war's devastation from afar. The sun was setting, which caused the blue sky to burn with red and orange hues over the calm waters. Nevarria's silhouette against the fiery clouds had changed drastically from what it once was as plumes of smoke streamed into the air.

The differing districts of the city all had unique forms of destruction brought upon them. The business district that she frequented was in shambles, with most of the buildings broken beyond repair and vines had reclaimed the structures closest to the forest. The entertainment district had been leveled completely with only small buildings still in place as steam tracks and tanks fought with no regard for their surroundings.

Seeing the residential district from this vantage point sent chills down Kiera's spine. She recalled the first time she saw her own house from here, how happy it made her to be able to pick it out of the cityscape among all the other buildings that surrounded it. Now it lay in rubble, along with the family and everything that she lost. A single chimney stack stood in the pile, nothing more.

"This place is always so peaceful, why can't the rest of the world be like it is here?" Alexis asked as she followed closely.

"It would be nice, wouldn't it?" Kiera replied solemnly.

Her tail began to sway once more as Alexis' optimistic joy helped her come back to the present. The smell of the ocean came along again with a gentle breeze that caused Kiera's hair to dance in the wind. The atmosphere of tranquility was enforced by the waterfall's low roar and the sound of Sofie's violin that grew louder with each step the pair took.

As they emerged from the tree-covered pathway and into the temple's exterior garden, they stopped to take in the sheer majesty of their surroundings.

The garden itself was situated into three platforms that were surrounded by water on all sides and connected via arching wooden bridges. The water flowed toward the cliff and formed a singular waterfall that surrounded everything. There was a lower reservoir that caught the cascading water and powered a large water wheel that could hardly be seen from where they stood. The enormous fountain was working as it always had, using the wheel's power to pump water back to the gardens from the lower level.

The water below was deep enough to catch anyone who might fall into the tides, and there was a stairwell for maintenance so that the area could be easily accessed. Kiera, however, was guilty of using the waterfalls recreationally on more than one occasion.

Sofie stood alone on the furthest garden platform and danced with a flow that was just as fast-paced as the lovely music her violin produced. Her outfit looked nearly identical to what she had worn so long ago, complete with her black corset and a tapered green ankle-length skirt.

Kiera and Alexis walked across the wooden bridges leading to the platform Sofie occupied. However, they stopped before crossing the final bridge so they would not interrupt her performance. The silver on her ankles and wrists reflected the setting sun, as twilight provided just enough shade to display the purple Amethya crystal shards set in their metal. Trapped spirits within moved like clouds beneath its surface and produced a faint, churning ethereal glow.

She was the same age as Kiera and Alexis, though she physically looked to be a cycle or two older than the other girls. Sofie had a habit of removing her moccasins whenever she came out to the garden. Dancing barefoot was something that she always felt would help her feel a stronger connection with the greater life energy of the planet. Her moccasins lay next to one of the three stone benches that were evenly placed around the circular platform. On the bench was a staff made of brown iron oak and topped with a green Amethya crystal that had the same glowing clouds of mixing spiritual energy trapped inside.

Her music had lulled all of the nearby Mek'Vatir into a false sense of security. They were drawn in to watch their goddess dance to the violin's upbeat tune and remained unfazed by the danger. Not a single Mek ran to a safe distance, even when her careless steps would land close enough to reach out and touch. Beady black eyes gazed up at her as she moved around the little speck of a creature at her feet who had avoided death by sheer luck up to this point. That luck was fleeting, as the ball of her left foot came down directly in front of her adoring fan.

Before it even had the chance to blink, her heel came down like the ax of an executioner. The dusty skin of her arch forced it to its back instantly. She hadn't fully shifted her weight onto that side though, so the Mek'Vatir was simply pinned down as it struggled to be set free. Its fate was sealed as Sofie's bow slid across the strings of her violin in her radiant bliss.

Dancing along, Sofie's heel began to repetitively tap on the ground. The casual and unrelenting torture went on for what seemed like a lifetime as the violin's tune resonated through her.

The Mek could feel air sliding across its body as she unwittingly teased it with freedom time and time again. Light would fade for mere moments before coming back to the small one's black eyes as its tiny heart feverishly pumped black blood and adrenaline through its veins. The simple act of shifting her weight from one foot to another was a death sentence. The soft and dusty skin it had been fighting against became rock solid as she settled her weight down, and its struggle was extinguished.

Sofie was fairly exhausted as her daily practice session came to an agreeable end. The dark green markings that adorned her arms illuminated with a pulse of spiritual energy, followed by all of her jewelry's purple Amethya crystals where the excess energy was stored. She then slipped the violin around her body using a leather sling like one would a rifle and sheathed the bow on her hip like a sword. With every new Acolyte uniform she obtained, Sofie fashioned a loop on the side of the corset to make carrying her instrument easier. Cheers and applause came from the two Aluni watching as they finally approached.

"Hmm?" Sofie uttered when she looked up from her home-made bow sheath to Kiera and Alexis as they strolled toward her on the stone platform.

"You've come a long way, comrade!" Alexis said in a chipper tone as they came closer.

"Alexis?! Kiera!" Sofie squeaked as she jogged over to the two, wrapping her arms around Alexis tightly.

"You have a staff now?" Kiera said as she motioned toward the iron oak staff next to her moccasins.

"Oh yes! I'm an Advanced Acolyte now. I've even seen the Sanctum Astrona's lower catacomb."

"That's fantastic!" Alexis said as she stepped back while still holding the Acolyte's arms. "I'm so proud of you!"

Pearl hopped off of Kiera's shoulder to the ground and quickly found a new victim to play with. The closest Mek was running away from the feline, which immediately caught its attention. The animal easily apprehended it, batting it to the side before patting it into the ground repeatedly with its forepaws. When Pearl discovered the Mek was abnormally strong, its cloud-like tail began to slyly sway and the animal trilled with joy.

"How adorable! A lunamir!" Sofie squeaked as she crouched down to beckon the feline over.

"So that's what they're called," Kiera said as she folded her arms and watched.

Pearl noticed the call and picked the Mek up by its hair. Then, it proudly trotted over to the Acolyte and curled up at her feet. The lunamir dropped its toy to the ground and promptly pinned the Mek's upper body down underneath one of its forepaws toes. Once its prize was immobilized, the animal began to lick at the Mek's lower half like a treat to be savored.

"Yeah," Sofie said as she carefully ran her claw tips through the purring feline's fur, "they're pretty rare to come across in the woods, but they're so adorable. If she's following you around, that means she's bonded to one of you."

"Looks like you have a daughter now, Kiera," Alexis jested, nudging her friend a bit while chuckling.

"I'm ok with this," Kiera replied with her arms folded across her chest while her tail swayed.

"Have you named her yet?" Sofie asked as she looked up from her crouched position.

"Kiera did! Her name's Pearl," Alexis said and crouched down to pet the fluffball as well.

"Sofie...." Kiera said in a low voice. "I know we should proably have come up here to visit a bit more often, and I'm sorry for that. But we didn't come here to catch up."

"Oh?" the Acolyte replied curiously.

"There's an Aestellan soldier who was shot at the pub. She's a friend, and probably won't make it without the help of a doctor or a Terra Medi."

Sofie nervously looked to the setting sun that was slowly disappearing over the horizon. The rings weren't visible from where they were, as the overhanging cliff face blocked them from view. The Acolyte stood up and looked back to Kiera with her hands behind her back.

"The beasts of the forest should be waking soon," Sofie said quietly. "I might be able to protect us during a night journey, but that would be inviting danger and I may be forced to kill them to keep us alive. It'll be much safer if we left in the morning, and we wouldn't have to contend with the wildlife. Do you think your friend will survive until tomorrow evening?"

"She's in good hands for now," Alexis said as she continued to pet Pearl. "Are you able to leave with us? It won't interrupt your studies, will it?"

"My studies can wait if it means saving a life."

"She's an Aestellan. That won't be a problem for you, will it?" Kiera nervously asked.

"Acolytes and Paladins are protectors of Cerolia as a whole. Nationality means nothing to us here, we're all Cerolians no matter what banner we fly. I'll do my best when we arrive."

"Thank you," Kiera said, bowing graciously after.

"You two must be hungry after your trip here! I'll go get my stuff and maybe we can share some aquamelon in the garden?"

"That sounds great," Kiera replied, then let her arms fall to her side as she looked back to Alexis and Pearl.

The Mek was trying to crawl away from its fluffy predator, though its feeble attempts to run were thwarted when Pearl's paw reached out and drug it back into the fray. Sofie bowed her head slightly, then she stepped over the lunamir on her way to retrieve her moccasins and staff. Her right shoe had fallen over when she took it off earlier. After stepping into the one that was upright, she kicked the other moccasin over so that she could don her footwear without having to kneel.

The rough jolt startled a Mek that had taken up temporary residence inside. The little one had fallen asleep to the tune of her music, having burrowed into the cotton-like fabric of the moccasin's interior. While the rather off-putting scent of the Acolyte's sweat was still abundant, the area was warm and dark enough to host a comfortable place to sleep. Some of the cotton had risen where her digits would normally rest, making it a perfect place for the little being to surround itself with warmth.

She could feel the Mek struggling within the cotton beneath her pinky toe as her heel slid into place with a light *'thump'*. They were the only creatures on the planet that the Acolytes and Paladins were trained to kill without remorse, as they represented raw energy that could be used for spells both mundane and extraordinary. She attempted to extinguish it, though her moccasin's fabric was too soft. Her actions buried it in the cotton to the point where it was unable to move, ensuring that it would never escape on its own. The tiny creature's plight was little more than a passing distraction, one that the Advanced Acolyte chose to ignore for the time being.

"We have someone else we want to show you tonight," Kiera said as Sofie returned with staff in hand. "It's a bit of a long shot, but maybe you can tell us more about him."

"Wait... *Someone* else?" Sofie replied quizzically. "Did you bring another person?"

"Well—" Kiera began.

"Welcome back," a familiar voice said from behind, "I must apologize, the Paladins on the walls have orders to report all visitors to me before allowing them access to the grounds."

"Lady Zara!" Alexis shouted excitedly as she hopped to her feet and gave her elder a formal bow.

Kiera and Sofie followed suit, and Zara returned the gesture with a polite bow of her own. The High Paladin's hair was almost unnaturally black and policed into a ponytail by a single silver hair tie. A long horizontal sky-blue Amethya crystal was wrapped around the band's center, which was constantly illuminated by the cloudy spirits of the deceased. As she came up from her bow, her crystalline blue eyes locked back on the three Aluni that stood before her.

"I'm glad to see you two are alright," Zara said softly. "To what do we owe the pleasure of your return?"

"We need Sofie's help," Kiera replied, "someone's been shot and they need a Terra Medi."

Zara's expression shifted from one of joy to concern as she held her white iron-oak staff. The black Amethya crystal which was fastened to the top swirled like a dark abyss as the Mek'Vatir's souls trapped within churned among each other. Like Sofie, she too looked off into the setting sun.

"It would be irresponsible of me to allow you three to travel tonight without protest," Zara said as she graciously motioned back toward the dirt path leading to the temple. "Your decision will be respected of course. However, you're all more than welcome to enjoy our hospitality until the morning."

"We were just talking about that," Kiera said, "do you have any beds available in the visitor's quarters?"

"Of course, though I would like you both to join me for dinner in the Sanctum Astrona."

"Really?" Alexis squeaked in shock.

"Are you sure, High Paladin?" Sofie asked.

"Perhaps it's time to share some of our wisdom with trusted outsiders. Not all, of course."

"Can we take Pearl inside too?" Kiera asked as she motioned to the lunamir who was still playing with her toy.

"We would be delighted to have her," Zara replied. "Sylvia just started preparing dinner, so there's no rush. We usually have plenty of extra, and some berries for Pearl to enjoy. Let's walk."

Lady Zara then turned to head back the way she came as the others followed suit. Pearl looked up and saw everyone leaving, so she snagged her toy Mek by its hair between her teeth then ran after the group.

Lady Zara

S A N C T U A R Y

C H A P T E R   I V

The black gates were now open, allowing the party to enter the temple's exterior complex. As soon as everyone was safely inside, the portcullis fell and the doorway began to close. The temple's entryway had been reconstructed in the time they were gone. They were corralled to the left and forced to pass through a secondary gatehouse that was made of the same jet black stone as the first. It was sealed once they passed as well, and the path snaked back to the right to a final gatehouse. Paladins lined the ramparts above as they watched over the killing zone through the protective slits of interior machicolations. As soon as they passed through the final doorway, two Paladins armed with long black swords fused the dark stone with a combined blast of blue and red spiritual energy.

"That was new," Kiera said as she looked back to the interior door as it was dramatically sealed.

"We've had to fend off several assaults from Aestellan airships and ground forces since the war began," Zara said as she began to ascend the main stairwell leading to the central building. "They've since stopped their assaults, but a more secure defensive posture helps ensure we don't have to retreat to the Sanctum Astrona for safety during attacks."

"Why don't you strike back?" Kiera asked.

"Do you not remember our tenants?"

"It's been a while."

"Paladins wander Cerolia in search of threats greater than those posed by political powers. We are sworn defenders of the planet, and mustn't allow ourselves to sway the tide of war."

"People are dying down there."

"It's tragic," Zara replied mournfully as she motioned toward a newly constructed residential area off near the protected interior wall. "We've taken in many refugees from the chaos below, but Paladins are not soldiers and should never be used as tools in any conflict."

"We don't even take the lives of animals for food here," Sofie added from behind, "if we got involved, we'd be responsible for the deaths of so many — regardless of who we sided with."

"Understandable," Alexis said as Pearl hopped up the stairs around her ankles.

"I apologize," Kiera said solemnly, "I shouldn't have said anything about it."

Young Acolytes and Paladins alike wandered the footpaths with brooms and swept up any dirt along with broken carcasses of the Mek'Vatir. Some wore a uniform that differed from what Sofie had on. It consisted of a long, emerald duster-type jacket with silver accents and a black vest beneath. Just like the corset, their black vest had six brass chains draped horizontally across the abdomen. Beneath this they wore a long-sleeved emerald button-up shirt with ruffled cuffs, also adorned with silver accents and stitching. The details could only be truly seen on those who weren't wearing the duster. They had soft black pants, and matching black moccasins with gray soles.

The group reached the top of the stairwell in good time and entered the monastery's main temple. It was recessed into the mountain, only open on three sides with cloisters that surrounded the main garth in the central area. There was a single, large straw mat platform that was lowered slightly from the gardens and surrounded by a soft vertical berm. Acolytes and Paladins surrounded the exterior as glowing clear Amethya crystals illuminated the area like torches with no fire. The youngest of the Acolytes spread Mek throughout the platform as though they were sewing a field with seeds.

"I almost forgot about the Astral Dance," Kiera said.

"Tonight's dance is a unified advancement test. Would you like to stay and watch?" Zara asked as the group came to a stop.

"Yes!" Alexis excitedly replied.

"You don't happen to have some decent alcohol by any chance, do you?" Kiera asked.

"We do, why?" Zara replied. "Have you even been practicing your suppression techniques?"

"Alcohol works better and it's easier."

Sofie ran off the way they came, quickly disappearing around a nearby corner as Zara folded her arms in disappointment. The High Paladin lowered her head and sighed, before looking back up to the young purple-haired Aluni standing in front of her.

"You can't always rely on alcohol in a crowd, have you at least *tried* to apply what you've learned here to your life?"

"Only when it's convenient. Alcohol's more convenient."

"I understand why you would choose that route when it's available, but please try and practice your meditation and inner control when you can."

"Here!" Sofie shouted as she ran up with an oddly shaped bottle in her grip. "Sweet Avriberry Spirits, we make it right here at the temple. This one's my recipe."

"You're a lifesaver, comrade," Kiera said as she wrapped her arms around Sofie.

The Acolyte pulled the cap to her brew off and dropped a pair of Mek into the burning liquid before offering it to her friend. Kiera accepted Sofie's offering and immediately took a swig of the strong liquor. She didn't even flinch as the burning liquid passed her lips, and Zara shook her head disapprovingly.

"You've obviously had quite a bit of practice," the High Priestess said with an unimpressed tone.

"I live at a bar and my new family loves me," Kiera replied as she licked the liquid from her lips. "Maya knows it helps and she doesn't make me feel bad about it... Much."

"Do you like it?" Sofie asked.

"It's fantastic, I'll be numb in no-time."

Lady Zara motioned toward a nearby empty bench that was close to the edge of the arena, though it was surrounded by Acolytes and Paladins of all races and ages. Kiera took another abnormally long pull off her new bottle of alcohol, let out a contented sigh with a smile wide enough to show her fangs, and followed the High Paladin's lead as the group made their way over to the open seats. The spectators were courteous, making a path for them to pass through as they approached.

The High Paladin was the first to make it to the bench. Just as she came to a stop in front of her seat, she felt the pop of a Mek's body beneath the ball of her foot. Ignoring it entirely, she sat down with her staff in her right hand and crossed her legs so the tiny creature was suspended in the air.

The Mek was still among the living, though everything below its upper chest had been crushed and broken. It weakly clawed at the space between Zara's great toe and first, just as a black shadowy mist came from her skin. It engulfed the Mek's body in a torrent of pain, tearing it asunder with a focused smoky whirlwind. Within seconds, the darkness subsided leaving only ash and the perfect figure of a tiny body. There were dozens of other silhouettes, as her snowy white skin made their profiles stand out well against the ash they left behind.

Zara was unique among the Cerolians, as she was the only person known to have no patterns on her palms or soles. Black crescent-shaped marks on Zara's biceps and calves produced that same dark mist that trailed behind her movements as she adjusted her posture to get comfortable. Kiera and Alexis sat on either side of Lady Zara, while Sofie chose to stand among the closest Acolytes to their seat. They welcomed her with open arms and spoke in whispers out of respect for the test that was about to unfold. Pearl curled up on Kiera's lap, still holding her toy Mek by its hair between her lips as Kiera drank her booze and pet the lunamir for comfort.

Five young Acolytes were wearing a different uniform than the rest. It was a single black dress with no sleeves and a high collar around their neck. The fabric was parted down the middle and tied together with little white bows from the collar to their ankles. None of them wore shoes, nor were they wearing any form of crystalline jewelry. Each of the Acolytes had different attunements, and represented different races as well.

An Elder Paladin wearing a white version of the Acolyte's formal dress stepped forth into the ring, and as she did so, her dark green hooves and horns illuminated with the soul of a Mek transferring into her body. She still looked to have maintained her youth like Lady Zara, though she was likely hundreds of cycles old. The sun had just fallen, leaving the colorful night's sky in its stead. As the white-furred Edoraii entered the arena, she crouched and sent out a wave of green energy across the lowered floor. The Mek'Vatir all fell to their backs as the pulse washed over them. They were frozen in place as the elder stood back up and looked to the five Acolytes before her.

"We come together on this wondrous night to bear witness to the progression of these five Acolytes, on the ever-evolving journey of their lives," the elder began. "Each of these brave young Acolytes has toiled to overcome their adversities. They would not be standing before us today if we did not believe they were ready to take this step toward their future."

The elder then paused and looked around to the other Acolytes and Paladins that surrounded the arena. With a smile, she put her hands behind her back before continuing.

"For the young Acolytes in attendance, watch and learn from your peers on this night. We train both as individuals and as one unified force. Tonight's test will showcase the sheer necessity of cooperation to control your Æther Projection. With enough training and dedication to the craft, one day you too will be where they stand. And after you preform the Astral Dance for the first time in earnest, you will be ready to construct your staff from the great iron oak trees and become an Advanced Acolyte."

She then turned her gaze back to the five young ones who stood just outside of the ring in front of her, and held her right hand out toward the Acolyte that stood furthest to the left.

"Abigail Vari, please enter the arena."

The young Edoraii stepped down directly onto a Mek'Vatir just as the Elder had. Her bright-blue hooves and curved horns illuminated, shining down on her soft white fur. She held her hands to the side and streams of pale blue energy emerged to surround her in ribbons that floated independently around her.

"Kylie Lyn, please enter the arena."

Immediately, an Aluni with dark brown skin hopped into the arena and onto the nearest Mek to siphon its spirit through its death. Neon-green patterns across her arms illuminated the area around her as she too allowed bright green ribbons of energy to surround her body. She pulled her long, green hair back behind her pointed ears and bowed to her Elder respectfully as her fluffy green tail swayed.

"Tristan Vari, please enter the arena."

A white-furred Kavar with their wings folded down over their shoulders stepped into the arena, careful to target a Mek so that they could get enough energy to perform an entry display. As the Mek'Vatir was killed, they spread their wings and the dark blue membrane around the interior acted like a temporary area light around them. It shimmered twice as they accidentally killed another and took a powerful stance with their legs wide and arms spread. Ribbons of blue energy spun around them, emanating from the ground and working their way up.

"Willow Lodbrok, please enter the arena."

The Acolyte did as she was asked, hopping down on the nearest Mek she could see. Being a young Incana with soft paw pads, the creature didn't die immediately from the impact. The pink-furred Acolyte spun on one foot, twisting the Mek into a smear as her dark green paw pads illuminated with its soul. Her eyes had a green glow as well when she came to a stop with a sharp stomp on another little victim with just enough force to partially break it. She pulled her paw back quickly so that her pads could glow again, and sent green waves of soothing energy out to her friends in the arena.

"Julia Grace, please enter the arena."

The last Acolyte stepped forward as her thick, overly fluffed tail swayed behind her. The rings around it were alternating colors of pink and red, with a black tip that was nearly invisible from where the group sat. The moment she set foot in the arena; Willow's green tendrils of energy arched over toward her to give her the same boost that she gave all of her other comrades. Julia tucked her long dreadlocks behind her rounded ears and made sure the red and black strands were secured so they wouldn't interfere with her performance. She then stretched her arms toward the sky, yawning as her fur-coated paw found its mark on the ground.

The interior of her mouth and the long strands of red dread-locks, as well as her paws and hands, began to glow deep crimson. The Acolyte then fell to one knee and set her hand on another immobilized Mek on the floor. Strands of glowing red energy surrounded her while she drew the life directly from the little one on the ground without physically harming its body. When she stood back up, the Mek she had under her palm was a dead husk driven to its end by over-stimulation.

She made sure she was in line with the others, all of whom were still surrounded by their glowing energies. The Acolytes walked in unison toward the center of the arena, and each step they took caused their Symbiont patterns to glow as they restored their drained energy. All except Willow, who used her powers to carry the Mek'Vatir along under-paw like a glowing green adhesive. She was far more methodical about her con-sumption, executing those trapped in tow via over-stimulation just as Julia had done.

The five reached the center of the arena and knelt together in unison to the Edoraii elder that stood before them. She stepped backward without looking, and out of the lowered arena.

The moment she did, the Mek'Vatir that were temporarily stunned were allowed to resume wandering.

"Begin."

They all moved with absolute purpose, like martial artists fol-lowing the steps of their Kata. The ribbons of color followed their movements with ease as they adapted their maneuvers to match the scurrying Mek'Vatir below. Lights melded together, mixing their colors to change their vibrant hues. Rays of cyan and magenta filled the area, occasionally reaching a level of combined energy to produce a pure yellow color as the power grew.

Occasionally, Willow's energies would reach out to her nearby comrades to transfer the souls she collected directly to them. The ribbons then turned to colored balls of flame, each masterfully controlled as the energy twisted and turned around them. The energy moved as if it had agency, though everyone knew the Acolytes were pulling the marionette's strings.

The more they progressed, the more they allowed glowing dust-like particles to accumulate on their black training dresses. Eventually, all five of the Acolytes shimmered like the stars above as their Symbiont's continuously lit up the night. They dodged and weaved like self-contained cosmoses as their colorful burning comets darted around before transforming back into the ribbons they once were. The glowing spectral ashes remained as the five spun in unison, each positioning themselves so that they made up the five points of a sacred star.

They then moved in a clockwise fashion, sending their ribbons up in a tent-like spiral to meet together at a single focal point. The colors faded to a brilliant white as the ribbons touched together at the apex. They danced around the central axis for a few moments in perfect harmony, and when the tip of the star they created was pointed toward the elders, they all crouched again. The ribbons fell to the ground quickly, but instead of fading away, they scattered across the entire arena and up into the spectators. The energy would bead up wherever it landed before it dissipated, as it wasn't enough to be properly absorbed by anyone who wasn't a direct target.

Kiera chuckled when she saw Pearl pawing at the floating ashes of spiritual energy as though they were the insects that she hunted. When it was clear she wouldn't be able to catch any of them, she turned her attention back to the struggling toy she had acquired earlier. The Acolytes, still crouched, looked up to the group of five elders that were judging their merit during the dance. They all stood from their chairs in silence with their arms behind their backs. Each of them had the task of focusing on a single Acolyte, and the Edoraii elder that had initiated the dance earlier was in the center of the group. They all reached toward the darkened sky as the pulse of spiritual light in nearby crystals shimmered off of their uniforms. Then, their hands all illuminated with focused energy that extended a meter from their palms. Roaring applause from all of the spectators filled the arena as the Acolytes nearly leaped from their crouched positions in joy. They had all passed, and in unison, the five walked across the arena toward their elders. Glowing spiritual dust spread like a wake of water behind them, though it was fairly short-lived after the display was finished.

Even with the alcohol in her system, Kiera could feel their excitement and the overall joy of the crowd bombarding her from all sides. Pearl, as if sensing her companion's discomfort, stood in the Aluni's lap and nuzzled up to her arm while purring loudly. Kiera watched from her seated position as the Acolytes were given a special feather showing their progress. Her attention was quickly diverted to the feline in her lap, and the abused little Mek that was trapped dangling between her lips still by its hair. Pearl's intuition helped immensely, as Kiera's somewhat intoxicated state and the animal demanding her attention kept her from feeling most of the emotional barrage.

Sofie made her way over toward the five through the crowd to congratulate them on their success. Zara stood up as well, though she didn't immediately follow suit. She looked down at Kiera and Alexis with her staff in hand, and her tail swayed slowly behind her.

"You two are welcome to stay here or come with us," Zara said, "we won't be very long."

"I'm alright staying here, thanks," Kiera replied as she took another long drink of alcohol while petting the feline on her lap.

"I'll stay too," Alexis chimed in.

Zara then walked off into the crowd as Alexis stood and stretched. She had the urge to draw some energy from her comrade underfoot, but decided it would be best to avoid drawing attention with a prolonged glow. Someone like Sofie might be able to get away with it, but neither Kiera nor Alexis had a command of their Æther Projection strong enough to do that without any form aid.

"How's Adriel?" Kiera asked, looking up to Alexis.

Alexis tapped her shoe on the ground a few times, wiggling it about to see if she could coax a response from her passenger.

"He's still moving and breathing, poor thing. I hope I wasn't too hard on him today."

"We can ask him later...."

"Sorry," Alexis said sheepishly, "I should have asked you before volunteering that we stay."

"It was worth it. A bit overwhelming there at the end, but Sofie pulled through for me."

Kiera then displayed her nearly empty glass bottle of alcohol with a rosy-cheeked smile, before bringing it back to her lips to finish it off. She then capped it and set it aside while Pearl continued to bother her for more petting.

"She's a needy little one, isn't she?" Alexis said as Kiera nuzzled up to Pearl's fur.

"I think she's trying to help."

Alexis watched the crowd of people as they slowly dispersed, returning to their nightly duties while Sofie and Lady Zara stayed with the five. Her tail slowly swayed as she listened to the sound of muffled talking and insects chirping off in the distance. The young Acolytes who had dispersed the Mek in the arena now had brooms and were sweeping them up into small dustpans. All who attempted to escape were swiftly stamped flat and swept up with the others to maintain the pure appearance of the arena.

"Are you ready?" Sofie asked as she approached the two with Zara close behind her.

"Yeah," Kiera replied.

Pearl took her little chew toy and set it down on Kiera's lap, then stood up and stretched. The Mek weakly tried to escape by crawling away, then rolled off onto the floor as Kiera stood. The lunamir's ears perked up as she watched her favorite little tough-bug fall, and she immediately hopped to the floor to retrieve it. Weakly, the little Mek gasped for air as it tried to gather its breath and the strength to flee. The feline circled it once as the Mek finally stood, then knocked it to its back so that she could set her hind paw on its little body. She held it down just long enough for the Mek's skin to adhere to the soft purple paw pad, while its head was buried in fluffy feline toe-fur.

The lunamir then pranced after the group with her head held high, easily catching up to the five as they ventured toward the large black gate that separated the outer facility from the myste-rious Sanctum Astrona.

Pearl

SANCTUARY
CHAPTER V

"This is so exciting," Alexis nearly squealed as her tail swayed back and forth feverishly.

The fluffy whip nearly smacked Kiera as she struggled to walk in a straight line. She managed to get alongside her friend though as they approached the black doorway, then she took her arm for support. It was an attempt to be subtle but the alcohol hit her harder than she expected.

"This door looks smaller than I remember," Kiera said as she tried to maintain balance while looking up to the top of the solid black stone.

"Of course it does, you've grown," Zara said as she stepped out in front of the group.

They all came to a stop as Zara placed her hand in the center of a spiral glyph carved into the doorway. Her black markings began to seep dark smoke before the stone split down the center in a perfect line and separated so the group may enter. To Kiera and Alexis' surprise, the darkened doorway was nearly silent as it glided to an open position. Beyond it was a single descending staircase lit with glowing veins of white crystal that extended along the walls.

"This is so pretty," Alexis said in awe as she stepped down to the stairwell, running a fingertip along one of the smooth crystal veins as she passed.

Lady Zara took the lead and everyone else followed suit. Alexis continued, keeping close to the wall while still hold-ing Kiera so that she wouldn't fall down the stairwell. Behind them all was Pearl, who hopped down the stairwell one step at a time in quick succession. The sound of the wind, as well as the Paladins and Acolytes going about their business, faded to a cold silence replaced only by their footsteps.

"Isn't there an elevator we could have taken?" Kiera asked, keeping her eyes down to the stairs below so that she wouldn't misplace a step.

"There's really no need," Sofie replied from behind. "Tired?"

Pearl, weary of hopping down the stairs, leaped into the air and spread her ethereal wings. She glided over to Kiera and landed on her shoulder, curling up against her chosen compan-ion's neck to get a free lazy ride to the bottom.

"The trip here took a lot out of us," Kiera replied in defeat. "How much longer before we reach the end?"

"There is no end."

"Excuse me?"

The group came to a stop as Kiera looked to Alexis for affirmation, already able to feel the unease coming from her comrade.

"What are you talking about? Of course it has an end," Alexis said, perplexed by the comment.

"It's a defensive mechanism," Zara said calmly as she looked up to the two on the stairwell, "one of many precautions used to ensure the sanctity of our home."

"I was wondering if Zara was going to show you," Sofie said with a chipper tone as she continued down past the two. "This place is one of several fractured locations beneath the surface. We aren't completely on Cerolia anymore."

"I'm too drunk and tired for this," Kiera said dismissively, "what are you talking about now?"

"I did make it a bit strong, didn't I? Sorry for not letting you know in advance, comrade."

"Next time make it stronger; I can still see," Kiera said, then chuckled. "So if we are not in Cerolia anymore, where are we?"

"Cargasso?" Alexis asked with a tinge of wonder in her tone.

"No. Reality beyond the Veil," Zara replied calmly. "Cargasso has nothing to do with it."

"Solumna?" Kiera asked.

"Interesting...." Zara replied under her breath as though she were speaking to herself. She positioned her staff out in front of her and held it vertically with both hands firmly gripping the white iron oak. A light-headed sensation filled the two, followed by a dizzy spell that made Kiera's mild drunkenness much worse than it was. Then, reality set back in.

Alexis regained her equilibrium first as she held Kiera up while leaning on the wall herself. Pearl shook her little head and yawned while Kiera finally stood without assistance. They both looked back the way they came in unison to the black doorway that had closed long ago. Two large crystals illuminated the solid sheet of otherworldly material, allowing them to see it clear as day. They looked back to Sofie and Zara who now stood before them on the short, straight stairwell that seemed to only descend a few stories.

"Kiera?" Alexis asked nervously, "You uh...."

"Yep," Kiera replied breathlessly.

"Welcome to the Sanctum Astrona," Zara said as she turned to walk back down the stairwell.

Sofie followed quickly, but Kiera and Alexis hesitated so that they could process everything. Pearl impatiently hopped off of Kiera's shoulder, extending her glowing wings again to gracefully glide down to the end of the stairwell. When the feline softly landed, she turned around and sat down while her wings disappeared into spiritual dust.

Kiera and Alexis moved together, and as they reached the bottom of the staircase they entered an enormous antechamber.

The walls were covered in what appeared to be the roots of a large tree. Carved into those roots were runes that meant nothing to the newcomers. They pulsed with life as though they were breathing the spiritual essence that illuminated the room.

At the other end of the antechamber stood a single Latherian guard clad in silver and black armor. He held a halberd, and within the dark blade at the top of his polearm was a thin sheet of dark blue crystal. He wore an ornate sword on his hip that matched the silver ensemble, and over his heart was a small circular marking that Kiera and Alexis didn't recognize. His jagged horns reflected the glowing light around him. The sentinel cut an imposing figure and looked well trained, ready to strike at a moment's notice if needed.

"Welcome," the sentinel said with a deep voice that echoed throughout the chamber.

Sofie hurried over to the sentinel and wrapped her arms around him while still holding her staff. He looked down at her with a warm smile across his lips as his free hand came to rest on her back. However, the singular red eye in the center of his forehead remained trained on both Kiera and Alexis.

"Kiera, Alexis," Sofie said as she turned to her comrades. "This is my friend Ramus, one of the two guardians of the Sanctum Astrona. He's really nice."

The newcomers bowed as Pearl took the opportunity to climb back up to her perch on Kiera's shoulder. Sofie stepped away from the friendly sentinel as Ramus returned the gesture. He wasn't the first Latherian the two had met, though they were extremely rare to come across.

"A pleasure to finally make your acquaintance," Ramus said, his voice still booming. "Sofie has told me much about you two. Even in your absence, you've made quite an impression on her."

"Really?" Alexis asked as Sofie sheepishly held her staff close.

"Yes. I think, maybe?" The Advanced Acolyte squeaked before she looked up to Ramus. "How's Ivar?"

"He's doing quite well. I believe his daughter and husband are currently in the Natalin Suites enjoying a performance."

"That sounds wonderful, anyone I know playing?"

"I don't believe so. You've been on the surface for quite some time, haven't you?"

"Have I?" Sofie replied as her tail swayed. "We should get going though, my comrades are famished. Catch up later?"

"Of course," Ramus replied.

The door behind the guard did not open to allow them access; it simply vanished. Kiera and Alexis were taken aback not by the door's disappearance, but by what it revealed. It was a city-sized cavern illuminated by crystalline monoliths that protruded from a lake in the center of the chamber. There were thousands of stone structures built into the walls that were connected by walkways. The crystal lake was constantly replenished by a large waterfall on the far wall, providing the subterranean colony with a clean source of water. Several small farms could be seen in the distance, though neither Kiera nor Alexis could recognize their crop. The sky was filled with flight-capable races such as the Sarin and Kavar as they went about their nightly lives.

Zara led them down a short flight of stairs and into the subterranean city. When they were all clear of the aperture, it was replaced with a solid wall of stone marked only by the same glyph that adorned Ramus' plate armor.

"How does a place like this even exist?" Alexis asked curiously. "We didn't actually descend too far. The ceiling of the cavern goes well beyond what the top of this mountain could contain."

The city's ground was not nearly as pristine as the temple above. Mek scurried around the floor like ants to be lost under the denizen's footfalls. It was the only familiar thing to the two newcomers in this strange place.

They eventually came to a stone bridge that extended across the lake and into the waterfall that cascaded off in the distance. The path itself was shielded by a large stone structure that surrounded a pristine white doorway at the end. Lights below the water's surface caught Kiera's eye as they walked along the pathway, causing her to stop and take a quick look. Pearl hopped back to the ground and leaned over as well, then began pawing at a small fish that swam just below the water's surface. Alexis wandered back to her friend's side and joined them, while Sofie and Zara patiently waited.

The water itself was crystal clear, allowing them to see to the rocky depths below. Strange bioluminescent fish swam among colorful coral and other odd filter-feeders that covered the lake's floor in an assortment of vibrant hues. Aquatic attuned Paladins swam through the depths as well, seemingly taking great care to both study and preserve the breathtaking display without the need for an underwater breathing apparatus. Researchers toward the bottom, however, were wearing full diving suits and seemed to be taking regular trips into spherical structures. Instead of using hatches, they opened transcendental portals that likely allowed them to pass through without decompressing the structure itself.

Along the walls, in areas that were more desolate and devoid of life that could be harmed by construction, were glass windows surrounded by stone structures which seemed to be living quarters. The largest structure was off to the side around thirty meters beneath the surface. It was mostly made of glass with supporting pillars of smooth stone to help push against the force of the water above. The stone building looked like a theatre, set in a perfect place so that it wouldn't disturb the ancient coral yet all who attended could see the picturesque display in all its glory. Every structure beneath it was spherical in design.

"The Natalin Suites," Lady Zara said as she approached the two and stood behind them.

There were Mek'Vatir swimming just along the surface that had likely haphazardly fallen in. Small fish that leapt out of the water from time to time would occasionally find them, eating them whole before descending back into the depths.

"Where do all these fish come from?" Kiera asked.

"Beneath Cerolia's crust is an entire world of cavernous self-contained biospheres," Zara replied. "This is just one of the many undiscovered subterranean regions. It's connected to a vast network of caves and tunnels teeming with life."

"What if something big and angry shows up?"

"We direct it elsewhere. Our abilities work underwater just as they do on land. The underwater life nearby seems to be more prone to mildly stinging our researchers if they aren't careful."

"How old is this place?" Alexis asked curiously, looking to Zara for an answer.

"Older than the Ali themselves," Zara responded.

"Older than the Ali? Is this...." Kiera said under her breath as she stepped away from the railing and looked up to the High Paladin before her.

"A Substation," Zara calmly stated as she motioned toward the doorway at the end of the bridge. "I'd imagine we gave Sylvia plenty of time to prepare for our arrival. Let's continue."

Kiera and Alexis nodded in unison as Zara and Sofie resumed their trek across the well-maintained stone suspension bridge. Two towers that supported the entire structure came out from the wall on either side of the enormous lake and joined forming a point at the top.

The roar of the waterfall at the other end grew louder as they approached. Kiera had expected the white doors beyond the archway to disappear or warp into some strange entity, but to her genuine surprise, they functioned as normal doors. Sofie and Zara held them open for their guests to pass through, and once they closed the sound of the waterfall was muffled to the point where it was nearly inaudible. They now stood in another ante-chamber lit by the same crystalline veins along the walls.

"Are these lights all powered by souls?" Kiera asked.

"Every single Mek that's killed has a purpose here, nothing is wasted. Follow me to the dining quarters," Zara replied as she led the group along the pathway.

As Zara walked along, another Mek disappeared beneath her footfalls. The black mist gently rolled from her patterns once more, and by the time her foot lifted from the ground, the Mek had been reduced to another ashen outline.

There were several ornate doors along the walls, and a glowing crystalline chandelier overhead. Zara lead the group to the left and through one of the passageways. As soon as they entered the smaller room, they realized they were standing in Zara's home. Before them was a large table that was only set for two, as she wasn't expecting visitors. The savory smell of an active kitchen drifted through the room, immediately lifting the girl's spirits even higher than they already were. Kiera's stomach growled and her mouth salivated at the prospect of having a full meal.

     CEROLIAN SAGAS

There was a kitchen adjacent to the dining hall on the left, and the chef inside was preparing a dish that smelled simply entrancing. When the doors shut behind the girls, another door in front of them opened to reveal an Acolyte. She wore the secondary Acolyte's uniform – a green long-sleeved formal button-up shirt with ruffled cuffs, a black vest, and black moccasins. As a Sarin, she was nearly twenty centimeters shorter than the others even though they were roughly the same age. When she saw the additional guests, she froze in place.

"Sylvia, can I trouble you to make three more meals tonight?" Zara asked her politely as she made her way over to the corner of the room to set her staff aside.

"Of course, Lady Zhar," Sylvia replied in a sheepishly low voice. "I was preparing enough to have leftovers, so there should be plenty to go around."

After she finished her sentence, the girl politely bowed and turned toward the door she came through. She tucked the long sky-blue hair that had fallen out of place between her ears and the two gray horns that curled down around them. Two patches of thick green crystals adorned her back. The vest and shirt she wore were both specifically designed to contour to them so that she could summon her wings at will. Kiera had met several of the Light Sarin before, though she had only seen them summon their wings once in passing. Sylvia seemed extremely meek, though, awash with anxiety that was nearly palpable.

"Is she alright?" Kiera asked. "She seems a bit anxious."

"Sylvia isn't generally comfortable around newcomers," Sofie said as she pulled a chair out for both Kiera and Alexis.

"That's relatable. Just like me in big crowds with no alcohol, speaking of which...."

"You don't need any alcohol here," Zara said primly as she took her seat at the head of the table, "it's just us."

"I didn't say I needed it, just that I wanted it."

Sylvia returned with two plates in hand, as well as two clay cups that were lined with crystals and filled with silverware. Without saying a word, she set the plates out in front of Kiera and Alexis then placed their utensils on the table properly.

"Thank you," Alexis said, prompting a silent bow from Sylvia before she returned to her kitchen.

There was enough space at the table for six or seven guests to have a nice meal, and more could potentially be accounted for if need be. Sofie sat down across from Kiera and Alexis, then placed her staff to the side on the unoccupied chairs. Kiera took her rifle from her back and propped it against the table, keeping it close even though they were likely several kilometers below the surface. She then took off her backpack and hung it on the chair, before sitting down herself.

"So, is this substation a functional one?" Kiera asked.

"Not anymore," Zara replied as she crossed her legs and leaned back in her ornate chair.

Sylvia Tate

"How? I mean..." Alexis stammered. "The staircase? How deep are we?"

"I'd like to talk about something else. To begin with, how do you know about Solumna?"

"I read about it in a book," Kiera said confidently.

"Really? What can you tell me about it then?"

"Oh, uh..." Kiera mumbled. "It's a thing that I read about. Thoroughly. Very thoroughly."

"You are a terrible liar."

"Alexis asked a really valid question, maybe we should focus on that instead?"

"Alright, I suppose where you heard the name doesn't quite matter," Zara began. "When the substations were destroyed long ago, they created areas beneath the surface of Cerolia that we refer to as fractured zones. Before the Temple of Aludra was constructed; Ivar, Ramus, and I surveyed each of the affected areas. This site was the only one where the fracture reached close enough to the surface for us to construct a temple, as well as a secured passage through the fracture to reach the substation."

"What happened to the original entryways?" Alexis asked.

"There were passageways into all the substations once, but they were destroyed. They've since been overtaken by the elements and would take a nation's worth of labor and a lifetime to excavate. There may be alternative entrances through from the sea, but we've yet to find any."

"So, this tunnel. That's what Ivar and Ramus guard, and the runes are there to keep it open?"

"Essentially. That region is the space beyond the veil, it's only safe to traverse because we have made it so. Ivar and Ramus protect the temple in shifts as they always have, they are my eldest friends and closest confidants."

"How old are you exactly?" Kiera asked.

"That's not something I would like to reveal. Old enough."

The doorway to the kitchen opened to reveal Sylvia holding a large plate with a single roll of kelp-wrapped sticky whitegrain. There was a sweet sauce drizzled over the top, along with a side of little toothpicks that had Mek'Vatir glued to the end with a sweet nectar facing outward. Steamed vegetables were in the center of the whitegrain rolls, and there were four bowls of soup filled with noodles and thick blue veggies balancing on the edge of the large plate.

"That looks fantastic, you're a really good cook," Alexis said as Sylvia retracted her arm.

"Thank you, I'll be back with the rest," Sylvia replied meekly before quickly dismissing herself to return to the kitchen.

Lady Zara reached forward and distributed all four bowls among the group while Sofie began splitting the roll up so they all would get an equal share. They had enough for everyone to have five rolls and ten 'Mek Sticks,' though Alexis happily gave the ones she received to Kiera as they weren't appetizing to her.

She was thankful that the noodle bowls weren't made with Mek swimming around inside, though. There was a ceramic spoon next to each bowl for drinking the broth.

"Aren't we going to save some for the chef?" Alexis asked curiously as she noticed that the entire roll had been divided among the four of them, with none left for Sylvia to enjoy.

"It's quite alright," Sylvia said as she stepped backward through the kitchen door with another large plate of food. "I've already taken my share to my quarters."

The plate had a fresh loaf of black bread swirled with white, a pot of tea on a miniature heater, a small bowl of fruit with Mek sprinkled on top, and a bottle of Sentoberry liquor. Two small dishes that had labeled covers were set to the side. One was black with the phrase *SweetMek* written on the top, while the other simply just said *Mek*. Alexis leaned back as the Sarin took the bowl of fruit from the table.

"You can eat with us if you'd like."

"I'd rather not," Sylvia replied as she stepped back from the table. "Please don't take it as an insult, I just..."

"You don't have to explain yourself," Kiera said as she slipped one of the Mek Sticks between her lips like candy, "thanks for the food, it looks wonderful."

"You're welcome. Excuse me, please."

Sylvia bowed her head respectfully before setting the fruit bowl on the ground. Pearl ran over and immediately lifted a piece of fruit with her forepaws to begin nibbling at it, tearing a Mek in half in the process. After gently patting the feline on the head, Sylvia left the room to go enjoy her own meal.

Kiera's patterns began glowing as she rolled the Mek's nectar-coated body between her molars. When she removed the stick from her lips, there was nothing left aside from a tinge of black blood. Sofie took the tea kettle and strainer from the table then filled her cup, catching all of the stray leaves in the wire so they wouldn't sully her drink. She then walked around to each person and did the same for them. While she poured the tea, Kiera took the bread and split it into even sections. She also procured the Sentoberry liquor for herself and filled her cup.

"May I ask a few more questions?" Alexis said as she lifted the teacup to her lips.

"Of course you may," Zara replied.

The High Paladin took one of her Mek Sticks and gently pressed it into the center of the warm whitegrain. The heat dissolved the nectar that bound the little one in place. When Zara pulled the pick out and set it aside, the Mek was left trapped with nowhere to go. She did this with a second Mek Stick before picking the roll up with her fingertips and taking a bite. The black markings on her shoulders let loose a soft and dark mist as her teeth crushed both of the tiny creatures trapped within.

"The people here look like they're doing a lot of research on the area," Alexis said, "and you seem to know a lot about what this 'Solumna' really is. Why haven't you shared that information with the general public? Surely you've found something that could benefit the rest of the world here, right?"

Alexis started to eat her noodles while she listened for a response, lighting up at just how good they tasted. They weren't quite the same as what Lain could whip together, but they were still a savory delight. The smell they had taken in when they entered must have been the broth, which had a perfect balance of savory and sweet flavors to it.

"We have no intention of withholding any information that could benefit the masses if we come across it," Zara began, taking a sip of her tea before continuing, "Solumna, on the other hand, is a beast best left undisturbed."

Kiera took the little black bowl labeled 'SweetMek' from the tray in the middle of the table and set it next to her plate. With her spoon in hand, she lifted the lid from the dish to reveal a pile of Mek'Vatir that had been stunned and soaked in alcohol. She carefully scooped out a spoonful of them and mixed them into her noodles, before replacing the lid and returning it to its original spot. There were a few that had fallen to the table like grains of sugar, though since they couldn't move too far on their own, they were promptly ignored.

"Why is that?" Kiera asked as she stirred the Mek into her noodles until they were evenly spread. "What's so dangerous about people knowing?"

"The last time we disturbed Solumna resulted in the extinction of the Mek'Va and the Ali. It's both a physical realm and a sentient entity that reaches all across the cosmos. The less the outside world knows of its existence, the less likely it is to set its gaze on Cerolia again."

"Oh..." Kiera meekly said, turning her attention to her food.

She brought a fork-full of noodles from the bowl, watching as the Mek'Vatir struggled to hang onto the strands like little gray bits of seasoning. The hot bath was enough to reinvigorate most of them, but their plight was lost on her. Her patterns flickered to life intermittently as she ate, swallowing some whole while others were crushed to death between her teeth. Sofie had just finished most of her whitegrain rolls and half of the Mek Sticks. Now, she was discarding a healthy scoop of the SweetMek into her steaming noodles.

"Wasn't it Cargasso though?" Alexis asked. "We've always been told that our ancestors linked up to Cargasso, not this 'Solumna' creature-realm thing."

"That misconception has helped to keep the planet safe, and we've never felt the need to correct it. The Anunnari mentioned Cargasso in their texts, so when the Mek'Va were able to create a stable link to another location using the substations they simply assumed that to be the case. The error has persisted through generations of research."

"So, what's Cargasso then?"

"A construct world, named after the race that created it. Last I knew it was in orbit around the star we know as Osiria. It's been quite some time since I've spoken with the Cargassan Union so it's hard to say."

"Wait," Kiera said quickly, "You're telling me the word we use for the afterlife is actually the name of a race's home world?"

"Indeed. The Cargassans tended to find our classification of them a bit quaint. I'm sure my limited experience with their race isn't indicative of their entire culture, but I was assured the way we use their world's name is acceptable when I met their king."

"You met an alien king?"

"His name was Ares Rahelin, though there's no telling who sits on the throne of Cargasso nowadays. I'm not particularly proud of that part of my life though, so I'd appreciate it if we could speak of something else."

"Of course," Alexis said as she took another sip of her tea.

With her noodles mostly gone, Kiera brought the bowl to her lips and drank the broth. Most of the Mek'Vatir that remained were swiftly carried along in the tide and disappeared, leaving only two at the bottom of the damp bowl. The strange sensation of movement against the inside of her upper lip caught her attention, though, and she traded the bowl for a small wooden pick. One of the Mek'Vatir that had been caught in the noodles was stuck in the space between her teeth. It writhed in pain against her long, white fang with its lower half crushed nearly up to her gums. Kiera pressed the tip of her wooden pick into its body, impaling it in the process of freeing it from its confines.

"Sylvia is a good chef," Kiera said as she discarded the sullied pick. "If she's interested in learning from a professional, Lain needs some help at the pub. Maybe it's something you can talk to her about later? I'm sure she'd be more than welcome, and we wouldn't force her to interact with the guests."

"An excellent idea," Zara said brightly. "I'll let her know that it's an option, but she's working toward her next rank here at the temple. She may not want to leave until she becomes a Paladin. Cooking does seem to be her passion, though."

The lunamir was having a wonderful time with her little fruit meal as the strong Mek she had found in the gardens earlier was still fastened tight to her hind paw. It was still alive, its abnormal strength turning out to be a curse rather than a boon at this point. The fruit was almost gone, leaving only a few Mek'Vatir struggling in the juice at the bottom. They tried their best to climb the slick walls as Pearl's tongue lapped away at the ones closest to the center of the bowl. She would lift her head whenever she got one, chomping down on it before moving to the next. Once they were all finished, she blissfully pranced over to Kiera and hopped up on her lap for more attention.

Kiera didn't have much left on her plate aside from a single roll and four more Mek Sticks. She set them all inside of her empty cup and poured the remainder of the sour Sentoberry liquor inside. While they soaked in the alcohol, Kiera's attention moved to the Mek that had fallen from her spoon earlier. It was slowly dragging itself away from her, clearly still stunned from whatever alcohol it had already been soaked in before. Its escape was foiled as the tip of Kiera's index finger came down on its back, forcing it face-first into the wooden table. With minimal effort, its tiny body popped and stuck to her fingertip.

Alexis had finished the last of her meal and had sat back to enjoy her tea. When she looked over to Kiera, her eyes widened and she slid closer to her comrade.

"Kiera, are you alright?" She asked.

"What?" Kiera replied, looking up from the table as she casually slipped her fingertip into her mouth.

"Oh my goddess, you're bleeding!" Alexis shouted, her voice tinged with both shock and concern.

Confused, Kiera brought her finger from her lips to gently wipe beneath her nose in case it was a nosebleed. There was nothing, just the soft skin of her upper lip. The black pupils of her eyes disappeared, replaced with a yellow sheen marking an adrenaline rush. Still not sure what was going on, she looked up to Zara who had already stood up with a tissue and was running over to her side. The High Paladin's black markings were starting to smoke as she prepared to heal her guest.

"I... I guess I am...." Kiera stammered as Zara brought the tissue to her neck.

Kiera could feel blood soaking the collar of her shirt. When Zara's tissue touched her skin, a sharp jolt of pain shot through her body as though she had been cut deeply. Their voices faded into low mumbles as Sofie ran over to assist.

She knew they were all speaking, but she couldn't understand any of it. Her vision slowly faded to white, her ears painfully rang, and she could feel the others trying to get her attention...

To wake her up.

The Treaty of Nevarria

Daybreak | Alerio 12, 1240
The Temple of Aludra – Natalin Suites

"The Immortal...." a raspy voice cut through the darkness as Kiera's senses slowly came back to her.

It felt like only a few seconds had passed. Her memory was hazy as she rolled in her bed and tugged the sheets up slightly. She could hear someone moving around nearby, but brushed it off as Alexis getting ready to go up to the pub or something. Her eyes shot open when she felt something hop up on her bed, immediately bringing her back into the realm of the conscious. She propped herself up on her left elbow as Pearl came striding down the length of her bed.

"Oh, good morning," Kiera said as Pearl gave her forehead a little headbutt then curled up near her arms.

Kiera gently ran her fingertips through the animal's fur as her recollection of the night's events came flooding back to her.

Realizing she wasn't at home, she glanced around to her surroundings. The walls were made of smooth white stone and
there were two tables with blank scrolls nearby. A bookshelf
filled with literature was set between the two desks, which had
ink quills for the room's occupants. Next to her was a second bed
that was unkempt, as well as Alexis' shoes which had her dirty
socks balled up and stuck in them. There was a single nightstand
between the two beds with a small door above built into the wall
that said 'cold storage.' To her right was a large pane of glass
obscured by closed blinds.

Pearl hopped over to the nearby end table and let the Mek she
had in tow fall from her hind paw. It was still alive, despite having
been trapped there all night and being maliciously mauled by the
creature. The animal then gently pawed at the little one, nudging
it toward Kiera like an offering. Pearl sat proudly with her cloud-
like tail swaying behind her while the Mek writhed.

"You're sweet. Thanks, Pearl."

Kiera gently reached out and picked the little one up between
her index finger and thumb. It struggled weakly with its head still
free from her grasp. This one was a bit strange, notably tougher
than the others she had come across but still not strong enough
to escape. She pinched it, forcing its white innards to come up
from its mouth while Pearl leaned in and cautiously sniffed at
the mess. Kiera parted her inky black fingertips, and the lunamir
happily licked the corpse clean leaving nothing behind.

She could feel bandages wrapped around her neck with a dirt-like grit beneath, likely something that was used to keep her from developing an infection. Kiera touched the bandage with her fingertips and winced as a jolt of pain shot through her. She found it strange that she hadn't been healed completely, especially with the High Paladin and her medically attuned friend right there at the table. Without dwelling on it for too long, she sat up and set her feet on the cool floor below. Kiera leaned forward and looked to the ground, keeping her hands together as she felt something struggle beneath her right foot. As she cocked her ankle to the side she saw a Mek stuck to her arch.

"Well, that makes two," Kiera said sarcastically as she set her foot back down and stood.

She then stretched, going up on her tip-toes as her arms reached toward the sky and her tail quaked. Even with a wound, she was feeling quite rejuvenated. Her clothes were folded up neatly on one of the tables nearby with her black boots on the ground next to them. Instead, she was wearing a black silk night-dress that had ornate silver stitching around the seams. The room was illuminated with crystalline lamps and white veins of energy that ran overhead through the ceiling. There was a lever on the wall between the beds, and one near the entryway that controlled the flow of spiritual energy. She didn't know exactly how it worked, just that it was an interesting design that she hadn't seen anywhere else.

Kiera cautiously made her way around the edge of the bed toward the closed curtains. Her tail slowly swayed behind her as she peeked through the center. Immediately, her eyes widened with wonder when she was greeted by the sight of colorful coral and wandering sea life. The young Aluni threw open the blinds to reveal the majesty of her surroundings in their fullest form. A large, serpent-like sea beast swam past the window heading toward a hole in the rock face nearby as a school of brightly colored glowing fish spiraled like a little whirlpool among the other bizarre underground ocean life. There were bone-like crab creatures on the window walking up the side, and enormous mollusks that were adhering to the bottom corner of the glass near the other stones.

"Oh, hey!" Alexis said with excitement as she wandered out from the washroom while toweling off her hair. "Glad to see you're up! We washed your clothes while you were asleep."

"Thanks," Kiera replied before turning back to the window. "This place is absolutely amazing!"

Kiera looked up toward the surface, pushing herself against the glass so she could see as much as possible. The city from above looked like it was so far away, though the suspension bridge could still be easily seen from where they were.

"After we patched you up and made sure you were alright, Zara thought it would be nice to let us stay down here in the Natalin Suites. She had to leave, so she left me in charge of you."

"She *is* running an entire settlement down here. Anyway, what happened to me?"

"We don't know... Sofie and Zara both tried to heal you but they couldn't do anything to actually stop the bleeding. We had to resort to contemporary medicine to get you taken care of. The good news is that it wasn't very deep, they said if it scarred it wouldn't be all too noticeable unless you were looking for it."

"Oh...." Kiera nervously said as she touched her neck again.

"Adriel is doing well too!" Alexis exclaimed as she ran over to her bed to throw her clothes back on.

"Oh?"

Kiera and her comrade both walked back over to their beds and sat down. Alexis then picked her shoe up from the floor and pulled the balled-up sock out of it, before reaching in to remove her modified insole. Adriel looked disheveled, his white hair was a matted mess and his tail was ground into the insole as there wasn't much of a place for it to be. She carefully lifted him from his crevasse and set him on the bed, before removing the cutout she made from the strap near her shoe's heel.

She tied the string back onto her shoe before gently pressing the cutout into place where he once was. The little metal bars engaged to keep it from falling out unless she bent the insole properly. Alexis waved it around in the air as a test, and when it didn't fall out, she put her shoe back together and looked down to Adriel with a smile. Even with his scruffy appearance, the little Ætherbug looked fairly content as he sat up. Pearl hopped up to Alexis' bed as Kiera searched through the nearby drawers for a comb.

"So you got to talk to him a bit this morning?"

"Briefly. I was worried about him last night since he had such a rough time the night before. Instead of just stuffing him in a box and assuming he would be alright through the night, I asked what he'd like to do. He said he was comfortable where he was at so I left him in my shoe and checked up on him this morning. Our little comrade was still cheery!"

"What a cute little oddball."

"Right?"

Alexis then reached down for him so that she could see about straightening up his hair and cleaning him off a bit, only for her hand to connect with the soft fabric of the crumpled bedsheets. She looked around her bed curiously, then to the ground nearby to see if she could find him.

"How long was I out?" Kiera asked, unable to find anything to comb her hair with.

"Just for the night. Hey, did you see where Adriel ran off to?"

"No. I was distracted, sorry."

"Huh... Well, I think Sofie is going to be here soon, so you should probably get dressed. Sylvia's preparing us a quick packed breakfast so we can eat on the way and said she would meet us in the concourse."

"Do you know where my rifle's at?" Kiera asked as she got back up and wandered over to her clothes to change.

"Sofie has your backpack and rifle with her, she held onto your stuff to make sure it wouldn't get lost in the ruckus."

"It's alright as long as they're returned."

After Kiera changed back into her clothing, she respectfully folded the nightdress she had been afforded up and set it where her clothes once lay. Then, she made her way over to the wash-room to continue her search for a brush while Alexis made the beds. Once the room was clean and everything was in proper order, Alexis got comfortable on top of her bedsheets and gazed up to the glowing crystalline veins.

Shortly thereafter, Pearl hopped up onto the nightstand and carefully started to make her way over to the pillow Alexis was using. The feline crawled up onto her abdomen and curled into a ball, purring as the Aluni began to pet the lunamir's back.

"Hey," she said as her tail lethargically flopped around on the bed next to her.

She looked down just as a drop of liquid fell to her stomach. Pearl was looking back at her with a proud expression on her face, curled up with Adriel trapped in her maw. The little one's tail had been ripped clean off and his glowing purple insides were nowhere to be seen, leaving a cavity where they once were. She was holding him by his leg as he dangled upside-down. His white hair was soaked in glowing purple blood like the bristles of a paintbrush, and his ears were twitching along with what remained of his little limbs.

"Hey!" Alexis yelped as she quickly sat up.

"What?" Kiera replied, stepping around the corner while running a brush through her hair.

Alexis carefully reached out and took Adriel's broken body from the feline's maw. Pearl gave him up readily, licking the sweet purple blood from her matted lips as she sat up with pride like a noble little huntress. The moment his blood touched her palms, she felt a soothing energy radiate through her hands and arms. Kiera watched, chuckling from the washroom corner as Alexis held him in her cupped hands.

"I found Adriel...."

"Well, you didn't need to yell about it."

Kiera returned to the washroom to freshen up more while Alexis let out a defeated little huff. The glowing aura shrouded the little Adriel's body as he lay in tatters on her palm, and when it receded, he was whole once more. She gently pet the top of his head with her index finger, flattening his little black-and-red ears while his tail swayed against her palm's skin.

"Are you alright?" Alexis asked. "I'm sorry I let her get you, I should have been more diligent."

"I'm fine," Adriel replied as he tiredly lifted himself onto his elbows. "Pearl seemed to have quite a bit of fun playing with me."

"I'm sure a lot of animals would."

"I don't mind, really. You should have seen how her eyes lit up when she got a hold of me. She wouldn't stop purring the whole time until she came over and offered me up to you."

"Your tranquility is otherworldly, squirt. Does anything actually bother you?"

"Being trapped and alone does. I really don't know why, but it makes me panic."

"You were alone all night last night in my shoe. Are you sure you were alright, little comrade?"

"Yeah," Adriel replied calmly, "I know it sounds contradictory, but I think—"

"You don't have to explain yourself," Alexis chimed in, petting him atop his head once more. "All that matters is that you're comfortable and happy. To me, at least. You can ride with me anytime you'd like."

"Thanks."

The sound of gentle knocking on their door echoed through the room. Pearl hopped off the bed and ran over to the doorway, sitting down and looking up in anticipation of a visitor. Before Alexis could get up to answer the door, Kiera stepped out of the washroom and opened it to reveal Sofie standing there with her staff in hand.

"Kiera," Sofie said as she bowed her head. "I'm so sorry."

"Don't worry about it. Apparently, I'm just beyond help."

"She's not wrong!" Alexis shouted from around the corner.

Kiera glanced back into the room with a smirk before looking to her comrade in the doorway. Along with a staff, Sofie had her violin on her back and Kiera's rifle slung over her shoulder.

"I'm glad you're alright," Sofie said meekly as she stepped forward and wrapped her free arm around Kiera in a tight embrace.

Kiera could feel the self-doubt and worry seeping off of her. She wrapped her arms around Sofie and brought her in closer, her tail swaying gently while the Advanced Acolyte's tail was motionless. Pearl climbed up to Kiera's shoulder to nuzzle at Sofie's face as well, bobbing her own cloudlike tail. The blood on her mouth had stopped glowing, virtually disappearing before it could be seen by the newcomer.

"It's alright, I mean it. Not even the High Paladin herself was able to do anything about what happened."

"Yeah...."

"Let's take some of this weight off you. Come in, comrade."

She stepped to the side as Sofie took the rifle and backpack off to offer them back to her comrade. Kiera simply set them both in a nearby corner, taking care to balance the rifle so it wouldn't fall over as Sofie entered their temporary abode.

"I took the liberty of packing some extra food and a few bottles of alcohol for you to take home for yourself. Two big bottles of Sentoberry and Avriberry Spirits from my collection, and I refilled the canteens you had with water."

"Isn't Sylvia making something for us to eat?"

"Yeah, I just wanted to give some extra."

"Thanks," Kiera said as she shut the door. "We have someone we'd like to introduce you to though."

"Someone? You mentioned that before. Did you bring someone else into the Sanctum Astrona?"

"Sort of?" Kiera nervously responded. "You'll see."

Kiera walked over to her nicely made bed and sat on the edge, motioning to Alexis as the Advanced Acolyte stepped around the corner. She made her way over to Alexis' bed and sat down next to her, curiously looking to what was in her friend's cupped hands. Adriel sat in the center of her palms, his tail swaying back and forth quickly in response to seeing the newcomer.

"By the Goddess," Sofie said breathlessly.

"His name is Adriel, and he's an Ætherbug," Kiera said as she crossed her legs and Pearl hopped down to her lap.

"I've never seen anything like him."

"Watch this," Alexis said softly.

The red Symbiont markings on her hands and face began to glow as she felt the influx of energy from Adriel coursing into her body through her hands. Alexis let out a soft sigh as she enjoyed the soothing sensation his life force gave to her.

"He's immortal," Kiera said. "On top of that, he likes being treated like a Mek. Complete with extended stays in footwear."

"I wore him all the way from the pub to the temple," Alexis added as she sat up next to Sofie so she could see him better.

"Fascinating," Sofie replied in awe. "May I?"

"Of course."

Sofie gently lifted Adriel from her friend's palm and let him lay in hers. The redhead smiled down to the little one, who was just recovering from Alexis' energy drain on his body. He weakly pushed himself to a seated position, his tail still swaying across her palm while his ears were cheerfully perked up.

"So this little creature survived the entire day in your shoe without being crushed to death?"

"He can come back from anything," Alexis replied, watching to see what her friend would do.

"Is all of this true, little one? Would you like me to treat you as we do the Mek'Vatir?"

"Yes," Adriel replied, "it's all true, and I would be honored."

Sofie's fingers coldly closed around the little one in her hand until she had him held in a fist. Adriel watched as his sight was obscured entirely by her skin, forcing him to lay lengthways on his back as the pressure continued to pour on from all sides. Bones began to snap and crack before his skin split. As Adriel's purple blood poured onto her skin, a soothing jolt of energy ran up Sofie's arm causing her to gasp in shock.

"That didn't take much convincing," Kiera said sarcastically as her tail swayed.

"Who am I to refute his desires? If this is what he wants, I'll happily oblige."

Sofie squeezed as tightly as she could, watching the glowing blood dribble out onto the ground as her fingers twisted to inflict as much damage as possible to the little one. Her green markings were glowing continuously as she drew in all the spiritual energy Adriel could give. Her Amethya crystals were all shining at once, including the crystal at the top of her staff. The little one was almost unrecognizable when she opened her hand and looked to the mess she had made.

"Feels good, doesn't it?" Kiera asked as she stood up from the bed and cradled Pearl in her arms.

"Quite...." Sofie replied, trailing off in awe.

"You can wear him on the trip back if you'd like. Of all of us, I think you're the best equipped to use his powers to their fullest."

"Wear him?"

"Yeah, in your mocs," Kiera said.

Sofie watched the little mangled mess in her hand as white light began to surround his body. He returned to normal in seconds, leaving him panting in a puddle of his blood as he tried to regain the energy he had lost. Adriel's vision turned green as Sofie's energy clamped around his arms and legs, lifting him into the air with thin tentacle-like strands that extended from her palm. Adriel didn't struggle, though he knew it would be useless for him to try with his legs and arms spread. He felt like a puppet hanging from strings as he watched her remove her right shoe and look back to him, then to the blood on her hands.

The glowing had already begun to dissipate and the purple color was fast fading to a clear water-like sheen. She casually wiped it off on her skirt, then turned her attention back to the little being trapped in her glowing embrace. Without so much as moving her hand, the Advanced Acolyte slowly lowered the little one down to the mouth of her moccasin below. The moment he neared it, he could feel the warmth emanating from within. It was almost as though he had passed an event horizon as he was brought deep into the confines of her footwear.

"Neat isn't he?" Alexis said as she stood up and walked over to Kiera's side, playfully bumping her in the process.

"That's an understatement," Sofie replied as she slid her moccasin back on.

Her tail swayed quickly when she felt Adriel's against her skin, struggling to breathe from the ambient pressure. Smiling, she greedily took in all the energy he could give while she sat looking at her glowing palms. All of the self-doubt Sofie felt was gone, replaced with an intoxicating sense of wonder as she stood from her seated position.

A pulse of soothing energy cascaded through her body as she felt Adriel's abdomen burst open. The sensation encouraged Sofie to lift her heel and press down with all of her weight to draw as much blood as she could and prolong the feeling. It was as though he had disappeared entirely after she felt several more pops and snaps, leaving nothing but a damp spot in her moc.

"Well, I'm hungry," Kiera said as Pearl's little forepaw hands tugged at her shirt.

"I am too, ready?" Alexis added cheerily.

"Of course."

Sofie walked on like nothing had happened, utterly unfazed by Adriel's presence underfoot. Her lack of care for his condition made healing impossible as his still-sentient body was ground deeper and deeper into the cotton's fabric. She exited the room first while Kiera retrieved her backpack and rifle, and Alexis donned her gun belt.

Then, they were off to the concourse.

Pearl clung to Kiera's shoulder as the group walked down a long hallway that ran parallel with one of the underwater cave's passages. The ceiling was made of glass panes, each having a steel plate set on rails that looked as though it could seal the area in the event of an emergency. Just beyond the glass was a rocky passageway illuminated by marine fungi, bioluminescent plant life, and various stygofauna. After taking in the view, Kiera's attention turned to the people walking around them going about their day. Some wore the same outfit that Sofie had on, while others preferred the duster and vest.

It wasn't long before they came to a grand staircase that widened as they ascended. The steps were made of white pearl accented with jade floral designs, and at the top was an enormous hall lit by ornate crystal chandeliers. There were large panes of glass off to the right separating the concourse from the nearby cavern. Directly in the center of the chamber was a large tree that had sprouted from a plot of soil, and in front of that, Sylvia knelt with her hands toward the flowers below. A dark green mist surrounded the base of the tree, and the green crystals on Sylvia's back were glowing steadily. Next to her was a stack of three wooden boxes with a small box on top, all wrapped up with string so they would be easy to carry.

"Hello, comrade!" Kiera said, approaching from behind.

Sylvia let out a squeak, jumped up, and turned to face the group all on one haphazard motion. She almost fell into the bed of flowers behind her. It took a second to catch her breath while holding her hands over her chest. Her gray eyes were wide, and slowly the Sarin's anxiety waned.

"I'm so sorry," Sylvia quickly said in her reserved tone.

"I'm the one who should be sorry," Kiera replied, "are you alright? I didn't mean to startle you."

"Yes, thank you."

The green mist began to dissipate from a bed of flowers that shared the same soil as the great tree. Leaves high above started to close, shielding a soft membrane inside that had presumably opened for access to sunlight.

"Did Lady Zara talk to you about coming to study under Lain at the pub?" Kiera asked.

"She did! I would like to finish up here and become a Paladin before I go anywhere else though, if that's alright. I still have a lot to learn."

Sylvia plucked a pair of Mek from the pouch on her hip and knelt back down before slipping them into her ankle-height moccasin. She gathered the boxes of food from the floor that she had packed and stood back up, offering them to Kiera with a nervous smile. Her patterns shimmered, as one of her sacrifices had been crushed beneath her heel to replenish the energy she used in taking care of the flowers and the great tree. The other was still alive, though it wouldn't likely last long.

"Thanks," Kiera said as she accepted the gift.

"There's some fruit for Pearl in the small one, and I baked some Mek into choco bark candies this morning," Sylvia replied, bringing her hands behind her back. "They should survive a few days before they suffocate in the chocolate. Oh! I mixed some Mek in with Pearl's fruit too since she seemed to like it."

Pearl hopped from Kiera's shoulders over to Alexis' and cuddled up with her neck. The animal kept a tight grip on her shirt though so it wouldn't fall, and let out an exaggerated yawn before nuzzling her more.

"We really appreciate it," Alexis said as she gently pet Pearl underneath her chin.

"May I accompany you to the surface?"

"Of course," Kiera replied.

The group made their way around the tree toward another ascending set of stairs. A sign that read 'Sanctum Astrona' hung over the staircase's entry. Sofie led the group up the stairwell, which looked impossibly short for the vast distance they needed to travel. They could see the waterfall off in the distance and people walking by the other side, but it was unnaturally silent. Kiera noticed the area around them distort as they passed under an arch halfway up the stairwell. When the soft roar of a waterfall filled her ears, she stopped in her tracks.

"Is everything alright?" Sylvia asked quickly.

"It happened again, didn't it?" Kiera replied with a question of her own.

"What?"

"Sorry, I should have warned you," Sofie said as she turned to her friends behind her. "All of the stairwells like this link the different chambers our researchers find."

"I think it's neat," Alexis said in a chipper tone as she resumed her trek up the stairwell.

They emerged from the tunnel near a beach on the Sanctum Astrona's lake. A few residents were lounging in the water while children ran around, splashing each other and playing in the gray sands. Some built tiny structures for the Mek to crawl around in while others fed them to nearby schools of fish. The sight was eerily reminiscent of Nevarria's beaches before the war came to their pristine shores.

It looked as though they would have to walk over a kilometer to return to the subterranean city's entrance. The prospect was distressing, as they still had so far to walk to get back to the pub. Before the group could move, though, Sofie turned toward another archway that led to a solid stone wall beyond.

"What are you doing?" Kiera asked. "We've already spent too much time messing around. Rina's condition might get worse, let's get going while we still have time."

"Wait," Sylvia said softly with her hands behind her back.

There was a single wide brick on the stone archway that was jet black to the right. Sofie gently traced the tip of her index finger along the dark surface, leaving a trail of glowing green energy behind. When she was finished, her drawing of a stylized glyph was automatically surrounded by a circle of white energy. The stone wall faded away, replaced with a staircase leading upward.

Sofie led the group up the stairwell. It was half the distance of the other one, and led directly to a black doorway at the top. When Sofie reached it, she set her hand in the center of the structure and her markings began to glow. It split in half and parted, revealing the temple's exterior courtyard and the same arena the Acolytes danced in the night prior.

"Well, that was convenient," Kiera said as she stepped through to the surface.

The doorway sealed behind them as the group continued through the open-air pathway and came to a stop at the top of the stairwell leading down to the main gate. Off in the distance, Nevarria looked like a mere shell of what it once was. The pub wasn't visible though, as the trees obscured it from their line of sight.

"So where are you headed, Sylvia?" Alexis asked.

"Oh, uh... The terraces. We're running low on whitegrain."

"We could have taken you there through the archway paths," Sofie replied, tilting her head a bit.

"I still could use them, but I wanted to fly."

Sylvia then stepped forward and wrapped her arms around Sofie, before backing up and turning to face the other two. The unease Kiera felt from her wasn't nearly as intense as before, though she still moved in a stiff and guarded manner. The second Mek perished when she bowed to them, causing her green crystals to glow as Kiera and Alexis both returned the gesture.

"It was a pleasure meeting you, comrade," Alexis said, smiling brightly to their new friend.

"Y-Yes. I'd ask you to stay for a while were the situation not so dire. That would be selfish of me, though."

"We'll see you again soon, I'm sure."

"I'd like that."

Her hands dark green markings began to glow again. They looked like deep cracks in her skin with sharp, jagged edges as opposed to the Aluni's soft spirals and twists. Six enormous sky-blue tipped white wings came from the crystals on her back.

They stretched out nearly twice her body length in each direction before folding up neatly. All six were of different sizes, with the smallest at the bottom tucked away under the others. Sylvia smiled again, gently waving to the group.

"Goodbye," Sylvia said, then turned to the stairwell.

She ran and jumped, easily gliding through the air and away from the group. Pearl followed, leaping off of Alexis' shoulders with her glowing wings spread at length. When the lunamir noticed that everyone else wasn't flying along she banked back around, landed at Kiera's feet, and hopped a few times in place. Sylvia flew off to the right and over the white walls, catching the attention of the paladins that were stationed there. The group could barely see them waving up to her as she soared past them on her way toward the whitegrain fields below.

Now, it was time to begin the journey home.

THE TREATY OF NEVARRIA
CHAPTER II

Noon | Alerio 12, 1240
Industrial District – Nevarria City

The frontlines were eerily quiet as Aurora stood outside the command tent. She still had her rifle on her back and her skin was covered in dirt and sweat. The consular was alone, watching her soldiers get settled in after successfully completing their most recent assignment. Some made their way directly to the racks while others went to the recreation tent to drink and smoke their worries away. It was technically against regulations, but none of the command officers here enforced such things.

Long blue hair fell down as she pulled out the two hair sticks that were holding her bun in place. Still shaking from adrenaline, she slipped them under her belt for safekeeping. Her blue tail gently brushed against the tent behind her as it swayed. Like the rest of her, it was unclean and matted from combat.

She was briefed on the state of the war when she returned. Their outpost received communication from Admiral Victoria Lozen, who was en route to the Nevarrian Theater with a fleet of air-superiority forces. Osa Eastern Command had successfully defended the city of Kalahai from an invasion force and was prepared to continue the fight in the skies of Nevarria. With reinforcements, they planned to quickly retake the city and travel north to support Admiral Luther Blackthorn. Another invasion force was attacking the western coast of the continent as well in an attempt to take Sanova City, Novalus' capital. They gained some ground initially before Admiral Creed Deimos' fleet forced them back to the sea. Further south still, an invasion of the city of Kusagrad was thwarted when invaders vastly underestimated Admiral Feather Rossi's training forces garrisoned nearby at Obalysk Southern Command.

Aurora closed her eyes and let her head hang low, filling her lungs with a long breath of the crisp day's air. The base had a small breeding shelter for the Mek, so it wasn't surprising to see one of them on the floor near her boots when she opened her eyes. The little one was having a difficult time scaling the side of a fairly flat rock. After a few moments of trying, the tiny creature made it to the top. It looked around, standing still as though it had forgotten the reason it wanted to be up there in the first place. They were blissfully ignorant of the world's struggles, and for that, she somewhat envied them.

"Consular?" A familiar voice came from behind.

"We're in private, Tanya. You don't have to be that formal," Aurora replied as she looked up with a smile, her blue hair covering part of her face.

Tanya and Aurora were twins, a rare happenstance where two children are born from the same crystal. They were nearly identical, only differing by a few key points. Tanya lacked her sister's Prime Attunement, her eyes were emerald green instead of dark blue, and her hair was black at the tips.

"Get me anything fancy from the city?"

"We're here to protect the place, not raid it. Did you need something?" Aurora said, glancing down to see that her Mek 'friend' had disappeared.

"When was the last time you stopped to take in the beauty of the world around you?" Tanya asked with a smile, stepping up to her sister with a cigarette in hand. She took a deep puff from the stick of tobacco, lighting the embers at the end as her lungs filled with dark smoke. Casually, she let the smoke roll from her lips as her focus shifted up toward the sky above.

"I don't have time to look at the wrecked architecture. It was beautiful once; we'll make it that way again someday."

"I meant the rings, idiot. We're in a warzone, but I think if we don't take the time to appreciate the little things like that, we may forget what we're fighting for," Tanya said softly as she kept her gaze up toward the sky.

The sparkling rings arched across the sky like an enormous bright-blue rainbow while wavy clouds accented it all around. Each layer could be seen from here, with several gaps where shepherd moons had cleared a path of their own. The light sparkled like thousands of gems twinkling together to form a single superstructure. Aurora joined her sister, taking in the majesty for a few fleeting moments before speaking.

"To think, we just sent our first real Cosmonaut up to the rings a few cycles before this war came to our doorstep."

"Ever wonder what's out there? Maybe another sentient race or something, like us."

"I bet there are. Andromeda is a big galaxy and the texts in Zian have really helped us further our understanding of the cosmos. Milky Way, Circinus, Centaurus. Ever wonder how they named all of those galaxies back then?"

"Would be nice if they let us study the library firsthand."

"Someday. The Sarin have the star charts…. I wonder if they even know where they came from."

"Well. I need a drink, and you look like you need one too."

"I really shouldn't," Aurora protested, looking her sister in the eye, "last thing I need is a hangover now, I'm sore as it is."

"Shut up and be irresponsible with me again," Tanya said as she took the final puff of her current cigarette.

Looking to the ground, she saw a Mek'Vatir scurrying across the rocks near her feet. She dropped the tail end of her cigarette in front of it, causing it to fall over as she swiftly snuffed them both out underfoot. The crimson markings on her hands and neck shimmered to life as she twisted her foot back and forth before she started toward the recreation tent.

"We're all family here," Tanya continued, "you fight alongside family, you should relax with family."

"I don't—"

"Relax?" Tanya interrupted with a chuckle. "I know, and it sucks… And you should. We'll just keep you hydrated and you can ride a buzz if you're worried about a hangover. It'll be good for morale, I promise."

"Fine," Aurora sighed, "I'll have a few drinks later."

"Trust me, sis. It'll be good to actually relax!"

"Lady Consular…." Another voice came from the tent. The two were both standing out in the open, looking toward a Kavar officer who was standing in the entrance holding the fabric back.

"Yes, Sindri?" Aurora replied, her tone shifting from shy and lighthearted to her usual serious demeanor.

"You are being summoned by the Consul," they said sternly, their golden eyes locked on the consular as she came toward the command tent. The Kavar had long white hair pulled back into a high ponytail between their thick, curled horns. Their tawny fur glistened from the light inside the tent as they beckoned the consular to come inside. It was obvious by the look on their face that what the Consul had to say couldn't wait.

Aurora and Tanya followed the Kavar officer into the command tent. Sindri sat down at the communication's table, which was covered in wooden equipment embellished with brass accents. Coiled wires atop the device ran to a dish that was used to receive communications from throughout the country. There was nothing visual about the device, since most of the comms had to be sent through encrypted channels and be decoded by the communications officer.

"Let's have it, Lieutenant," Aurora said calmly from behind the Kavar, who had slipped the brass headset underneath two large horns that curled around their ears so it would rest comfortably atop their head.

"Exigo Tower. Sanova City," they said, "Communication codes authenticated as Consular Ina, Foreign Affairs. The war is… Over as of 0900."

"They surrendered?" Aurora asked softly.

"No...." Sindri replied softly. "Cease hostilities immediately. Nevarrian Theater no longer under Novalin control. City was surrendered to Aestellus in exchange for a cease-fire. Aestellan Forces have withdrawn from Valinayask and Ranovograd. All forces within the Nevarrian Theater are ordered to fall back and maintain a border around the city."

"Send a message back to them...." Aurora said, her tone sharp. "Consideration Advised – Authentication Alpha Vector 1864. Current theater operations have a significant advantage over enemy forces, victory imminent. Surrender or cease-fire is ill-advised. Repeat, surrender or cease-fire is ill-advised."

"Sent," the officer replied solemnly.

Their command tent was eerily silent.

The only reason they still had this city was due to the armed population resisting the Kingdom of Aestellus' initial invasion. Those without firearms were armed by both the local police forces and their neighbors, giving the Nevarrian Defense Force time to assemble a proper defense of the city. It brought them to where they were now, and simply giving the city to the enemy seemed like the ultimate betrayal. This was something nobody in the tent seemed willing to do without protest.

The white light atop the communications machine lit up, indicating another incoming transmission.

"Authenticated. Consular Ina, Foreign Affairs," Sindri said softly. "Consideration Noted – Orders stand."

The silence in the tent continued as Aurora and Tanya stood over the communications table, gazing at the light that flickered out. It was almost as though they weren't even breathing. None of the officers in the tent knew what to make of the orders at all. Not only that, the cold and angry look on Aurora's face said much more than her voice ever could. She was holding herself back, not wanting to make too much of a scene for the more junior officers in the tent.

Inside, she was screaming.

"We're with you, Lady Consular," One of the soldiers toward the entryway of the tent said, breaking the silence.

Aurora turned to look at her soldiers, every one of them gazing upon their leader with ferocity. For the first time in her career, she didn't know what to say immediately. Their eyes seemed to pierce her, paralyzing her on the spot. She knew what everyone was thinking, and they all knew what was going through her mind as well. However, she gently shook her head.

"We have our orders," Aurora said sternly. "Have all ground forces regroup here for redeployment along the city's border. I want the 103rd Infantry to meet with me at the Triana Airstrip to oversee the civilian evacuation. Everyone else, get this base ready for decommission and prep the Steamtracks for transport. When all of our troops have been redeployed, I want the command staff here to meet with the 103rd and I at Triana for new orders. Is that understood?"

"Yes, Consular!" the most senior officer in the tent said, snapping into a sharp salute before life returned to the command tent. The mood was still solemn, but they all understood what they had to do.

"Lieutenant," Aurora said sharply, turning to Sindri who was still sitting at their post in front of the communications equipment, "I want you to send a message to the Aeon Technical Institute on an encrypted channel."

"Consular?"

"Address it to Rozetta Makoto. Request four R.A.E.S. Agents to meet me at Triana Airstrip as soon as possible. Be sure to let her know we'll be willing to pay for her agent's services."

"Right."

A few moments passed before the white light illuminated as a response. The remainder of the officers within the tent were moving to make her orders a reality, while the Kavar lieutenant at the communications desk deciphered the special encryption code. It took longer, as the Aeon Technical Institute used a separate type of encryption.

"What do we have, Sindri?" Aurora asked softly.

"Authenticated. Rozetta Makoto, Aeon Technical Institute CEO. It's good to hear from you, comrade. The Reconnaissance Assault and Espionage Service is at your disposal. Agents will be en route immediately."

"Good," Aurora said with a sigh as she turned to look to her sister. "Tanya, come with me."

Aurora led her sister out of the command tent to an empty circle of chairs set around a wooden crate. It was behind the tent, a special area that the officers used during their down time when they didn't want to be bothered. They were far enough away from the tent that nobody inside would be able to eavesdrop on the conversation they were about to have. In the center of the wooden crate, was a large and well-used ashtray. Tiny crushed bodies lay smeared in the ash beneath several cigarettes, showcasing the cruel game that officers played every so often while they relaxed. Among the carnage, only two had survived. They were unable to escape from the death pit due to the steep walls, yet neither had given up the hope of escape.

Aurora took a seat next to their makeshift table first, leaning back in her chair as her sister sat opposite her and pulled a new cigarette from her pack. She took a Mek from the pouch on her hip and forced it into the end so that it wouldn't be able to escape, then struck a match. With the cigarette between her lips, she set it ablaze, sighing contentedly as the Mek was incinerated at the end. Her red patterns shimmered as its soul was absorbed into her hand. After a few long drags, Tanya brought the ashtray closer to her side.

"Do the Mek add to the experience?" Aurora asked, pulling a Mek of her own from a pouch that was on her hip. "I don't think I've ever asked."

"They do actually. Makes the first drag taste different depending on what flavor you get."

Tanya flicked her cigarette over the tray, showering the tiny creatures below in ash as they continued to search for freedom. Aurora crossed her legs and discarded her Mek into a small one-way chamber that was flush with the back of her heel. She felt the little one tumble like a living pebble between the insole of her shoe and her grimy sock. It gave her something to fiddle with while she tried to relax for a moment.

"Good to know."

"How many Mek have you had today?"

"This makes two that I know of."

"You know you need more than that, Miss Prime. I can get away with two, you can't."

"I'll get more later," Aurora replied as she patted the side of her boot gently.

"You're going to forget, and I'm going to have to remind you again when you complain about your head hurting."

"Alright, alright."

Aurora pulled another from her pouch and tossed it onto the wooden table in front of her. After it recovered, she pinned it down with her thumb and began to press. The little one resisted for a moment before its little body collapsed with a tiny pop. Aurora lifted her thumb to show her sister as the white markings on her face illuminated brightly.

"Happy?" Aurora asked, before wiping the Mek's body off of her thumb and onto the black uniform that she wore.

"Maybe. So we're giving up the city."

"We don't have a choice," Aurora said softly, looking back up to the rings high above.

"Everyone here would follow you to Cargasso and back. All you have to do is say the word — even the admirals respect you more than they do a bunch of idiots sitting comfortably in a black tower halfway across the nation."

"We can't throw a fit every time we get an order we don't agree with. I don't have control over foreign affairs, just military doctrine and tactics," Aurora said as she gazed into the sky, her blue hair hung freely over the back of the chair. "We can still help."

"Aeon Tech?"

"Yeah. The civilians fighting underground will be lost if we don't leave them something to hope for. R.A.E.S. Agents acting on our behalf under the radar will go a long way in their eyes."

"Smart."

"Tanya, I need someone that I can trust without question for a quick assignment."

"Do I get hazard pay?"

"I need you to deliver a letter to an asset I have at a place called 'The Isarean Pub.' It's near the Southern Gothan Forest, which is occupied territory so ditch your uniform. She usually plays live music for the dance floor at night and slips us the information the pub's owner gathers throughout the day. Get yourself a drink and wait for the lights to go down."

"Spy work... Hazard pay?"

"She won't give you her real name if you ask, so don't bother. Her appearance changes constantly, including her hair color. However, you can identify her by the three horizontal markings on her neck. She's an Aluni as well, aquatically attuned. Once she has the package, finish your conversation if you started one and return to the command center."

"But… Do I get hazard pay?"

"You're my bodyguard, you always get hazard pay."

"Double hazard pay?"

"Really?" Aurora said, chuckling as she leaned forward in her chair. She looked over to Tanya as she flicked more ash over the scurrying creatures in the tray below.

"I really wanna get a new… Something really shiny? I dunno, I'm just trying to extort my sister because it's fun. Why can't you send her an encoded message or something?"

"I am. You."

Tanya took the last breath of her cigarette and looked down at the ashtray, noticing the two Mek who were crawling aimlessly through the ash. She went to extinguish her cigarette, subconsciously targeting one in the process.

Hot embers engulfed it in the blink of an eye as she violently twisted down into the smooth glass tray. Tanya added some force, hearing a quick hiss as the ash sizzled out in the Mek's blood. It seemed like an eternity for the little one as its body was partially crushed and horrendously burned. The crimson patterns on Tanya's hand began to glow as she absorbed the little one's soul. With that death the landscape of the tray had been changed, giving the survivor an avenue of escape.

"Sophisticated technology you have there, boss. State of the art," Tanya jested as she exhaled the remainder of the smoke in her lungs. "I'll get the message to her, you can count on me."

"Don't take any unnecessary risks, alright?"

"Of course," Tanya said as she stood from her seat and made her way around the table to her sister's side. Extending her hand, she offered to help the consular to her feet. "Will you do my hair? I need to clean up a bit for the mission."

"I haven't done your hair in cycles," Aurora replied.

She took her sister's hand and stood up, crushing the Mek that was trapped inside her shoe. The swirling white markings on the left side of her face illuminated as she took in its soul. Aurora smiled, showing a fang as her long tail swayed for the first time since she heard the news of the war's end.

"Yeah, and I miss it."

"I can't guarantee it'll be any good."

"I don't care," Tanya chuckled as she wrapped her arm over her sister's shoulders and began leading her to the rack tent. "As long as we get a few more minutes together before I go."

THE TREATY OF NEVARRIA
CHAPTER III

Thick fog refused to lift throughout the day as the girls walked beneath the canopy's shade. The sun's rays cut through the enormous leaves, creating pillars of colorful light as it mixed with the various bioluminescent plants below. They had already passed the river and were in the small clearing where the Ishar were resting the day before.

"Ishar?" Sofie said as she knelt in front of paw prints that were left in the dirt.

"Yeah," Kiera replied, "we came through here on the way out to the temple and got through without a problem."

"You were lucky. They've likely claimed this area as their hunting grounds. We shouldn't stay here for too long, they're prone to returning to places like this through the season."

A Mek was left to die, half-crushed in the center of a paw print on the ground in front of Sofie. When she saw this, the Advanced Acolyte set her hand in the print, which fit perfectly in the main pad's indent. She then sent a pulse of energy into the little one, overwhelming its aura until its heart gave out. When she stood, she dusted her palm off and continued along toward the wooden city wall nearby.

"I can't imagine how bad it would have been if they decided to attack us back then," Alexis said. "One swipe probably would have been enough."

"No use dwelling on that," Kiera replied.

It wasn't long before they returned to the wooden walls that protected the city from the larger beasts of the forest. Kiera stepped over to the rope that was still hanging and gave it a few rough tugs. It was damp from the morning dew that hadn't subsided, but other than that, it was secure.

"Should we take a break?" Alexis asked, looking up to the canopy where the rope disappeared.

"If you'd like," Sofie replied, sitting down in the damp grass.

"Alright. Not too long though, we'll probably make it home by evening as is." Kiera said as she set the boxes of food on the ground in front of Sofie.

Kiera and Alexis sat down cross-legged while Pearl hopped off of their shoulders and started sniffing around through the grass. The lunamir found the patch of crushed Mek that was left from before, but they had all decomposed and were of no use to her. Their bodies were spent, having spawned new young that already disappeared into the woodlands nearby. She continued her hunt, prancing through the grass in search of stragglers.

"I'm surprised we went so far without eating," Alexis said, eying the boxes of food.

"I just wanted to get back. Honestly, I forgot I was hungry," Kiera replied as she untied the laces.

She set the smallest box aside for Pearl then handed the other two boxes to her companions. Alexis opened hers first, revealing that the wooden box was separated into five distinct chambers. In one was a small bushel of freshly grown berries that looked like they had been picked that morning. There were homemade whitegrain cakes sprinkled with sweet seasoning inside the largest container, and a sliced cinnamon muffin in another. Dark green noodles mixed with seeds and bright pink kale filled one of the remaining chambers, while the last had a few slices of choco candy bark with living Mek trapped inside.

"Here," Alexis said as she took the choco candy bark, offering it to Kiera, "Want a few more?"

"Of course!" Kiera replied as she took one of the choco candies and slipped it into her mouth.

She pulled the canteen off her hip as she let the choco melt in her mouth before beginning to chew. The Mek were still very much alive despite their inability to breathe while trapped inside the candy. It took away all the energy they had to escape as her teeth tore them asunder. All of the little salty bursts added to the sweet taste of her choco, and she let out a contented sigh.

"Good?" Sofie asked curiously.

"I haven't had choco bark like this in ages. She's really good making this stuff, isn't she?"

"Sylvia loves making sweets."

"Lain does too. We haven't had the supplies to make anything like that for a while."

Pearl came around to Kiera's side and rubbed against her hip, meowing loudly before coming over to sniff at the little box of hers. Without hesitating, the Aluni untied her box to reveal another little container filled with fruit and stunned Mek. The lunamir purred as she sniffed at the fruit then sat down, nibbling it to pieces. Each time she caught a Mek, the crystal on her fore-head would shimmer as it absorbed another soul.

They remained fairly silent for the rest of their breakfast meal, quickly eating the contents away section by section until they were finished and full. Kiera took the string and the empty boxes, tied them up, and fastened them to her backpack so she didn't have to carry them herself. When she stood, she dusted her pant legs off and turned back to the rope behind them.

Pearl looked to the woods nearby, slowly licking her lips clear of the sweet juice as her blue eyes scanned the area. The hair on her back stood up as she arched her back and let out a sharp, loud hiss before running over to Kiera's side and leaping to her shoulders. The lunamir kept her eyes on the woods, even from her new perched position.

"Hey, what's wrong?" Kiera asked as she tried to gently pet Pearl and comfort her.

"Let's go, quickly," Sofie said as she ran toward the wall, stopping just short of the rope.

Kiera and Alexis followed as they heard the sound of leaves rustling in the bushes all around them. Whatever it was, they were surrounded. Pearl hopped off Kiera's shoulders and spread her ethereal wings, prowling the ground nearby as the girls prepared to climb their way to safety.

"We don't have time for this!" Alexis said while pacing back and forth with her tail between her legs and ears lowered.

"You're right," Sofie replied calmly, though Kiera could feel the fear welling inside of her.

Sofie slid her right foot forward and drew as much energy as she could from Adriel. The patterns across her arms and legs illuminated as she threw a hand forward, creating a thin staircase that only reached three meters in height. Kiera saw what her friend was doing and ran up the stairs, followed quickly by Alexis as Pearl remained on the ground.

When they were almost at the end, Sofie ran toward the stairwell and the lunamir followed close behind. Just as she did, the sound of a large beast moving quickly toward their position caught her attention. She turned toward the source, extending her staff in its direction which cast a wall of green energy back to the woods. An enormous black-furred Ishar threw itself roughly against the barrier, which gave way like an ethereal net. Energy wrapped around the Ishar's body and forced it to the ground as Sofie slowly backed up the stairwell. Pearl hissed and slashed at the beast trapped beyond the barrier while she spread her wings in an attempt to look bigger than she was.

"Pearl, let's go!" Kiera shouted down as more Ishar began to close the distance.

Sofie made more steps leading up the side of the wall, allowing the ones they had already passed to disappear as the group ascended. The lunamir hopped atop the disabled black Ishar just as three more of the beasts ran out from the woodland areas toward them. Pearl jumped into the air, flapping her wings quickly enough to gain the lift she needed to escape. The nearest black-furred beast swatted at the lunamir, missing by mere centimeters as it came crashing back down to the ground.

The Advanced Acolyte lifted her staff, removing the bindings from the first Ishar so that she could create a wall to keep them away from the bottom of the stairwell. Her eyes shimmered with green light as she concentrated. Maintaining so much was taking a toll on her mentally, even if she had an unlimited power source in the form of a sentient smudge inside her moccasin.

Instead of flying back up to Kiera though, Pearl dived back toward the Ishar. The giant beasts stood two meters tall as they haphazardly tore through the woods like tanks at full speed. They were larger than the pack that Kiera and Alexis had come across earlier, and far more aggressive. The lunamir strafed the beasts as they ran around the ground below, pestering them and drawing them away from the escaping trio.

"Pearl!" Kiera shouted. "Pearl, get back here!"

"Keep moving!" Sofie shouted back up. "She'll be alright."

"How do you know?!"

Kiera crouched and pulled her rifle from her back. She aimed at the nearest beast as it ran toward the feline. As she pulled the trigger, Sofie reached out with her energy to force the beast to the ground. The bullet impacted its back, though it was deflected into the ground by Sofie's shield leaving the Ishar unharmed.

"Just go!" Sofie commanded.

Kiera put her rifle onto her back again in frustration and ran up the stairwell. As Sofie made it high enough for the green barrier on the ground to no longer be useful, she let that fall and focused primarily on making the stairwell reach the topmost level. Kiera made it up to the battlement first and drew her rifle again, while Sofie stood just below the canopy.

"Goddess," Alexis said after she fell to her back, panting as she lay on the moss-covered walkway that surrounded the city.

Sofie watched as Pearl swooped down again, then reached out with her energy. She managed to dispel the lunamir's wings and bind it like she had done with Adriel earlier that morning. Quickly, the Advanced Acolyte pulled the feline over to her and ran up the remaining stairwell to the top. When everyone was accounted for, she let the green pathway turn to glowing dust that rained down over the canopy. Her eyes stopped glowing when all she made dissipated.

Kiera took Pearl and cradled her in her arms. The lunamir was shaking as she used her forepaws to pull herself closer to her chosen companion for comfort. Sofie walked over to the wall's edge and looked down to the forest canopy. Her tail was tucked between her legs, her ears were lowered, she was coated in a nervous sweat, and she was shaking more than Pearl.

"I've seen black-furred Ishar before but these ones looked really different from what I remember," Sofie said softly. "I don't understand why they would be so aggressive during the day."

"Sorry," Kiera said as she came up to Sofie's side, "I should have trusted you. I was just worried."

"I panicked. I should have been able to protect us more on the way up. There must have been a better way."

"We're all still standing."

"I'm not," Alexis chimed in, raising her hand as she continued to lie on the ground.

"Well, we're mostly still standing."

"Right," Sofie replied, finally relaxing a bit as she turned to look back toward Kiera. "I shouldn't be so critical of myself."

"We can look back and figure out what we did wrong and how we could have done it better or safer as much as we want. That's how we improve. Just don't beat yourself up over it, alright?"

"Yeah. How's Pearl?"

"She's doing alright I think, still shaking a bit."

Kiera turned away from the battlement, not wanting to get close enough to make Pearl uneasy as she tried to comfort the trembling creature in her arms. Sofie walked over to Alexis and helped her back to her feet.

"Are you alright?" Sofie asked her.

"Yeah," Alexis replied while dusting the dirt from her back, "it's just nerves. I've never actually been chased by those things."

"Ready to go?" Kiera asked as Pearl climbed back up onto her shoulder and nuzzled against her neck.

"I am."

Kiera nodded in response before turning back to the north. She spent most of the trip trying to keep herself from worrying about Rina at the pub. They could only go so fast, and she knew if they had attempted this trip the night before they would be under a constant assault from the Gothan Forest's fauna.

Now, it was time to get back to their comrade.

Now, it was time to get back home.

Kiera picked up a flat stone as they walked along the river-bank. She stopped long enough to toss it into the water toward the north, skipping the stone five times before it disappeared beneath the surface. She had enough of a lead on her comrades that she could afford to stop for a moment. The sun had just disappeared beyond the horizon to the west, and now that she was facing south, she could take in the ring's majesty as they arched high above the mountains. Their icy celestial dust looked as though it had caught fire as stars started to twinkle through heralding the night. All along the river, the spectral flowers were starting to glow and reflect their light to attract insects of the night for pollination.

"We're almost there," Kiera said as Alexis passed her by.

"It's probably about time for the lights to go down," Alexis replied in a joyous tone.

"What do you mean?" Sofie asked, keeping behind the group.

"You'll see when we get there," Kiera replied as she started to walk alongside the Advanced Acolyte.

"I should head directly to the pub, if that's alright."

"We just have to put everything away and change into something a bit cleaner. We'll meet you there, sound good?"

"Of course."

Sofie ran up the side of a dirt embankment and through the brush before turning back to look at Kiera and Alexis as they continued along with the riverbank with Pearl. As she bowed, they returned the gesture with a wave and Sofie turned to focus on what she had to do.

The muffled sound of a guitar attached to the audio system inside the building could be heard pulsing through the air as she approached the side of the pub itself. Around twelve people were standing out in front of the building, smoking and laughing with each other. Instead of entering from the front though, she decided to play it safe and head around toward the rear entrance. She didn't notice the silhouette of someone sitting near the back entrance as she came around the corner.

"Can I help you?" Heather asked.

She sat alone with her legs crossed. A pair of black boots were on the ground nearby with socks balled up inside. The inspector was on break, resting her sore paws while she enjoyed a small meal of her own. There was an empty plate of food with silverware next to her, a small dish of Mek, and she held a nearly empty glass of Aquamelon juice in her left hand. She was wearing a red vest with a black tank top beneath that was tight around her neck.

On her hands were gray gloves and she wore a pair of gray military breeches. A pair of leather tassets was held up by a series of belts, along with a single pouch of Mek on her right hip and a revolver on her left.

"Hello, comrade!" Sofie replied. "I didn't see you there, sorry. Is this the rear entrance?"

"Are you a Paladin?"

"Oh, uh. Not quite, I still have a few more cycles of training before I reach that point."

"I've always been fascinated with what you do at the temple."

"I can't talk much about my training with outsiders."

"Apologies," Heather said as she took the last swig of her drink, "I didn't mean to imply I wanted your secrets."

"I really should get going," Sofie said as she took the handle of a nearby door.

"Hold a moment, luv. I'll come with you."

"Right, of course."

The Incana took the small bowl of Mek'Vatir next to her and began plucking them out one by one, then retrieved her balled up socks. Straightening them out, she dropped three in each side and set the bowl on her plate along with the now empty glass. Heather donned her socks and boots before standing, her tail undulating in the air behind her as she felt the Mek writhing both in her fur and under her pads. Already having had her fill of energy for the day, she used them to help her paws feel better during the long hours she put in at the pub. Heather wasn't normally heavy enough to kill them outright, and her paws were far too soft to crush them without walking for a while.

"The door you were about to go through was the employee entrance. You passed the patrons entrance on your way over."

"Sorry."

"I was just finishing my break. We'll start serving again in a few hours, but the bar is open."

"A few hours?"

"We're expecting an air shipment soon," Heather replied as she gathered her things and stepped over to Sofie. "You can come with me though."

"Thank you," Sofie replied.

Heather opened the door and stepped through with Sofie, then locked it behind them so nobody else would enter. The Advanced Acolyte waited to be led through the storage room to the main area, as she had no idea where to go from here.

"To what do we owe the pleasure of your visit?" Heather asked her politely.

"I know the owner and her family. Met Kiera and Alexis long before the war started."

"Haven't seen either of em' all day. They're probably gallivanting out in the city," Heather replied as she passed Sofie to grab a small glass of pain pills and set her dirty dishes aside for a moment. "Hopefully they've heard the news."

"Are you hurt?"

"Just sore."

"I can help if you'd like."

"Medi?" Heather asked, setting the glass back on the shelf.

"Mmhmm."

"Sure," Heather replied, "I'm completely knackered and we're only halfway done with the night."

Sofie lifted her hand as her patterns began to solidly glow. She abstained from drawing in Adriel's energy, instead choosing to use the energy she had stored in her staff and jewelry. Green mist began to surround the inspector's arms and legs before it dissipated into sparkling dust, leaving her rejuvenated for the moment. Heather sighed, stretching up toward the ceiling on her tip-toes as her red markings shimmered to life. She felt one of the Mek flatten under her pad and grumbled at how easily the little one broke.

"Ah, drat. Another weak little bugger...." She said in disgust.

"Excuse me?"

"Sorry luv, I meant the Mek," Heather replied, stamping her boot to jar the remaining occupants back to life. "They break whenever they bloody-well feel like it."

"I really should get going."

"Eager to see Maya?"

"Yeah, it's been a while," Sofie said with a smile. "I had a long walk from the temple, too. Just a bit tired."

"Right, sorry to keep you," Heather replied as she picked her plates up and started down the hallway. "This way. Maya's working the bar tonight as always."

Both of their patterns shimmered randomly in the dim hall as they walked over the Mek'Vatir that wandered the floor. She led Sofie past Maya and Lain's bedrooms, as well as a few other unmarked doors. When they came to the hallway's end, Heather pushed the door open to reveal a full house. Nearly every chair was taken in the entire facility, with people standing around near the walls holding their alcohol while they enjoyed their visit.

Heather pointed toward Maya and gave Sofie a gentle pat on the back before walking back off toward the kitchen. She needed to prepare for the first official shipment the pub has received since the war began. Sofie's garb immediately caught Maya's eye as she finished up a patron's drink order. She gave the Kavar soldier their drink before leaving to see Sofie.

"Goddess, is everything alright?" Maya whispered.

"Everyone's safe."

"Good," Maya said, trying to keep from looking too worried, "we held a room for you upstairs, comrade. Here."

Maya gave her a card for room number eight with all of the information she would need on the back. She then motioned toward a doorway near the kitchen, before starting toward the bar to resume her duties.

"Thanks Maya. It'll be nice to take a breath after the trip."

"Hurry back."

After she shut the stairwell's door, Sofie ran to the upper level of the pub. She came to a hallway with thirteen doors, all with large numbers above and small brass card-reading devices attached to the wall next to them.

She walked toward door number eight and set the card in the device, unlocking it to allow her access. Rina lay on her back, resting alone with an IV hung from the wall which ran fluids directly into her body. Her shirt was off and the blankets only covered her lower half, while her chest and back were wrapped in cloth. All of the blood that was matted in her fur was now cleaned, and she looked well taken care of given the circumstances.

"Are you Sofie?"

"I am. How do you feel?"

"Positively gutted."

Sofie nodded solemnly as she approached the injured Edoraii, her staff held tightly in hand.

"I'm going to try and ease your pain before we proceed, comrade Rina. Just do your best to relax," Sofie said softly.

She then shifted her stance, planting her feet firmly on the ground and spreading them far enough to ensure her stability. She couldn't feel Adriel at all, though she knew he was still there in some capacity. After taking a moment to mentally prepare, the Advanced Acolyte took in a deep breath and brought her staff in front of her.

Closing her eyes, she focused all of the control she wielded over her Symbiont up through her body to her hands. The green markings visible on her arms and legs started to glow as her crystalline system feasted on Adriel's soul. This, however, was notably different from her usual displays of power. Green haze came from her hands and covered the Edoraii's torso, which was brighter and far more concentrated than what she used to help temporarily soothe Heather's aches. The glowing dust adhered itself to Rina's fur like beads of dew rolling down grass in the morning before it was absorbed by her skin. The relief on Rina's face was apparent in seconds.

"That feels lovely," Rina said in a soft tone.

"Good. May I see your wound?"

Rina nodded and slowly rolled to her front so that she was laying on her chest with her head resting off to the side. There was a dark spot of dried blood in the cloth that was larger than the rest. A ribbon of green energy came from her hand and slid across the fabric, slicing just the cloth in half so that Rina would not have to sit up so they could remove it.

When she peeled it back, she saw what had become of the wound. It was filled with a dark paste, likely something Maya used to help prevent infection and stop the bleeding. Despite the pub owner's best efforts, there was a discoloration of her skin setting in. The wound was infected, and the infection was spreading. Sofie let out a soft sigh, her patterns still glowing as she used

Adriel to maintain her powers. She was nervous, having never actually dealt with a wound of this severity in her life. It was a far cry from the scrapes and bumps she regularly dealt with.

Then, she held her right hand over the wound with her palm facing down. Several small green tendrils of energy began to flow from her palm and into the site of Rina's injury.

Seconds turned to minutes as the Advanced Acolyte searched for all the fragments lost deep within the Edoraii's body. Rina was as comfortable as she could be given the situation. It felt like someone was running cold water over her back with each movement she made. Sofie then sealed the wound, leaving a tinge of glowing green energy to fight the infection that had set in.

After gathering all of the bullet fragments, Sofie went into the washroom and came back with a wet rag. She wiped all the dried blood and emergency powder from her back, then sat down in a chair nearby.

"It's done," Sofie replied, clutching her staff in hand.

Rina pulled her blanket up over her chest and tossed the rest of her bandage off to the ground by the bed. The Edoraii was shivering as she held the blanket close for warmth, then looked over to Sofie who stood up once more.

"Is this normal?"

"Just breathe and relax," Sofie replied, "Try and get some rest, we'll come back up to get you when it's safe for you to leave."

"Alright."

"May I ask you a question?"

"Sure."

"Are you planning on defecting?"

"I..." Rina paused, turning away from Sofie in her bed. "I don't feel like I can go back home. Not without her."

"Alright. If you need a haven, you're welcome to seek me out in the Temple of Aludra."

"I'll keep that in mind."

Sofie bowed to Rina, then started toward the doorway so the Edoraii could rest.

"Hey, wait," Alexis said as she ran up to Kiera's side. "You've come undone, dork."

Alexis knelt down to tie the laces on Kiera's hip, which ran up to her arm like the laces of a shoe. When she finished perfecting the little bow she had made, she stood up and swayed her tail back and forth with a proud smirk. Kiera smiled back in turn, gently patting the top of Alexis' head before they laughed together and resumed their walk toward The Isarean Pub.

The sun had set and the sky was clear. Stars and colorful nebulae lit up the night's sky along with the bright rings that arched across the pathway in front of them. A glowing Amethya crystal sign could be seen off in the distance, along with a group of casually dressed Aestellan soldiers. Most were smoking, while others looked as though they were ready to return to their barracks.

"Looks like the lights haven't gone down yet."

"Yeah. They should soon though," Kiera replied while walking alongside Alexis.

As the low chopping of airship propellers filled the sky, the pair looked behind them to see the source of the noise. A large airship held aloft by an air bladder was heading south from the city. It was lightly armored, with repeating small arms and large cannons on all sides of the lower section that was built into the bladder. There was a section in the center of the airship that was cut out and replaced with a crane system, which held a large storage container. On the bow of the ship was *Olga V* written in stylized reflective paint. The armor had been dented severely, it was scratched and weathered, but it was still flying strong and on its way to make a delivery at the Isarean Pub.

"James!" Kiera shouted excitedly, hopping and waving at the glass cockpit of the airship as it soared overhead.

Both Kiera and Alexis ran toward the pub, bumping into each other playfully as they did so. Alexis' silver dress flowed in the wind behind her as she darted past the soldiers. Kiera cut off to the right and hopped over a wooden fence, gaining some distance on Alexis as they ran to the back of the facility. Heather, Sofie, and Lain were all waiting behind the pub talking among each other as the airship maneuvered high in the sky.

The booming sound of a deep air horn echoed through the forest as the airship spun into position and the propeller blades rotated to help push the ship to the ground. As the *Olga V*

James Dorsey

descended, they could see the silhouette of someone moving around in the cockpit of the airship. The air horn echoed a few more times before the airship itself touched the ground. Lain and Heather each quickly took a rope and walked over to the base of the airship. They hooked them into loops on the side and did the same thing for two more so that all four corners of the *Olga V* were tethered to the ground. The propellers slowly came to a stop as Sofie came to Kiera's side.

"How's Rina?" Kiera asked.

"She's healed," Sofie replied. "I think she would have been ok for a day or two, but the infection she had would of spread quickly after that."

"Infection?"

"It looked like Maya did a good job at cleaning and maintaining the wound, but sometimes you just can't help it."

"How much did you tell Heather?"

"Nothing. I didn't recognize her so I was careful not to say anything about Rina."

"Good."

"Why?"

"She's an Aestellan intelligence officer. If she found out we had her here, we'd all be in trouble."

Heather opened up two large doors on the back of the airship, then hopped on board. She found a leaver and pulled it, causing air to hiss through the system as a platform lowered into position to create a ramp on the back. She then turned to the storage container, took note of its seal, and cut it off with a knife before opening it up. She was engulfed in a cloud of cool fog as she revealed pallets of supplies inside waiting for them. Lain was busy opening the pub's main storage room. She had started the temperature control engine a few hours ago in preparation for the airship's arrival. It hadn't run since the beginning of the war, since it was older than the one in the shed.

A small metal ramp extended from the personnel door to the grass below on the side of the airship. As the door opened, both Kiera and Alexis ran over as fast as they could. Kiera vaulted toward the person who stepped through, landing on him in a tight embrace while Alexis stopped short. James let out a hearty laugh as he hugged her back before setting her down in front of him. He was a Vel'Nahar, one of the thirteen races of Cerolia and one of the rarest.

"You've grown a *bunch* since I last saw you, *right!*" he said, his long ringed tail swaying behind him.

"You know it!" Kiera replied. "How have you been?"

"Holdin' in there, flying high and keepin' it in the wind."

"I didn't think I'd see you so soon!"

"The *moment* I heard the war was done I booked a load headed right here. You can't keep me from Miss Lain's cooking. Best Laya steaks I ever tasted."

"The war's over?"

"Sure nuff. Just heard this morning and I was already gettin'
loaded up in Sola to come here."

"James Dorsey," Lain said as she came over with her hands
behind her back. "You don't know how relieved I was when I got
a message from the *Olga V.*"

"You're lookin' the same as the last time I saw you," James
replied. "You know I'd be here the second I heard."

"You going to need help unloading?"

"Naw. You and your friend just need to worry bout' what you
do best in there, *right*! I'll get it done quick."

"How much extra for the unload?"

"As long as you get me a good steak and a place to sleep
tonight I'll do it for free."

"Can I help?" Kiera asked.

"Alright. How bout' you count what I pull off and sign the bill
of lading after, gimme a hand, eh?" James replied as he pulled a
piece of paper from the pouch on his leg and handed it to her.

Kiera took the paper and nodded, before heading to the back
of the airship to speak with Heather about the seal number. The
second that Alexis had a clear path to James, she walked over
and wrapped her arms around him. He patted the top of her
head gently and chuckled.

"Welcome back."

"I still gotta' teach you how to fly."

"You remembered?"

"You know it! I ain't gonna forget something like that."

"Are you going to be here for a while?" Alexis asked hopefully, looking up while still hugging him.

"Long as I got a warm bed I sure will. Gotta' be careful though, if Lain keeps giving me good food I ain't *never* gonna' leave."

"Good."

"Alright, now watch this. I got something you've gotta see."

After Kiera verified that the seal number matched up with what she had on the paperwork, Lain and Heather went back inside to reopen the kitchen. Sofie followed suit, eager to get in and actually relax for a little while. James went to the back of the airship and stepped up onto the ramp, while Kiera and Alexis stayed on the ground. They watched their old friend pull open a sliding door off to the side, revealing a machine made of brass and steel. He gripped a cord on the side of its engine and gave it a strong pull to get it to start. With a single attempt, the machine began to sputter and pop with life. He then pulled a skeleton key out of a pouch on his hip and put it into the machine, twisting it as a command override to allow him to drive the vehicle.

When James took a seat on the vehicle, he pulled his tail up onto his lap and connected a large brass object that was on his left shoulder to the vehicle. The red orb on James' chest turned green once he was safely strapped in and he gripped two large leavers on either side of his chair. Then, the machine hissed as six mechanical legs began to lift the vehicle from the ground.

"Pretty cool, right? It's called a Tusk Crawler," James said as the two watched him walk the machine off its chamber.

Kiera and Alexis both nodded in agreement. The machine's legs were set low to the ground and allowed him to move without worrying about terrain. It had two tusk-like blades in the front that were controllable via levers for moving the freight. James walked the machine into the opened cargo container and positioned it in front of the first pallet of goods. It wasn't very large and it moved quickly with a counterweight on the back so the tusks at the front could lift freight safely up to five meters.

He backed out, moving the freight so that Kiera could read the code and mark it off on the paperwork. After, he walked the pallet into the building to set it in the refrigerated storage unit.

"This makes things a lot easier," Kiera said as James walked the machine back outside.

"Yeah," Alexis replied, "remember when we had to pull them in on steamjacks?"

"I never want to see another one of those things again."

"Hopefully James isn't the only one with a Tusk Crawler."

It wasn't long before they had the entire shipment taken care of and the storeroom was completely stocked. Kiera wrote down her signature on the bill of lading, marking that everything was received in good order. As James returned, he came to a stop next to Kiera so she could hand him the signed paperwork. She kept a version for the pub's records safe in her pocket so they could be sure to add the shipment to their inventory and knew how much to pay the Vel'Nahar airship pilot.

"That's how it's done!" James said. "Tell you what. Here...."

James reached into his pocket and pulled out a small one Cen coin. He handed it to Kiera, who took it and looked to him with her head tilted to the side and tail still. Then, he pulled a canteen off his hip that still had a bit of water in it, pulled off the lid, and handed it to her as well.

"What's this for?" Kiera asked.

"Go put these on the ground over there on the cement. Don't worry, you'll see."

She walked over to a cement pad near the doorway and set the coin down while Alexis followed along. Kiera then put the canteen next to it so that it was standing up on its own. James' Tusk Crawler moved into position in front of the two, and he lowered the flat tusks to the ground so the right one was in front of the coin.

"Alright, now watch this," James said confidently.

Kiera crouched and Alexis folded her arms as they both watched on intently. Metal clacked together as James brought the right tusk of the vehicle over the coin and lowered it until it was no longer visible. After a few minor adjustments, the Tusk Crawler stepped back. The coin flipped perfectly from the floor onto the flat tusk before he lifted it to around chest height for the girls to see. Kiera and Alexis both clapped, watching in awe as the tusks were lowered back down to the canteen. James then managed to jump the tusks just well enough to let the coin fall into the open top and splash to the water below.

"That was great!" Kiera said as she picked up the canteen and handed it back to James on the Tusk Crawler.

"Right!" James replied. "Why don't you two head on in, I'll park it and see y'all there."

Kiera waved as James walked the Tusk Crawler over to dock it with the airship in its miniature cargo bay. Alexis ran over to the employee entrance and opened it for Kiera, who was already mentally preparing herself to deal with the large gathering of people inside. Alexis wrapped an arm around her as she passed, keeping her emotions close so Kiera could comfortably adjust.

"Rough Ruska, on the rocks," Maya said proudly as she finished mixing the last drink that had been ordered. "Can I get anything else for ya, darling?"

The Jalar bartender set the glass in front of a soldier, who was the only one there in full uniform. He was a Raki, one of the masculine races of the planet Cerolia. His long, slender black tail swayed behind him on the barstool while the sharp crystalline arrowhead-like tip gently grazed the ground. The soldier looked down at the glass in front of him as it was presented. His eyes were crimson, so bright they almost looked as though they were glowing against the black backdrop of his sclera.

"No, thank you," The soldier said as he took the drink.

He pulled a single Mek from a pouch on his hip, gripping it by its hair between his ghostly white fingertips. In a quick motion, the Raki tossed the writhing creature into his drink. It bounced off of the glass, landing directly atop one of the ice cubes without falling off into the liquid.

"You have something on your mind? Don't have to tell me what's bothering you, but if you feel like chatting; I'll listen."

As he shifted himself in his seat, his long brown dreadlocks fell over his collarbone. The markings on his uniform differed from the ones Maya had seen before. Ground troops usually had a cross on their shoulder; the color of the cross and the number of lines beneath it designated rank. His uniform has a set of wings where the cross would normally go. The golden color and lines underneath told Maya that he was likely one of the highest ranking officers she's dealt with to this point.

"I worry for the future," the soldier replied.

He watched coldly as the Mek struggled to stay on the block of ice and above the burning liquid. After a moment, he started moving the glass in a circular motion on the bar to force the little one beneath the surface.

"What's your name, soldier?"

"Azron."

He looked strong, easily twice the size of the Raki soldiers that Maya had been serving throughout the night. Azron gently lifted the glass from the counter to take a small sip of his drink. After he set it back down, he pulled some dreadlocks which had fallen out of place back behind his long pointed ears and tucked them in front of a pair of black horns that curled downward.

"Well met, comrade Azron," Maya replied. "I'm Maya Isarean. Have a last name?"

"Why are you so interested?"

As he took another sip of his drink, he could feel the Mek struggle against his upper lip to keep from falling in. The door to the back opened, catching his attention momentarily as Kiera and Alexis entered the pub.

"Illegal to be curious now?"

"Refill!" a soldier several seats away shouted, slamming his glass on the table.

"One moment comrade," Maya said to Azron before walking over toward a rowdy group of soldiers.

Three little escapees scurried behind the bar, their tiny legs fluttering over the floorboards as they ran together toward safety. None of them expected Maya to walk toward them as they ran, casting them in shadow as her bare paw lifted ominously in the air. Time seemed to slow as they ran, still focused on getting to a safe place.

Thump.

A gust of wind knocked two of the Mek to their back, while the third was nowhere to be seen. They scurried to their feet in search of their lost friend as Maya continued through. Her paw lifted from the ground to reveal the soft layer of fur that was beneath. The white strands of fur shimmered with dark blue energy as the lower half of their lost companion's body fell to the floor. The rest had disappeared, hidden deep inside the black fur of her heel.

"You've already gone far beyond your limit, comrade," Maya explained to the soldier who called her over. "You know I'll need to see some Cen before you get any more."

"I'll stop when I'm done, 'comrade'. Not a Cen before then."

The two remaining Mek on the ground ran together toward their goal, a small crack in the wall that had been used as a path for them to enter the bar earlier that day. The three of them were captured together to be cooked and had cooperated in their escape from the kitchen. Now there were only two left from the group of survivors.

Snap.

The Mek who was leading fell to the ground as its ankle became lodged in a crack on the wooden floor. Its tiny mouth opened in a silent scream as its friend came to help. They were both stopped in a very bad place, directly in front of where Azron was sitting on Maya's side of the bar. The Mek's voiceless cries did nothing to help as both tried to free its twisted ankle. They couldn't hear her approach, her soft paws muffled by fur.

"Are they always like this?" Azron asked Maya as she returned to the bar in front of him.

Maya leaned on the edge of the counter with her elbows and tried her best to ignore the soldiers who were causing trouble. The two Mek beneath her were lucky as the Jalar settled into where she stood. They both occupied the three centimeters of free space between her paws.

"Well, the mouthy one walked out on the tab once. Told me that his artillery service was scheduled for a test soon, and if I didn't want any accidents that I should keep my mouth shut."

"How much does he owe you?"

"84 Cen," Maya said as she glanced to the bar-goer down the way whose fist clenched tighter the longer Maya let him sit without another drink. "I doubt he'll pay. You soldiers sure know how to steal from honest folk trying to make a living."

"Unacceptable," Azron stated as he shot back the last of his drink and set the glass back down gently.

The struggling Mek disappeared into the soldier's maw with such ease that Azron didn't even notice its presence. Without another word, the officer stood from the barstool and gave Maya a kind bow before walking down toward the trio of soldiers.

The two creatures on the floor were now in the shadow of Maya's left paw, which was resting against her right ankle with her heel raised slightly. The free Mek didn't flee even though it could feel the fur of Maya's paw on its back. She hadn't been out of her boots long, which made the air around the two warm and unpleasantly musky. The crack that the Mek had been stuck in was larger the further it went toward the bar's counter, but neither could get the little one's trapped ankle to budge.

"Good evening, friends," Azron said as he approached.

He towered over all three of the army grunts as he stood with his arms behind his back. The two soldiers who were around the obnoxious Raki were both Kavar. They had their bat-like wings wrapped around them like a cloak so they didn't hit anyone with them by accident. The Kavar on the left tucked their short light-blue hair behind their ears to keep it from getting in their eyes, while the other had just finished pulling their white hair back into a ponytail.

"How proper," The Raki grunt said, leaning toward the table with an elbow on his empty glass. Azron could tell that he was intoxicated by the way he swayed in his chair. "Why don't you do something useful, Officer? Get this wench to make me another drink, free of charge."

"Soldiers of our grand nation should always be paragons of honor, otherwise it reflects poorly on the empire. Would you not agree?" Azron said with a calm, collected smile.

"Honor? These people aren't any better than the Mek on the bottom of my shoe. They owe us for bringing 'honor' back to their pitiful little city," The grunt replied sharply. "Why should we pay for anything here?"

"Leon, just pay her," The white-haired Kavar said as they nudged their friend. "We shouldn't be getting into trouble."

"No," Leon replied, "we deserve this after they all fought back like they did."

"Do you honestly expect to win the hearts of a foreign populace through threats and theft? Referring to the good people here as 'wenches' and likening them to the Mek'Vatir? Even if you're out of uniform, you will always represent the Kingdom of Aestellus. We are a glorious empire, not petty thieves."

"We aren't paying," The thin Raki replied sharply.

"You will pay your debts, and I will buy you all a hot cup of tea to help you recover for the morning. The civilians of Nevarria are due the same respect as all the civilians of Aestellus; they're just people trying to live their lives in peace," he said with a stern, fatherly grace. "Refusal would be... unwise."

The song that the musician was playing on her guitar ended as Sofie took a seat next to her with her violin out. The conversations that were going on all around did not cease, and after a few seconds of silence, the music came back. Leon said nothing in that time as the tension rose between the two. The thin Raki then jumped forward, using the bar to push himself toward Azron as fast as he could to get a punch in. He was confident that his companions would come to his aid as they had throughout the war, and he was partially right. Both of them saw his movements, but the white-haired Kavar threw up their arms in protest while the one with blue hair stood to fight. They thought Azron wouldn't be well versed in combat as an Aeronaut.

They were wrong.

He read their movements perfectly, bringing his left hand up in time to get a death grip on Leon's wrist. Azron stepped forward himself, bringing his right arm up to the other Raki's neck to lift him off the ground by his throat. In one fell swoop, he sat the soldier back down on his seat and turned his attention to the blue-haired Kavar who was standing to fight. The other had shifted themselves away to avoid being involved.

When Leon was forcibly reseated at his spot on the bar, Azron brought his forearm toward the other Kavar in a quick strike. He cut it short, just barely touching the bridge of their nose, causing the Kavar to stop in their tracks. Leon was so stunned he didn't attempt to get back up; he could hardly breathe from the tight grip Azron had used on him to put him back in his place.

They all froze for a moment. Azron had moved with such grace that nobody at the bar even noticed the fight start. The blue-haired Kavar could feel the rough crystal of Azron's forearm beneath his uniform. If that strike had connected, it was unlikely that they would be conscious still. The white-haired Kavar on the other side had returned to their drink and was shamefully ducking down, trying to distance themselves from the others and not get any more involved then they already were.

"Tea," Azron stated calmly, "and I won't report you to the Ministry of Investigations for attempting to strike a superior officer and extorting the local population."

"Tea sounds good," The Kavar with blue hair said meekly as they sat back down.

"Good," Azron replied, letting go of Leon's wrist, "You'll find that Valong Tea is a wonderful way to prevent a hangover."

Heather was watching the scene unfold from the corner of the room while leaning up against the wall on one paw with her arms folded. Her red eyes began to glow as one of her trapped victims was crushed beneath her, unable to take the full weight of her heel pad for a prolonged period. As soon as she was sure the situation was under control, she pulled the lever down. Parts of the ceiling shifted in response to reveal glowing blue crystal, much like the pub's sign that hung over the entryway. Trapped souls constantly churned inside to produce an ethereal glow, and the patrons of the bar erupted in cheers and jovial shouting. She pulled a secondary lever, which dimmed the electrical lights so the crystals above were the only thing illuminating the pub.

Most of the patrons had worn clothes that accentuated their patterns for this reason specifically. As the darkness covered the room, they all began to glow brightly with each life they casually took. Every Mek that was crushed turned them into a glowing, beautiful beacon. Every soul they devoured was another excuse to show off their natural beauty.

Maya watched the scene unfold from afar, smiling a bit at the thought of the trio getting their comeuppance. Her left paw idly slid back onto the ground as she shifted her weight, devastating the two creatures fighting for freedom below her in a quick and careless motion. The crack was large enough for the Mek's body to safely be forced into while its ankle twisted nearly to the point of amputation. Musky white fur covered its entire body. Its companion, however, was not so lucky. It had no place to take refuge as Maya's paw ruthlessly pressed it into the wooden floor. The surviving Mek could hear its selfless companion's body slowly squelch and crack as black blood drained over it.

"Violent pacifism?" Maya chuckled as Azron returned.

The Mek that had been consumed alive finally succumbed to the torturous acid of Azron's stomach just as the one beneath Maya's paw was crushed to death. The white fur that surrounded the survivor trapped in the floorboards began to glow its dark blue color, as the deep red crystalline patterns on Azron's palm produced their eerie glow. They both laughed heartily at the timing as Azron took his seat.

"One hundred and thirty-two Cen," Azron said as he inadvertently bathed the coins in glowing red light. He then reached into a coin pouch on his hip and added some more to the pile. "I promised them all a pot of your best Valong Tea."

"Just when I thought you were starting a brawl," Maya shyly replied. "Thanks for keeping it civil."

"I wouldn't dream of damaging your wonderful establishment. If you would like, I can have a small security detail posted here to keep the peace."

"Oh, that won't be necessary, comrade. Inspector Christoph is already taking care of that. She would have stepped in if you hadn't, I'm sure."

"Inspector Christoph?"

"I think she was already forming a report on their conduct."

"Better to handle it this way I think. If they continue, I would recommend pursuing an official recourse," Azron replied. "Your hospitality is much appreciated."

"If you don't mind my saying, Soldier. Your patterns look fantastic under this light when they glow."

"And yours look as lovely as the blue spectral lotus along the riverbanks at night."

Maya stepped over toward a cabinet behind her. The surviving Mek was forced to watch as its companion's body was taken along with her. Its broken limbs dangled lifelessly from the fur that concealed most of its carcass before it was too far away to see in the dark.

"This one's on the house," Maya said slyly as she filled a new glass with the brightly colored liquid.

"You're most kind," Azron replied as the drink was set before him. "May I ask what it is?"

"Tal Varoi, part of my personal stash."

The Mek beneath her was once again engulfed in a wall of unpleasant fur, which fell upon it repeatedly as Maya nervously tapped the heel of her paw on the ground.

"Once again, your hospitality is matched by none."

"You never did tell me your last name, comrade Azron."

"Major Azron Klaha, Chief of Security aboard His Majesty's Airship *Levant*."

"Hey," Kiera said as she approached quietly from the side, behind the bar.

"Did everything go well with the shipment?" Maya asked.

"Of course. Why don't you let me tend the bar for a while? It's about time we opened up the pit. Maybe you can show your new Aeronaut friend around and prepare the Mek?"

"The pit?" Azron asked curiously. "Sounds fascinating."

"That's sweet of you dear," Maya replied meekly. "We won't be too terribly long."

"Take your time, I've got all night," Kiera replied.

Azron stood from his chair after finishing off the Tal Varoi and slid the glass over toward Kiera, who took it and set it in a sink nearby to be washed. Maya made her way out onto the main floor and over to him, before taking his hand to lead him toward a large lowered platform near where Sofie and the guitarist were playing music.

Requiem for the Lost

REQUIEM FOR THE LOST
CHAPTER I

Night | Alerio 12, 1240
Nevarria City – Isarean Pub

A thick, glowing mist rolled in over the lowered platform as the Mek'Vatir wandered aimlessly. The longer the mist stayed around them, the slower their movements became as the muffled sound of laughter and music began to fade more and more. It was already hard to move on the softer padded surface, but now it was simply grueling.

"There," Maya said as she ushered Azron over to a wall filled with small personal lockers.

"What's this now?" he asked curiously.

"No shoes on the dance floor."

"Why?"

"Well, it feels better for one."

"Oh?" He replied. "Is there another reason?"

"The floor's designed to absorb the Mek's bodies and gets softer as it's used, so shoes can damage it."

"Well then, if you insist."

"House rules, dear."

Azron did as he was asked, taking off his boots and socks to set them inside the small locker he had been offered. He took his uniform jacket off as well, revealing the black roll-neck sweater that he wore underneath. The soldier neatly folded his uniform top and set it inside, making sure not to wrinkle it in the process. She closed the door and handed him the key after he was finished while her fluffy tail swayed briskly.

"It's been cycles since I've been on a dance floor," Azron said. "Forgive me if I'm a little rusty."

"I think you're just being modest."

"We'll see, won't we?"

The glowing mist had nearly frozen the little one in place as it lay on its back looking up to the swirling tides in the air. Time had slowed for them all, making the Mek react sluggishly to everything around as the fog's chemicals worked to subdue them. Then, a wall of pale white skin cut through the mist directly above where it lay. Azron reached up to Maya to offer her his hand. As he did this, the thick red crystalline formations that were on his forearms and his shoulders, as well as his sharp spade tail's tip, began to glow. He could feel the mist rolling around his ankles on the lowered platform as she stepped in as well.

The music slowed as Sofie took over entirely, and all eyes were on the two on the dance floor.

"Why are we the only ones out here?" He asked softly as they walked toward the center, their patterns glowing at random now as they trampled those lost in the fog below.

"Because, this is the first time I've been out here with a patron."

"Then this is truly an honor."

Azron held her close as they took each other's hands. The music from Sofie's violin echoed through the room while they danced together in a slow circle. As the mist continued to wrap around their ankles, Azron became progressively aware of each Mek that fell beneath his footfalls. He could feel their spirits roll into him, traveling up through his entire form.

"What is this mist, if I may ask?"

"Valteritoxin. It slows the Mek down and disorients them. For us, it heightens our sense of touch and our awareness of the spirits inside of our bodies."

Deep in the mist at their feet, a Mek struggled to get its footing before falling beneath Maya's arch. Pain ran through its body as the majority of its bones shattered in an instant, leaving it a quivering mess as the pair turned in their dance. Then, it disappeared beneath Azron's toes only to be lifted from the ground and crushed in his next step. The crystals on the top of his foot that ran up his ankle illuminated, and he could feel every second of its spirit's journey as it spread through his system.

The little one had been in darkness for as long as it could remember before the machine was turned on. It could hear fresh Mek'Vatir getting poured into a basin at the top for patrons, then the groaning engine had enough air built up to begin the process it was designed for. A gust of air forced the little one down a small tube that led to the dance floor. It got to its feet the moment it landed, quickly trying to orient itself in the mist.

The giants were everywhere, dancing in every direction the little one had available to it. Their ankles were like the trunks of massive trees disappearing into the fog overhead as they danced without care for those below. It watched helplessly while others ran for their lives, disappearing beneath footfalls as they were reduced to black tattoo-like splatters on the patrons' skin. With no way for the Mek to tell which route would bring it to safety, it had to trust its instincts. The little one picked a direction in the fog and ran as the sound of a violin playing in harmony with a guitar filled the air. Its heart pounded in its chest as its lungs took in the poison, slowing down its reaction time immensely. It saw another Mek in its way, but it didn't matter.

Thump.

As an Aluni's heel landed in front of the little one, it ran into her and fell to its back. White fabric draped down into the mist from above as she continued to move, lifting her heel in her dance to reveal an assortment of inky blood-splatters. Her crimson patterns lit up as the Mek it had seen a moment ago was now nothing more than a smear of grime. It was the only carcass she carried, as the floor had taken the rest in her stride leaving only bloody outlines in their shape. The black tip of a tail swayed overhead, with some blue barely visible beyond that.

If it stayed, she'd surely kill it.

The Mek's movements were slow and sluggish as it got to its feet. It was determined to survive, to live on even if that meant another day of strife. Pushing itself beyond its limits, the little one ran past the dancing Aluni in the direction it was going toward before. It ran over the bodies of its fallen comrades as others tried to survive in the chaos nearby. Those who were still alive didn't last long in the mist before succumbing to the poison, which meant certain death as they fell to their backs. Just as all hope felt lost, as the poison entering its lungs began to take hold entirely, it saw an opportunity to climb above the mist.

A blue dress slid along the ground in front of it as another patron danced nearby. Another Mek had the same idea, though it had fallen and disappeared beneath the swaying fabric. When the dress moved away, it revealed the Mek who had been crushed into the ground. The longer the little one stayed here, the more the poison gripped its body. It ran over, leaping onto the fabric it used every ounce of its strength to climb up and out of the mist toward the fresh air above.

Once it was free of the oppressive fog, it was able to see its surroundings better. She was dancing near the edge of the pit!

CEROLIAN SAGAS

With one last feat of strength, the Mek jumped from the dress and landed free of the dance floor. It then stumbled over toward the wall, walking along the edge in search of an exit. There was another crack near the base of the wall with just enough space for it to slip into. The Mek felt as though it had done the impossible. It was safe, for the time being.

This was the first night in cycles that Tanya felt she could relax and let loose, even knowing she was surrounded by enemy soldiers. She could feel the mist around her ankles as she danced to the upbeat tune of the violin and guitar that played in unison. The souls of the Mek she killed slid up into her body, and the alcohol she had taken in helped her take the edge off her aches. She was loving every second of this assignment. It had been so long since she felt the smooth flow of a white silk dress on her skin. It was a far cry from the uniform she was used to wearing in the grime of the warzone, a grit she carried with her still.

She was starting to tire, though, and she wasn't only here to have fun dancing and drinking.

The soldier collected herself, smiling ear to ear as she made her way over to the edge of the dancing pit and stepped out of the mist. The light from her deep red patterns cut through her thin white dress with every Mek she killed along the way. Tanya walked over toward the bar, leaning between two soldiers so that she could be easily seen by the bartender.

"What'll it be?" Kiera asked, noticing the Aluni as she fin-ished pouring a glowing blue drink.

"I'll have a Blue Nevarrian," Tanya replied, looking up to the young bartender behind the counter.

She could feel her entire body tense up when she saw who it was. The long purple hair, the golden yellow eyes. Kiera wasn't oblivious to Tanya's quick change of emotion, but it didn't reg-ister as anything too odd. The young Aluni bartender mixed up another tall glowing blue glass, dropped a few Mek inside, and set it down on the bar in front of the blue-haired patron. She even chuckled to herself at how perfect of a drink it was for someone with blue hair to order.

"That'll be five Cen."

"Thanks," Tanya said as she slid the Cen on the bar. "I mean it. Thanks for everything."

Kiera gathered the money and nodded, looking directly into Tanya's eyes as the soldier took her drink and walked away. The sincerity in her voice was enough to get the message across. Kiera knew who she was, she was able to recognize her by that one sentence alone.

As Tanya made her way over toward the lockers to retrieve her shoes, she passed behind both Sofie and the guitarist. Casually, she pulled out a small white envelope from her dress' pocket and let it drop into a partially closed guitar case. Without stopping to chat or do anything more, she continued to her locker and pulled out a small key she had in her other pocket.

"I need a damn smoke," She said to herself as she retrieved her pack of rolled cigarettes.

She dropped her flats to the ground and stepped into them, not bothering to dust the bodies from her feet as she did so. Tanya's mission wasn't completed until she was sure the target had her letter in hand. After she shut and locked the door, she walked back through toward the bar.

She looked out to the dozens of people dancing their cares away in the middle of the glowing fog. As Tanya passed by the two songstresses, she pulled a Mek out from her pocket and tossed it to the ground. It was a good enough excuse to look down without looking too suspicious. She watched as it tried to run away, then gently set the front of her flat down on the little one and twisted it out like one of her cigarettes. As she did so, she glanced over to the guitar case to ensure that the letter was gone. It was, and since she was sure there were no other people over in this corner near the performers at this point, her mission was a success.

Tanya powered through her drink, swallowing the Mek that Kiera dropped in whole as she did so. She walked her glass back over to the counter, set it down, and made her way outside the pub. The moment she stepped into the open, she pulled out her cigarette pack and opened it up. Unlike the issued cigarettes she had earlier, these were her own blend.

Within the confines of the tobacco-leaf wrapping, she had rolled her cigarettes in was a soul awaiting death. It was packed so tightly that it was nearly impossible for it to move. However, it hadn't been given the proper motivation until now.

She struck a match before holding it up to the end of her cigarette. The flame caught easily as she inhaled, surrounding the creature inside with smoke and robbing it of its oxygen. No matter how much it struggled for its life, the tobacco kept it from moving about. Within minutes it was burning alive with its charred legs sticking out of the red-hot cherry at the end. The Aluni leaned against the building and took two more long drags of her cigarette, and her red patterns began to glow. She then gently flicked the cigarette using her thumb so that the ashes would fall to the ground.

The streak of a shooting star in the sky caught her attention as she took another puff of her cigarette, enjoying the end to a very productive night.

"How's the food?" Heather asked as she sat down at the table across from James.

"Better than I remember. You taking another break or what?"

"Just have to get off my paws for a minute."

Four Mek had survived, writhing and crawling around inside the inspector's socks. Her long, slender tail swayed along the floor as she allowed their movements to soothe her aching paws. Occasionally she would bob her paw to get the ones underneath to move, or flex her toes to stir those trapped in the oppressive fur between to life.

"*Right?*" James replied, "You're an inspector, aren't you?"

"Maybe."

"You can't fool ol' James now. I might not know you all that much, but I think you got a good head on your shoulders from what I've seen."

"Is that right?"

"Sure is! You ever think about bein' an Aeronaut?"

"Not particularly. I like being on the ground."

"Right. Now, how long you been a soldier?"

"Long enough."

"There ain't nothin better than flying through the skies," James said as he sliced into a juicy bit of his steak. "You ever been up?"

"No, I came over on a battleship with the Aquanauts. I don't trust the airships as they are now."

"You know in a cycle or two they're leaving the ol' air bladders behind? After this run, I'm parking it in a shop and turnin' a wrench until I get the *Olga V* airworthy without it."

"Oh?"

"Yep. The skies are going to look different here soon."

"Well," Heather said, pulling a small jar of Mek'Vatir out of her pocket. "I did bring you this. Noticed you didn't have any with your meal and was wondering if you needed a jar."

"Nah. I already had my two this morning. I don't need any."

"Suit yourself," Heather said as she slipped the jar back into her pocket for safekeeping.

"I just came here for good food and good company."

"Are you the one they call the 'Sage of the Skies' around here?"

"Kiera and Alexis are the only ones who call me that anymore. I used be a captain in the Novalin Defense Force before retiring from the military. Now I just fly freight where it needs to be and keep food on people's plates. It ain't as glamorous as fighting in the skies, but it's worth it."

"They speak highly of you, luv. Is there anything else I can get for you before I get back to work?"

"Fat bag of Hundred-Cen coins please."

Heather laughed politely while she enjoyed the few minutes of respite she had, looking around to all the tables she needed to take care of. The pub was slowing down significantly at this point, much to her relief. Most of the patrons had already paid their bill, so all that needed to be done now was to walk around and collect the dirty dishes nearby.

The aches and pains from being on the go all day were relentless, even after getting a quick jolt of healing from Sofie earlier.

 CEROLIAN SAGAS

Heather closed her eyes, leaned back in her chair, and focused on the Mek she had trapped. She hoped that they would survive long enough in there to help soothe her walk home too. Since she didn't drink, and she tried to avoid taking medication, they were the best form of painkiller she had access to.

Reluctantly, she stood to start the last leg of her shift.

Rausia Liviana

REQUIEM FOR THE LOST
CHAPTER II

"You play pretty well, comrade," Rausia said as she set her guitar back into the case next to her. "What's your name?"

"Sofie Caren. Yours?"

"Holly," Rausia replied, giving out one of her many aliases.

The red-haired spy pulled a small Mek'Vatir from the pouch on her hip and slipped it into her dangling black flat. The Mek landed on its back and slid down to the heel of her shoe as she sat with her legs crossed. There were other little gray splats on the fabric, all in varying states of decomposition. The red tip of her long black tail dusted the ground as she pulled her guitar case up onto her lap so she could strap it down and set it aside.

"I had fun playing with someone else for once," Sofie said brightly as she put her violin on her back. "There aren't many musicians where I'm from."

"How long have you been practicing?"

"Oh! I got my first violin when I was ten cycles old and I've been playing ever since. There are a few other musicians at the Temple of Aludra, but we don't really get along very well most of the time. It's really sad because I do love playing with others."

"Having a good session always helps me unwind. I don't have many people to play with either, especially not someone who can keep pace with me and make stuff up on the spot like you."

Her passenger tried to steady itself where it was while gazing up to the strange blue diamond pattern in the center of her arch. She had her legs crossed and was dangling her shoe by a strap in the center, her idle movements made certain that the Mek's attempts at escape would never come to fruition. It sat in the heel of her shoe with its back against the insole while trying to keep from being tossed around too much.

"Are you going to stay for a while?"

"I don't know, really," Rausia said as she put her guitar on her back while still seated. "I've been around here for a while and I'm starting to get a bit stir crazy. The walk in isn't really all too bad. I'm just used to getting out, flying around to other cities, and playing at other venues."

Rausia then uncrossed her legs and slid her heel back into place within her footwear. The little Mek inside had nowhere to go as her heel descended. Her skin was dry and calloused, the result of a life dedicated to martial arts coupled with a lack of care. The rough and cracked skin of her heel settled down onto its chest with a huge amount of weight. Its tiny legs were forced vertically along the interior wall of her shoe as well, putting the little creature into an incredibly uncomfortable position beneath her foot.

"Well, you want me to walk you out?" Sofie asked.

"Sure. Maya already paid me for today so I don't really need to stick around."

"Well then, lead the way!"

Rausia stood from her seat and shifted the strap of her guitar case across her chest until it was comfortable. The little Mek's thrashing came to an end as its insides squished out into the cracks of her rough heel. It caused the blue stripes on her neck to shimmer as her Symbiont feasted upon another soul. Once her guitar was secured, she straightened her black vest and fixed the cuff of the red dress shirt beneath. Then, the pair began to make their way toward the door.

"Maya!" Rausia shouted when she saw the pub owner.

The Jalar had returned to the bar and was cleaning up while Azron was straightening out his uniform jacket. The three soldiers who were causing a ruckus earlier were just finishing up another cup of tea after having enjoyed some time on the dance floor together, and everything just felt right for the night. Rausia waved over toward Maya, who returned the gesture in passing before returning to her work as the two stepped out the front door of the pub.

"Next time we're both in town, we should absolutely get together and play," Sofie suggested as she stood under the light of The Isarean Pub's glowing sign.

"You got it," Rausia replied, then turned to make her way back to the occupied city. "See ya soon I hope."

"Take care, Holly!" Sofie said as she waved.

Rausia returned the gesture, waving without turning back to look at The Isarean Pub. The moment she had the opportunity to do so, she cut off to the right of the pathway and started walking through the woods. She had hoped to keep her interactions with the local military forces to a minimum, so avoiding the main path was a good priority. The sun reflected off the planets glowing rings and bright moon overhead, which illuminated her pathway enough for her to see with confidence.

"Rausia," a feminine voice said from behind.

Quickly, she drew a pistol that was hidden on her hip in the direction of the voice, but stopped herself from pulling the trigger on the newcomer. She then let out a sigh and holstered her handgun after she recognized who it was.

"It's Holly around here," Rausia replied. "Glad to see you anti-social bastards crawl out from your little corner of the galaxy to grace us with your 'divine' presence."

"Well then. We have a proposition for you, Holly."

She looked a lot like an Aluni at first glance, though there were some very significant differences. Her ears were rounded, furless, and small enough that they were hidden beneath her white hair. Her current form had no visible tail, and her golden eyes had a single slit down the center as opposed to the Aluni's unique inky spot.

"I'm not interested in saving the world again, Astaroth. I cut ties with the Cargassan Union a long time ago. Tell your brother my debts been paid," Rausia replied sharply in a hushed tone before turning her back to continue away from the main path.

"We will complete our objectives with or without your assistance. Your involvement will simply ease our task," Astaroth replied calmly. "At least listen."

"Fine. I'll listen, but I have important business of my own to tend to. If you want me to work for you, I need something really shiny. Walk with me."

"You'll be compensated," Astaroth said as she began walking alongside her companion. "Solumna's activity in this region has increased dramatically and we need to know why. We've narrowed down the sources to several planets within this arm of the galaxy but the Union is spread too thin to cover them all. Each of the planets that have seen heightened activity houses technology built by the Anunnari."

"So, you need me to keep an eye on Cerolia for you while your fleets check out the other worlds?"

"Most of the other marked worlds have no sentient races on them that we are aware of. We're reaching out to all agents on worlds we have contact with to keep us up to date. You're the only being on this planet that my brother trusts."

"If I'm going to be your agent on the ground, you need to equip me," Rausia replied sternly, "with things I can keep."

"After I leave, my sister will be your contact on the ground. We'll be outfitting you with a communications device and any technology that she deems important enough for you to have. When we're convinced that Cerolia isn't a threat to the greater galaxy, you may keep what we equip you with."

"Why would the king of a galactic empire send his siblings to do his bidding, and not… literally anyone else?"

"Freya requested the post as your liaison. She knows how to use the technology we will be outfitting you with, and you know this world far better than any of our observers since you're a denizen. Your help would be appreciated."

"And what's your story? You just in the neighborhood to give me the good news?"

"My fleet is currently on course for Arturia 4. I'm transmitting this message directly to your mind, using your Symbiont."

"Why not just use that instead of some fancy communications device you might outfit me with? That sounds like some pretty awesome tech."

"Because it requires a starship's power supply to operate."

"What made Ares change his mind about letting me play with your toys, anyway?"

 CEROLIAN SAGAS

"Necessity, and the trust you've gained by paying off your debts to the Cargassan Union," Astaroth replied. "I've given my sister command of an advanced reconnaissance starship called the *Loriss* with a crew of six specialists. When she arrives, she will contact you for further instructions and training. Work with her and you will be rewarded in ways no soul on Cerolia can hope to offer."

"I never said yes."

"Freya will contact you shortly, I don't have time for your indecisiveness," Astaroth replied before disappearing entirely.

"Right… fine, whatever," Rausia grumbled as she continued toward Nevarria City.

Midnight | Alerio 13, 1240
Nevarria City – Isarean Pub

"More tea?" Maya asked from behind the bar as she held up a steaming teapot.

"That would be lovely," Azron replied.

Maya tossed a Mek into the empty cup of tea, then lifted a strainer to the spout of the teapot before she began to pour the hot liquid on top of the creature. Steam rose from the teacup as it filled, and when it reached the top she set the teapot back on the heating coil she took it from.

"There."

Azron took a sip of the tea as the steam rose from the liquid. He felt the Mek slip into his mouth and fall between his teeth. The Raki bit down and enjoyed the soft sweet taste of the specially prepared little one, then took another sip of tea.

"Fantastic. Did you brew this tea yourself?"

"I did."

"This is very delicious, and the perfect temperature."

"You said you were from an airship?"

"Yes, the *Levant.* One of the first military vessels to fly without the use of an air bladder. It's a marvel of engineering."

"Anyone special on the ship? Or back at home?"

"Not particularly. I live alone in a small logging town called Sheffingham on the northern coast of Aestellus. That's where I spent my childhood, with Commodore Falk."

"Commodore Falk?"

"She's the commanding officer on the *Levant.* Kari and I have a long history together. We both fought in the War of Aestellan Unification on the side of the north. 'The Aerial Kitsune' is what the south called her."

"Are you two together? If you don't mind my asking, of course. I don't mean to pry."

"No, it's quite alright," Azron heartily laughed, then took another sip of his tea. "The Commodore and I have a strictly platonic relationship. I give her counsel when she needs it, and we support each other quite well, but we've never been romantically involved. Besides, it would be improper to form a relationship with a superior officer."

The poor soul beneath Maya's paw was still trapped in the wooden floorboards. She and Kiera had both been unknowingly trampling the little one throughout the night, but the crack it occupied kept it safe from death. It simply gazed up from its hole in the ground as the fur of Maya's heel hovered so close to its little body that it was touching the skin of its arm. Then, the Mek reached up with its weakened little hand and grabbed onto the nearest bit of fur with all the strength it could muster.

Heather came through the batwing doors from the kitchen with a jacket slung over her forearm. She looked quite tired, but she knew she had to make the long trip back to the city tonight to finish up some paperwork in her office. Leaning up against the wall near the lever she pulled earlier to dim the lights, she tapped the toe of her left boot on the ground to see if she had any survivors along for the walk. The motion caused two little Mek to writhe — one caught under the main pad of her paw, and the other trapped in the gray fur along her arch.

"Hey Maya," she said, looking up to the two near the bar, "Lain said something earlier about the pub not opening tomorrow?"

"Yeah. We're taking inventory on that shipment we had and just planning on catching a breath after how busy tonight was. You can come back on the 14th around noon or so if you'd like."

Heather shifted herself and tapped her other shoe on the ground a few times, feeling only one still alive in there squirming in the soft fur between her digits. She smiled, happy that she wouldn't have to replace them for her long walk home. If they survived, she might even be able to use them later.

"Alright, if you need anything, you know how to contact me."

"Have a safe trip back, comrade."

"Cheers."

With that, Heather disappeared into the hallway leading to the back of the pub and Azron shifted in his seat. There were no other patrons left, and he knew the only reason he was allowed to stay after was that he had caught Maya's eye.

"What are your plans for the night?" Maya asked.

"I'm on leave for the next few days. We're scheduled to be in the region for a fortnight before we start on our next assignment."

"Which is?"

"It's a state secret, my apologies."

"Understood."

"Do you have a room available for the night?"

"If you did stay, I'd have to run you off early in the morning before we get to work on the inventory. Besides, I'd hate for you to waste your only days on leave watching us count boxes."

"Say no more."

"Hold on a moment," Maya said as she turned to the cupboards behind her.

The Mek in the floorboards was still holding on tight, and the sharp motion was enough to rip it free from what very well could have been its tomb. Its weakened grip faltered the moment it was released. The result was a rather graceless plummet to the wooden floorboards below. Maya was long gone by the time it had lifted its weakened body again, and the Mek used the last of its strength to crawl to the safety of the bar's edge. Adrenaline pumping through incredibly thin veins kept it from feeling any sort of pain, but its foot was still broken from the ordeal.

To its surprise, the little survivor felt someone lift it from the ground. Not a giant, but another of its kind. The wounded little one gazed weakly up to the black eyes of one of its companions. Neither of them could truly comprehend the heroic act, but they could still both feel for each other.

It was going to be alright.

"Here," Maya said as she returned with a thermal canteen and set it in front of him. "You can have this if you'd like."

She then put a strainer on top of the canteen's opening and poured tea into the container. Leaves fell onto the mesh netting as it was filled until there was nothing left in the pot to pour. Maya set it aside, dropped a few Mek into the container for the road, and tightly capped it.

"Are you certain?" Azron asked.

He lifted the thermal canteen to see 'Maya' engraved into the bottom along with a replica logo of The Isarean Pub's Amethya sign from outside. It was about the same size as a standard-issue military canteen, though it was made from far stronger material. Small Amethya crystals adorned the top, each alternating an attuned color against a glossy and pristine steel backdrop etched with intricate swirling patterns.

"I am. It works well for both cold and hot drinks. I've had it since I started the business here, and think you might get better use out of it than me. There's an Amethya layer as well, so any Mek that die inside won't go to waste."

"I couldn't possibly take this from you."

"Keep it, comrade. Just in case you can't get back here."

"Well, if that's the case, I humbly accept your gift. Now, allow me to return your kind gesture."

Azron pulled his canteen off of his hip to replace it with the one he was gifted. He set it in front of her as the spade tip of his tail slid across the ground behind his barstool. His wasn't nearly as fancy as hers, made of thin sheet metal that had been dented and worn from cycles of military service. She picked it up and looked at the bottom to see 'Azron Klaha' etched into the metal by a knife.

"Perfect," Maya said brightly.

Sofie enjoyed watching the dust roll across the ground as she swept the upper floor hallway clear with her broom. The bodies of Mek'Vatir that had been crushed came up easily, rolling in with the dirt as she walked the halls with a dustpan in hand. She came to a stop in front of the room she had for herself and knelt with pan in hand, sweeping the dust up that she gathered from the entire walkway. It was late, she was quite tired from the long walk, and she was ready to turn it in.

"Hey," Kiera said from behind as Sofie slid her keycard into her doorway's mechanism.

"Hello, comrade."

"You were amazing tonight."

"Thanks."

Sofie opened the doorway and stepped in, holding it open for Kiera to enter as well. She made her way over to a nearby bin and tossed the dust and bodies away. The Advanced Acolyte then set the broom next to her staff in the corner, stepped out of her moccasins, and sat down on her bed. The violin was sitting upright on one of the two nearby chairs along with her bow.

"I don't just mean your playing," Kiera said as she sat down in the other chair and crossed her legs. "We really have a lot to thank you for, comrade. I just wanted to let you know how much we appreciate everything you've done."

"I'm just glad I could help."

"How was Adriel?"

"I had a hard time remembering he was even there, to be honest," Sofie said as she slid herself up in the bed, using pillows to prop herself against the wall.

Kiera leaned over, picking up the moccasin she knew he was in from the ground since it was close enough for her to reach. She moved it so that she could see inside, pulling the heel section down a bit to let in light. Sofie's footprint was clear as day along the cotton insole of the shoe, and the bodies of dead Mek'Vatir were easy enough to pick out. She could see one Mek still alive, trapped in the toe section still struggling in the cotton print.

His tunic was spread out on a dark smudge that vaguely represented a person's shape. Adriel's white hair was spread around in the cotton as well, and his tail's fur was nowhere to be seen. It was almost as though he had disappeared, crushed so thin from all of the walking she did that it was impossible to tell where the little one was exactly.

"Blegh," Kiera groaned as she set the shoe down on her lap, "I wonder if he's alright."

"I was still able to use him when I needed to, so I would imagine he's fine," Sofie said calmly.

"Why hasn't he healed then?"

"I'm not sure how his healing actually works. Wasn't very worried about him though since he volunteered for this."

A soft shimmer of white light caught Kiera's eye coming from inside the moccasin. As she looked down, she saw Adriel dragging himself out from the deep by his arms. He was back in his little tunic and covered in dark grime. The little one rolled over onto his back, panting with exhaustion as Kiera gently pulled him out and set him on her lap.

"Are you alright, comrade? You look broken."

"Never better," He said between breaths. "Was I helpful?"

"Immensely," Sofie chimed in, barely able to hear him from where she was on the bed.

Adriel curled up against Kiera's hand, pulling himself close to her index finger in an embrace. She smiled, gently petting the top of his head to help him recover from what he had just been through. The little Ætherbug wasn't quaking at all; he didn't seem to be afraid as he relaxed. Kiera set Sofie's moccasin neatly next to its mate and stood up with Adriel in hand.

"I'm glad we were able to get here on time." Sofie said, pulling her covers up over her chest.

"Likewise. I'll see you in the morning. Sleep well."

Kiera gently slipped Adriel into the Mek'Vatir pouch on her hip for safekeeping and bowed to the Advanced Acolyte, before walking toward the doorway.

It was time for her to get some rest.

REQUIEM FOR THE LOST
CHAPTER III

The sound of steam pistons hissing filled the hallway as the stairwell lifted upward. Kiera waited patiently with one hand on a nearby switch and the other holding her worn combat boots. With how tired she was, it felt like an eternity for the machine to reach its set position so that she could turn the lights off. When she did, the soft hum of the generator was all that could be heard in the darkened corridor. Slowly, she opened the doorway to her bedroom and stepped inside. It was far from the first time she had to creep around so that Alexis wouldn't be disturbed. She used all of her acquired skills to close the door silently, then turned in the direction she knew her bed to be.

Pat

She took her first step, and she immediately lit up the room with her glowing blue markings. Kiera knew her friend wasn't as sensitive to light as she was to sound, so instead of worrying about where she stepped, she was more concerned with how she did so. She kept her striped socks on to help muffle her footfalls, and slowly continued toward her bed.

Rurr

She had been spotted! A soft, silky coat of fur ran across her left leg as Pearl circled her on the ground. Kiera could hardly see the silhouette of the little creature, though she couldn't help but crouch down and bring her hand close enough to the ground for the feline to find it. The lunamir immediately ran her forehead up into Kiera's palm and was rewarded with a thorough yet gentle back-scratching.

She meticulously continued her walk to her bed, illuminating the room again as she tip-toed atop a Mek by accident. Each breath she took was planned and quiet, every movement was calculated to try and keep her friend sleeping.

"Did you get Adriel?" Alexis asked, her voice low and tired.

"Yeah," Kiera sighed as she stood up straight. "I didn't mean to wake you up, sorry."

"It wasn't you, but thanks."

Kiera set her hand on the pouch on her hip and began drawing energy from him to illuminate the room around her. The glowing patterns gave her plenty to work with as she went to turn on the small electric light between their beds. Once that task was done, Kiera sat down on the bed next to her friend.

"Is something wrong?" Kiera asked.

"It's my leg again."

Alexis curled up, holding her pillow close as Kiera unstrapped the Mek pouch from her hip and tossed it into the air. When she roughly caught it, she looked to her friend with a smile.

"I know a few very small folk who can help with that."

"Maybe just one?" Alexis meekly replied.

"Just one Mek? I'll need more than that, comrade."

"No, I mean Adriel."

"You want me to use him instead?"

"Please," Alexis said as she peered over the edge of the bed-sheet she was mostly under.

Kiera slid down the bed toward the lumps where her friends feet were located. As she pulled back the covers and slid close, Alexis stretched out so that her heels were on her friend's lap. Kiera then opened the Mek'Vatir pouch and looked inside.

"Oh, Goddess." Kiera said as she stifled a laugh with her hand.

The exhausted little Adriel lay on the bottom of the pouch while the Mek used him in their attempt to escape. They hopped all around on him with no regard for where they stepped, keeping him buried and hardly visible like a living little floor. Kiera reached in, pulling him out by his tail and shaking him so the clinging little Mek wouldn't escape on their own.

"What?" Alexis asked.

"Nothing," Kiera replied quickly, still trying to keep herself from laughing aloud.

Alexis let out a sigh as she felt Kiera's hands wrap around her foot. She pulled her covers up a bit and watched as her friend's light-blue markings began to glow at a constant rate once again. The clawing, needle-like pain that was wreaking havoc on her slowly began to subside, replaced with a familiar yet powerful euphoric energy. Not used to being used as a focus in such a way, Adriel started to writhe between them as he was both drained and overwhelmed with new sensations. Alexis closed her eyes, taking in every minute movement as Kiera used the little one like a massaging stone.

"Is there anything else bothering you?" Kiera asked quietly.

"I talked to James about taking me to Sanova."

"Oh... So, uh..." Kiera replied, clearing her throat. "You're really going through with it then, huh?"

"Rina is coming too. She wants to defect, so we'll both go together to Sanova City with the help of the Sage of the Skies. I'll be able to apply for the Novalin Defense Force there, and she wants to see about getting into politics."

"They'll ship you to Vale from there, I think."

"Vale Western Command would be great, but I want to see if they'll send me down to Obalysk Southern Command. They train officers there, ya know? Hopefully I'll be able to get into the Aeronaut Officer Candidate School."

"I know you have what it takes," Kiera replied confidently. She flinched a moment later as she felt one of Adriel's bones crack under her palm. "Have you brought this up with Maya and Lain?"

"Yeah."

"And?"

"Maya was glad that I had a plan to get out of the city, and she trusts comrade James well enough. Lain was sad, though. She's not against it, but I can really tell she'll miss me a lot."

"I will too. I won't be able to help you sleep like this when you're gone," Kiera solemnly replied.

"I know."

"You'll come back and visit?"

"That I don't know. I'm really not sure how that works, especially with this now being Aestellan territory."

"I understand."

Kiera used both of her thumbs to press Adriel as hard as she could against her friend's skin without breaking him any more than she already had. She could feel his lungs empty and was careful to shift the pressure on him so he could still breathe.

"I'll write as much as I can though, I promise."

"You'd better, or I'll come find you."

"And when you find me?"

"I'll give you a stern lecture about how you should write more. Then probably a hug."

"By the Goddess, I should be careful." Alexis chuckled.

"It'll be a terrifying hug and a boring lecture. The stuff of nightmares, I promise."

"No doubt. Do you have any idea what you'll do after I leave?"

Adriel's squirming was stifled as Kiera placed her thumbs on his back and slowly pressed him directly into the center of her foot until glowing purple blood burst from his abdomen. They both felt the rush of soothing energy from direct contact with the glowing liquid wash over them as Kiera gently kneaded him into her comrade's soft skin.

"I want to go back to where I found Adriel and look for clues about where he came from. Maybe there's something at the hotel that can tell us about the Sarin, or something we can find to clear up his past."

"Just be careful, alright?"

"You're the one going into the military."

"Yeah, into a controlled training environment. You're talking about gallivanting around in occupied territory, and our excuse to wander the city is gone now. Heather's going to be keeping a close eye on you and the last thing we need is her finding out about the little squirt."

"I'll be fine."

"We should cut a spot for him in your boot. Like I did with mine... Have we even fed him since we found him?"

"Oh Goddess, I don't think we have."

"I think we should tell Maya and Lain about him tomorrow after we've finished breakfast."

"You're right," Kiera said softly. "They deserve to know."

"Ahh...." Alexis sighed as she cuddled closer into her pillow. "Why couldn't we have met him cycles ago. This feels divine."

Kiera smiled enough to show one of her fangs as she warmly sat at the edge of her friend's bed. She was careful not to hurt Adriel any more than she already had, though. Instead, she used her thumbs and palms to dig into Alexis' skin in an attempt to help lull her to sleep. The more her friend relaxed, the more Kiera's worries began to eat away at her. Alexis had been there for her through every traumatic experience in her life up until this point. She could feel her eyes watering as the true gravity of their situation finally set in.

This could be their last night together under the same roof, and although she felt like she could fall asleep at any moment, she couldn't bring herself to get up and walk away. So she sat there, with Adriel's broken body in her hands that were covered in his glowing blood.

She had a soft smile on her face as the tears dripped from her chin to the bedsheets below.

Alexis forgot everything about her dream the moment her consciousness came back to her. The light that they were using earlier hadn't been turned off, and Pearl had taken it upon herself to lay beneath it. Adriel was there as well, his head pinned beneath the feline's front paw as she slept peacefully curled up around her new prized toy. His tail was still swaying even though his limbs all looked as though they had been gnawed on for several hours.

"Good morning, comrade," She whispered, noting how his tail's pace quickened in response.

She shifted to her left to get into a more comfortable position while still in a general state of grogginess. The motion was stifled by a weight she hadn't expected. Alexis yawned, slowly sitting up to see what was blocking her from achieving a more desirable sleeping arrangement on the bed.

Her friend's violet hair came into view immediately as she propped her weight up on her elbow. Kiera had fallen asleep right there, sprawled out across the bed laying on her back with no covers to speak of. She was asleep, with her mouth wide open and her hair sprawled out behind her on the comforter.

As Alexis carefully pulled her legs out from the covers, she caught the attention of a weary Mek trapped in the grimy fibers of her slipper. The last few days seemed like an eternity, and having been worn last night, the little one was now barely breathing. Every tiny bit of air it took in was foul, as the lingering scent of cycles worth of use surrounded its little body. All it could do was watch as the red swirling patterns of Alexis soles came into view, and entombed it between a layer of skin and fabric once more.

Trying to be as quiet as she could, Alexis went over to Kiera's bed and balled up the covers into a single large mass. It took a few attempts, but she eventually managed to wrest them up into her arms and begin walking back over to where her friend lay. She stumbled a bit, stamping down on the Mek that was trapped inside her slippers.

Its death went completely unnoticed.

Her red patterns added to the yellow tinted light of the room as she dropped the sheets on her bed and spread them across Kiera's sprawled form.

"There...."

She pulled her pillow over toward Kiera's head so that she could use it if need be, took the Mek pouch from the nightstand, and made her way over to her sock-stuffed boots.

"Sorry little comrades." She said as quietly as she could to the two little Mek she pulled out by habit, and dropped one in each of her boots.

Alexis was still incredibly groggy and hardly thinking straight. She yawned as she donned her socks and shoes. Then, she turned off the light that was over Pearl and walked in darkness to the door. Her patterns illuminated the room every so often, giving her a good idea of where she was concerning her goal.

Alexis yawned again as she wandered behind the pub to the grassy field that still had its morning dew. James' airship was still anchored in the ground with all of its doors sealed up tight. The sound of a shovel digging through dirt echoed through the air as she approached the single enormous tree that grew near the back of the field.

There was a small hill leading up to the tree's base, and the hole was being dug far enough away that the root system would not be an issue. It was already a meter deep by the time she had arrived at its edge.

"How long have you been out here, comrade?" Alexis asked as she looked down into the grave.

"I'm not stopping," Rina replied coldly as she struck the dirt again with the metal shovel blade. She still wore her bloodied uniform, which was now soiled with sweat and caked in dirt.

"I wasn't going to ask you to. How long?"

"I don't know," Rina said as she stopped digging for a moment to catch her breath.

"You know what? I'll be right back," Alexis said quickly, and had disappeared before Rina could question her intent.

She returned from the small shed near the aquamelon patch with another shovel, and without asking permission, she hopped down into the meter-deep hole and plunged the steel spade deep into the ground.

"You don't—"

"I'm not stopping," Alexis replied sternly.

Rina was leaning on her shovel as she pulled a Mek from the pouch on her hip and unceremoniously smeared it between her red hoofed fingertips. The Edoraii was simply gathering the strength to continue and realized there wasn't much point in trying to talk Alexis out of helping. Silently, she turned back to her side of the grave and resumed the task at hand.

Kiera clutched Adriel in hand as she approached The Isarean Pub's front entrance with her tail tucked between her legs and her ears lowered. She was still a bit groggy, having slept in far longer than she expected to. The illuminated sign was still bright as the souls trapped within swirled around inside the Amethya crystal design. On the doorway itself though, was a secondary sign made of the same crystal that read 'Closed' large enough to be seen from a significant distance.

After stopping in front of the doorway, she opened her hands and let Adriel take a deep breath of fresh air.

"Are you alright with this?" Kiera asked in a whisper.

"If you trust them, I do too," Adriel replied as he sat with his legs crossed in the middle of her hands.

"I just don't want them to take you away and ship you off somewhere for science or something."

"Do you really think they would do that?"

"Well, no."

"Then I would be delighted to serve them as I do you."

Kiera hesitated for a moment before taking a deep breath. She gently wrapped her fingers around the little one, then pushed her way into the main room. James was sitting at a table to the left talking with Rina, who had changed into one of Maya's old dark red dresses. Sofie had a broom in hand and was sweeping up dirt and debris on the floor that the Mek'Vatir scavengers hadn't managed to pick up themselves.

"Well good morning, sleepyhead!" James bellowed as he saw her enter the pub.

"Where's Maya and Lain?" Kiera asked meekly.

"Why? You do somethin' wrong? You look pale as snow."

"It's nothing like that. I just slept in a bit longer than I expected, wanted to check in with them and talk about something pretty important."

"You sure missed a great breakfast there, *right?* Lain and Alexis are both with Maya in the boss' bedroom talking about 'something pretty important' already. I think they're waiting for you so you'd better get on in there."

"Thanks," Kiera replied, bowing with both of her hands in front of her.

She ran off toward the hallway door that led to the employee's exit and quickly went through. Instead of following the pathway around to the right, Kiera jogged over to the embellished and reinforced doorway that was directly in front of her. She opened it to reveal a fairly lavish room with a double-wide bed and a vanity off to the side.

"Yeah," Alexis said as she sat on Maya's bed, "I wore him through the whole trip and Pearl even played with him a bit."

"I'm here," Kiera quickly said as she jogged over.

Lain was leaning against the wall nearby while Maya stood in front of Alexis with her arms folded. A strange mixture of concern, amusement, and wonder permeated the room to the point where Kiera couldn't place the emotions with their source.

"That's quite a story," Maya said softly.

"I believe them," Lain quickly said as she walked over, her tail swaying behind her. "Where is he now? Trapped in one of your shoes? In your pocket?"

"How much have you told them?" Kiera asked Alexis.

"Pretty much everything," Alexis nervously replied, shifting a bit closer to her friend.

"Well then...." Kiera paused as she opened her hands to reveal the little one as he struggled to stand up. "Maya, Lain. Meet our little friend Adriel the Ætherbug."

Lain stepped closer and crouched near Adriel with a wide smile as Maya watched. The little one in Kiera's hands graciously bowed, his tail swaying as the chef reached out her index finger to gently touch the top of his head. The amusement and excitement seemed to roll off Lain in droves as she gently scratched at his matted white hair.

"Ah! He's so adorable!" Lain squeaked before standing back up. "I can't wait to make incredibly tiny dishes for such a cute little *doll* of a creature!"

"You can hold onto him if you'd like," Kiera offered.

Without hesitation, the chef reached over and offered her hand so the little one could step over. Adriel made his way onto her fingertips and walked over to her palm, and the chef squeaked out in joy once again.

"Oh Goddess his tiny footsteps are so adorable and weird I absolutely love it!"

Lain brought her hand up so she could see him closer with such haste that Adriel fell to a seated position. She bit her lower lip to stifle a giggle as she gently brought her other hand to caress his long, white hair before toying with the black fur of his tail.

Maya watched on, and the concern Kiera felt from her began to fade. They all allowed Lain to have a few minutes with the little one, watching how she spent most of her time rolling him around in her palm trying to find the ideal place to pet.

"So you say he enjoys being crushed?" Maya asked, looking back at Alexis.

"You can ask him if you'd like," Alexis replied.

Adriel was adoring every second of Lain's attention as her claw tip found its way to the base of his left ear. He pushed himself up into the scratching while his tail wildly swayed, and the chef continued to simply radiate joy. When she realized they were all waiting on her to stop, she meekly pulled her hand away from the little one and smiled to the group.

"Sorry. Didn't mean to distract him."

"It's no problem, comrade. You were having fun," Maya replied softly before turning her attention to Adriel. "So, is it true? You actually want us all to treat you like a Mek, and you enjoy it?"

"It is," Adriel replied nervously.

"Goddess!" Maya joyously laughed, shaking her head a bit as she looked down upon the little one. "I still don't know what to make of you, little comrade. You speak so very well for a being of your stature. If I were you, I'd be terrified of being crushed."

"You should try him out, see for yourself," Kiera suggested.

"Sure!" Maya said as she put her hands on her hips. "I'll put him under-paw if he wants."

Lain's smile disappeared as she held the little one close. Her tail slipped up between her legs as she ran through all of the possibilities in her head. However, the chef had known both Kiera and Alexis long enough to realize that they wouldn't make something like this up for a cruel laugh. She cleared her throat a bit before crouching down and setting the little one on the floorboards in front of Maya.

"Alright," She said meekly as she stood back up and watched.

"Don't worry," Alexis said softly, reaching up to take Lain's hand, "he'll be alright, I promise."

Maya looked down at Adriel as he lay on the ground. She still had her hands on her hips as she lifted her paw over the little one and set it down on him gently so that his head was between her toes. Adriel tried his best to take in the musky air as the soft fur engulfed his face on all sides. Her weight made it very difficult for him to breathe as the pub owner hesitated.

"You mentioned something about his blood being euphoric. How intense is it?" She asked nervously.

"It's like a strange wave of soothing energy that just washes over you," Kiera replied. "Different from manipulating someone's aura. More intense, but it's still a very different experience."

Maya continued to bide her time a bit, pressing down on him in a few little tests. She could feel his breath puff up between her toes with each application of pressure, something that reminded her of a toy she had when she was a child.

After stalling for a few minutes, she lifted her heel and pressed down on him with all of her weight. The fur between her toes began to glow purple as blood filled the gap.

She immediately let out a shaky, soothed sigh as her blue tongue and the inside of her mouth began to glow. She was inadvertently drawing energy from him as she squeezed her toes down, crushing his little skull between them.

"Goddess...." Maya said as she put her hand on Lain's shoulder and lifted her paw to take a look at what he had become.

The white fur near her toes and the ball of her paw was continuously shimmering and pulsing with a blue glow as his purple blood matted the strands. She spread her toes, though Adriel's head was smashed up into the webbing so much that only his white hair and black ears could be deciphered from the mess. He was quickly engulfed in the same healing light as always though, and in seconds the little one had been restored to his previous self. Carefully, Maya reached down and took him by the tail. She peeled him from the bottom of her paw and rolled her wrist so the little one was discarded into her open palm.

"How many people have you told about him?" Maya asked.

"Other than the people here, Sofie is the only other one who knows about him," Kiera replied.

"I think it would be best if it stays that way, at least for a while. Be extremely careful of who you tell, someone like Adriel could cause a lot of trouble if he falls into the wrong hands."

"May I?" Lain said meekly as she snuck up to Maya's side.

Lain gently picked Adriel up from her companion's palm and held him in her hands once more. The chef immediately resumed petting the little one, who was still adoring the attention even though he was recovering from Maya's step. She then looked up to the two seated on the bed in front of her and meekly smiled.

"Can I hold onto him for a while? Please?" Lain asked, "I'll be sure to take care of him and wear him while I'm in the kitchen."

"I uh...." Alexis stammered. "You really want to wear him? *You?* I mean—"

"Of course you can," Kiera quickly chimed in. "Speaking of which... I haven't really had breakfast yet, would it be a bother if we went and cooked something up quick?"

"I saved some breakfast for you," Alexis replied.

"Thanks, comrade."

"You want to ride with me?" Lain asked the little one in her hand as she gently scratched under his chin with her claw tip.

He nodded, his little tail swaying as Lain stepped out of her left moccasin. She cleared her throat a bit as she gently lowered him inside. Adriel could feel the intense, muggy heat radiating around him as he descended into the moccasin before being set on the soft insole. He looked around inside the new environment. The print was worn in deep from cycles of use, but to his genuine surprise, there was no sign of Mek'Vatir at all.

"Are you sure you want to do this?" Maya asked as Lain nodded in response.

"He won't be crawling around like the Mek do, so it'll be different. I think."

Lain stepped back in her moccasin and pulled it up her calf until her foot slid into place. She could feel him breathing against her arch holding onto the stirrup of her black silk leggings. Although his breath was clear on her skin, he wasn't climbing around or squirming. Her tail began to sway yet her ears were still lowered as she cautiously stepped down. Like Maya before her, she let out a slight gasp when she felt his blood on her bare skin.

"I hope he's alright," She said nervously.

"Don't worry about him, he's been through worse," Kiera said as she stood back up. "So what did we have for breakfast?"

"It's a surprise."

Lain took the first few steps toward the door, faltering a bit as she tried her best to keep her weight off of Adriel before just giving up and walking normally. The others followed, and it was off to the kitchen to prepare Kiera's breakfast.

R E Q U I E M   F O R   T H E   L O S T
C H A P T E R   I V

Evening | Alerio 13, 1240
Nevarria City – Isarean Pub

Everyone stood together underneath the large tree behind the pub as the sun fell below the horizon, filling the sky with an amber glow. Cerolia's rings seemed to be set ablaze while the clear skies yielded to nebulae that surrounded their active region of the galaxy. Twinkling stars danced overhead like sprinkled paint along the orange-tinted horizon as purple celestial clouds started to canvas the sky from the opposing direction. It was as though they were chasing away the light to herald the coming darkness.

Normally, such a calming sight was a wonder to behold and served to soothe whatever ailed Kiera's heart. This evening, as she watched the glowing green platform lower the body of a fallen soldier into a makeshift grave, she was far too overwhelmed to bask in the glory of the cosmos.

Rina stood beside her at the foot of the grave with Alexis at her other side gently holding her hand. The Edoraii's gaze was lifeless yet her emotions were powerful. She remained quiet as the body of her comrade finally reached its place of internment, and the glowing green platform that Sofie had created dissolved. There was a moment of silence before Rina finally spoke.

"It wasn't right," She whispered as Sofie held her staff tightly in hand at the head of the grave. "I just... I don't believe it."

Sofie took a deep breath while she replenished her energy via her Amethya crystal jewelry. Sweat began to bead on her forehead as she tightly clutched her staff and mentally prepared for what she had to do. This was the first time she had ever preformed this ritual in earnest, and while she had plenty of training at the temple, she was far from confident in her abilities.

"Are we ready?" Sofie asked, trying her very best to speak in a clear and concise tone.

As Rina nodded in response, Sofie brought her staff out in front of her. The fur on the Edoraii's cheeks became matted as tears streamed from her eyes, making it harder for her to see the proceedings. She grit her teeth in an attempt to keep herself from breaking down, cleared her throat, and used her free wrist to wipe the tears away.

"At least she will have a proper burial," Rina whispered, her breath shaking as Kiera handed her a tissue. "Most soldiers don't get that out in the field."

Sofie took a step away from the grave to begin the Ritual of Passing in full. Five ribbons of energy were let loose as she swayed her staff through the air in a slow and methodical dance. They all arched up over the group and came to the ground where the five tips of a star would naturally sit, then erupted into a small controlled ethereal flame. When the flames were lit, Sofie began to sing in a language none of them had heard before. The haunting melody felt as though it pierced Rina through her heart like an arrow. The sight was alluring and graceful, yet she loathed what it came to represent. As the crystal atop Sofie's staff trailed energy through the air, the grave's green mist lost its color to resemble a white and glowing low-lying fog.

"Make your peace, if you so will it," Sofie said solemnly.

There was a long moment of silence as Rina reached into a pocket on the side of the old dress she wore. When her red hooved fingertips emerged, she was holding onto her blessed green Amethya necklace.

"Sandra..." She began, her voice cracking as she spoke. "This wasn't supposed to happen. I should have refused your offer that day and stayed behind the wire where I belonged. If I had, maybe we would be on our way back to the vineyard now... back to our special place beyond the moonlit waterfall and under the sea of stars. I have a feeling I'll always regret that decision, that I'll always regret taking this necklace off. We never got our ceremony, but I know you'll always be with me, my love."

"By the Goddess..." Maya whimpered out, "I—"

"No..." Rina said somberly. "It's alright. Sandra said she found this crystal in our special place. It's her color, so she thought it would be a fitting betrothal gift when she asked me to...."

Rina couldn't finish her sentence, not immediately at least. She took a deep breath after she gathered herself and continued.

"She said it was like a part of her would always be with me," Rina finished, her voice cracking and quivering as she spoke. "She was the best. I know what you all got to see of her was absolutely horrendous, but she really was. We lived together for most of our lives at the Vineyard. She was far more attuned to the planet than I ever was, way more peaceful. I… I always found her in the woods. I loved her so much."

"I'm sorry," Maya said softly.

"That wasn't her.... It wasn't!" Rina replied sternly. "She would never have done what she did. It wasn't...."

She trailed off, turning from the grave to gaze directly up to the ring that had come even more prominently into view. The sun had set, and the bright purple nebulae had all but taken over the night's sky. She used the tissue that Kiera had given her to wipe her eyes again, her hand shaking as she tried to make sense of it all in her head. Seconds seemed like hours to her, and when she was ready to continue, she turned back to the grave and looked directly to her betrothed with her hand clenched around the crystal of her necklace.

"I swear to you," Rina said sternly, "I will do everything in my power to help bring about peace on Cerolia. I... I want our legacy to unite people, not divide them. I know you would want me to go back to the safety of our home island, but I can't. Aestellus isn't going to be the nation I can make a change in, and I need to make your death mean something."

With trembling hands, she brought her necklace back around her neck and secured the clasp. She cleared her throat, closed her eyes, and then took a deep breath.

"You always wanted to dance in the stars and explore the cosmos," She continued. "Spread your wings and fly, my love, wherever your heart desires. I'll join you when I can."

Rina looked up to Sofie and nodded gently. There was another short pause as the Advanced Acolyte allowed time for anyone else to speak their piece, but nobody did. When she was certain everything had concluded, she stepped back and resumed the chilling melody of passing. The mist lifted, rising in a cloudy funnel of swirling energy as she danced along. It spread into the leaves of the tree above them, and she brought her staff close to her chest to conclude the ritual.

"With this, the passage through the veil has been fulfilled," Sofie said softly.

"Thank you," Rina's voice was still quite shaky as James and Maya began to fill the hole with dirt. Nobody spoke from then on, as the sound of shovels echoed through the night.

Kiera was trying her best to distance her own emotions from everyone else's as she looked up to Rina, who was holding the crystal around her neck tightly. The Amethya was glowing beneath the Edoraii's fingertips, but before she could say anything about it, the light faded.

Night | Alerio 13, 1240
Nevarria City – Isarean Pub

Kiera sat at the bar with a mug of honey wine in her hand. She gazed into the liquid solemnly as she tried her best to drink away everyone else's emotions. Sofie sat at a nearby table with her legs crossed and the staff still held tightly. There were a few crushed Mek'Vatir bodies on the table, smeared by her fingertips as she regained the energy she had used for the funeral. On the other side of the bar, Lain stood next to Maya to comfort her as the Jalar kept an eye on the front door to the pub. After a few moments of silence passed, the door creaked open.

"Come tomorrow mornin' ain't nobody gonna be able to tell we dug that spot up," James said as he stepped through, holding the door open for those to follow.

Rina entered next, her hooves clopping against the wooden floorboards as she walked over to the chair next to Kiera at the bar. Maya offered her a shot of alcohol, but the Edoraii gently waved her hand to dismiss it.

"It's a shame we had to do that," Alexis said as she stepped through, hugging James. "I'm just glad we had a Terra Botanical around to fix up the grass and that the inspector wasn't here."

"I still think Heather has a good heart."

"We shouldn't take chances anyway."

Alexis ran over to the chair on the other side of Rina as James let the door shut behind them all. He walked over to sit near Sofie while the others got comfortable, and Kiera took a long drink of her honey wine. The Edoraii's slump was disturbed when Alexis set her hand on her back. The sensation seemed to reassure the ex-soldier enough to coax a half-hearted smile.

"I don't know how much Sandra told command, but I can't go back anyway," Rina said. "Hopefully it won't be too hard for me to gain citizenship in Novalus."

"They have a defection program at the Exigo Tower in Sanova City," Maya said in the most upbeat tone as she could muster given the circumstances. "I'm sure they'll be proud to have you."

"I really don't think she said anything to your command," Kiera said, still gazing down at her drink.

"What makes you think so?" Rina replied.

"Hypothetically. If they did know, then Sandra would have been here in an official capacity. Heather would have been informed, since she's the resident whistleblower. I doubt she would have been so relaxed over the last few days if she knew a few soldiers came here and turned up missing shortly thereafter."

"You're right," Rina replied, folding her arms. "Soldiers turn up missing on combat zones all the time. We're probably just considered MIA until I make myself known in Sanova. For now, I should keep my head down."

"What about your family?"

"My sister will be fine and the winery won't die without me. I'll just write home to let them know I'm alright. Hopefully we'll open up our borders and be able to travel freely between nations someday soon. Until then, I have work to do."

"You can still go back, though. You don't have to stay here to fix things that aren't really your responsibility."

"I've made them my responsibility now. I can't go back there and live in that place without her. Not with everything we've been through... I don't think I would be able to keep myself going if I just turned my back where I could make a difference. I need something bigger than the winery to keep me from... I mean—"

"Sorry," Kiera said softly. "Please, I didn't mean to make you feel that way. I know this is going to sound really selfish but I really can't take much more of this tonight. Just forget I asked."

"I got a message over the TelCom a few hours ago," James said. "Found a load heading right for Sanova that's picking up near the Triana Airstrip."

"Good. I already have all my stuff packed," Alexis said, her hand still on Rina's back.

"Are you sure you want to go?" Maya asked.

"I don't think I'll get another really good chance to join the Novalin Defense Force, and since it's a cease-fire we'll be in peacetime when I do. They'll take me."

"I think it's a good idea," Kiera said as she looked up from her mug to Alexis. "Nevarria's not going to get any better anytime soon. If she goes into the military, she'll have food and a place to sleep every night no matter how bad it gets here. Not to mention she'll keep her citizenship with Novalus."

"There's room for y'all on the airship," James chimed in.

"This is still our home," Maya replied in a hushed tone. "Are you going as well, Kiera?"

"I get free alcohol here," Kiera replied as she took another drink from her mug. "I don't like the idea of being told what to do by a commanding officer much either. Not unless I know who they are and don't want to beat their face in."

"What are you going to do, Sofie?" Lain asked from behind Maya. "Back to the Temple?"

"I have a lot more to learn," Sofie said with a smile. "I might as well get as much information as I can before that happens. I'll make regular pilgrimages down here though."

"I don't trust air bladders, be careful," Kiera warned.

"The *Olga V* ain't seen nothin' that can take her down," James quickly said. "She'll get us where we need to go and then some."

"Well then," Lain chimed in, "I'll get to cooking up something good for dinner before you go."

Rina stood behind the pub with a hand held to her chest as the grass licked at her fur-covered ankles. Her betrothal necklace fit perfectly, allowing the vibrant green crystal to rest in the center of the white diamond-shaped patch of fur she had on her neck and chest. As the wind blew through the leaves of the tree high above, she gently touched the crystal she now counted as her most valuable possession.

"I'll keep my promise, somehow," she whispered.

The Edoraii was having a difficult time holding back her tears, but she was managing to keep a level head. Her Aestellan uniform was packed away aboard the *Olga V* already, and she had changed into a less formal outfit. A simple brown skirt that almost reached the tuft of white fur on the back of her ankles shifted in the gentle night's breeze. She tightened the white sash around her hip that concealed her standard-issue Aestellan revolver as she looked down to the grass on the grave that was already starting to grow.

Rina heard footsteps approaching from behind, but she didn't turn to face them.

"Ready?" Alexis asked as she handed her a pouch of Mek.

The Edoraii graciously accepted the offering and affixed the pouch to the side of her brown leather corset so that it could be accessed. She paused for a moment, took in a deep breath, and then turned to Alexis with a smile.

"I think so," Rina replied.

"We can stay longer if you need to."

"It's fine, we have a long way to go."

Rina then walked past her companion toward the *Olga V*, which was being prepared for launch. Alexis didn't follow immediately though. Instead, she looked up to the monolith in front of her. It was strange that she never noticed how perfect the rings looked from here, and now this mighty tree was a gravestone.

Quickly, she turned and ran back to Rina's side as the two made their way toward the pub's rear entrance. Maya was taking an inventory on the few supplies that they were offering up for the trip, while Lain was sitting and fiddling with the moccasin Adriel was still trapped inside of. When they neared the doorway, Kiera stepped through and waved.

"You look nice," Kiera said with a smile.

She was wearing a black pair of pajamas, her hair was disheveled, her combat boots weren't tied, and she wasn't wearing any socks. She had a mug of aquamelon juice in her left hand, which had several Mek'Vatir swimming around inside the sloshing cool blue liquid.

"You look relaxed," Alexis replied, nudging her friend a bit.

Kiera's markings shimmered to life as the shift in her weight flattened a Mek trapped inside of her boot. She stumbled a bit and giggled before giving Alexis a playful shove in return. When they were done, Kiera took a drink of her aquamelon juice and smiled to her friend.

"I work very hard to maintain my appearance, it's an art," Kiera jested. "You wouldn't understand."

"You have a little someone between your teeth."

Alexis chuckled and pointed toward her left fang, which caused Kiera to bring her claw tip to the space between her teeth. There was a Mek that was relatively uninjured, with only its arm caught in a minute gap. The claw landed on its chest, crushing it into her tooth before flicking most of it away. As she slid her tongue across the area to wipe up what remained, her patterns shimmered as she smiled once more.

"Did I get it?" She asked.

"Yep. I'm glad you're drinking aquamelon juice and not something a bit… harder."

Alexis quickly stepped over to her friend and wrapped her arms around her. Their tails both swayed behind them as they tightly hugged each other.

"I've had enough for the night. There's plenty of drinking to do tomorrow! And the next day! And the next."

"Alcohol poisoning is a thing."

"Myth."

"Fact."

"You ain't gotta' give us all this stuff for the trip," James said as he stepped down the ramp of the airship. "We'll be able to get some food once we actually get underway. Nothing as good as what Miss Lain can whip up though."

Lain was bobbing her foot around a bit with a bright smile on her face when she heard her name. She instantly perked up, looking to James as her swaying tail came to an abrupt stop.

"What?" She squeaked.

"Just sayin' you've got the best cooking I ever tasted! I'll have to talk to you about a recipe I made and show you what cooking where I'm from is like."

"I'm from where you're from," Lain laughed, standing up.

The moment she felt Adriel compress again, she instinctively lifted that foot off the ground. Sheepishly she stepped back down, and since he had slid underneath her heel on accident, she just kept her weight forward to give him space to exist. She looked like a baby Laya trying to walk for the first time, which got a strange look from James.

"You okay there, Miss Lain?"

"Yep, never better. Don't mind me, sorry."

"Right."

Kiera and Alexis snickered a bit as they walked over toward the entry ramp for the airship. Before they could reach that point, the sound of a twig snapping nearby caught their attention. They looked over toward the woods to see Sofie walking over with a big basket in her arms.

"I found some really nutritious fungi and berries!" Sofie said happily. "There really was so much around here. I'm surprised you never went out foraging!"

"You went out there at night?" Kiera chuckled.

Sofie was covered in dust, while dirt was caked up beneath her red clawed fingertips from digging up the fungi. She smiled brightly as she walked, letting tendrils of green energy sprout from her ankles to illuminate the area around her.

"It's safe here. Near the temple is a different story."

"Fair enough."

"Here," Sofie said happily as she brought the big basket over to Rina, who took it in her arms. "I hope you get some good use out of it!"

"Thank you so much," Rina said happily. "I'm sure they'll keep us for a while on the trip."

"I know how to cook fungi!" Alexis chimed in brightly. "Lain's been teaching me here and there."

The peaceful air of the night was disrupted by the sound of an explosion off in the distance. Immediately after, the familiar sound of popping gunfire echoed once more. It caught everyone's attention as they all looked back toward the city.

"Is the war back on?" Sofie asked innocently.

"Naw," James said with his arms folded, "freedom fighters and militia, probably. It ain't gonna be safe here for long."

"Ironically," Maya solemnly added, "I think with the war finished, things might even be worse than they were before."

"I'm not worried," Kiera replied confidently.

Alexis had already made her way to the basket that Rina now held in her arms and was peeking inside. There was a bit of movement in there—a few Mek that were on the bits of fruit when they were plucked from the vine. They looked confused and dazed. As she turned around though, one of the Mek'Vatir inside flew out after her. Its small, thin wings carried it whizzing by her right ear.

Bzzz.

She cringed away from the noise as she approached the ramp leading to the airship. Looking up and around, she tried to pinpoint the source of the annoyance.

Bzzz.

This time she saw it and quickly batted her hand in its direction. The little winged Mek'Vatir was struck directly, sent plummeting down to the steel ramp below. It landed on its back with its wings twisted as Alexis swiftly lifted her boot over it. Time seemed to slow for the little Mek as it saw the paw pattern on the underside of her shoe. Cast beyond it was the celestial mix of color and stars, and in that last second, it knew it had accomplished its goal.

"May the Goddess bless your path, friends," Sofie sweetly said as she gave them a gentle bow.

The red markings on Alexis' face didn't shimmer as the insect managed to survive her stomp. The texture of the ramp had spared it a quick death, leaving it to suffer. She had identified it as the stinging sort, and the last thing she wanted to have to deal with now was an insect bite before such a long trip.

"Thank you, Acolyte," Rina said graciously as she returned the bow with the basket in hand. "I can't begin to thank you enough for saving my life."

"I'm glad I could help."

Before Alexis could turn and give her friend a bow as well, Kiera's arms wrapped around her tight from behind. She yelped, then quickly turned so she could wrap her arms around Kiera. Both of their tails swayed gently back and forth in rhythm as the rest of the world seemed to fall silent around them.

"Take care, alright?" Kiera whispered.

"I'll send a letter the moment I get to the city and let you know we're safe. And I'll be back one day, I promise."

"Sanova's a big place. Don't get lost or anything."

"The government headquarters is a giant swirling black tower in the center of the city. I don't think we'll miss it," Alexis chuckled as she ran her fingertips down Kiera's armored spine.

Kiera did the same to her, allowing her energy to trail as she manipulated Alexis' aura for one last time. Alexis didn't return the favor though. She knew Kiera never liked that sort of thing, and it wouldn't work on her anyway. She closed her eyes and enjoyed the pleasurable sensations that radiated along her back as Kiera danced her fingertips along her shirt. As Kiera stepped away, she trailed her fingertips just below Alexis' ribcage as a bit of a parting gift for her comrade.

"I'll be waiting," Kiera said somewhat solemnly as Alexis nodded in turn.

"Alright then," James said as he made his way up the ramp to the cabin of his airship, "Let's get this show on the road."

Rina followed, accidentally stepping on the winged Mek in passing. Her hooves and horns shimmered as she set the basket down near the entryway, then turned back to Kiera and Alexis who were still standing at the bottom of the ramp. Alexis leaned forward, going up on her tip-toes to reach Kiera's forehead so she could plant a friendly kiss. She then reached up to the top of Kiera's head and quickly messed up her hair even more, before running up the ramp to the top and turning back with her tongue sticking out from between her sharp fangs. They both laughed as Alexis waved to her comrades and swayed her tail.

James disappeared into the cockpit as Lain worked to undo the straps that tethered the airship to the ground. The chef then ran over to Kiera's side and waved as well, while Maya stepped up behind them both. She set her hands on the young Aluni's shoulders as the airship began to rise into the sky.

"Alexis! You'd better keep that promise!" Kiera shouted up to her as the ramp began to close. "I'll be expecting you back someday! And you'd better come back with your own airship."

"I will! I love you, sister!" Alexis yelled back. "Keep everyone safe for me!"

As soon as the doorway sealed, Kiera saw Alexis peeking out through one of the windows waving at the group as the airship gained altitude. It ascended quickly, turning into nothing more but a darkened silhouette among the sea of stars and glowing multicolored nebulae. The tears came back, though this time she had her family to support her.

Maya gently wiped them from Kiera's face as Lain stood at her side. While the *Olga V* crept out of sight behind the shadow of the clouds, Kiera couldn't shake the nagging suspicion that Maya was right earlier.

That the worst was yet to come...

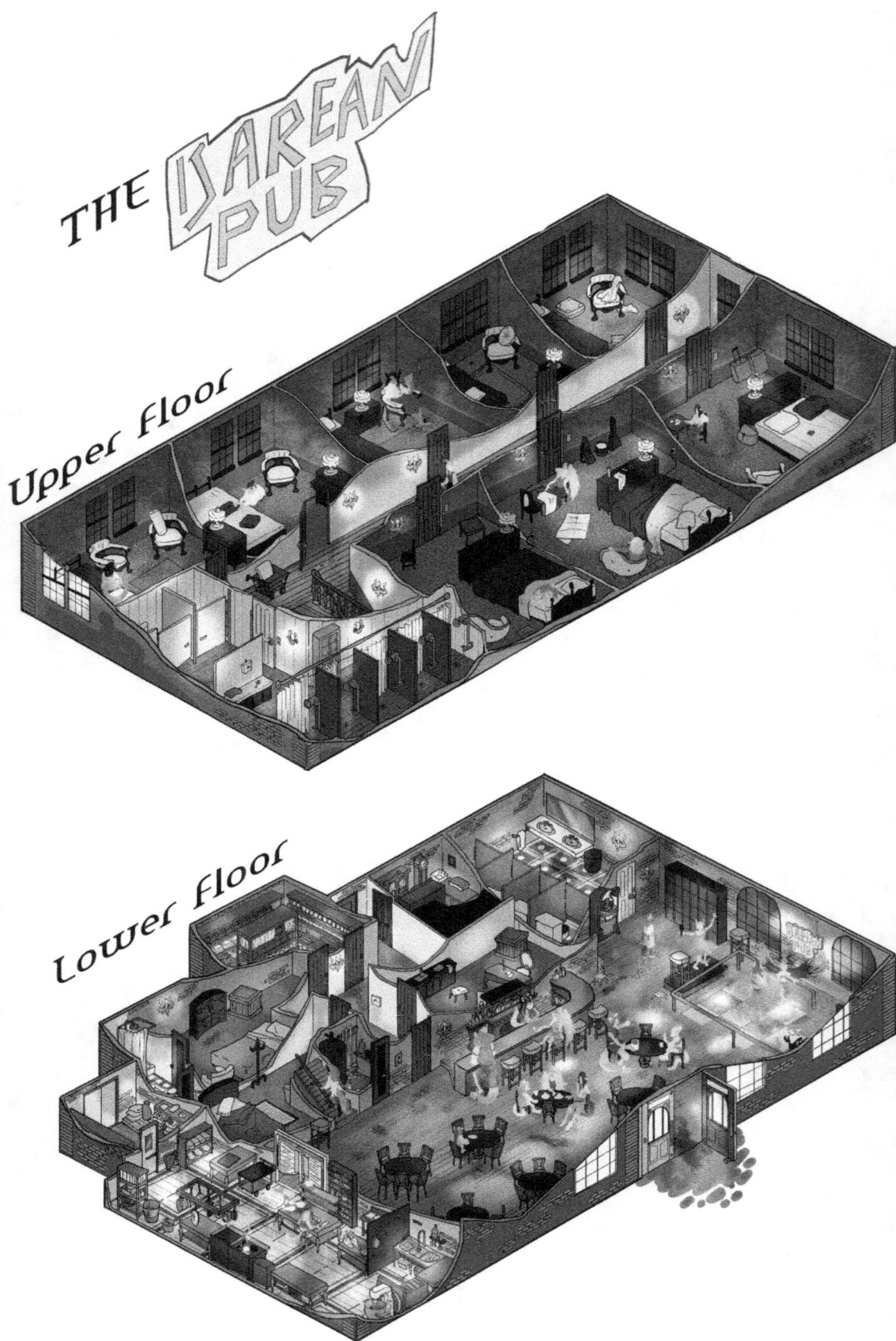

 CEROLIAN SAGAS

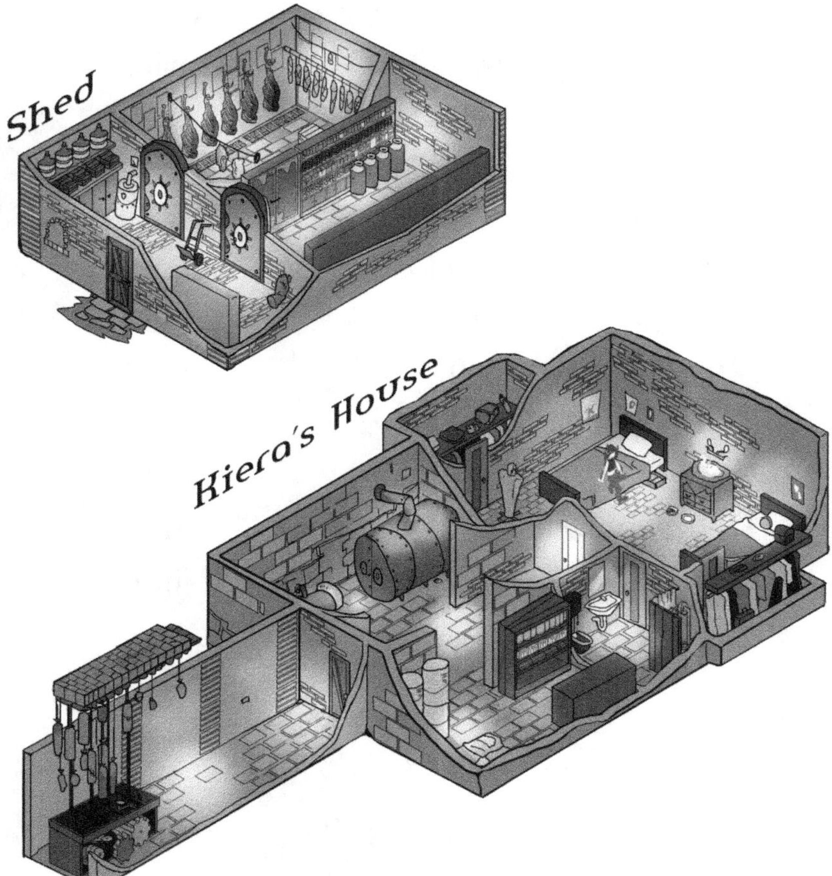
Shed
Kiero's House

CALENDAR & PLANET

Agusta	(44 Days)	Winter
Feyra	(43 Days)	Winter
Noxtra	(42 Days)	Spring
Bostai	(40 Days)	Spring
Viano	(44 Days)	Spring
Alerio	(39 Days)	Summer
Pixan	(40 Days)	Summer
Ronta	(45 Days)	Summer
Ibexar	(40 Days)	Fall
Kosta	(43 Days)	Fall
Obex	(42 Days)	Fall
Indar	(42 Days)	Winter
Ultir	(43 Days)	Winter

1 Cerolian Cycle = 1.5 Earth Years (Approx. 547.5 Days)

Gravitational Pull - .79g

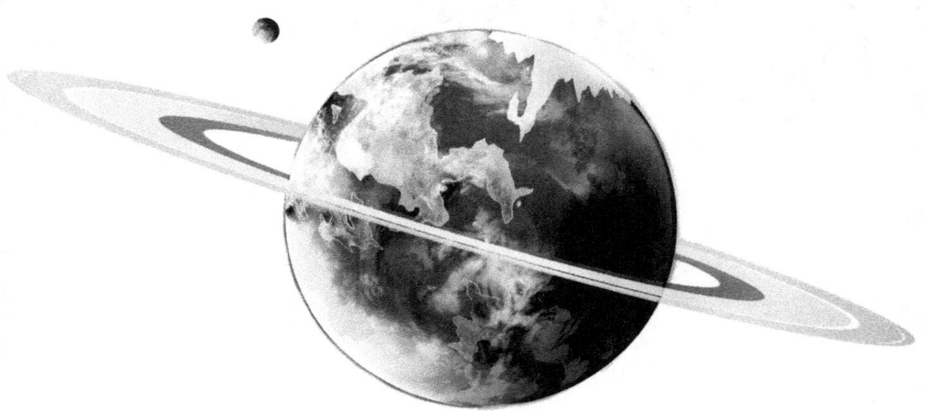

UNITED REPUBLIC
OF
CEROLIA
JUSTICE
SACRIFICE
RETRIBUTION

CEROLIAN SAGAS

About the Author

Mathew Ruley (AKA Vieryon) is an author, a gaming YouTuber, and an over-the-road truck driver from Michigan. The Cerolian Sagas is a series that is very close to his heart, as most of the characters within have been with him since its inception in 2007. He created Cerolian Arts and cultivated a small group of friends to help him create the series outside of any major publishing house.

In his down time, when not thinking about the series while driving across the United States, he spends time playing and recording video games for his YouTube channel "Cerolian Republic" (formally 'The Gaming Cinaflix').

ACKNOWLEDGMENTS

I couldn't have done this without the help of various contractors that I have had the pleasure of working with along the way. These are people that I consider to be dear friends, and look forward to working with on all of my future endeavors in *The Cerolian Sagas*.

Mylene Olavere (Mikurei) is a fantastic artist who is from the Philippines and has been my de-facto concept artist for the series. She does a wonderful job bringing the characters from my imagination to life, and is absolutely one of the best artists that I have ever worked with. She lives with Mon Macairap (Hachiimon), who is simply one of the best environmental artists I have ever seen. Together, they make an unstoppable duo of artistic creativity who can overcome any challenge!

Most of the characters in The Cerolian Sagas were created long ago through roleplays I've had with Eleanor Mathews (Spelledeg) and her incredible cast of characters. She's the creator of a comic series called 'Now Hiring', which you can get updates about by using the QR code to the right! On top of being a wonderful artist, she's always been my go-to individual for map and graphics design.

I'd also like to thank Brenda Mallette, who I met during my time in truck driver training school. Not only has she helped a lot by simply listening to me ramble on about Cerolia, but she introduced me to her daughter-in-law Heather Romanowski!

Heather Romanowski has been wonderful to work with when it comes to copyediting and ensuring that everything falls into place the way it needs to. She is the owner of Book Realm Revisions, and she absolutely has the credentials to back up her work. Heather holds a Bachelor's Degree from Oakland University in Writing and Rhetoric, an ACES Certificate in Editing, and has completed many EFA courses in copyediting, among other things. She is a proud member of the Editorial Freelancers Association and the ACES Society for Editing as well. You can check out all of her credentials on her business' website for more information by using the QR code below!

SPELLEDEG

BOOK REALM REVISIONS

MIKUREI

HACHIIMON

Beta readers are one of the most important aspects of a book's development, as they can absolutely help keep you from making major mistakes in the long run – even if that advice prompts you to rewrite the entire manuscript. Jia Yue He has had a major impact on the series as a whole, and this series simply wouldn't be the same without her words of wisdom. It's always fantastic to see all of the comments and critique that she has to offer. Jia Yue He isn't afraid to tell me when I've faltered, and I am incredibly thankful for that.

One interesting thing about being a truck driver is that you never really know who you'll meet. I'll never forget the time I met Daniel Kinsman at a company terminal while we were both waiting for service on our trucks over the weekend. We commandeered the company television in the driver's lounge to binge all of Blood-C in a single setting, and have been friends ever since. With his time in the United States Marine Corps has made him a fantastic and reliable military advisor for the series. Whenever I have a question about tactics or military equipment, he's always ready to enthusiastically answer. He helps me ensure that all of the military aspects of The Cerolian Sagas are in line.

I haven't forgotten my friends and family: my father Jon Ruley, my mother Kathy Ruley, my brother Sean Ruley, my sister Rachel Ruley, my stepmother Becky Ruley, and my grandmother Dorothy Schallhorn who I talk to every day. Not to mention my good friend Jordan Keeler, who helps keep me sane while I drive across the United States. *To everyone who has ever supported me, I love you.*

Last but not least, I'd like to thank James Dorsey. I met him in orientation four years ago when I first started at the company I work for now. We would keep in touch on a daily basis, and whenever our paths crossed we would take turns paying for a nice steak dinner. He was incredibly enthusiastic about this project. The first thing he wanted me to do after it was published, was send him an autographed copy because he believed that this series would take off. He made sure to let me know that he appreciated me every time he had the chance. His last request to me was to write his biography for him. I'm not a biographical writer, and without him around to tell me his stories, I'm afraid that I won't be able to accomplish what he asked… not exactly. He was a truck driver and a great friend who taught me so much along my own journey. My friends at home, when they saw pictures of him, even gave him the title 'The Sage of the Road'.

Now, through this story, my friend lives on.

NOW
HIRING
JOKER
JOKER
STORY&ART BY
SPELLEDEG